WHAT ONCE WAS MINE

WAS MINE

A TWISTED TALE

WHAT ONCE WAS MINE

A TWISTED TALE

What if Rapunzel's mother drank a potion from the wrong flower?

LIZ BRASWELL

DISNEP · HYPERION
Los Angeles · New York

Printed in the United States of America
First Hardcover Edition, September 2021
3 5 7 9 10 8 6 4 2
FAC-004510-22087
Library of Congress Control Number: 2021936057
ISBN 978-1-368-06382-1
Visit disneybooks.com

For all librarians everywhere

I would not be the writer I am today without
the special librarians in my own life:
Wunderly Stauder, Peter Salesses, Jane White,
Eleanor Malmfeldt, and Rita Braswell.

—L.B.

The Story

The last notes of a pop song faded out over the movie credits, and the real world re-formed itself around Brendan.

In place of a happily-ever-after kingdom full of flowers and birds and kings and queens, there was a small, cold cubicle of a room, bare and icy white. Inside there was barely enough space for a single chair, a small cart, a tower of IV tubes and pumps—and the hospital bed where his twin sister, Daniella, lay.

Brendan had tried to brighten and decorate the room the way he always did when he sat with her during chemo treatments. He hung multicolored fairy lights over her bed (battery operated), placed a bouquet of outrageously bright flowers on the cart (fake; real pollen and allergens were bad for the immunocompromised), and laid out a stack of bagels and tub of strawberry cream cheese if she felt like eating lunch (she never did).

These things kept most of the scary away, but not all of it.

It was not the worst cancer. It wasn't even in the top twenty. That didn't make Brendan feel any better when his very weak, very tired sister—who had been sitting up while watching the movie, with wide, interested eyes—fell slowly back onto her pillows in exhaustion.

In the silence brought on by the movie's being over, the noise of the IV pumps clicked loudly over everything.

Daniella opened her mouth but didn't quite yawn.

"Okay, *Tangled* viewing number three: check!" Brendan said with a smile that wasn't quite forced. "What do you want to do now?"

"Read to me?" Her sleepy brown eyes lit up for a shining moment. How could he say no to that?

. . . and then he saw the book she shook at him and his face fell.

"Come *on*," he groaned. "We just watched the *movie*. Can't we read something else?"

"No, I want to hear about Rapunzel," Daniella said,

sticking her lower lip out (with, Brendan was actually glad to see, a little bit of her old sisterly self coming through). "*AGAIN*. Unless you don't think your sixteen-year-old sister who has cancer deserves it . . ."

"Oh. My. *God*." Brendan took the book reluctantly. "Okay, I get the whole reverting-to-childhood thing. But why *Rapunzel*? Like, so much Rapunzel? Your hair is—was—black. And you don't even have it anymore."

Only her brother could talk to her like this: her brother *had* to talk to her like this. When he got all weird and gentle and sad-faced like her boyfriend and Mom and Dad, and used the strained words nurses did to talk around what was really happening, *that's* when Daniella got scared and angry. None of the terrible things happening to her seemed to really get to her as much as her obnoxious brother being all sweet and nice.

But he had caught her, just once, looking in the mirror at the few puffs of hair that remained on her head, all that was left of her shining piles of box braids. Her throat had distended like a bird eating fish as she swallowed again and again to keep the tears from coming.

"Read. The. Book" was all Daniella said now. Tiredly. She was making her eyes shoot lasers at him with what little oomph she had left.

Brendan sighed and flipped to the beginning. He shivered. They kept the little chemo rooms cold for—some medical reason he couldn't remember. He always brought along Daniella's old Tiana quilt; now it was tucked closely around her along with the hospital blankets a kind nurse had autoclaved so they would be warm.

He looked at the opening page.

Then he closed the book.

"Brendan," Daniella said, sleepily but impatiently.

"What about this?" he said, getting an idea. "We've read this book like a *hundred* times. . . ."

"Twice," Daniella corrected, eyes closing.

"What if I tell it to you—differently? Like, *my* way?"

Her eyes shot open; she glared at him suspiciously.

"Uh-uh. You're going to make it dumb and have Storm-troopers jump out or have the characters swear at each other and then aliens land and ruin *everything.*"

"No I won't! I promise. No silly anything. The exact same story, but . . . different."

Daniella narrowed her eyes at him.

"With Mother Gothel as the bad guy? And Flynn falling in love with Rapunzel? And Pascal? And the guys from the Snuggly Duckling? And *magic*? No robots or time travel?"

"All there. I *promise.* No robots."

"All right," Daniella said. She still sounded unsure, but

definitely more awake than she had been a moment earlier. "We'll try it."

"Okay," Brendan said with a smile. He opened the book as if he were reading.

"Once upon a time . . ."

A Fairy-Tale Beginning

Once upon a time when the heavens still had some truck with what happened down on earth, the sun shone so brightly that on one fine spring day he shed a tear of pure joy. Where this drop of sunlight fell there grew a magical golden flower. It glowed warmly and softly like morning sun and had the power to heal the sick and injured.

. . . only it never had the chance to. *Once upon a time* those who knew the forest and were desperate for a miraculous cure sought its magic. But then war after war ravaged the countryside in those dark ages, and the plague took entire generations of wisewomen and ancient hermits. In time the Sundrop Flower almost entirely disappeared from memory.

Many years passed. The world moved on. Yet eventually one clever and evil young woman, guided by story and rumor, did find the flower again.

Her name was Gothel.

She could have done many things with the magic. She could have become a great healer—or at least a highly sought-after physician who tended the rich and royal. Instead she kept the flower entirely to herself, using its magic to halt her aging, allowing her to remain eternally young.

A hundred years went by.

There was peace again in the land. King Frederic and Queen Arianna, fair and wise beyond their years, ruled their kingdom well. And just like in so many fairy tales, they had everything they could ever want . . . except for a child.

(While this was of course distressing to the king and queen, the lack of an heir also unsettled the good people of the kingdom; without a clear path of succession, all would be thrown into chaos and bloodshed again. The neighboring baronies were always restless, hungry and greedy for bigger holdings.)

After consulting goodwives, doctors, priests, and charlatans, the queen finally conceived. There was at first great rejoicing in the castle—but sadly, as happened all too often in those *once upon a time* days, she grew sick as her time drew close, and seemed likely to die.

Once again the king called upon goodwives and doctors and priests and charlatans, and it was one last old crone who remembered the story her great-grandmother had told her about the secret of the Sundrop Flower.

The king immediately sent all his horses and all his men to comb the countryside for this magical glowing bloom. Each night from dusk until dawn, every able-bodied citizen was drafted into the search. Willingly, because the king and queen were good and their people wanted them to be happy; willingly, because all wanted an heir and no return to the chaos of the previous centuries; willingly, because there was a mighty reward.

And so the flower was found, and a tisane made to soothe the fevers of the ailing queen. She soon recovered and bore a beautiful baby girl, and all across the kingdom they celebrated, ignorant of the mistake that had been made.

For it was not the Sundrop Flower that a newly rich peasant had found.

It was the blossom of the *Moondrop*.

Memorial Sloan Kettering

"Wait, *what?*"

Daniella slammed her arms down in the blankets on either side of her. The IV tubes rattled but luckily nothing came out.

"The *Moondrop* Flower," Brendan repeated patiently. "They picked the wrong flower. I told you the story was going to be different."

"Yeah, but—how'd they pick the wrong flower? It's the Sundrop Flower! It's golden, and it glows, and everything."

She frowned and crossed her arms, pouting at the stupidity of a character who hadn't even been named—and who was now probably rich off his mistake, with more goats and gold than a peasant really knew what to do with.

"Okay, look, both flowers *glow*," Brendan said, leaning forward to defend his anonymous character. "They were told, 'Go find a glowing flower.' So they did. There was just more than one. A long time ago the moon also shed a tear, or something, and a plant grew from that, too."

He saw the look of understanding and intrigue start to cross his sister's face and tried not to revel in his triumph too overtly.

"Are there Stardrop Flowers, too?"

"I dunno. Maybe. Why not?"

"What does the Moondrop Flower do that's different?" Daniella asked, trying not to sound eager.

"Why don't you just relax and *listen*, dummy? You'll find out," Brendan said, opening the book again—this time with a little flourish. His sister looked unsatisfied but settled herself back into the pillows, swallowing once or twice loudly. There was something weird in the chemo that made her taste and smell things that weren't there. Brendan made a note to get her more of the Sour Patch Kids from the vending machine next time he took a bathroom break. They weren't her favorite, but they were strongly flavored and helped a little.

"And so a healthy baby girl, a princess, was born. After a week of waiting—as was custom in those days, when there was high infant mortality—they named her: *Rapunzel*, for the field of rampion or bellflowers where the magic flower was found. There was joyous celebrating all over the kingdom; feasting and dancing and picnics and presents were given out to everyone. The king and queen launched a flying lantern into the sky. For that one moment, everything was perfect.

"And then that moment ended."

Rapunzel

The new princess was healthy, vigorous, and vital, and showed no signs of sickness (or *desire to escape the sinful world of man and return to Heaven*, as some said). A wet nurse was promptly found for her—and just as promptly sent away by Queen Arianna, who wanted to care for the baby herself. And who could blame her? Rapunzel was jolly and fat, had pink cheeks, and loved a good snuggle. The only thing at all strange about the newborn was her hair—it was a beautiful silvery color and already several inches long when she was born.

Old Nanna Bess, in charge of the maids and servants and widely thought of as the mother of the castle, dismissed superstitious rumors about its potentially demonic origins;

it was first hair, infant hair, and would probably fall out in a week or so to be replaced with the girl's actual color. Arianna had been born with a fuzz of coal black covering her scalp and within a fortnight it was gone, a month later replaced with the chestnut locks that would stay.

But Rapunzel's hair was fine and troublesome, prone to tangling in tiny baby knots that were a devil to get out (made worse by prodigious baby drool and baby spit-up, which even the most precious infant princesses produced).

The day of her baptism was marked out for one of great celebration across the kingdom. King Frederic, an amateur stargazer, noted that in the evening there would be a new moon; the night when the sky was blackest for lack of her light.

"We should send up *more* candle lanterns!" he declared. "We should fill the sky with them! To celebrate!"

A trade caravan from the East had introduced these wonders to the kingdom a few months before: brightly colored and painted paper lanterns that flew like clouds up into the sky when their wicks were lit. Frederic had bought the entire lot and begged them to come back with more.

(Also bought were fireworks, silk, tea, and a range of spices the castle cooks had never even heard of before—but quickly made great use of.)

Lanterns were distributed to everyone in the kingdom with instructions to light them from boats in the harbor as soon as the sun had set.

All the land was swept up in preparation for the night: garlands of flowers were hung from the houses; the *chanci* painted bright mandalas on the plazas in chalk. Musicians tuned and polished their instruments, everyone readied their best dresses and tabards, women braided their hair with brilliant white lilies that only sadly approximated the glow of the Sundrop Flower.

(Moondrop Flower.)

But little baby Rapunzel was not enjoying *her* preparations for the celebration.

She didn't mind wearing the snow-white christening gown that had been tatted from the finest silk by a dozen of the country's most skilled lace makers.

She didn't object to the rose water that was sprinkled on her chubby folds to keep her as sweet smelling as idiots imagined babies *should* be.

She didn't even object to the very careful trimming of her tiny fingernails so she wouldn't scratch her face.

What she hated was all the fussing with her hair.

"How can a newborn already have so many knots?" Nanna Bess wondered, holding Rapunzel close while the young maid Lettie tried to tease the tangles out with a silver comb. Queen Arianna looked on with a smile, secretly rejoicing at the feisty screams and surprisingly strong kicks from her daughter. Fury meant *life*, which wasn't always guaranteed in the youngest. Fury meant a strong will— which was especially useful for girls and women and even queens, who had to fight for what was theirs.

King Frederic paced the room impatiently, constantly checking the work of the court painter, who was doing a quick sketch of the scene. Which would have been charming behavior in a new father—if only he hadn't also tried to have the poor artist sketch Rapunzel's first bath, Rapunzel's first lie-down in her royal bassinet, and even Rapunzel's first royal diaper change.

"Stay still, pretty thing!" Lettie pleaded, trying to gently hold the baby's head so she wouldn't be hurt by the beautiful comb.

"Easy there, love," Nanna Bess said, dandling the infant a little on her hip.

"All right, just one more knot and we're done," the maid said through gritted teeth.

She *might* have yanked the comb a little hard to get through it quickly. Rapunzel let out an angry cry and jerked her head, causing the tangle to get stuck on the comb.

"Oh, darling!" Lettie cried, putting her hand on the baby's poor red scalp.

Rapunzel's face also turned red. Beet red with infant hurt and pain. She opened her pretty pink lips wide and *howled* . . . .

. . . and the maidservant dropped dead.

The room was silent except for the infant princess crying, which really wasn't all that loud—she was a newborn, after all.

"What . . . ?" The normally silent Frederic spoke first.

One of the guards thought fast; he rushed over, dropped to a knee, and felt the maid's cheek. "She's already growing cold—call the physician, though I think it's too late."

The other guard saluted and went shouting through the halls, demanding the summons of Signore Dottore Alzi, who treated the castle and staff.

"Rapunzel!" the queen cried, leaping up. Like any mother, confused and faced with violence, her first instinct was to grab her baby.

But Nanna Bess turned aside, clutching the baby close and holding her away from the queen.

"Your Majesty, no," she said, her quick mind making sense of the situation faster than anyone else in the room— save, perhaps, the guard. "You must keep away."

"Give me my child," Arianna demanded, a bit of her

daughter's will bubbling up through her otherwise terrified black eyes.

"No, my queen," Bess said firmly. "There's something strange afoot here—you saw it. Lettie tugged Rapunzel's hair and now she is dead. In truth the babe seems to be calming now, but let me hold her until we know that it's safe."

Arianna started to move forward anyway—but Frederic held her back.

The artist continued sketching the scene: a bleak, silent room full of chaos and despair . . . and a rosy-cheeked baby, who was already gurgling and making content little noises to herself, the moment of hurt utterly forgotten.

The artist was *not* invited into the king's solar, where the scene of despair continued—though it was now tempered by thought and worry. Frederic and Arianna held each other close while their daughter slept nearby (in the bassinet that had been carved from rowan wood to keep her safe from bad fairies). Signore Dottore Alzi was there, as was the castle priest, and Nanna Bess, and the guard who had discovered that Lettie was dead.

"I'm inclined to think it was an unhappy accident," said the doctor tiredly. He had wire glasses and kind eyes.

"Perhaps this maid had a heart condition, or something in her brain. The stress of the moment caused the blood and humors in her body to boil and agitate until her weak condition could bear it no more."

"You think *that* was the first time she experienced stress?" Nanna Bess shot back. "Tell me, Signore, have you ever actually talked to a pretty young maid from a poor family?"

The doctor shrugged. He didn't have an answer.

"The devil is at work here," the priest said. "This is what comes from relying on magic plants and witchery to save you, and not the word of God."

King Frederic rubbed his prodigious brow tiredly and squeezed Arianna's shoulder, comforting her before she could react to this.

"You there, guard," he commanded. "You're the one who understood what was going on first, going over to the poor dead girl. Tell me exactly what you saw."

Royal guard Justin Tregsburg (known as "Maximus" in the Roman fashion because of how he towered over his siblings) was young, but experienced enough not to show emotion. "Your Majesty, to my eyes it looked like the princess grew angry—and the maid immediately died. I saw nothing else save the fact that the maid was touching the baby, the baby's hair to be exact, when it happened—but

Bess was holding the baby and lived. I could not tell you *how* it happened."

"The princess's *hair* . . ." Arianna slowly rose and went over to the bassinet. Rapunzel's silver locks—still with that last knot—were spread out on the pillow around her, strange and, yes, unnatural in the child of two parents with hair as brown as the mane of a fine Arabian steed.

Witchy hair.

"Maybe it *was* the flower," Signore Alzi mused. "Of course I don't believe in such things—Arianna is a fine, healthy woman who probably recovered on her own. But let us suppose this Sundrop Flower was magical, and its essence was transferred to the queen upon her ingesting its infusion. Would it not follow that the baby too would consume its essence, as she ingests the food and drink her mother eats while bearing her?"

Arianna and Frederic exchanged a worried look. She put her hand without thought on her belly, now empty of its charge.

"A child cannot control her rage, Your Majesty," the priest said gently. "Whether this is the work of the devil or Alzi's ridiculous scientific ideas, if she has the power to kill she will do so again, thoughtlessly, as babes flail and squirm in their tantrums."

Frederic tried to control his feelings by frowning and

thinking like a king, the way his father taught him, and his father before that.

"But what is there to be done? Do any of you actually have any *ideas*? Tregsburg?"

At this the guard looked uncomfortable. He had been raised deep in the hinterlands of this country, on the folklore of the people there. And now he wore the garb of any fairy-tale hunter or executioner who might be tasked to take a baby out and . . . deal with it in the woods.

"Sounds like she could present a credible danger and threat to you and the queen, Your Majesty," he said reluctantly. "Or Nanna Bess, or anyone who tends her."

Arianna stifled a sob.

Nanna Bess looked at the baby wistfully. "Think of it, though. A princess who lived with such powers . . . a queen . . . she'd be a right powerful ruler, wouldn't she? That would be a sight."

"She needs to be raised *safely*," King Frederic said, repeating aloud the only thought that was clear or made any sense in his head.

"Safe for her—*and* everyone else," Alzi added quickly.

"In a safe, godly community. With nuns," the priest suggested.

"Maybe by someone who knows about these sorts of things," the guard disagreed as politely as possible.

"She is *my child*," Arianna cried. "I will go with her!"

"You are the queen, beg pardon, Your Majesty," Bess said with a low curtsy. "You have a responsibility to many children besides yer own. A whole kingdom of children—and their parents, who need your leadership."

"She's not wrong," Signore Alzi said.

"You are a shepherd to your people," the priest said.

"Perhaps we could keep her nearby so you could visit," King Frederic suggested . . . but in that suggestion was the note of finality in his thoughts on the matter. "Until she has grown out of such things . . . or has learned to control herself."

Arianna glowered at him with her own unmagical fury. Then she wilted.

"Tregsburg—put the word out. *Secretly* this time," King Frederic ordered. "To all the real goodwives and wit—uh, women, who have knowledge of these things. Dangerous magical things. Find one who will care for Rapunzel like her own child and teach her well, protecting her from the world and the world from her."

"Yes, Your Majesty. Absolutely, Your Majesty." The guard saluted.

"And what shall we say happened here?" the priest asked, indicating the baby—and the unseen, unmentioned, but unavoidable body of the maid.

"We will say she died trying to save the princess," Signore Alzi suggested. "A noble act, but too late. A serpent or venomous lizard got them both."

(Signore Alzi had happily fled the insidious courts of the Medici for the less scheming and poisonous land of this kingdom, but he had well learned the art of the lie, and the power of rumor and gossip.)

"Let it be done," Frederic ordered.

Then he took his weeping Arianna in his arms, and held her tightly until night fell.

Mother Gothel

The assortment of goodwives, doctors, priests, and charlatans to choose from was much smaller this time because of the need for actual expertise on the matter, not just hearsay. When it came to magic, there was a very small—but very significant—difference between *belief* and *knowledge*. The average sort of hedge practitioner, the kind who silently wished for powers like the Sundrop Flower bestowed but in reality concocted useless love philters for starry-eyed teens (while dispensing reasonably good advice), just wouldn't do this time. Nor would those who read the fates in cards or those who could do tricks for kings, either.

Necromancers were right out.

It was down to a very slim selection indeed when, one dark evening, a cloaked, black-haired woman appeared like a fairy tale at the castle door. The guards unlocked and opened it, and she wasn't even paying attention; she was admiring the shadow of her—admittedly comely—body, cast large by the flames of the torches in the wall. She posed and tossed her head like a much younger maiden.

"Sorry. My little hut has absolutely terrible light," she said with a winning smile. "Just tallow candles and sunshine to admire my girlish figure."

Tregsburg was not drawn in by her smile, nor her beautiful full black hair, nor her large eyes. Yet he also did not have the sadly common prejudices of a peasant; he didn't care if she was from the Romi or the Judisce or the mountains or someplace south. There was just something . . . off about her. False.

Still, he ushered her in like all the others. She looked around at the tapestries, the suits of armor, the resident nobles' finery, with interested eyes—but a strange little smirk on her face. As if she thought it was all delightful yet largely unimportant: *How silly for the inhabitants to treasure such things!*

"Your Majesty," the guard announced, "Mother Gothel."

"*Sister* Gothel, really," she corrected immediately.

"Not that I don't yearn to be a mother to my own little babe someday, but . . . 'mother' just sounds so . . . *old*, doesn't it?"

She remembered to curtsy only at the very last minute.

The king sat in his comfiest non-throne chair; Arianna was perched drawn and pale on a settee with one hand on the bassinet. Nanna Bess stood close by, one hand on her queen's shoulder. The priest and the doctor lurked in the shadows.

"I'm so *delighted* the queen pulled through her ailments and delivered such a *beautiful* baby girl . . ." Gothel said, standing on her tiptoes to peep at the baby. "After the tragedy of not finding the Sundrop Flower . . ."

"But we did," Frederic said, confused. So much so that he forgot the formal speech he had already recited a dozen times. "We found the flower, plucked it, and made the tea, and the queen drank it—and this is the cause of the problem, we believe."

"Um, what, Your Majesty?" the woman asked, also confused. "The Sundrop Flower *can't* have been picked! I still have . . . I mean, I feel like there would have been a *sign* or a portentous omen . . . I would have, uh, read it in the tea leaves. . . ."

"A royal celebration and minstrels proclaiming the magic of a healthy birth wasn't enough?" Nanna Bess asked archly.

Ignoring her, Gothel went over to the baby. She gazed at the princess with greater interest and intrigue than before.

"Her hair . . ." she said slowly. "It's silver. Not golden, like one would expect if she had drunken the essence of *golden* petals. And you're sure it was the Sundrop Flower?"

"Yes, unless there is another shining blossom out there somewhere," Signore Alzi interrupted impatiently.

Gothel remained silent.

"Here is the situation." King Frederic pressed on. This was the hardest part of the ordeal; recounting again and again the story of what happened. Arianna turned and buried her head in Bess's aprons like a child; the old woman put her arms around the queen like a mother.

Gothel said nothing, but her large eyes grew even wider as the king told the truth about Rapunzel and the death of Lettie.

When it was over, Gothel studied the baby a moment silently before she spoke.

"Such power . . ." she murmured. Her eyes narrowed in thought. "In the right . . . or wrong . . . hands . . . Some would pay for such a pretty little weapon, not lock her away. . . ."

"*What* did you just say?" Arianna demanded.

Gothel turned to face the king, a grim look on her face. "Sire, you are correct to be so concerned. The power of the heavens is now terribly concentrated in the heart of such a . . . cutie-wootie little baby. She needs to be *protected*. But also kept safe from those who would use her for ill. Though it is a dangerous undertaking, I would be honored to take on such a burden as my own, and lift the responsibility from Your Majesty's shoulders."

"Rapunzel isn't a *burden*," Arianna said, fingers tightening on the bassinet. "She is an *infant*. She isn't a *responsibility*, she's a child."

"Your Majesty, one can tell you're an . . . excited new mother with all of the resources of an entire kingdom at your disposal," Gothel said with a curtsy and a wink at Nanna Bess. "*All* infants and children are both responsibilities and burdens. . . . It is why those of us who practice the arts often don't have time for them."

Bess didn't disagree but shifted uncomfortably at the familiar tone the goodwife took with her mistress.

"So you have never cared for a child before," King Frederic said.

"Oh, don't let these girlish looks deceive you," Gothel said, laughing and spinning coquettishly. "I am far older than I look and have lived a long hard life before now. My experiences are too many to list."

"That's not answering the question," Signore Alzi pointed out.

"Here," Gothel said in answer, turning to the baby and leaning over her.

She stroked Rapunzel on the cheek and murmured soft words . . . and then lifted her up.

Everyone in the room gasped.

But the baby, first woken in surprise by a stranger, immediately saw she was in no danger. She tried to lift her head off Gothel's shoulder to get a look around. When she saw her mother, she relaxed, snuggling back down.

"You see now?" Gothel cooed quietly, bouncing the baby a little. "I'm quite good with little ones. And my knowledge of things like the Sundrop Flower will allow me to raise her safely, away from people, where she can hurt no one."

"Until she has grown out of it," Arianna said, carefully repeating what Frederic had said before, as exact and superstitious as a child afraid of being cheated out of a promise. "Or she is old enough to control herself."

"Ah, Your Majesty, I'm afraid where this sort of thing is involved *growing out of it* isn't a question," Gothel said, making her lips purse sadly. "Her powers will grow and become even more, ah, powerful. Until she is deadly just to be near—you won't even have to be touching her."

"*No!*" Arianna cried, standing up, clenching her fists.

"Afraid so," Gothel said with a sigh. "Honestly, it's a ridiculously dangerous thing for me to take on. You hear about it all the time in the circles I travel in. Someone takes in a cursed foundling, then dies at its hands. . . . I probably wouldn't even bother unless I thought I would be compensated enough for my family to be taken care of in the probable event of my accidental death."

"Of course," the king said, missing Tregsburg's poor attempt to not roll his eyes. "We will provide for you—and your family, in the event of your . . . Do you really think she would do that?"

"No," Arianna whispered, gazing at Rapunzel, who looked no more dangerous than any sleeping babe.

"Where do you live, Gothel?" the king asked, trying to sound businesslike. But his eyes were bright with tears.

"Oh, you know, a little hut in the Deiber River Valley," Gothel said carelessly. "Maybe not the best place for such a dangerous—er, pretty little princess. But I know *just* the spot. A hidden place in a beautiful dell, full of wildflowers and soft grasses. An ancient place, a ruined fort . . . with the sort of, ah, keep one might need to protect the darling."

"Where is it?" Tregsburg demanded.

"Maybe it's best not to tell. Kidnappings and ransom are common with the little ladies of the court, aren't they? And what if the people revolt and want to destroy her?"

"But I want to *see* her!" Arianna said, standing up. "I want to see her grow up! Even if I can't . . . *be* with her."

"We could of course arrange visits," Gothel said soothingly. "But maybe, for her—and your—peace of mind, without her knowing about it. At least at first. I'll let you in and you can gaze at her to your heart's delight."

"You should leave tonight," Frederic declared. "Alzi—fetch the treasurer. We must make sure our child lacks for nothing and provide her with the lifestyle we cannot oversee ourselves."

"You're too kind, Your Majesty," Gothel said, curtsying with the baby still on her shoulder.

"Tonight . . ." Arianna said—with no tears, for they had already been used up.

A layette was quickly assembled and packed. Blankets and gowns and snuggly hats and the softest diapers were folded into trunks. A handsome, gentle donkey was saddled up with a basket for the baby and a cart for the provisions—and gold.

Although the guards tried to stop her, Queen Arianna would not be held back from giving her princess a final kiss.

"We are doing the right thing," Frederic said, holding her shoulders.

"For the kingdom, maybe," Arianna said. "Maybe for

our own safety. But *not* for my baby. Do not for a moment fool yourself into thinking that."

And so Mother Gothel set out like a thief in the night, the princess tucked in safely for the journey.

The next day the story was made public of the sudden and terrible death of Rapunzel, and the brave maid who had tried to save her from a venomous serpent. All who had actually been in the room at the time were sworn to secrecy. The entire kingdom mourned for a fortnight, and the ceremonies ended with the release of the sky lanterns as a tribute to the poor deceased princess. The king declared that they would do it every year to mark the anniversary of her death.

Life gradually returned to normal for the kingdom . . . but not for its king and queen, who were still kind and fair, but now sad and prone to silence.

A Fairy-Tale Interruption

Late one night, not too long after these events, a light but decisive knock sounded upon the gatehouse of the castle. A guard opened the door to find an old woman waiting patiently there. She was wrapped in layer upon layer of undyed wool robes and shawls, and grasped a walking staff made from the gnarled root of a tree in her gnarled hands. Her hair was long, swirled in black and white, and bound up in braids around her head. Though her face was pouchy and cheeks and nose red with the cold, she peered up into the guard's face with bright, interested black eyes.

"I'm here about the baby?" she said.

The guard blinked at her in surprise for a moment and then went and fetched his superior. Corporal Tregsburg (promoted because of his calm—and quiet—handling of the princess situation) ushered the old woman inside quickly, taking her to a small side room where they could talk and not be heard.

"That crisis is over," he told her. "We found a caretaker for the princess weeks ago—how is it you are just coming here *now*?"

"Oh, I live in the woods and rarely hear the news, and when I *do* hear it, I often forget it for a day or two," the woman said, not really apologizing. "There's always something else to take my attention . . . mostly the goats, of course. Or baby dormice who need tending, a brownie that got lost, a patch of ground that was forgotten by spring . . . you know."

Tregsburg did *not* know. What he did know was that this sort of thing really wasn't in his job description *or* worldview, and he wished it would all be tidied up—by someone else—and sooner rather than later. He had a servant bring the woman a nice bowl of broth and a tankard of cider, and if she were an angel or a sorceress in disguise, he felt that he had done all that was right by her.

She happily tucked into the soup . . . and grew chatty, to the corporal's dismay.

"Well, as long as I'm here, pray could you tell me what the truth of the matter is? Your messenger made it sound urgent, and here I am, miles away from my cozy hut."

"I am sworn to secrecy on the matter, which has now been attended to."

"Ah, yes, but if I had been here on time you *would* have told me. And anyway you could take my tongue out with a single lop of that fancy steel sword of yours—so humor an old lady. You found the Sundrop Flower, you fed it to the queen, she grew healthy and had a baby girl, and—then what?"

The corporal sighed and told her what happened.

The old woman frowned.

"*Killed* the poor maid? And the baby had silver hair, you say? That is not the mark of the Sundrop Flower, nor its power. Either it was a rogue mushroom the queen ate instead, or, by my guess, the bloom of the Moondrop."

Tregsburg looked at her in dismay, his mind racing. This goodwife was not a tenth as comely as Gothel . . . but spoke candidly and certainly, like she actually knew of these mystical things. The other woman, now that he thought about it, had not said much at all about the flower or the strangeness of the situation. She had just taken the baby—and left.

"Where is the princess now?" the woman asked interestedly, sipping the broth as if this were gossip at a pub.

"The king and queen found a goodwife who arrived *on time* and promised to care for her safely."

"Hm. And then you made all this fuss about the princess dying to hide what really happened?" she asked, waving her spoon around. There was still black crepe hung here and there throughout the castle, though outside it the people of the kingdom were slowly taking the bunting down and continuing with their lives. "Strange choice. Not *wrong*, just . . . not what I would have done. But I choose to live in the woods and talk to plants. Say, this is a *nice* spoon," she said, suddenly looking at it in her hand. "Well balanced. *Metal.* So who is this goodwife who took her?"

Tregsburg debated secrecy for a moment. But the old woman already knew most of the story at this point—and seemed to have guessed the rest. She might have seemed like a daft old hermit, yet her mind was sharp.

"Mother Gothel," he finally admitted.

"Never heard of her," the old woman said with a shrug. "There was a family of Gothels who lived . . . oh, a while ago, on the other side of the river. . . . But no goodwives among them."

The corporal tried not to let his frustration show. It seemed that a terrible mistake had been made—but what was done was done, and not by his choice. The kingdom had already gone through enough turmoil and tragedy. And if Queen Arianna suddenly thought she had made a bad choice, or Frederic . . . the revelation of this would kill them. And despite all else, the Gothel woman seemed a good enough nurse.

"Well, nothing for me here now, I guess," the goodwife said. She had finished her soup and was looking around a little uncomfortably. "I sort of . . . you know, I sort of was looking forward to having a baby. I had one once—a long time ago. He died before his second birthday. . . . It would be nice to have some bright eyes and a merry laugh around the house. I was thinking about it all the way here. Where I'd put her bed, the best herbs to ward off pox, how to get help from the river spirits . . ."

"I'm sorry, Mother," Tregsburg said, meaning it. "I'm sorry for many, many things here. But there is nothing more to be done. May I find someone to take you by cart as far as you need, back to your home? Some supplies for the way, perhaps?"

"Oh, you're too kind," she said with a smile and a wink. "Nice *and* quite a build. If I were younger, laddie . . . But I think I'll spend some time in the capital, as long as I've made the trip. See the sights, visit a few old trees, buy some trinkets. Hey, can I keep the spoon?"

The guard blinked at the sudden change in conversation.

"What? I suppose. If you must. A gift from King Frederic, for your time."

"Lovely, just lovely," she said with a sigh, gazing at its

bowl. "*Nice* workmanship. Solid. All right then, young man, just see me to the door and I'll be on my way."

"At once, Mother," he said with a bow.

The old woman rose carefully, holding her new prize, and waddled off toward the exit.

"Oh, you might want to tell whoever is taking such lovely care of those bellflowers on the ledge there that a cold snap is coming, three days hence—an untimely freeze," she called over her shoulder as she left. "She should take them in."

"But it's June!" Tregsburg said.

And that was the last he saw of her for many a year.

But in three days the bellflowers were dead, their pale blue blossoms frozen and thawed to pastel-colored tissue that melted in the rain.

Memorial Sloan Kettering

"Hold up a second."

Daniella didn't move anything except her lips, didn't even open her eyes, too cold and exhausted to do much more than speak. But her voice was adamant and demandy and went through Brendan's skull like nails on chalkboards—and for that he was extremely grateful.

"What about the queen?" she asked.

"The queen?" Brendan asked, confused. "She was, you know, sad about what had to be done and went back to ruling the kingdom with her husband, stoic but forlorn all her days . . ."

"Uh-uh. Nope." Daniella shook her head just a little. "It's one thing when your baby has been stolen and you don't know where she is and you keep looking; it's totally different when *you've* made the choice to give her up. The queen knows who has her baby, and might even know where—you can't tell me she doesn't want to at least check up on her own child!"

"Okay, that's a good point," Brendan admitted, thinking about it. Would he have given in so quickly if she hadn't been sick? Would he even have bothered to consider the point? He liked to think he would have.

"Your male gaze is affecting the story," Daniella said with a smirk. She could read him, even when half asleep. "The great patriarch here only cares about the plot, the *driving* elements of the story, and doesn't understand how events might affect those who aren't the central hero with a thousand faces. . . ."

"All right, all right point taken!"

"Imagine if it were Mom."

"*I said okay,*" Brendan said, trying not to laugh. "Okay, here goes, and forgive me, great Goddesses, Keepers of the World Tree and All Relevant Subtext.

"Queen Arianna, bereft of hope . . ."

Queen Arianna

. . . bereft of hope, mourned just as hard and long as a kingdom would expect her to for the loss of her first—and in all likelihood only—child.

Of course no one but the king and their closest advisers (and that one guard) knew the real truth, or how her mourning was different from that of a woman whose baby had actually died: she had *chosen* to give up Rapunzel. The princess would grow up bathed by someone else, having her hair brushed by someone else, being taught to walk, run, sing, speak—*everything* by someone else. Another mother. That mother would nurse her, feed her, dress her, sew little flowers on her dresses, sing her lullabies at night.

The queen could scarcely move off her bed, so sick with longing and sadness was she.

Signore Dottore Alzi suggested that they encourage Arianna to get a hobby to distract herself. Maybe a dog; a tiny fluffy one.

The king said no.

The priest suggested that the queen bury herself in good works and prayer. Maybe the donation of a nice new wing at the kingdom's second-largest church would help.

The king said it was a nice idea, but it wouldn't really fix anything.

Old Nanna Bess suggested that nothing could cure a mother's loss; even those who lost child after child to starvation, disease, and foreign wars never grew used to the heartache of each passing.

The king said no, that couldn't possibly be true; please, he couldn't bear it.

As for Arianna herself, when she could no longer bear the hole in her soul, she begged Corporal Tregsburg to secretly take her to see her child.

He tried to dissuade the queen as much as his station allowed him to. The guard had a fine, strapping nephew of ten and a beautiful and clever niece of fifteen, but he had lost another niece, who came into the world already dead.

Mostly they were a healthy, happy family, but his sister still put flowers on the sunny spot where they had buried the infant, thinking no one saw.

"Your Majesty, no good can come of this," he said, trying to use the words his sister had suggested. "It will not make you feel better—only worse."

"Thank you, but it must needs be done," Arianna said, gracious as she was in all things, despite the raw pain on her face and in her heart.

Reluctantly he took her deep into the forest.

Where the path divided, the woman Gothel was waiting for them. She curtsied low and behaved *just* respectfully enough—but seemed to enjoy the act of blindfolding the queen a little much.

"Is this really necessary?" Tregsburg demanded. He couldn't put his finger on it, but there was something about the woman that made his skin crawl.

"It's for the good of the kingdom," Gothel reminded him in a tone he also didn't like.

"It's all right," Arianna said, with a ghost of a smile at his concern.

From there she followed the goodwife, one hand in hers, down a path she could not see, not trusted with the secret of where her own child was now hidden. So Tregsburg stayed and guarded their spot as best he could, but it wasn't really necessary. No one came by except for one mushroom forager, who was obviously curious but fearful enough of the soldier to just touch his hat and walk on.

Arianna, meanwhile, was led silently through the woods, into what seemed like a moist, close area of rock—a tunnel? A cave? Her baby had better not be in a cave! But they finally came out into a wider space; sounds echoed differently and a breeze blew across her face, scented of meadow flowers. The two women padded across soft grass and through a wooden door . . . and then *up*. Up and up and up tiny, tight spiral stairs, the only handhold a knotted rope that hung straight down into the depths. Despite her sadness and anticipation, Arianna did feel a little curiosity: where *were* they exactly?

But every time she opened her mouth the witch shushed her, or laid a finger across her lips. Not a gesture appropriate to make with a queen, but her finger was soft and smelled of precious oils, so it wasn't the worst thing.

At last they reached what felt like a space to step out, albeit a confined one. Gothel removed the blindfold and for a moment Arianna was dizzy and confused; all was still black. Then there was a noise of something being slid aside, and a rectangle of light revealed a strangely serene scene beyond what was (now) obviously a peephole.

There was a large, well-appointed, sunny room,

decorated with expensive curtains and such furniture as the queen had provided. A window revealed blue sky and a few puffy white clouds—and nothing else. They were so high up!

In the middle of the room was a soft bassinet. In it lay Rapunzel, silver hair glittering in the light, bright eyes dancing as she tried reaching for a mobile of pretty sparkly things that hung just out of reach.

Gothel came into view and picked up Queen Arianna's baby, cuddling and cooing at her. She swayed over to where the queen was hidden and held the happy infant up to—but not facing—the slot where the queen looked out.

The baby sighed then threw herself hard against Gothel's shoulder, for the sheer delight of moving.

"Oh, that's a good girl," Gothel murmured. "There, there, aren't we feisty?"

Arianna reached a hand out, only to have it touch the cold wood before her. All energy, light, feeling, spirit, vanished out of her, down to her feet. She would have collapsed to the floor but didn't want to miss a moment of seeing her child.

When Gothel put Rapunzel down and came back to the hidden room for the queen, Arianna said nothing. She silently wept during the endless descent down the stairs, along the path back to the guard. When she took the blind-fold off it was heavy with tears.

"Never again" was all Arianna said aloud.

Without another word she let herself be led away.

Tregsburg tossed Gothel a sack of coins, which she caught with an ironically courteous smile.

Although the visit was supposedly secret from the entire castle, some knew even without asking what had occurred. The king said nothing but held Arianna in his arms deep into the night. The doctor and the priest played a long game of chess as the hours drew on, casting weary and saddened looks over at the royal apartments.

A month later, Nanna Bess had just about enough.

She caught Queen Arianna gazing out the window at some servants' children playing in the courtyard, a strained look on her face. The old servant sensed this was a turning point for the beleaguered queen and approached her gruffly.

"You know, Your Majesty, there's many a babe who has suffered the loss of a *mother*—as well as other mothers who have lost their children. Why don't you pay a visit to the poorhouse and do charity for those who are in far more dire straits than you? Or the orphanage? The nuns barely keep it going with such meager funds as they have."

"Orphans?" the queen asked, blinking. "We send food. . . ."

"And is it just food you think an ailing, motherless child needs?" the nurse demanded, folding her arms. She knew she was pushing it. But she loved her queen, and her kingdom, and these were precipitous moments. Everyone knew how the Countess Bathory had turned out without anyone to talk back to her.

"I . . . Take me to one of these places," the queen ordered.

Which showed her underlying strength of character and the goodness of her heart: she was not so far gone with her own troubles to ignore a lack somewhere in her kingdom.

At the orphanage she picked up a baby covered in sores and cuddled him to her chest—despite the horrified pleading of the nuns and nurses. She looked around at the dim and dingy room where babies and toddlers were confined, and past it to where older unwanted children hung about listlessly. These adolescents were occasionally sent to farms that needed workers, or wealthier families who needed servants.

The queen's eyes, previously as empty as her heart, were forcibly opened.

"This is my cause," she murmured.

And so it was.

Arianna still mourned the loss of her daughter and spent many sleepless nights in the last room where she saw her, one hand on her cradle. But her days were spent building the finest orphanages that anyone in the world had ever seen. She made sure there was enough food, clothes, and nurses to take adequate care of the kingdom's motherless youngest. Books (mostly Bibles) were provided, and teachers with them. The habit of sending off the older children to work was stopped; couples who could not have children, or families who genuinely wanted more children, were encouraged to come—but carefully vetted.

"See?" the doctor said. "I told you a hobby would distract her."

"See?" the priest said. "Good deeds have calmed her soul."

Nanna Bess just rolled her eyes.

Rapunzel

It was summer, so the sun appeared in the bottom left-hand corner of the big window at quarter past six.

Ish.

It was hard to tell exactly until the sun rose just a *little bit* more, enough to send his beams through the holes carefully bored through a piece of wood, above which the hours were marked off in beautifully painted flourishes. This simple timepiece hung from the ceiling off a stick hammered sturdily in, because a string would have let it spin and therefore fail its task of tracking the sun.

The wind chimes, however, assembled from more bits of wood, and pieces of metal, and shaped and dried bits of pottery, were free to swing and tinkle as they pleased. These were surrounded by celestial bric-a-brac that also dangled from the ceiling and spun with abandon when the breeze found them: papier-mâché stars, comets of hoarded glass shards and mirror, a very carefully re-created (and golden) replica of the constellation Orion, a quilted and embroidered cloth model of the sun, and several paintings on rectangular panels hung such that they faced straight down. So that the viewer, in bed, might look up at them and pretend they were windows or friends, depending on whether the subject was landscapes or faces.

Rapunzel woke up to the dazzling, sparkling, gently chiming display with more cheer than anyone really should who had spent the last six thousand and approximately nine hundred days in a lonely tower.

"*This* birthday is going to be *great*. I just know it!"

She only really knew about birthdays because she had read about them in one of the thirty-seven books she owned: Book #3: *Stories from Rome and Other Great Empires*. Marc Antony apparently had *splendid* birthdays, and Cleopatra gave him the most cunning gifts. Anyway, they seemed like a marvelous idea, and she had adopted this time of year as her own.

Had there been anyone around, they would have been

amazed at the hermit's beauty. For one thing, her cheeks were surprisingly rosy for a girl who had been indoors her whole life.

(This was because on sunny Wednesday and Saturday afternoons she carefully followed the window-shaped spot of sun around her room, lying down and soaking in the warm rays.)

Her eyes were large and green because of parents she had never known.

Her lips were usually set in an expectant smile because she was Rapunzel; good-natured, lighthearted, with a quick mind that constantly refused to be crushed by her circumstances.

"No birthday yet, though," she told herself. "Chores first!"

Putting off something wonderful—even a little bit—always made it more delicious later.

She sprang out of bed, the ornaments in her hair tinkling and jingling, making tiny versions of the noises of the chimes above her.

And that was Rapunzel's most striking beauty: her hair.

Miles of beautiful, sparkling, *silver* hair.

Bound in plaits and whorls and buns and knots and twists as tightly as she could manage. Some of the braids were so long they hung in loops that she put her arms through; they hung at her sides like giant sleeves or tippets from an ancient dress.

Decorating all of this were dozens of charms—also silver, like her hair, but some with exotic stones like lapis and turquoise. Bells, tiny moons, hands, suns, six-pointed stars, eyes, and anything else Mother Gothel could lay her hands on at her daughter's request.

By these amulets Rapunzel desperately tried to control her hair, bind her hair, disempower her hair, and unenchant her magic hair.

Ten of the thirty-seven books she had were devoted to magic: sorcery, spells, folklore, the wisdom of the ancient Egyptians, wise men and women before the time of Christ. Sadly, none of those ten books spoke specifically about controlling magic hair. They described talismans made with the lock of an innocent child's hair, spells for love bound with a strand of the desired one's hair, incantations for revenge involving the braid of an enemy's hair. But nothing about hair that was *in and of itself* magical.

She tied a kerchief around her brow to keep the frontmost strands off her forehead and the tiny dangly bits from annoying her.

Then she dove into the morning cleaning.

There weren't many rooms in the tower, which made

it easy, but she liked to be thorough. Sweep, mop, polish. The garderobe and her mirror got sparkly from scrubbing with a bit of vinegar (a trick she learned from Book #14: *Useful Recipes for Master Servants*). She transferred a day dress that was soaking in a soapy bucket to a clean water bucket, scrubbing out the bit of lingonberry juice stain from breakfast on Monday.

7:00: Personal ablutions. She washed her face and nails and applied cream to her cuticles and everywhere on her face but the T-zone, which was, despite her fairy-tale beauty, just a tad prone to breaking out.

8:00: Reading. She (re)read Book #26, *Sidereus Nuncius* by Galileo. More a pamphlet than a book, but it counted.

8:30: Art! Lacking a proper canvas (or piece of wall space) she chose to spend her painting time decorating the mop handle. It might not be dry enough to actually use the next day, but that was all right. Birthday weeks meant the occasional break from routine—that was part of the fun! She took out Book #24: *Symbols, Runes, and Motifs of the Sámi People* and propped it open so she could study the designs while she worked. She didn't copy them exactly but found them extremely inspirational. The book had runes of enigmatic, powerful gods; she drew lines of girls with long hair she imagined as friends or cousins. The book had pictures of birds that looked like dark messengers; she made her own birds into the tiny singers that she saw from her window: quick and gay and full of no meaning beyond their own world. The book had images of strange creatures with giant, dangerous-looking antlers. Rapunzel preferred the sinuous lines of a mink or weasel as it wound round and round the handle of the mop, chasing a pink frog with absolutely enormous ears.

(Though it should be noted that she wasn't exactly sure of the physical details or actual names of any of these animals; she had seen almost none of them in real life, and the illuminations of them in her books were often exaggerated and always different.)

10:00: Preparation for the night's astronomy! Rapunzel knew exactly when her adopted birthday was coming because of her careful tracking and observation of the heavens. What had started out as a child's interest in the longer days of summer and shorter days of winter had progressed into a study that would have been the praise of any university professor. She knew all the constellations, of course; which ones came and went with the seasons (Orion), which ones stayed wandering the heavens forever (the Big Bear). She could predict when Jupiter would rise. She could predict some lunar eclipses. She had astrolabes and pendulums and squares and straightedges and compasses for measuring the precise height of an astral object above her window ledge.

Besides the actual science and math part, Rapunzel also liked creating seasonal paintings based on astrological signs—the constellations that the sun moved through as the months passed, especially the ones said to have sway over a person's life. Among her ten books of magic was #5: *The Annular Tarot*, and it had been a favorite of hers four years ago, for the pictures as well as its instructions on how to predict the future.

(Until, of course, the tall dark stranger, the finding of great treasure, and the travels to a misty and mountainous land had all failed to materialize. She still liked the illustrations, though.)

Tonight, according to her astronomy notebook (#4 of her notebooks, which were even rarer and harder to come by than actual books, according to Gothel), the moon would be new, meaning not there at all; the sky would be black but for the stars. And in a few days *the floating lights would appear.*

They came at the same time every year. Even when it was cloudy, Rapunzel could see the telltale pinprick glows of their presence, gold and pink against the clouds. Which meant they were of the earth; below the moon and stars. How far *up* the lights floated she could never tell; they drifted into indifference when her eyes could no longer make them out against their sparkling stellar counterparts. Whether they were a natural phenomenon like rain (that went the wrong way) or some sort of magma or volcanic spew (Book #8: *Naturalis Historia* by Pliny the Elder, Complete with Letters and Notes by Pliny the Younger—including, of course, the Elder's death by volcano), or something else entirely (pixies? Titans?), Rapunzel had no idea. She only knew that they came every year on what she had decided was her birthday.

This year she would go see what they were. Herself.

Just thinking that thought caused the normally cheery and relentless Rapunzel to pause, bringing a flush to her face. It was a heady thought, a decisive thought; an insurrectional thought.

She swallowed and moved on with her day as best she could.

11:00: Plants.

Long accustomed to watching the green world outside her window ebb and flow with the seasons, Rapunzel had made the bold move some years ago of bringing some of them *in*side. Plants changed, and change was fascinating when you were stuck in a tower for your entire life. On the shelves around two of her windows she had a nice assortment of well-tended greenery, some gifted from her mother and some stolen from the wind and the tower wall itself. She had Tiny Ivy, Dandy Lion, Rebecca (a bugloss, and happy that it was mostly shaded), Cedric the Sedge, and a host of tiny vegetal offspring from supper leavings that came and went with the month. Most were annuals. But sometimes the onions flowered and they were beautiful, and the regrown lettuce made pretty rosettes that were fascinating to paint; they were the inspiration for dozens of pastel mandalas on the floor. Carrots made fun feathery tops that she liked to brush along her cheeks.

"Oh! You have a tiny shoot, Mr. Celery! Or wait, is that a root growing the wrong way? No, that is definitely a shoot. Good for you! And hello, Dandy, how are you today? Going to bloom and smile for us twice this year? That would be lovely!"

Et cetera.

Last to check was her namesake: a rampion or bell-flower, Campanula rapunculus—*little turnip*. All by itself in a beautiful Spanish clay pot with a bright blue glaze. Its blooms were pinky-purple stars, tiny but perfect and delicate.

Sometimes, if she was feeling down, Rapunzel would secretly break off a leaf and chew it, the sour/bitter taste comforting her through the worst of the drab winter months when nothing else grew.

Bugs were welcome, even the ones that ate leaves. If they stuck around, she named them as well.

(She also named the moose that had somehow made its way up into the tower, into her pantry, and nibbled through all her nuts in a matter of days—but the tiny, fluffy-tailed thing left after only a week.)

She had tried to get her mother to bring back an earthworm or two to live in her pots, or a newt, or, better yet, a lizard. But despite the specifically witchy cast to her adopted mother's physiognomy, the woman had laughed herself silly at the idea of her hands touching such "slimy" and "noxious" creatures.

Rapunzel, isolated from gossip and wives' tales and the ridiculous social constraints foisted upon girls, couldn't figure out Gothel's prejudice. These were still just creatures, after all, the same as the beautiful birds she saw. Only smaller.

And moister.

11:30: Morning calisthenics! And light exercise.

From Book #23, *Imperial Armies of the Known World and Tactics of the Greatest Strategists*, Rapunzel had learned all about how the Romans exercised when they weren't actively in battle, the training routines of the Spartans, and the dance-like moves of warriors in great countries to the east. Putting them all together in a way that felt right,

Rapunzel stripped down to her undergarments, tied a different kerchief around her forehead, and worked out with a paintbrush as a military baton.

When you had all the time in the world, you could literally isolate each muscle, feel how it differed from its neighbors, and learn to flex it individually.

She could also stand on her right tippy-toes for over an hour, eyes closed. Which sometimes she did.

12:00: Snack. Usually a piece of fruit, sometimes a leftover piece of bread or pastry.

12:15: More reading. Today, Book #13: Brother Gaudi's *God and the Natural World*. Bees were always interesting.

1:00: Hair.

Once a week, Rapunzel took down *all* of her hair, all of it, undid the braids that could still be undone, uncoiled the matted masses in the back, worked her fingers down to its roots, separated the coils, arranged the tresses, found all the buns and whorls, and brushed it completely from top to bottom. That was a six-hour affair at least.

But *every day* she attended to the lengths that still came out easily, the bits that framed her face, and the very, very, very longest of long braids that she coiled under and over her arms and shoulders like a vest. The one that also had a serious transport function.

She worked the fancy powder her mother had given her

into the roots and down to the ends, freshening and plumping her tresses. She looked into her somewhat dim mirror to check the placement of all the charms and crystals and bells; she tugged each to make sure it was solidly in and wouldn't come out. She shook her head to double-check, and the tower filled with happy silvery chimes.

2:30: Guitar practice. She was working on a piece of her own composition, something with lots of notes that was about the sky and birds. She sang along with half-formed words she hadn't quite figured out the meaning of yet, and apologized to the nameless medieval composer whose original piece she had stolen bits from.

And then at 3 PM sharp, French studies until . . .

"Rap*unzel* . . . Rapunzel dear! Let down your hairrrrrr!"

Mother Gothel was home.

Gothel

But where was Gothel when she *wasn't* with her daughter?

She always told Rapunzel she was taking care of the family farm, buying necessities at the market, and checking on her kitchen garden—which was liable to go to the aphids if not carefully watched.

If there were any white lies about where she actually went, they usually involved a certain dark mountainside where a certain glowing flower grew. Gothel would sing and stroke its petals, and her skin plumped up and her hair sleeked. Safe and young for another week! She always felt so old after visiting Rapunzel. The girl positively wore her out with her demands and wild emotions.

And doe eyes.

And rosy cheeks.

Anyway, the Sundrop was her normal secret.

But *this* time . . .

Deep in one of the few still-standing ruins on a deserted hillside, torches flickered and a fire blazed in an ancient hearth that hadn't been lit in a thousand years.

Between these two sources of distinctly human luminescence was a ring of uncomfortable but well-dressed people—and their much rougher-looking guards. Although several tried to disguise their faces and the sigils of their houses with veils and cloaks, it wasn't at all hard to recognize the Baron of Smeinhet, the Duke of Kraske, the Countess Bathory, and a number of the lesser lords of the lands surrounding the kingdom. Shifty eyes in well-fed faces looked from one to the other suspiciously.

Standing between these ridiculous figures and the hearth fire—so she was all silhouette and no detail—was the woman who had gathered all these wretches in gold and silk.

Gothel.

"All right, I'm here and my people are getting nervous," the Baron of Smeinhet snapped. "It had better be good."

"Oh, it is good, I assure you," Gothel said. "The girl is approaching her nineteenth birthday. *Marriageable* age."

"Long past marriageable age," a masked duke scoffed.

"Shut up, swinehound," the Countess Bathory snapped.

"Or *what*?" The duke snorted. "What possible thing could a *woman* do to me?"

"I could use my *vérhounds* to track down all your mistresses and cause a scandal for you—and then bathe in the girls' blood."

The man, who had a rich wife from a powerful family, many mistresses, and no standing army, went white.

Gothel hid her own disquietude at this interchange. Selling her ward to the highest bidder was one thing; princesses were always married off to people they barely knew. Selling her to a sadistic, well-known murderer like Bathory was too much—even for the very flexible morality of Mother Gothel. There wasn't a smallholding within a hundred miles that didn't scare their children into good behavior with stories of Bloody Lady Bathory, and how she kept her skin so young, and how young girls often disappeared from the villages around her castle.

"Folks, please. Can we focus on the important thing at hand?" Gothel said, waving her arms for attention and trying to change the subject. "Which is how much one of you lucky people is going to pay me for her bride price."

"I find this whole matter of bidding for her hand disgusting," Countess Bathory growled, flashing an angry look at the duke she had bickered with. "Wives aren't chattel to be sold as objects. . . ."

"You make an excellent point, My Lady," Gothel said with a curtsy. "And as a freethinking woman myself, I applaud your speaking out for our sex's rights."

". . . so I will bid for her as a maid," the countess finished. "As is appropriate. *Servants* are chattel and property. As are the children of the destitute and poor."

"All right, that wasn't exactly where I thought you were going with that," Gothel admitted. Not that she was entirely surprised. "But I take your point. The auction will be for a bride, servant, or licensing fee, whatever you want to call it. Blind bidding, three rounds only, less if there is an offer so generous that it can reasonably be understood to preempt the process. Have your servants drop off your bid, stamped with your house sigil, at the giant oak with the cross-shaped gash on the road leading to Leipserg.

"And please, before you complain, let me remind you: the girl's power has grown greatly, now that she is nearly an adult. As her guardian and the person who tirelessly raised her for nearly twenty years, *caring* for her and *listening* to her . . . Well, it's only fair I be recompensed for the burden of responsibility of such a dangerous—and talky—young person. Plus, how she *eats*! Why, her teenage appetite alone costs me more than—"

"You *say* she's powerful," the Baron of Smeinhet interrupted. "We have no proof. Only your word, and wives' tales."

"Yes," a marquess said. "We've traveled here at great risk twice now with nothing to show for it."

"You don't trust me?" Gothel asked in mock offense. "Really, does this look like a face that would lie to you? Don't answer that, I'm teasing.

"While I'm hurt, I'm not entirely surprised. How about this: you choose amongst yourselves a single witness you *can* trust. He—or she—will return with me to observe the deadly magic of my powerful ward . . . and report back to you lot."

"How do we choose someone we *all* trust?" an old earl called out. "None of us trusts each other—much less anyone else's servant."

There were several muttered agreements to this.

"But that is precisely the answer," Duke Kraske spoke up. "We need someone *no one* can trust—so everyone will. Viscount Thongel, that horrid spy is now with you, I see. What's his name? Crespin?"

The spy in question, sort of disguised as a common

servant accompanying Thongel, looked startled at the mention of his name—but not displeased.

"Crespin worked for Smeinhet over there until Thongel offered him more, and he worked for *me* before that," Kraske continued. "I dare say he has worked for us *all* at one time or another and been clever enough to save his own neck time and time again. I say we send him, with the usual rewards and threats if he betrays any of us along the way or tries to disappear."

The spy nodded, the large head on his spindly neck bobbing like an apple on Samhain.

"That makes sense," Smeinhet murmured, crossing his arms.

"I agree to it," Thongel added. One by one all the deplorables nodded and assented.

"Excellent," Gothel said with a grin. "It's a day's journey. We should get started tonight."

She looked through a crack in the ceiling to gauge and gaze at the waning, whisper-thin moon dramatically. Its light fell on the white, white teeth in her smile, creating her intended effect: it made even the hardiest, most sadistic souls there wonder at her mysterious powers.

Halfway there, she thought. She had the nobles—and Rapunzel—right where she wanted them.

Rapunzel

Mother was here!

Too many emotions coursed through Rapunzel's head, like the winds in fall that whipped clouds into rapidly changing shapes.

Excitement!

Visits from her mother were always a welcome diversion. Since Rapunzel had grown older, Gothel only spent part of her time in the tower. Mostly her visits were on Tuesdays and Thursdays, after three. But sometimes she would show up suddenly, unannounced, a surprise! Almost like she was checking up on Rapunzel, making sure she was still there. Which of course was absurd. Where would Rapunzel go?

Excitement, also, because sometimes Gothel brought a

gift—Rapunzel at nineteen was still young enough to hope for such things—but even if there was no material present, the older woman always cooked something delicious; beautiful vegetables from her garden, game from a huntsman, or other lovely things foraged and found in the woods around her cottage.

But . . . lately . . . added to the *excitement* was something else, something just the slightest bit off, a daub of grey in sunny yellow paint. Something unsettled and anxious. It might almost have been . . .

Trepidation.

Younger Rapunzel had accepted Mother Gothel in all her forms and all her moods, listening closely and taking her words to heart no matter what they were—and always assuming they were said with love. But some of the things Gothel said with a laugh, *funny* things, just didn't seem that funny anymore. They hurt. Even after she apologized or told her daughter not to take it so seriously (but also accused her of being too sensitive). Sometimes Rapunzel would spend hours in front of the mirror once her mother had left or gone to bed, wondering what she meant about "snub nose" and "funny-shaped freckle" and "sort of angular, unwomanly hips."

And besides all that, there was now the Question, about the floating lights.

Which kind of led to *Nervousness*. Maybe even *Panic*.

How would Gothel react? Would, by the end of this day, Rapunzel be sadly disappointed—or transported by joy, about to set out on an amazing adventure?

She was pretty sure it would be the second thing.

"Rapunzel, I'm waaaaaiting," her mother called out in a sort of cheerful voice. Cheerfully annoyed. Exasperated, but not alarmingly so.

"Coming, Mother!" Rapunzel said, rushing over to the window. With the smooth movements of long practice, she uncoiled the longest braid of her hair and strung it like a lasso over her right arm. She narrowed her eyes, gauged the distance, and threw.

Of course she could have just dropped the length of hair down, but she liked getting it to sail through the air, unraveling its coils prettily as it went, a silver streak in the sky like a rain cloud spun into yarn. The end of the braid, soft and fringed like the tail of a fairy-tale donkey (the only kind Rapunzel knew), just brushed the ground before falling back against the tower with an incredibly satisfying *thwack*.

(To dry the massive amount of hair after her monthly washing, she would throw *all* of it over the side of the tower and whack it repeatedly against the stone wall, sending waterfalls of droplets down to the ground.)

She braced herself against the wall—being careful not

to injure any of her plant friends—and waited. There was more jostling and pulling than usual; Gothel was having an awkward time coming up. Rapunzel peeped over the side. The woman had a giant basket hanging off her arm.

Could it be?

Had she actually remembered it was Rapunzel's birthday?

She closed her eyes tight, grinning, and tried not to dance. It was all going to work out. Everything was pointing to *yes*. Everything was, in short, amazing.

"What a *trip*!" Mother Gothel said, finally pulling herself up and over the ledge. As soon as she caught her breath, she brushed down her clothes and fixed her (own) hair. "The things I *do* for you, dear girl. The things! You have no idea."

Rapunzel carefully—mindfully—pulled her hair back up the tower, coiling it around her shoulders once again. She had to wait for Gothel to settle before trying to hug her.

But she just couldn't help herself. Strongly and gleefully, she wrapped her arms around the still-panting woman.

"All right, all right, don't let's overdo it now . . ."

Gothel pulled away and straightened her dress again, a well-sewn gown in burgundy that perfectly fit her tiny waist and torso. She had no cloak today, nor thong to tie up her thick black hair. Rapunzel drank her in for a moment, this woman who had been her mother and sole companion for nineteen years. She hadn't aged a day; there wasn't a single silver strand amongst her lush locks. The only submission to time was some shrinkage: while she was still taller than her adopted daughter, it was by a slimmer margin every year.

Gothel was too busy primping herself to notice this study of her form at first; when she finally did, she playfully hit at Rapunzel.

"What are you staring at little old *me* for?" she asked coyly. "Is something wrong? Do I have—is there a wrinkle?"

She dashed over to the mirror in sudden worry, pulling back the skin around her eyes with the tips of her fingers.

"No, Mother, don't be silly," Rapunzel said, kissing her on the cheek. "I was just . . . thinking about you. Us."

"You look like a cat with a bird to spit out," Gothel said a little suspiciously. Then she brightened and picked at something in her daughter's hair. "Is that a new charm? Oh, it's very fetching."

Rapunzel put a finger to the one she thought her mother meant, a little *Hamsa*. "Um, no? You gave it to me last Christmas. Where would I *get* a new charm?"

But the other woman was already turned around and doing something else, no longer paying attention. "It's getting a little . . . jungly in here. You know, dear, two of us have to share this space. At least part of the time. *Roomies*."

Rapunzel was thrown by this change of subject—but only for a moment. She looked left and right, as someone raised among other actual people and not puppets might do when looking for an ally, support, a shared eye roll . . . but of course no one was there.

"Mother," she said, taking a deep breath. "Mother, we need to talk."

This was exactly how it went when she rehearsed it, and a quick sideways glance into her mirror confirmed that she even looked the part she had imagined: back straight, serious expression, hands modestly clasped, chin firmly out. Mature. Sensible.

"What? Rapunzel? Stop mumbling," Gothel was inspecting the plants she had just maligned, picking irritably at their leaves. "Why don't you ever grow any flowers? Something to brighten up the place?"

"I'm *not* mumbling," Rapunzel began, and then quickly tamped herself down. She didn't want to seem like an argumentative little child.

"Mother," she began again, much more clearly but not louder. "Do you know what today is?"

"Blursday?" her mother asked lightly, and then laughed

at her own joke. "Who cares, darling? Weekdays are for peasants."

"It's my birthday," Rapunzel pressed on, deciding not to dwell on whether her mother actually knew that and was teasing—or had entirely forgotten it after all.

"Oh, we don't know that for certain," the older woman said with a sigh of obviously giving in. "When I took charge of you, you were already a few days old. You *know* that, Rapunzel. I've told you the story *so many times*. Don't you ever listen?"

"Well, it's this week, anyway," Rapunzel said, determined. "And I chose this particular day years ago. But . . . never mind! The point is . . . I am turning nineteen this year."

Gothel had left the plants and was now playing with a little moose figurine Rapunzel had made during the Six-Month Whittling Intensive she had put herself through two years ago, modeled after the one that once got caught in her pantry.

(She was sad to see the tiny, chittering thing go—but it wasn't happy in the tower.)

"And?" she asked distractedly.

Rapunzel was again taken aback. Gothel never spoke in short sentences—and she *always* argued about age and years. She hated being reminded of them, and her daughter's growth, and the passage of time.

Strange that she wasn't disagreeing or putting up a fuss now.

"Well, turning nineteen means that I'm an adult. By any definition," Rapunzel continued, standing up as straight as she could. "Grown up, and responsible, and . . . things.

"Which brings me to my next point: Every year during my birthday week there are those floating lights in the sky."

"What?" Gothel asked, sounding honestly confused (or as though she was expertly feigning confusion).

"You *know.*" She grabbed her mother by the hand and led her over to the painting she had made years ago, when she first started noticing the yearly regularity of the lights. It wasn't a technically sophisticated piece: just pretty golden orbs with faint auras rising up into a night sky.

"Every year at this time, the mysterious glowing things float up into the sky in the west. *This* year it should be especially bright because it's a new moon tonight, which means the sky will still be pretty dark a few days from now, and—"

"And you want me to watch them with you, dear," Gothel said, making a moue of her lips and squeezing Rapunzel's hands. "How very sweet. But—"

"No, I want to go see them. Myself. *Our*selves."

Silence fell over the room, which was also suddenly dim and dusky as a dramatic cloud took the opportunity to pass in front of the sun. The two women stared at each other, both silent: one, now that she had finally spit out the words, with a pregnant pause of hope. The other with disbelief.

Gothel pulled her hands out of Rapunzel's. She spoke flatly.

"You know you can't. Why are you even asking."

"But, *Mother*," Rapunzel said, trying not to wheedle or whine. "I'm older now. I can control myself. I won't see anyone or anything else. I won't touch anything. You'll come with me. You'll take me there and you'll make sure I don't—"

"That you don't kill anyone else, like *your own mother and father*?" Gothel hissed.

Rapunzel deflated like a tower that had an inferno raging through it a moment before. Everything burned out; the soot, smoke, and heat sucked themselves back into wherever a fire's energy came from. Ashes clogged her nose; her body felt fragile, sapped of its inner structure.

"Mother," she pleaded weakly, looking at the ground.

"Mother indeed," Gothel said—but what she meant by that was unclear.

This was what Rapunzel had lived with for nineteen years. The silent secret that destroyed her inside when she wasn't strong enough to stop it. The thing that took all the color from her already tiny world, the light from the faraway sun, the small amount of air her lungs used.

Rapunzel was locked in a tower because she was a murderer.

Her beautiful, treasonous hair had killed her birth parents just after she was born, in a moment of infant rage.

The hair that she now bound, braided, knotted, and tangled with charms to keep under control.

She couldn't even cut it off; to do so would be her death.

So there it was: endless sparkling braids of it, knotted up with charms and wishes, reminding her every day of why she was imprisoned. How she couldn't be allowed to hurt anyone else again.

"Look what I brought, *for your birthday*," Gothel said coldly, reaching down and opening up the giant basket she had brought.

Rapunzel miserably leaned over, guessing what it was, afraid of what she would find.

A fat, beautiful old chicken, her egg-laying time now passed. A yard bird of mixed feathers and heritage. The hen looked up at her, blinked in the light, but didn't make a sound.

"I was going to wring her neck myself," Gothel went on. "Because I know how squeamish my precious, tower-dwelling princess is. But I think maybe it's time for another lesson on why you are *in* this tower."

"No . . ." Rapunzel begged.

"*Do it,*" Gothel ordered. "You need to do it. You need to remember just why you're here."

As if the girl with the silver hair could ever forget.

The woman took her daughter by the arm and steered her over to the armoire, slamming the basket onto a table there harder than was necessary—or nice. The chicken squawked quietly.

Rapunzel began to cry.

She reached into the basket to stroke the bird, unsure if that was a terrible lie or a final kindness. Murmuring softly, she picked up the thing that was to be dinner. What a wonderful pet the old hen would have made—

—but one look at Gothel's large, cold, set eyes made Rapunzel forget even the idea of asking.

She drooped, listlessly taking a single small braid out of its knot. She laid it across the chicken's neck.

"I'm sorry," she whispered.

She closed her eyes and reached out with her voice, humming a sad little nonsense song. Her mind went blank. She felt an icy blackness coursing from her head down her hair to its tips, like freezing water down a chute. Her silver hair pulsed with an unnatural glow, throwing little shadows everywhere they shouldn't have been.

The bird relaxed . . . entirely. Its feet changed color first; its eyes rolled up into its head.

It died.

"Do you see that?" Gothel whispered.

"Yes, Mother," Rapunzel said dully.

"Do you understand why you can never leave this tower?"

"Yes, Mother."

Gothel shook her head. She took the dead chicken in one hand and patted Rapunzel's cheek with the other.

"Darling, you *know* I'm only doing this for your own good. You're too dangerous to be around other people. You'll hurt them."

"Yes, Mother."

"You'll see, you know I'm right." She paused, her eyes narrowing.

"Mother knows best."

The Secret Room

"There," Gothel whispered to the spy hidden in the dark space behind the armoire. "You saw all that?"

She shook the dead chicken in front of his face.

"Nothing up my sleeves, no tricks, dearie, though I *do* think I'd make a lovely magician's assistant, don't you? Oh, I'm kidding." She playfully hit him with the non-chicken hand. "The medium *is* the message—and you have it now, don't you?"

"*Mein Gott,*" the man breathed. He was a veteran of many small wars and brutalities, treacheries and villainous acts; he had witnessed many a thing too terrible to be named in the light of day.

Yet the look on his face now was the very epitome of disgust.

All around the black spider hole were piles of tiny treasures too dangerous to steal even if the spy had a mind to. There were dusty stacks of the finest—child-sized—linens; sheets and blankets and pillowcases all embroidered with the sun—the emblem of the kingdom. There were *books*, a pile of them, precious and rare, each written, illustrated, and bound by hand. Stacked in the dust like blocks of wood.

There were gowns of escalating sizes in wool and silk, several stuffed bears with velvet fur, and cunningly carved toys that wound up, rolled, or bobbled. There were wooden bowls brimming with dainty princess jewelry: gold necklaces with heart-shaped lockets, barrettes made of mother-of-pearl and actual pearl, rings of bright colors, and all sorts of pretty little bracelets from jet to jade to pink ruby.

Gothel noticed his eyes roving over the things and misinterpreted his real intent: to look anywhere else but at her.

"Oh, yes, I *may* have forgotten to mention that my ward is the supposedly dead crown princess. My plan was to reveal that little tidbit as soon as the bidding slowed down. Think of it: a powerful witch girl *and* a claim to the throne when her parents die! Not bad, eh?

"You know, the queen herself once stood where you now

stand. And only once," she added with a dry laugh. "That was all she could bear, seeing her baby and being unable to touch her. I suppose it's like when a falconer takes a fledgling from a nest and the mother hawk has to watch while its child is reared by someone else. Or something. How she wept! And then she did what all rich mothers do—she turned her love into countless material objects. She sends box after box of this stuff I can't even sell because it all has the royal seal. . . ."

Gothel picked up a simple linen nightshirt: the iconic sun was woven into a band that faced the front. She shook it for emphasis and dropped it on the floor.

(Causing the spy to wince—it was fair to say that *he* had never had such fine clothes as a babe, and even a morally bankrupt soul such as himself couldn't stand to see the hard work of weavers and seamstresses treated like pig offal.)

"I give her a book from time to time if she begs enough— can't let her get too greedy. Children can be so *demandy*. Just look at this stuff . . . useless!" Next came a bright (or gaudy) bracelet of large red coral beads; some of the beads had the royal sun motif painstakingly carved on them by someone with incredible sight, and the clasp also had the sun on it in violet enamel.

"Actually," Gothel said thoughtfully, taking another

look at the bracelet, "this would make a nice nineteenth birthday present. It's not like I actually got her anything. Oh, except for this chicken, of course."

She burst into a trailing titter of laughter. The spy was still silent, which wasn't unusual for a spy, so his distaste remained unnoticed.

"There's the stairs to get back down," Gothel said, taking a deep breath as if the laughter had winded her. She pointed to the trapdoor in the floor. "I will not be seeing you out, of course. Please report back to your various masters and mistresses on what you saw, *exactly*. Remind them that the bidding commences two nights from now. All right?"

The thin man nodded quickly and pulled up the secret door that led to the very, very narrow spiral stairway that spun down into the darkness. There were many questions and even some feelings in his quick and feral head, but he had to concentrate on the task at hand: to make it down safely, without slipping and falling.

In the way of spies, he opened the door at the bottom of the tower just wide enough to let his shadow-breadth of a body through before easing it silently closed again. He skulked his way across the clearing and into the black forest beyond, a tattered rag of a man, as common and unseen as a frayed sack, a trick of the eye, a breath of bad wind.

But as he raced back to the hands that fed him, Crespin's mind turned restlessly over many things, driven by the disgust he had mistakenly shown in front of the witch.

For it was not the death of the bird that disturbed him—oh, he had seen death, and he had even seen magic in his day.

Neither was it witnessing a sad and lonely damsel trapped high in a tower, far more powerful than she really understood, unable to escape—despite a set of stairs and her own length of hair.

Nor even was it the fact that she was really trapped only by the words of a cruel woman.

It was, most likely, that she still called that cruel woman *Mother*, and still hoped for love.

Memorial Sloan Kettering

"Hold up. I got questions." Daniella still didn't open her eyes, but she drew up her hands and began to tick things off on her fingers. This was the way chemo went: she had periods of wakefulness interspersed with longer periods of sleep or strange and hazy gazing at nothing. Her voice sounded almost normal now; her brain was working.

"I'm listening," Brendan said, both resigned and yet also almost eager to hear what she had to say. He was on a good roll, he thought, and didn't want to lose momentum.

"The Countess Bathory—we going to see more of her?"

"Oh *yeah*," he said enthusiastically. "Countess Elizabeth Báthory was a real person! Supposedly she murdered and tortured hundreds of young women and bathed in their blood. Like a vampire, but real."

"I know you like history and stuff," his sister said with a groan. "But why is it always nasty?"

"Hey, that's not fair. Rapunzel's shadow clock and her historically appropriate astronomical instruments aren't nasty," Brendan protested. "And all of her clothing has been incredibly accurate! I actually mention weaving."

"Okay, whatever. Next question," Daniella said, dismissing him with a wave of her hand. "*Where* is *Flynn*? And why don't you talk about the horses more?"

"I have plans to—wait, what?"

"If you're not going to give me Maximus straight up, give me at least a little about the other horses. You were all like—*and the guard dude and the queen go tromping off to see baby Rapunzel. On foot? A queen?* They were absolutely riding horses. So what color were they? What breed?"

Brendan felt like an idiot. One of the biggest disappointments about the cancer—maybe *disappointment* was the wrong word—was that Daniella had lost an entire summer of riding.

Her love of horses hadn't faded like it did with other girls as they grew older; she still begged to go to camps where they made campers *shovel out the stalls* and groom and feed the horses like real farmworkers.

This year, all the money she earned that didn't go into her college fund—along with a big birthday gift from their parents—was supposed to pay for leasing her own horse at Jamaica Bay Riding Academy.

Nope.

At least the academy had given her the deposit back, and even sent her pictures of the horse she had chosen ("Juno") wishing her a speedy recovery.

He was telling a freaking *fairy tale* and there really weren't any horses in it?

"Well," he said, thinking quickly, "we're coming to a bit about horses in a little while. But first, Flynn."

"Better be Flynn," Daniella murmured. "It's not *Tangled* without the *smolder*."

Brendan laughed quietly and began again.

Rapunzel

The next day Rapunzel sat on her favorite stool and looked out her window sadly.

For the very first time she actually looked the way she was often envisioned in the minds of fairy-tale-bedazzled writers: beautiful, wan, sad, delicate, yearning.

Stony. Unmoving.

It was very strange.

Because, as we all know, the real Rapunzel was never still in her three hundred square feet of freedom.

She rested her head on her hands, arms crossed on the cool ledge, and watched the world go by—very slowly; plant slowly. She was too sad to even put her thoughts into a painting.

She wasn't thinking about how she would never (ever) leave the tower. Nor was she stewing in disappointment over not getting to see the lights. She also wasn't mourning how her relationship with her mother had become complicated and unpleasant, picking over memories and discussions and trying to see where it had gone wrong.

No, right then she was still at that point of pure, undiluted sadness that prohibits all clear thought, distinct ideas, fully realized conclusions. Like a waterfall that drowns out all sound, it overpowered all the words in her head. Everything was just terrible.

And then *something happened*.

She almost missed the first few seconds of it, convinced she had invented the something out of her own misery—or that maybe she was finally going mad.

A man ran into the clearing!

Rapunzel almost pulled back from the window, frightened that he would see her.

Apparently *he* was frightened as well; he kept looking around wildly, behind himself and to the sides as if something terrible was near and unseen.

He was being followed, Rapunzel realized. Or at least he was scared that someone might be following him.

He stopped suddenly, spotting something.

A . . . tree?

A sick tree with a giant hole in it.

Rapunzel frowned, not understanding.

The man ran over to the tree and—threw something into its hole.

Rapunzel leaned forward, dangerously, straining to see. It must have been something valuable.

The man wasted no time: having stashed whatever it was, he backed away. He stood still and looked around the whole area slowly and thoughtfully. Probably memorizing his location.

She took his moment of stillness to study him intently. From an . . . *artist's* perspective. All she could see was his body at an angle: the top of his head (he had brown hair), and his arms when they were out (they seemed young and muscular and lithe). She wished she could see his face. The way he moved made her think that he was probably handsome.

(She couldn't have said why, nor did she bother to differentiate *think* from *hope*.)

The man ran to the base of the tower and touched it curiously. Then he disappeared out of her view, circling around the wall. There might have been some scuffling noises, a strange wooden *crunch*.

Rapunzel almost shrieked with frustration. What was he doing?

But even the frustration was exciting. Nothing like this had happened in any of her nineteen years.

(She had actually seen people a few times before this: a lost child, a confused shepherd, a dangerous-looking man with a sword and bow. But they all immediately hurried away from her and the tower, as if they knew the dangers it contained the moment they set their eyes upon it.)

The man reappeared! Running from the *other* way—he had gone all the way around the tower! And was now missing his jacket.

Strange.

He stood (posed?), hands on hips as if *very pleased* with himself—and then ran off, in a slightly different direction from which he had entered the clearing.

Rapunzel's heart raced. She gripped the window frame. The man might have left . . . possibly forever . . . but whatever he had stashed was still in the tree. Either he was going to return for it later or someone else would. Maybe it would be whoever was following him, maybe an enemy, maybe a co-conspirator. If she watched long enough, perhaps she would see the dénouement of this intriguing mystery.

But Rapunzel was tired of watching and waiting.

She thought about the hidden something in the tree and how she very, very much wanted to see what it was. To hold the mystery in her hand. To solve a birthday present.

In her excitement, her thoughts were a little muddled. But it *was* her birthday, and she was sad and disappointed and . . . well, this would go a long way to fixing things.

Lunch that afternoon should have been a dreary affair: she and her mother sitting across from one another, not speaking. Or rather: Gothel making fatuous and labored attempts at light conversation while Rapunzel presented a very un-Rapunzel-y sad wall of silence.

But now energy bubbled up from her hair to her toes and rosied her face, and she almost danced in her seat with the stirrings of hope.

"Well, I'm so *glad* to see you in such a better mood," Gothel said archly, somehow sounding like she didn't mean it at all. They were having the leftover chicken with some additions: mushrooms and herbs she had brought with her from the forest. Whatever else you could say about Gothel, she was a darn good cook with whatever she had at hand. "Of course I would *hate* to leave with you all gloomy and sulky like a ghost with bad digestion. Either way I still need to leave, get things done at the family farm, all the usual. But it's certainly nicer this way."

"I still want to see the floating lights," Rapunzel said, both telling the plain truth—and trying to draw out the argument as would have been natural.

Gothel rolled her eyes.

"No. No? *No*, you're a danger to others and can't be trusted to keep yourself under control." She said this matter-of-factly, almost sounding bored.

Rapunzel kept her head low over her dish, trying not to giggle. She was not good at dissembling. She had never learned how.

After dinner the two cleaned up side by side; life as usual for them. Their movements were almost synchronized and they had no need to talk. Although the washing was boring, an endlessly repeated task, Rapunzel almost wished that the moment could have gone on a little longer. No talking meant no fights, and no end to the dishes meant that she wouldn't do what she was about to. When she did that thing—when she left the tower—their relationship would change forever. Rapunzel would have an experience, a *secret* from her mother. Something new in nineteen years. She would be different.

And maybe it was about time, but it was also a little frightening.

Gothel was humming to herself, a little song about a flower gleaming and glowing. It was one of Rapunzel's favorites; her mother had been singing it ever since she was a baby.

When the plates and pots were clean and dried, Gothel

packed her basket and Rapunzel uncoiled her longest, thickest braid of hair.

"Darling, you *know* I hate disappointing you," the older woman said, touching her daughter's cheek before climbing up into the window. "It's just the way things are."

Rapunzel nodded, not trusting her mouth.

She looked outside to the forest, to the dark trunk with the hole in it, which was growing blurry and obscured with the first licks of shadow.

"Is it safe for someone to travel by herself, at night?" she asked curiously.

"What an odd question!" Gothel said, amused and suspicious at the same time. "I am not most women, Rapunzel. Fortunately for you, and me. Oh, here, I almost forgot. Happy birthday, darling."

She reached into her cloak and pulled out something so surprising Rapunzel's jaw actually dropped. It was a bright red bracelet, one of the most cheerful things she had ever seen. It didn't match any of her clothes or other accessories, and that was *wonderful*. It looked like fire, and the tongue of a cat in one of her books (or maybe it was a dog), and a really good sunset in autumn; happiness in a color.

There was even a cheery, many-rayed sun on the clasp. It was one of Rapunzel's favorite symbols, one she painted again and again everywhere in the tower. In her favorite color, too!

"Mother, it's beautiful! Thank you!" She threw her arms around Gothel and squeezed tight before the other woman could react.

Maybe the woman didn't love Rapunzel's hugs. Maybe she was too strict. Maybe she was a little domineering. Maybe sometimes she said things she probably didn't mean. But it was obvious—in her own, broken way—that Rapunzel's mother loved her. This bracelet was proof. She *had* remembered it was her birthday all along.

"I love you, Rapunzel," her mother said.

"I love you more," Rapunzel said back.

"I love you *most*." And with that Gothel leapt down the rope of hair and disappeared into the night.

Rapunzel

She bounced up and down while trying to predict time, do math on entirely unknown quantities, wondering if there would happen the extremely rare (but occasional) occurrence:

Rapunzel, I forgot something. . . .

How many times had Rapunzel similarly bounced with impatience—waiting and hoping for her mother to come *back*?

But now . . .

How long did it take Gothel to travel deep enough into the woods that she couldn't see or hear anything? How far was it? How many miles, or minutes of walking?

As a child, Rapunzel had constantly worried that

something would happen, that she would need her mother to return for some reason, that Gothel wouldn't hear Rapunzel yelling.

But now . . .

What *if* she came back? What if she had one last word to say?

What if . . .

(what if)

She weighed her worries on the one hand against creeping shadows on the other. The sun was forty minutes from setting, but the woods closest to the tower were already changing from the deep golden of late afternoon into the hazy blue of whatever you called the time just before evening. The hole on the hiding tree had gone from brown to black to deep Prussian blue; the leaves on the branches above it lost their gloss and grew matte.

Finally Rapunzel could stand it no more.

She took her long braid, the one she had never coiled back up again after Gothel had left, and tied the end around the armoire. It clung snugly to itself, and though she tugged it as hard as she could, it didn't give.

(Rapunzel, having no experience with normal hair beyond Gothel's slightly frizzy locks, wasn't at all surprised at this.)

Holding the silvery rope around her waist, keeping the

slack wrapped around her arm, she leapt up onto the window ledge. She balanced easily there, bare toes gripping the stone like a gecko's. Rapunzel had never worn shoes. Once Gothel had given her a pair of dainty pink slippers, which were pretty to wear and fun to prance around—and slip along the immaculately waxed floors—in, but aside from that she saw little use for the things.

Slowly, and perhaps unmindful of how much her hair might have somehow supernaturally eased her work, Rapunzel started down the tall side of the tower.

It was a little dizzying at first, but then again, she'd had nineteen years in a tower to grow immune to fear of heights and vertigo.

After not falling or slipping for at least a minute or two, she began to bounce. Just a little at first, testing her hair and her fear.

Soon she pushed herself off the wall, swinging back and forth. Her long hair spiraled around the tower while her legs shot out into the air and her head hung back like that of a fledgling unsure which way was up.

"WHEEEEEEEEEEE!" she cried out, forgetting for a moment that Gothel might not be far enough away yet—or might return.

She shut up immediately and concentrated on working her way down again, methodically but quickly.

Eventually her toes touched grass.

Her plan was to land, run for the tree, root around in its hole, grab whatever was in there, and then race back up to her tower before night fully fell or five minutes passed or Gothel returned or the man returned or those chasing him returned or Rapunzel accidentally killed anyone or anything that might have the ill luck to cross her path.

But . . . *grass*!

She wiggled her toes.

It was soft springy hard edges tickly.

"Gah!" she cried in joy, looking at the little stalks poking up between her footy digits.

She jumped up and down. She felt the earth push back. It was so different from stone or wood! Soft but hard. Warming quickly under her feet. *Sticking* to her feet . . .

She ran forward, just a little bit, to see how it felt.

It was *much* nicer than running in the tower.

Then she paused, realizing something.

She had never run more than seven Rapunzel-lengths in a row, which was the longest stretch of straight floor she had when all the furniture was moved out of the way for the Games Day Obstacle Course.

She couldn't run much farther now, with her hair tethered to the armoire back in the tower.

But if it hadn't been tethered, she could run—forever . . . ?

"WHAT'S THAT? I've never seen that flower before!!" she cried, forgetting her train of thought.

She bent over the blossom: a tiny little white star-shaped thing no larger than the tip of her pinky. There were a few scattered here and there, but they didn't grow in masses like bluets or brambles, so there was no way she could have seen it from her window.

She poked it.

Yellow pollen got on her fingertip.

Suddenly she grew frightened. What if she killed it?

Rapunzel jumped up off the ground, her second realization far more frightening and profound than her first:

Everything outside was alive.

She was standing on living grass and roofed by living trees. Bugs were flying past her, completely unaware of her deadliness. One *landed on her.* A bird chirped in a tree, a leaf fell from the sky, the threads of mushrooms wound under and through the grass and into the heart of the forest. Any and all of which could be killed by her without a moment's thought.

If she touched a plant and it died, would the bugs on it die? And the fungus intertwined with its roots? And . . .

But—nothing was dying. Not right then, anyway.

Mostly everything was ignoring her.

"Don't think of the chicken, don't think of the chicken," she told herself, trying not to think of whatever it was she thought of when she had to kill things.

A breeze blew a large bumblebee into her—smack! Despite her anxiety about harming the thing, she giggled as it shook itself and flew off again, slowly gaining speed as it recovered. It was fuzzy and yellow with enormous eyes and tiny antenna and looked like, if it were less busy, it might have been friends with her for a bit.

It had run into one of the thick braids coiling around her shoulders—even while she was thinking about / not thinking about / thinking about / not thinking about killing the chicken . . .

Cautiously she wrapped a tendril of hair around a finger.

She walked up to a tree and poked it.

"Ow!"

The tree skin was harder than she'd expected, never having poked a tree before. She supposed (sucking on her injured finger and its bent-back nail) that was why wood was hard.

But the tree endured her hair and even the beginning of her death thoughts—and didn't die.

Just like when she was able to stroke the chicken before having to kill it, or how she cared for her houseplants; no one was afflicted by her magical hair without her actively willing it.

"I just have to not get angry, or scared, or hurt," she said. "I can be careful and cautious."

She stood very still, drilling that order into her soul.

Then she spun around in joy, arms out to the clean, fresh breeze, inhaling pollen and beauty and possibly one or two small gnats.

"WHEEEEEEEEE!"

Not accidentally killing anything meant so many wonderful things!

She would *not* keep this a secret.

She would tell her mother.

She would tell Gothel all about her trip down to the outside world . . . and how nothing at all happened. She hadn't killed anyone or anything. She even petted a lizard—actually, she was doing it right then, before she could stop herself, even as she was thinking these things. She knew it was a lizard from pictures in the fairy-tale book, long and lithe and dry and scaly but with legs, unlike a snake (lizards were turned into handsome footmen in "Cinderella"). Probably a skink of some kind. The reptile bore her touch with the vacuous patience of a cold-blooded creature that liked to be warm and didn't smell anything dangerous like a fox or a hawk. Its experience with humans was minimal to none.

Rapunzel, of course, assumed this not-running-away meant it was a potential Wilderness Friend.

"I'm not going to kill you," she promised the little lizard and herself. "You adorable soft-skinned thing! You're *perfect*!"

She would tell her mother what she had done and then *show* her mother the lizard . . . and then it was only a matter of convincing her to take her to the floating lights. She wasn't a danger.

"Isn't that right . . . Pascal? I'm going to call you Pascal!" And with that she plucked the lizard deftly up and put him on her shoulder. Dizzy—and now petrified—he gripped tightly to her dress and stayed put.

With this daring new plan in mind and the floating lights practically in her reach, Rapunzel nearly forgot the reason she had left the tower in the first place. She shook her head at her own silliness and ran over to the tree with the hole—and stuck her hand in.

(Which only further demonstrated how little she really knew of the natural world, or the world outside her tower.)

Aha! Her fingertips brushed the smooth surface of well-worn leather. But she couldn't quite get a grip on it.

No matter. She undid a smaller coil of hair that had been carefully wound in the shape of a rune that was supposed to ward off evil. She retied it into a looping slipknot and danced it around the dark space, pulling hard whenever it hit something likely. Just like *fishing*, which she had read about. Eventually the loop tightened around something and she was able to pull it up.

(Again, none of this seemed strange to Rapunzel, who had only ever known her own hair.)

A leather satchel! Hastily closed and beautifully worn, barely containing whatever was inside it.

Now she would run back to the tower and hoist herself up as quickly as possible, thereby avoiding anyone returning for the bag, or accidentally killing anyone, or the extremely awkward scene that would occur *should* her mother come back early for some reason.

. . . Except that her hands were already opening the satchel even as she was deciding all this.

"No!" Rapunzel slammed the bag shut and yelled at her hands. "Come *on*, you guys! Can't you wait five minutes?"

She stomped back over to the tower wall, putting a look of stern disappointment on her face. She carefully—mindfully—wrapped the giant rope of hair around her waist and began the more difficult trip back up. It crossed her mind for the briefest moment that perhaps Gothel didn't know what she was complaining about when she said the climb was hard; Rapunzel and her hair did almost all of the work pulling her. She painstakingly and slowly hauled herself along, biting her lip and curling her tongue at the trickier bits—at one point carefully maneuvering around a nest that was tucked into some ivy, and then around a particularly slippery stone of Shiny Cloud Glass. (None of her thirty-seven books was about geology.)

When Rapunzel finally tumbled in through the window, she put a protective hand on Pascal so he wouldn't fall to the floor.

She leapt to her feet again and then, unsure why, spun around and looked out the window again.

Night was falling for real now; everything was much darker, cloaked in blues that had not been there just a few minutes ago when she was out in the green grass and poking the tree. The whole scene looked like a painting framed by the pointy-topped window.

Rapunzel felt a strange quietness come over her that she had never experienced before; something like wonder but softer. She had *been* out there. Down there. It was real and visceral and somehow normal when she was in the grass—and now it all looked like a picture. Delicate, magical, removed.

She wasn't sure what it all meant.

A secret part of her knew, and whispered:

Change.

Like the pause before a thunderstorm, or the hours before her monthly blood began.

She shook her head, clearing things from it she didn't understand, or want to.

"All right," she declared. "And now, *my birthday mystery*!"

She opened the satchel.

And honestly, fate couldn't have provided a better prize at the end of a scavenger hunt.

She pulled out a beautiful, sparkling crown.

Her large green eyes grew even larger. Despite the hour and lack of sunlight, its jewels still managed to shimmer and twinkle in a magical, expensive way. Rapunzel might not have had much experience with royal gems or any kind of precious stone, but it was very clear that these were those. The thing was straight out of a fairy tale, what a princess would be wearing when she was turned back from a swan. The giant diamonds were even shaped like swans' eggs. Under each was a round pink ruby, and threading between them was a strand of perfectly round pearls.

She turned it over in her hands, tracing the tiny, intricately wound gold wire that held it all together.

And there, in a small flat patch of smooth metal, was the artist's mark—*and a multi-rayed sun symbol*.

The same one on her bracelet clasp.

The same one that she constantly painted and dreamed of. The one that meant *life* and *happiness* and *energy* in the personal vocabulary of Rapunzel's soul.

Why?

She looked at her new bracelet. Even to an untrained eye it was obvious that the two pieces of jewelry had not been made by the same person, maybe not even the same studio.

For one crazy moment she imagined that it was all connected. What if it really was some sort of magical nineteenth birthday mystery scavenger hunt? What if Gothel arranged everything? The man, the crown . . . The bracelet was a hint. . . .

What other explanation was there?

And if so . . .

What if she *wanted* Rapunzel to sneak out?

Rapunzel reluctantly brushed that thought aside, feeling both silly and disappointed at the same time.

Her mother most definitely did not want her to leave the tower. Ever. She had made that abundantly clear. And she was definitely not the sort of person who hired actors for extravagant birthday surprises.

Rapunzel carefully unpinned the largest coils of hair piled on top of her head. Then she put on the crown and turned to look in the mirror.

She didn't *want* to think it . . . she wasn't that kind of person . . . but . . .

The crown fit her perfectly. The colors of the stones were accentuated by her own coloring, and the other way around.

She looked like a princess.

A princess with a lizard on her shoulder.

"Oh, Pascal!" she cried, ripping the crown off and putting a hand to him. "I'll bet you're starving—or dehydrated! I'm being so selfish here. Let's get you taken care of!"

So the crown went back into the satchel, the lizard got some leftover chicken (dangled at the end of a stick to make it look alive), and Rapunzel returned to her nighttime routines. She made herself go to sleep at her usual time, despite a head filled with crowns, lizards, mysteries, and boys . . .

. . . and the *best birthday ever.*

Rapunzel

She didn't want to wake up early the next morning.

She wanted to do all her usual things in their proper order, at the appointed time. Before she fell asleep she promised herself that she would hold off all the wonderful things—looking at the crown again, imagining how she would tell her mother, mentally planning their trip to the lights—until her chores were done.

Turned out Rapunzel needn't have worried; the only real excitement in her nineteen years had a profound effect on her mind and body. She passed out dreamlessly for ten hours and woke up having missed Morning Calisthenics.

Her eyes blinked slowly open, her mind confused by

the direction and intensity of light on the ceiling. She never woke up this late.

Pascal was not asleep, precisely, but still snoozing a little curled on her shoulder under her hair. Her Wilderness Friend had already become a bosom companion!

(Or, alternatively, the little thing was warmer than it ever had been in its entire life and had consumed more calories at once than it ever had, and therefore had no reason to leave.)

At once, like she was gulping thirstily from fresh, cold water, the events of the evening before rushed into her mind.

Her mother would be back around lunchtime. Everything had to be *perfect*. Nothing, not a speck of dirt, not a stray hair, could be allowed to darken her mood.

"Well, let's get cleaning!" she said to Pascal, pulling up her sleeves.

The little lizard said nothing.

By noon the tower rooms were sparkling, the linens freshened, the table set. Of course Rapunzel couldn't forage for herbs and mushrooms the way her mother did, but she was able to garnish the plates with a few leaves of the herbs she grew herself and tried to style the leftovers as prettily as possible.

And finally, when her mother called—

"*RAPUNZEL,* let down your *haaaair*!"

—she was already there, hair ready and waiting, and dropped the braid immediately.

"Oh, my dear girl, I don't know how much longer your old mother can do this," Gothel said as she came up, Rapunzel straining to pull her. "It might be that after this I need to take a little break for my back, you know, just a couple days. . . . You don't want to break *me*, do you? Just kidding, dear, of course I'm young and agile . . . but it *is* tiresome. . . ."

Rapunzel yanked extra hard at the end to get her mother quickly up over the top and managed, dancing on her feet, not to envelop her in a hug.

"Well, what's with you, bright eyes?" Gothel asked, looking her up and down. "You seem . . . unfortunately energetic today."

"Oh, Mother, I have the most *wonderful* thing to tell you!" Rapunzel said, unable to resist grabbing her mother's hands and shaking them.

"You? What could *you* possibly have to tell me? What has happened in one *day*?" she asked with—no, that wasn't a sneer, was it? It was just her peculiar sense of humor.

"It's simply amazing. . . . Wait, are you hungry? You must be hungry after your trip. How about some lunch?"

"I'm all right, thank you for asking—you don't keep your girlish figure by giving in to every little whim. Which, by the way, you could use a little more of. *Restraint*, I mean," Gothel added pointedly, looking at their still-clasped hands.

"Of course, Mother!" Rapunzel said, pulling away and laughing.

"Oh . . . *I* know what it is," Gothel suddenly said, her eyes widening in realization. Rapunzel felt her heart skip a beat. Mothers really did know everything! How did she possibly guess? "It's that . . . silly little lizard on your shoulder, isn't it?"

Rapunzel blinked, then put a hand to Pascal.

"You have a pet. Very nice." Before Rapunzel could respond, her mother had turned and was looking at herself in the mirror, fixing her hair. "Myself, I find they take way too much work and attention . . . always needing to be fed and coddled . . . like a child, you know? Who wants another one of those? So much work. Oh, I'm kidding, of course. But really, children *are* a lot of work. Utterly draining."

"Yes, but, Mother, don't you see?" Rapunzel fluffed her silvery tendrils over the lizard, who shook his head and sneezed. "Don't you notice anything? Important?"

Gothel looked at the image of Rapunzel and the lizard in the mirror, not bothering to turn around and look at her real self.

"You have a lizard on your shoulder. Is there anything

more?" she asked, impatient. "A praying mantis on your head? Something even worse on your foot?"

"He's on my shoulder," Rapunzel said with an exasperated laugh. "He's been there since last night! *In my hair! And he's fine! I didn't accidentally kill him!"*

Gothel was a woman who was used to talking performatively; smiling and pouting and waving her hands and swaying her hips. There wasn't an emotion that crossed her mind that didn't also cross her face. Even at her most devious, she completely and thoroughly believed whatever she said at the moment—that's what made it so believable to others.

So the thoughts, realizations, and reactions that birthed themselves inside her head now wandered across her face in symbols clearer to Rapunzel than the alphabet. Confusion, then slow understanding, then surprise (this was wide, wide eyes and raised eyebrows), then a *deeper* understanding.

And then wrath.

Her eyes narrowed until they were nearly invisible slits. Her hands went to her hips.

"What. Are you. Trying to say. Rapunzel."

Her daughter swallowed. Rarely had she seen her mother like this. There was more than fury in her face; there was *danger.*

"I just mean, I thought, but you see . . . It's just that . . ." she stammered, trying not to back away.

"Do not mumble. You know I hate the mumbling."

"I didn't kill him," Rapunzel spat out desperately. "He's been with me for almost a whole day, and he's fine! I'm old enough to control myself—I won't hurt anyone! We can wait another day if you want. I'll keep him on my shoulder just to be sure. And you'll be there to make sure I don't touch anyone anyway. You can tell people not to come near me. *We can go see the floating lights!"*

"Not this again," Gothel said tonelessly, and that was scarier than anything. "You cannot honestly be bringing this up again. We were finished with this subject *yesterday*, Rapunzel."

"But I didn't have Pascal yesterday!" She patted the lizard for emphasis, realizing her mother didn't know his name. "This changes everything!"

"This changes *nothing*!" Gothel hissed, cutting the air with her hand. "You are going *nowhere*. You will see *no one*. You will stay in this tower where you are safe and the rest of the world is safe from *you*. You think you can control yourself—young girls always do. But you *can't*. You can't control yourself when it counts. And someone gets hurt."

"We can test it, or—"

"Enough! I am your *mother*, Rapunzel. I know best. And *I forbid it*."

"But . . ."

Rapunzel thought about the crown.

It was kind of odd that her mother hadn't noticed the leather bag on the table. Nothing came or went out of the tower that Gothel didn't bring herself—or that Rapunzel did not create out of the things she had brought. And usually the things she created took days or weeks and were obvious in their coming into existence. Gothel always complained about the sawdust, the paint flecks, the experimental cheese curds . . . How could she not notice *this* new thing?

How could she not notice Pascal at first?

Wasn't it odd that in nineteen years a lizard had never accidentally climbed this far up into the tower? Why hadn't Gothel asked her where he came from?

How could she not *see*?

Something shut down inside of Rapunzel. It wasn't her will, exactly, or her personality. It was more like a riverbed, or banks of a stream that funneled her energy, thoughts, excitement, emotions, ideas to the outside world. Being filled in, dammed up didn't stop those things from happening; it just . . . cut off their release to an audience. To her mother.

Rapunzel really had been going to tell her all about her little trip outside of the tower.

And now—what would it do? What would be the point? It obviously wouldn't help her case. And if this was how angry her mother grew at the suggestion of leaving the tower, how would she react knowing her daughter had already left it? Better to stay silent.

Rapunzel wasn't used to controlling herself like this, and it felt a little like death.

One last attempt, one uncontrollable thought made its way out.

"But I really want to see the floating lights," she murmured. "More than anything."

That wasn't what she was planning on saying. It wasn't anything about the crown or the boy or being outside or running around on the grass without killing anything. But it was still the truth; in some ways a greater truth. And Gothel still had a chance to make things right, to answer like a *mother*, even if it wasn't the response Rapunzel had hoped for.

Oh, darling, said with feeling, would have worked.

I'm so sorry, I know you do, with a touch on her cheek, would have been more than acceptable.

No words at all, just a hug (and some tears from both of them) would have brought her comfort.

But this was how her mother responded:

"Well, you can't. So you had better just forget about it. *Forever.*"

Rapunzel swallowed something down—forever.

"Yes, Mother," she mumbled.

"Oh, the mumbling! And look at that, you've made me so frowny!" Suddenly Gothel brightened, all fury gone. "I'm not that kind of mother, you know that! Less with the *discipline* and more with the *girlfriend* kind of deal. Don't want premature wrinkles for either of us. Let's not ruin the day. Let's go have that lunch you offered."

Rapunzel slowly led the way into the mocking and cheery dining nook. She had even picked one of her precious few flowers and put it in a vase to fancy up the setting.

As she sank into her chair, she felt like she was all her paint colors pooling down to the floor in a messy, ugly puddle. She could *feel* hope draining out of her, her head emptying of dreams, wishes burning her weakening limbs like acid as they exited.

For the first time, *forever in a tower* began to actually mean something.

Of course humans can weather almost anything with love and companionship.

. . . and for the first time, Rapunzel was beginning to realize she might not actually have either.

She mechanically picked up her knife and spoon and put food in her mouth, because the only desire she had left in her was to not elicit any more comments or conversation from Gothel that she would have to respond to.

Mother Gothel gibbered on and on.

Rapunzel watched her, a little fascinated. She didn't hear any words; only saw the mouth and the eyes opening and closing—they were sensory organs, according to Book #22: *Of Human Life and Limbe.* She wondered if Gothel ever used them as such, or if they existed only to project her personality out into the world.

"You're very quiet," the older woman remarked, finally noticing.

"Mm," Rapunzel said, focusing on her spoon.

"But you're eating slowly, like a lady, so *that's* something. Oh, I got you this." Gothel reached into her basket and pulled out a rolled-up, rubbishy-looking parchment. "I figure you could paint over the surface, or the back, or something. Since we can't afford real paper too often."

We.

Like they were a couple, a team. Like Rapunzel had any way to make or earn money or receive anything she didn't beg from her mother.

She took the parchment with disinterest, unfolding it and viewing it with an artist's eye—really, it was too thin for anything more than charcoal sketches; paint would turn it to mush or blob up, tear the substance with its weight, and . . .

But her artist's voice shut down when she saw what was already printed on the front, from a large woodcut:

WANTED DEAD OR ALIVE: FLYNN RIDER, THIEF

ADDITIONAL REWARD FOR RETURN TO THE

KING AND QUEEN OF THEIR RIGHTFUL PROPERTY

And a perfect sketch of the man she had seen the other night.

All right, not *exactly* perfect. She was pretty sure they had gotten the nose all wrong. One of *that* size she would have seen, even from her window.

So . . . the crown had probably been stolen by that man and stashed quickly into the tree because they were after him! Whoever "they" were. The king and queen's soldiers, other thieves, anyone hoping for a reward . . .

Flynn Rider.

Now *that* was a name.

The perfect name for the sort of man who steals something and gets away with it, who hides out in the deep woods until the coast is clear, a man of adventure, a man of cunning . . .

. . . She bet he was *very good* at sneaking. . . .

A man who sneaked a royal crown out of a treasure vault could very easily sneak a girl through the woods and even villages without letting anyone see her, much less accidentally touch her.

A man like that could sneak Rapunzel to go see the floating lights. Safely.

Gothel, of course, entirely misunderstood the look of wonder and dawning delight on her daughter's face.

"See? I knew you would like it. Mummy's always thinking about you, darling." She smiled and bit into an apple. *The Rapunzel Problem, sorted,* she obviously thought.

"I know exactly what I'll do," Rapunzel said, talking to both her inner self and her mother. Her heart fluttered as she thought quickly, a skill not often needed or called upon in the tower. "But . . . I think I'll need some of that really special white paint. And I'm all out of it."

"Dear, it's a two-day journey to the Bone Coast and back to get the pigments," Gothel said with a frown. "It will wear me completely out."

"But it would be just perfect, and it would take my mind off of the floating lights. Maybe even for good."

Rapunzel risked looking directly into her mother's eyes.

She sort of meant it . . . just not the way Gothel thought.

"Oh, all right, all right—I hope you realize this shows just how much I love you." She heaved a great sigh and rolled her eyes wearily.

"I love you more," Rapunzel said, not really thinking about it.

"I love you *most*."

Rapunzel

The moment her mother was gone she began to pack.

"Isn't this exciting, Pascal?"

The lizard didn't answer. He tolerated her movements only because he was slung around the back of her neck like a kerchief; it was warm and soft there, he was full from a tasty egg dinner, and nothing was obviously going to kill or eat him in the next few minutes. As far as the lizard was concerned, all was good in the world—if a little a nausea-inducing.

Rapunzel pulled out all her maps of Europe, of which she had exactly three—each at least fifty years out of date. Baronies had been won, lost, or stolen; loyalties and boundaries switched around as if by magic. One of the maps had already been carefully rubbed out and reinked in several places. But the landmasses never changed: the mountains, rivers, lakes, and oceans. Rapunzel had a fairly good idea what direction the floating lights were in, but not how large or how far away they actually were. She hoped they weren't out over the sea. On the other hand, the idea of giant, antediluvian whales coming up from the depths on some unknown seasonal instinct to release golden glowing bubbles of blow into the air . . . well, that would be quite the thing to see, too.

Wincing, she carefully tore maps #1 and #3 out of their books, rolled them carefully, and stuck them in the satchel with the crown, which she stuck in a *larger* cloth bag that she usually used for keeping bread. Along with the maps, she also put in food that would last: the ends of some crusty loaves, roasted and dried beans, cheese, eggs she had boiled. Since she didn't have a waterskin like heroes had in stories, she had to make do with a clay jar of water whose lid she sealed on with wax so it wouldn't spill.

She carefully rolled up the wanted poster and slid it in the corner, along the seam where it hopefully wouldn't get too crumpled.

After some thought, she also threw in a quill, a tablet of

ink, and four daubs of paint dried on a palette made out of a shell (which her mother had found on her last trip to get the white pigment). Who knew? Maybe she would be inspired to paint something truly amazing she saw outside. . . .

A few little treasures, including some real coins and fake ones she had painted up for a puppet show.

Rope seemed handy, but she had her hair. A small knife, a bit of hard leather for sharpening, and several large cloths she could use as cloaks or—she whipped one around her head dramatically—to hide her giant pile of hair.

Then she saw herself in the mirror.

She was ridiculous.

It looked like she was hiding a second, smaller Rapunzel on top of her head: crouched down, covering herself with a blanket.

Rapunzel sighed and undid it.

Until she found Flynn—and probably after, as well—she would just have to be very, very careful.

She fastened her braid around the armoire again, got up on the windowsill, and reached behind her neck to touch Pascal for good luck.

Then she looked back at the room she was leaving.

It seemed so . . . small. And dark. But cheerful! Filled with everything that made Rapunzel. Paintings and mobiles and sticks and crafts and weavings and plants and . . . a blank mirror, which now reflected only the things in the room, not the person who lived there. Rapunzel felt strange, like she was a spirit departing an old body. It was a kind body and had done its job, but now it was a little too cramped to hold her and all her dreams.

A note!

She should leave a note!

But . . . what would she say?

Dear Mother, I've gone to find the floating lights. I'll be back.

Of course there was no obvious sign of a struggle, so it would be immediately obvious that she had left of her own accord. And Gothel would know where she was heading.

So was there any point in leaving a note at all?

So she jumped.

"Wheeeee!" she whispered, spinning around and around as she fell like a spider, enjoying her descent.

The landing on grass was even better this time, heightened by anticipation.

"Ha-ha!" she squealed, yanking her hair free.

When she was done with a few minutes of serious twirling across the grass, she checked on the tree with the hole in it. As far as she could tell with her extremely limited experience (none), there did not seem to be any tracks or signs of anyone else trying to find the crown: the only footprint she saw—which at first was first very exciting—turned out to be of her own dainty foot.

As eager as she was to begin her adventure, the hidden valley around her looked a little . . . dark. Foreboding. Full of rock, trees, and shadow, but somehow also empty.

"Mother comes and goes a lot, so there must be a path," she said aloud. "And if she found the poster on a tree, it must be a path used by other people. It would be wide, and easily seen!"

She walked around the base of the tower, keeping the tip of one finger on it—for fun? For comfort?—and thus immediately discovered two things.

One: there was indeed a path; a narrow one that led through a cleft between two natural rock walls, overhung and hidden by ivy. Easily missed if you didn't know what you were looking for.

Two: there was a door in the base of the tower.

"A *door*?" Rapunzel demanded in surprise and outrage. It wasn't much of a door, honestly; more of a sort of cabinet behind which you might put refuse or things you didn't need very often. But still! *Her tower!* Had a door! That she didn't even know about!

On it were all sorts of angry-looking signs:

KEEP OUT!

PLAGUE!!!

MENDICANTS AND POX VICTIMS HERE

DO NOT ENTER

This was confusing enough. But along with the signs, shoved in the gap between the door and its jamb was a coat—the coat that the young man, Flynn, had been wearing. And then suddenly *not* been wearing.

Rapunzel frowned at the mystery and tried opening the door.

It was locked, of course.

Rapunzel's frown deepened. Was Flynn trying to use his jacket to somehow open a locked door?

If so, maybe he wasn't the sort of clever adventurer she needed.

Or . . . wait, was he actually super, *super* clever? What if he was being pursued by the king and queen whose crown he'd stolen, *picked* the lock on the door, took off his jacket, and shoved it into the doorway *to make it look like he had somehow gone inside*? (And let his coat be caught in his haste?)

How many people would follow a man into a tower that had plague warnings all over it?

Even if they stood there trying to figure out what to

do, Flynn would have bought himself precious extra minutes to escape.

No, Rapunzel thought smugly, she was right to choose Flynn as her guide. This was precisely the sort of survival-minded, sneaky fellow she required.

(Not that she had much of a choice in the whole "guide" business.)

She left the coat where it was—after snaking an arm into one of the sleeves just to see how it fit her, out of curiosity—and headed down the path.

She did wonder about the door, however.

The tower was too narrow for any except the steepest stairs, and anyway, if there was a way up, why did Gothel insist on using her hair? Laziness? Or was there some other reason?

(Like: *not wanting Rapunzel to know there was an easy entrance and exit to the tower.*)

Of course, Gothel had managed to get up there somehow when Rapunzel was younger and her hair was shorter . . . but she couldn't quite remember how. And she'd never questioned it. The whole thing was strange.

Her ruminations didn't last too long, however; soon she was pushing aside the curtains of ivy, passing through the cleft, and stepping out into the forest proper.

It wasn't as dark as it had looked from above!

In fact, it opened up onto a trail as big as a road—she assumed, never actually having seen a road. Strange, straight marks deep in the softer dirt were probably made by wheels from a cart or wagon.

On either side of the trail, moss and pretty little flowers mounded around giant, squat trees with large leaves and friendly faces in the patterns on their bark. Light broke through the canopy of the forest in glittery patches, and tiny songbirds called, dancing in the branches. A small furry creature Rapunzel was *pretty sure* was a moose—like the one that had gotten caught in her tower—regarded her from a branch with its feral black eyes.

"Hello!" Rapunzel cried happily.

The thing let loose a high-pitched string of what sounded like swear words and took off, its bushy tail shaking.

(Pascal's feet dug into his mistress's neck. Moose were herbivores, of course. *Squirrels*, on the other hand, were opportunists who would not turn down a helpless fledgling or injured lizard.)

"And to you, too!" she called, curtsying. "All right, I can't be certain which way Flynn Rider went, so I'll just take the direction that leads sort of in the direction of the floating lights. If we see someone, Pascal, we'll ask."

The day was young and the sky above the trees was blue. She almost skipped, and wished she could let her hair trail out behind her as it so desperately wanted, gloriously free and silver. But . . . just in case . . . she kept it tied up. There were so many things to see—and touch—and talk to she could have spent a lifetime on the first mile; she who had spent nearly twenty years in two rooms.

Trees, for instance, were all different when you got up close. The painter in her was appalled at how thoughtlessly she had copied onto her walls what she thought was a good imitation of life. In reality they had differently shaped leaves, different shades of brown bark (and grey and black and even silver and white bark!), differently gnarled roots and patterns of branches.

Also intriguing were the plants that were neither tree nor grass; she knew logically that they were "bushes" but kept staring at them up close, wondering if they would have *preferred* to be trees or grass, these strange in-between things. One was a wild rose—she recognized that from her books— but no picture could have prepared her for the heady scent that enveloped her from blossoms caught in a ray of warm sunlight.

There were more insects than her mind could properly wrap itself around.

"Oh, look, Pascal!" she cried, spying something that didn't look like the rest of the forest. A regular shape and stark shades stood out against the fuzzy and organic back-ground. It was another wanted poster!

WANTED: FLYNN RIDER. DEAD OR ALIVE.

(TO BE CLEAR, *DEAD* IS PERFECTLY ACCEPTABLE)

"We *must* be on the right track if they're looking for him here, too!" she said happily, tearing the poster down. Then she frowned, regarding it.

"This one has a different drawing of his face—look, here the nose is even bigger."

She carefully rolled up the poster and put it into her bag next to the first one. There were recognizable tracks on the ground here, and fresher; many were large and deep, like shoe- or boot-wearing women had made them.

"Or men," Rapunzel realized. Honestly, except for her-self and her mother, she had no basis for comparison.

The land slowly began to change as she walked. Clear-ings became small meadows. The path grew flatter and more densely packed. And she got her first real look at any human structure besides her own tower: a rickety wooden fence that bordered a road intersecting with her own. Above the first post, swinging from chains, was a carved and painted sign of a beautiful golden duck.

"The Snuggly Duckling," Rapunzel read breathlessly. It was more or less what she herself would name an establishment, given the choice. This was probably a tavern. Or public house, or inn—something for weary travelers to stop in, like in fairy tales. Certainly a patron there could help her find Flynn!

She straightened her dress and the kerchief that hid *some* of her hair and followed the trail to a friendly-looking building. It was so old that a giant tree had grown partially into it and draped over the roof like a protective arm. The original structure had obviously been added on to haphazardly as space and time and tree permitted. Several large animals were tied up outside.

"HORSES!" Rapunzel cried, recognizing the fairy-tale creatures at once. She threw her arms open and was about to hug one mightily around its beautiful chestnut neck . . . but stopped herself at the last moment. "No, Rapunzel. You're on a mission," she told herself sternly. "Go in and ask about Flynn. Floating lights first, hugging horses *later.*"

And, firmly resolved, she drew herself up into what she supposed was a dignified and respectable pose and approached the Duckling.

Any reluctance she had to enter an unknown situation ended the moment she drew close. It sounded like the most magical place in the world. There were loud voices telling (unintelligible) stories, the merry plink of an instrument, some people singing one song, others another, peals of heavy laughter. . . .

Without even thinking about a life she had been denied, Rapunzel threw open the door with expectation and abandon.

All immediately became silent.

Her large eyes grew even larger as she took in the scene that confronted her. It was not at all like what she had imagined.

The giant room was dark, chaotic, and filled with enormous men in dark clothes.

These men gaped at her: scar-faced, pop-eyed, bald, hairy, bearded, beardless, muscled, weaponed . . .

She was the only point of color in the entire place, her lavender dress framed by the bright outdoor light that bent and rayed around her figure. From the looks of it, she might have been the only colorful thing to have *ever* been inside the Snuggly Duckling, despite its shiny yellow ducky sign. Some of the patrons seemed to actually wince at the garishness of her outfit . . .

. . . or maybe it was her hair. . . .

Rapunzel swallowed, briefly succumbing to a wash of different emotions. Fear, certainly; stage fright, definitely; but mostly guilt and embarrassment. She hadn't wanted their gay singing and laughter to stop and certainly didn't want to be the *cause* of its stopping. Had she done something wrong? Was this a private party? Was "Snuggly Duckling" the name of a family? Was this a men-only establishment?

No, she could see a couple of dangerous-looking women in the mix, and several serving drinks.

"What's a nice lass like you doin' in a place like this?" one of the men asked. He had a nasty smile and wore a little metal cap with horns that curved around and out on either side of his head; its points were sharpened and looked more like fangs than something that would grow on a cow or sheep or camel. (Rapunzel had no idea what kind of horns they were, only that large cuddly animals had once worn them.)

He flicked a fingernail along an evil-looking blade, slicing off moon-shaped bits of nail.

"All alone?" another man asked, this one with a huge nose. He had a hand on his sword.

"In a fancy dress," one of the women said pointedly. "With a pouch full of gold coins, no doubt?"

"*I* wouldn't touch her."

This was said with some finality by the scariest member of the crowd: a man with a broad, bald pate and a hook for his left hand. He turned his back to Rapunzel and very obviously sipped his beer, ending any potential interaction.

"She's a lady or a noble—nothing but trouble. Even if you try to return her to her parents for a reward, they'll just as soon gut an honest thug as pay 'im what he deserves."

The crowd—*thugs, ruffians*, Rapunzel could put words to them now that someone else had suggested it—began to mutter; sounds of reluctant agreement, disappointed noises, grunts. They all turned their backs on her, resumed their previous drinking and activities and discussions.

"Wait! I am not a lost lady!"

That sounded a little strange. But she decided to just press on.

"I'm not looking for help or my parents or anything. I'm looking for . . . *him*!"

And with that she dramatically pulled out the poster of Flynn, unfurling it with a snap of her wrist.

She waited for the appropriate reaction.

Everybody in the Snuggly Duckling began laughing at her, all at once.

"Flynn Rider!" one of the women hooted, cackling. "You're looking for *Flynn Rider*?"

"You and the *Stabbingtons*!" the man with the big nose cried, panting from his hysterics.

"You and the *king and queen*," a man whose muffled voice echoed from underneath a metal helm said. He was giggling.

"You and everyone in the kingdom who wants the reward!" the man with the horns roared.

Rapunzel looked at them, and then her poster. A single silver hair had loosened itself from whatever knot, braid, or bun it had been bound into. She shoved it back immediately and forcefully . . . not out of the usual irritation that came with a stray tendril, but the fear that came from a lifetime of worry about accidentally killing things with it.

"I'm not looking for a reward," she explained carefully. "I want to hire him for a job."

"No, you don't," the man with the hook for a hand said almost kindly—but still without turning back around. "You really don't want to. Free piece of advice, miss. Go on back home or wherever you come from."

"Wait! Please!"

But the chatter and discussion she had been so sorry to interrupt before started up again, with no regard for her presence or predicament.

This was a very strange moment for a girl who had spent her nineteen years in a tower by herself with only one other person to talk to.

There she had been forgotten and ignored by an indifferent world, cut off by the walls around her.

But there she had never been *actively* ignored by

anything (okay, maybe Gothel—a little), much less a crowd of strangers.

"Um, excuse me?" she said, waving her hand, trying to get their attention again. "Hello? I need *help*. . . ."

Her quick eyes saw coins being pushed across the bar, cloth pouches of silver and gold changing hands. She thought about the repeated mention of *rewards*, both the one on the poster for Flynn Rider's capture and the one the thug assumed would be offered for her return to her "parents." Apparently to get anything done in this outside world—or the Snuggly Duckling, at least—you needed money.

"Listen, I can pay! I'll pay someone to take me to him! I have, um, let's see." She dug around in the bottom of her bag. "A couple of six-sided coins, a coin with a hole in it, a slice of wood my mother brought me that kind of looks like a coin . . . ? I painted a face on it. Oooh, here's a little dragon I carved. . . ."

"Oh, go away," the man with the hook said, waving his hook backward at her like a pesky fly. "No one wants your trash."

"I'll take you to Flynn."

The words rang out heroically over the rabble.

Rapunzel was momentarily dazzled by one of the thugs,

muscled and comely, striking a heroic pose on top of a table, chin out, ivory teeth sparkling, hands on hips.

The rest of the thugs rolled their eyes at this and continued talking.

"Okay, yes, thank you! Finally! Yes!" Rapunzel said, trying not to jump up and down with excitement. "Um, which coins will you do it for? If you please?"

"First tell me . . . what do you need Flynn *for*?" The girl leapt down from the table. Her dark hair hung in a single braid down her back, wrapped at the end by a leather thong. She was even shorter than Rapunzel.

"I need a sneaky thief to lead me on a valiant quest."

"*I* can sneak!" the girl said, slamming her gloved fists down on the table in a display that was far less subtle than she might have wanted. "What's he got that I don't?"

"A . . . poster advertising his famous exploits?" Rapunzel ventured, holding it up as evidence.

"Hmph." The girl crossed her arms and looked piqued. "You got me there. *I'm* just starting out, though. He's been at this thuggery business for a while. All right, I'll do it. I'll take you to him. It'll look good on my résumé, beef it up a bit for future jobs."

Rapunzel tried to interrupt, but it was like it had all been decided and the girl was doing her a favor. "The name's Gina."

She stuck out her hand.

Rapunzel stared at it, unsure what to do.

"I'm . . . Rapunzel."

"Huh. Weird name. Okay," Gina said. "Buy me a drink so we can discuss details."

Rapunzel wasn't sure what she meant by *details*. She had said what she wanted—to be taken to Flynn Rider. What else was there to say? But the idea of sidling up to a bar and ordering something like a real adult human was entrancing.

The two girls pushed their way through the throng.

"Wow, I *really* like your . . . um . . . arm painting!" Rapunzel said to the man in the metal helmet as they squeezed by him. The picture was of a cupcake, with what looked like a whisk and a spoon crossed in front of it. "I *love* making cupcakes on rainy days when I'm feeling down!"

Of course she couldn't see the expression on his face as he turned to watch her go. And it was very hard to hear him whisper, over the background noise:

"She *knows*. Finally, someone who gets it. . . ."

Rapunzel and Gina

While you might think that year after year of talking only to herself and inanimate objects (and the occasional would-be arthropod pet) would make Rapunzel mad with a desire to communicate all the things that had been building in her skull for the last nineteen years . . . Well, you would be right.

But on the other hand, everything Gina said was literally new information for her.

Rapunzel was fascinated.

"Flynn's been working with the Stabbingtons this season . . . dumb of them, if you ask anyone, of course. You can trust Flynn about as far as you can throw him. But the Stabbingtons *are* dumb as a box of caltrops. They're good for pounding things and people—mostly people—into dust. No skills at all in sneaking or talking their way into anywhere. That's why they needed to team up with a thief like Flynn. Rumor has it they had a big heist, something at the castle. It's why all the wanted posters are up everywhere. He's been helping them loot the royal treasury, one treasure at a time."

"I don't know much about this sort of thing," Rapunzel admitted, thinking about her crown—so this was its origin story! "But the name 'Stabbington' sounds like someone you might not want to deal with?"

"Oh, big-time no. Even Hook Hand here won't cross 'em," Gina agreed, gesturing at the man. "But rumor is that Flynn *did* . . . double-cross them, I mean. He took the treasure and took off. The Stabbingtons are after him. We find the Stabbingtons, they find Flynn, we get to Flynn before their daggers do . . . easy peasy medlar squeezy."

"You sound like you've been, um, thugging for a long time," Rapunzel said with admiration.

"Actually, you're my first paying gig," Gina admitted. "*You're too young*, they say. *You're a girl*, they say. How am I supposed to *get* job experience if no one will let me in on a job? Literally the only thing I've wanted to do my entire life and it's a boys' club . . ."

"You've wanted to be a villain your whole life?" Rapunzel suddenly wondered if that was a polite thing to ask.

"Not villain, *adventurer*!" Gina said, not taking offense. "Living by the speed of my mind and the edge of my blade. I was always running away for adventure, even back in the orphanage. Oh man . . ." She laughed, slapping her thigh at a memory. "I was always diving out the window, tiptoeing on the railing . . . Yeah, that place was the *worst*, but it definitely honed my sneaking skills early on, know what I mean?"

"Absolutely," Rapunzel said, wishing that were true. "And you grew up there? At the—orphanage?"

"Nah, I was adopted. My mom's, you know, a nice lady. An old goodwife. Lives in the forest. She's a . . . she doesn't do well around other people. *Not* an adventurer."

"A hermit!" Rapunzel said in amazement. She wondered if there was a tower involved. "I'm adopted, too . . . but I didn't come from an orphanage."

"Yeah, looks like your adopted family has bit more money than mine," Gina observed with amusement, looking over Rapunzel's dress.

After they finished their drinks—Gina made Rapunzel get a kvass; she could tell the other girl wasn't used to pub life—the thug grabbed her own sack and a few more weapons, and they set off down a twilit road.

Her plan was to search all the spots where the Stabbingtons were known to hang out, find them, follow them, and thus find Flynn.

The first hideout was a small cave, dark but dry, with broken ale jugs and rotted bits of leather in the corners.

(This was *very* satisfying for Rapunzel; it looked just like what she imagined a ruffian's camp would be, down to the candle nubs on the ground.)

The second place they searched was a decaying woodsman's shack deep in the forest, spooky and filled with spiderwebs.

(Neither Gina, as brave as a Valkyrie, nor Rapunzel, innocent of the world, hesitated at barging in.)

The third was a colorful, noisy inn at the edge of the forest, full of music and shouting.

(Gina would not let Rapunzel go into this cheerful place, to her surprise and intense disappointment. "I think you're some sort of lady," Gina explained. "And really—it's not fit for a lady." "What about the Snuggly Duckling? I went in there just fine!" Rapunzel demanded. "This place is even less, um, lady-appropriate" was all Gina would say.)

By the time night truly fell they had seen neither hide nor hair of the brothers; only heard rumors of their whereabouts. Rapunzel was eager to continue their search, but her body was falling apart. She had never walked so much in her life, not even during the Cross-Country Trek on Games Day of three years before, when she was *pretty sure* she had walked half a marathon back and forth from her bedroom to the stove. At least that was the goal of the race, and she had done the calculations twice.

"I think we'd better bed down for the night," Gina said as Rapunzel walked into a tree for the third time.

"I'm fine," Rapunzel protested wearily. "We'll keep . . . going. . . . Don't villains do their . . . villaining at night? Easier . . . to . . . find."

"Yeah, but even *villains* sleep, even your famous Flynn Rider," Gina said cheerfully. "Here, this looks like a nice spot. C'mon, you make a fire and I'll go get us some game hens or something for dinner."

Rapunzel was immediately, fully awake.

"I'm not going to kill them!" she shrieked.

"Uh, no," the other girl said slowly. She frowned at Rapunzel and held up her leather sling. "The—stone— missiles—are—going—to—kill—them. If I do my job right. What's the matter with you?"

"My mother would bring me chickens . . . and it was my job to kill them. And I *hated* it." Rapunzel shivered and wrapped her silver hair tightly around her shoulders.

Gina stared at her for a moment, obviously trying to process this.

"Was she trying to teach you to be a good farmer? Like the whole circle of life thing? Know where your food comes from, treat it with respect, 'If you can't look your meat in the eye then you should stick to carrots' lesson?"

Rapunzel almost giggled at that and wasn't sure why. She knew nothing about farming save what she'd read in Book #34: *The Farmer's Book of Days* . . . and that Gothel generally looked down on it as an occupation.

But now that she thought about it . . . what kind of person brought *live animals* on long trips, to be killed by a young girl at the end of it? Why not wring their necks at home and then pack them, quiet and unmoving? Why would Gothel do that?

Because she wanted to teach another kind of lesson. Not about any circle of life.

Rapunzel, you're a killer.

Or . . .

Rapunzel, see what I can make you do.

How come Rapunzel had never just said no?

She shivered again and looked down at the fire.

"I . . . I don't think so."

"Huh, okay, well. Guess I'll . . . just . . . be back in a few, all right?"

Gina stepped away from their campsite—keeping a close eye on the other girl. Less like she was afraid her first professional job would sneak off into the night and more like there was a chance she would do something potentially destructive. Rapunzel pretended not to notice.

She made a fire—which would have been fun if she hadn't been so tired. Unlike the closed resource loop of her tower, where she had only what logs were brought to burn, here she could gather as much as she wanted. They weren't cut neatly, but that was all right.

Once it was burning nicely, she looked up at the stars directly overhead. That was new! Never in her life had she been able to *just look up* and see anything besides the mobiles she made herself to imitate the real stars and planets.

Now there was nothing between her and the heavens.

She felt the world spin and flung her arms out, digging her fingers firmly into the dirt to steady herself. A warm breeze blew, and for one crazy moment she felt like a bird, diving into infinity, into the air that was the warm breath of the celestial spheres, the wind between the stars. It was magic.

When Gina came back a couple hours later, Rapunzel was fast asleep and snoring; it took several gentle kicks to wake her.

"Mm? Fffr? Wha?" Rapunzel sat up, her crazy silver hair even crazier with leaves and twigs. The stars had shifted since she passed out, the heavens whirling above her, unconcerned with sleep.

Gina laughed softly. She had already taken care of the small birds she had killed; they were nearly finished cooking on an improvised spit. There were even some herbs stuffed in them, and that plus what little fat they had snapped and sizzled and smelled delicious.

"Wow, you can do everything," Rapunzel said with frank admiration (and a little bit of drool).

"I *said* I lived in the woods with my mom. It's mostly grow or catch whatever you eat. I tried to find you some mushrooms in case your thing about dead birds included eating them, but it hasn't rained in a while, and anyway the really good ones come later. But I guess that's not an issue."

Rapunzel had already taken the stick with the smaller bird and begun tearing into it.

"Ee gon' go 'fter this?" she asked.

"No, no point wandering around at night and getting lost. It's not safe. Fire will keep away the bears and wolves and other nighttime dangers. We'll rest and be off at first light."

Rapunzel considered this. It was the confidence with which Gina had spoken that moved her: not arrogance, just the simple assumption that it was obviously the right thing to do and anyone else listening would have agreed.

Which was strange, considering how Gina had said no one took her seriously and how hard it was being a young woman in a thug's world. She had sounded very *un*sure of herself then. Despite being well versed in the particulars of the business—hunting for dinner, setting up camp, where to look for their quarry—did people still reject and ignore her?

After dinner Gina banked the fire and threw the sticks they had used to cook and eat with into the woods so they wouldn't attract animals. The two sat up for a while, Rapunzel with her back against a tree, Gina watching the glowing coals, her face illuminated dramatically.

When she read stories or performed puppet shows, Rapunzel forcibly gave everyone different faces from her own, tried to imagine people different from herself. Gothel had laughed when once as a young girl Rapunzel had painted a family scene in which the children had blue hair. How was she to know the limits of human features? She had literally only seen her mother's black hair, her own silver hair, and brown hair from the few times people had wandered into her field of view below her tower.

Now that she had a chance to study another person, Rapunzel found herself trying *not* to see how different Gina was (shorter, darker hair and skin) but just how she *was*, from an artist's perspective. Lost in thought, not entirely relaxed. There was a flash of the fire deep in her clear brown eyes.

"Hey, you got a twig or something caught in your hair there," Gina said, breaking the silence, leaning over to take it out.

"DON'T TOUCH MY HAIR!" Rapunzel shrieked, scrabbling backward in the dirt.

"Whoa, all right, crazy person," Gina said, pulling back, eyes wide. "I wasn't going to. Do I *look* like the sort of girl who wants to come over and braid your hair or something?"

"I'm sorry," Rapunzel said immediately, biting her lip to keep from crying. "It's . . . it's a long story."

"I'll say it's long," Gina drawled, her eyes moving very specifically over the lengths of her braids. "Get it?"

Rapunzel managed a weak smile.

"This got something to do with the whole chickens thing?" Gina asked.

"What? No. Why would hair have anything to do with chickens? Or killing them?" Rapunzel said, forcing a laugh. "That's weird. Hair killing chickens."

Gina narrowed her eyes.

"Who said anything about hair *killing* chickens? I just meant that the sort of childhood where your mom made you kill the farmyard animals without a good reason might also have other strange things about it. Like you being forced to grow your hair long. Not letting anyone else touch it. Putting weird symbols and jewelry in it. Like you were raised in a cult or something."

"Um, no," Rapunzel said. "Sorry. I wasn't. I don't. I'm—uh, not."

"Oh," Gina said carelessly, snuggling down into her cloak. "Then what *is* the story with your hair, anyway? It's such strange color, and so long."

Rapunzel shrugged. "I was born with it this color, and I've never cut it."

"Huh."

She waited for Gina to ask more, hoped and feared Gina would ask more.

But all the other woman said was, "Must be a real pain to keep out of the way. I mean, it's pretty and all, but I'd probably cut it—not all of it, maybe. My mom's braid goes down to her knees when she undoes it. Maybe like that."

Her words got slower and softer, and were replaced in the end by the quiet breathing that suggested sleep. Rapunzel drifted off uncomfortably, new ideas making her soul itch as they sprouted through her skin.

Gothel

Of course she didn't travel two days to the town on the sea that had the shells that produced the special shining white pigment Rapunzel wanted. But she did know someone less than a third of the way there who often stocked the white paint and sold it on to traveling merchants.

He had it, she paid for it, and Gothel was back at the tower exactly when she told Rapunzel she would be there.

(With a quick stop at the Sundrop Flower for a youthful touch-up.)

Mother Gothel was in a great mood. She had three bids already, all of which were over fifty gold coins. She would be set for life even if the bidding ended soon.

But if truth be told, it wasn't the money that she really wanted.

Insofar as she wanted anything besides eternal youth, what she really enjoyed was meddling with the nobles and having them trust her. She loved being on the *inside* of the squabbles that determined the fate of this village or the burning of that village.

Only one person would win the auction, true. *But.* The rest would lose, and, having missed out on the chance for such a magical wife (or servant), they would feel they needed something else. Something just as good, or better. It would become an arms race. And oh, maybe Gothel had something else up her sleeve . . .

. . . or would find something . . .

"Rapunzel, let down your hai-air," she called out.

She was feeling generous. Two days was more than enough time for the teen to get over her sulk. And there was the paint. And Gothel herself was almost giddy from her shenanigans.

She didn't even mind that it was taking Rapunzel more than a minute to get to the window.

"Rapunnnzel, I'm waaiting," she yelled.

Still nothing.

"I'm growing old here . . . all right, not really, not a grey hair yet, but you get the idea. *Rapunzel!*" she snapped, her mood switching by the end of the sentence. Even if Rapunzel was in the garderobe, she could shout, mention that she would be right there. "I've been traveling constantly and Mummy is *exhausted*. Let me up."

That girl wasn't still sulking, was she?

A forest cricket decided to chirp after a moment, as if on purpose, to draw a line under the already obvious silence.

"*RAPUNZEL!*" Gothel screamed. "*NOW!* Come *here*!"

Not once did it occur to her that there might be anything *wrong* with Rapunzel (even though damaged goods might affect her auction). Rapunzel was nineteen and healthy; she had none of the sort of fits or hemophilia that often afflicted those of noble birth, and her monthly bloods were not unduly painful.

Gothel didn't even have a moment of panic that her daughter might have slipped on the overly polished floors and knocked herself out, or accidentally stabbed herself with the chef's knife, or been poisoned by a rare but not unheard of fungus that grew on wheat and caused those who consumed it to dance themselves to death.

No, Gothel thought none of these things. Only that *she*, Mother, was being kept waiting, probably for some selfish or stupid reason of her useless little ward's.

"Rapunzel! You have until the end of the *deep, calming* breath I'm about to take to show yourself or answer me!"

Gothel took that breath—but poorly, if anyone had been around to notice; through her mouth, and quickly, making more noise than actually letting air in.

"I'm going to count to six," she shouted. "If you're napping, that should be more than enough time for you to rouse your pretty little head and come help your mama.

"One!"

She put her hands on her hips. The basket on her elbow swung back and forth.

"Two!"

She angrily strode forward a step, face still upturned, facing the window.

"Three."

She stepped back again, still trying to get a view into the window.

"Four . . ."

She ground her teeth.

"Six!"

"All right, you leave me no choice," she growled.

Gothel had hoped that this day would never come—the day she might need to use the secret stairway. Years ago she had prepared all sorts of excuses and stories for just such an emergency, most of which relied on her generally spooky, vaguely magical deportment to authenticate them.

She could imply that she had turned into a crow and flown up there, or that pixies had spirited her through the airs, or that her spirit was called directly to the tower because she had sensed trouble.

All of which depended, of course, on her somehow getting out of the secret room and into the living area unseen.

Messy.

Unpredictable.

Gothel *hated* things like that.

She strode around the tower angrily to the door—and what she then saw caused her face to go literally white with rage, her mouth working unspeakable omens.

A jacket.

A *man's* jacket.

And it wasn't the spy's.

She picked it up gingerly, as if it were covered in filth.

It was not, and it was well made if simple, and spoke of a sleek build. A young man's coat.

Clues began to assemble themselves, perhaps incorrectly, in her mind. The conclusion based on them was obvious and inevitable.

With a cold fury, Gothel unlocked the door, threw it open, and clambered methodically to the top of the tower. Not stopping once to catch her breath. Now she no longer cared if Rapunzel found out how she got up. When she caught the little hussy and her man friend, they would *both* know her wrath.

Upset *her* plans, would they?

Despoil the girl *she* had been raising so carefully for nineteen years, isolated and protected from everyone?

Destroy everything *moments* before her long-set machinations came to fruition?

She would kill him.

As for Rapunzel . . .

"SHOW YOURSELF!" she shrieked, bursting out of the secret compartment behind the armoire. In her right hand she grasped a black dagger, evil looking and strangely curved.

Obviously she could never best a young man in a straight-up fight. And she didn't *really* have magical powers that could aid her, or spirits that would do her bidding. What she did have was a tiny bottle of a poison so strong that a single drop would paralyze an opponent for hours. More than enough time to finish him off. The poison had cost her dearly—the viscous, milky liquid was an extract from some frog in the deepest Sun Countries—but had already served her well twice before. She knew it would work.

She stormed out of the secret room and into the tower proper, seething. Her hair was wild, her clothes blown all about her. Her cloak tangled in a bit of Rapunzel's hanging garbage and she pulled hard, ripping the constellation of mica and papier-mâché out of the ceiling. Pebbles and planets went skittering along the floor, sounding like mice. Gothel roared in frustration. She was terrifying; a lioness protecting her cub. . . .

(All right, not exactly.)

But in the end it didn't matter; there was nothing. No amorous couple, no Rapunzel, no prince, not even a random and curious looky-loo.

"*RAPUNZEL!*" she screamed.

But no one answered.

She was gone.

Rapunzel

Rapunzel woke up outside.

While she was still half in her dreams, she heard bird-song close—*very* close—like, right above her. The air was fresh and cold and there wasn't a hint of the staleness that sometimes drifted invisibly through the tower like an old ghost, despite all the cleaning. Her back was achy because there was no soft mattress under it, only roots and twigs and hard, hard ground.

She opened her eyes and saw that beyond the treetops a streaky, messy, glorious predawn sky was trying to get its colors together before starting the day: pinks and blues and golds smearing into each other.

She leapt up, throwing her cloak off. "I'm *outside*!"

Gina stopped what she was doing and gave her a look.

"I'm just going to keep going with 'cult,'" she said dryly.

It looked like the other girl had already been up for hours. Her clothing was adjusted neatly, her blanket rolled and tucked away, her bag packed and ready to go. She was stamping out the remains of the fire and dragging a branch through, looking for sparks. How had she risen and done all this without Rapunzel hearing? It was like she was a bird or forest creature herself, able to work around the ugly and blunted human senses and stealthily go about her business.

"I think we'd better just get going—sorry, no time to hunt down breakfast," Gina apologized. "Trail snacks along the way if we can find any. Berries and stuff."

"CHEESE," Rapunzel said, suddenly remembering. "I have cheese. Do you want cheese? I will totally share my cheese!"

"I'd eat some cheese," the other girl said interestedly.

Rapunzel pulled out the (slightly moist) cheese and (very dry) bread. As she broke each and handed half to the other girl, she had a funny feeling—a funny *good* feeling, like the opposite of when her hair did the magic that killed the chicken. There was something special about this ritual: sharing her food with another person. Literally breaking bread.

Gina took it with a cheerful "Thanks!" and immediately

began eating it, apparently not noticing the specialness of the moment—or the dryness or moistness of anything.

"Mmm, cow's milk cheese, don't get that very often," Gina said with a contented sigh. "It's pretty much all goat all the time at home. I was right, your family *must* be pretty well off."

Rapunzel was about to object; she had a crown in her bag that obviously belonged to someone *actually* well off. But . . . her dress was made out of finer and more colorful cloth than Gina's outfit, and the other girl wore no jewelry at all.

And . . . to be fair . . . if you squinted, you could look at her tower and call it a castle.

Books were so simple about these things, fairy tales so straightforward! There were peasants, and then there were kings and queens. Sometimes there were people who made shoes or were soldiers. Occasionally there was a priest supported by the church. But that was all; all the types of professions, all the different economic classes of people.

Maybe, like hair color, wealth in the outside world was more nuanced and subtly shaded than her stories suggested.

"You know what we could do?" Gina said through a mouthful of cow's milk cheese. "After this Flynn thing is all over? You and me, we could *ransom* you to your parents or whatever. But you wouldn't have to go back if you didn't want to. We'd just split the money and take off. And you could do whatever you want with your share. I'd give half to my mom and buy a horse with the other half. We could go adventuring together!"

She seemed so excited by the possibility that Rapunzel hated to disappoint her.

"But . . . I *am* going back to my . . . parents," she said, voice trailing off as she said it. "My . . . mother . . ."

Gina gave her a look.

"Uh, okay. It just *sounds* like maybe you're a little done with the whole situation back home. Dead chickens and all. Whatever! Not my farm, not my pig. Er, chickens. You do you.

"But that doesn't mean we still couldn't ransom you and I'd still get *my* share. In fact, if you were going home anyway it would make it easier. You could still keep half—to buy more little jewelry things for your hair or whatever."

"I'll keep your offer in mind," Rapunzel said with a smile.

But as they walked on, she actually thought about it. The path was soft on her feet (not stone or wood), there was a real live person walking next to her who wasn't Gothel (or a puppet she had made), the space around her stretched out to forever (instead of five to seven Rapunzel-lengths).

It was always her intention to return home.

Or maybe she had just never considered anything else.

She hadn't really thought about anything beyond seeing the floating lights. And now that it was about to happen, and if it *did* happen, and she saw them . . . then what?

Or: if she *didn't* see them, then what?

Go back to the tower? When she had slept under the stars?

Go back to her mother, after their terrible fight?

After spending less than a day with this random criminal girl who questioned the way Rapunzel had been raised?

Criminal. That was exciting! That was something to talk about! That would take her mind off this.

"So—you actually know all of those other, ah, *thugs* back at the pub?" she asked.

"All the regulars," Gina said, nodding. "Hook Hand, Attila, Vladimir, Shorty . . . I don't know if you saw Shorty. He's super short, and super super old. He usually hangs out in the corner with a pint, if you know what I mean. Nice guy, though. Tries to cheat at bones—but always lets me win. He's the only one who really treats me like one of them."

Suddenly the girl stopped, putting her hand out to stop Rapunzel as well. Rapunzel shied backward immediately, not wanting a stray lock to hit her new friend.

"Hear that?" Gina whispered, cocking her head. Her black braid fell over her shoulder.

Rapunzel strained, and even tried turning her head to listen like her friend—but her own hair jingled embarrassingly. Pascal tightened his grip on her neck with obvious irritation.

"No," Rapunzel admitted, whispering back.

"Exactly," Gina said smugly.

"Um, I don't really—"

"Where are the birds and squirrels?" Gina whispered. "Why have their calls stopped? What's going on in the forest?"

As if in response, a single long chitter burst forth from an angry, or scared, or angry-scared moose (squirrel). A warning cry; even Rapunzel could figure that out.

When it died out there came the sound of something large and two-legged crashing through the woods.

This was quickly followed by the sounds of more and heavier crashing; whatever was running was trying to put *lots* of distance between itself and whatever things were chasing it. Quickly.

And then a third noise, almost silent at first but very rapidly growing to a crescendo:

"aaaaaaaaAAAAAAAAAARRRHHHHHHHHH!"

The cries of a man who very much wanted to attract attention, good or bad, anything at all. Something that would change his current situation.

Gina nodded smugly.

"Flynn," she said, no longer bothering to whisper.

Rapunzel's eyes lit up in excitement. Her plan was working! She was really going to meet the man who had come to her tower!

"This is going to be messy," the other girl told her. "You need to stay on top of Flynn. *Stop* him. I'll deal with the Stabbingtons. Or royal guards. Or whoever's after him."

"How am I supposed to stop him?" Rapunzel asked, quailing. "I don't have a weapon."

"Gee, I don't know," Gina said, rolling her eyes. "I'm sure a pretty girl in a fancy dress in the middle of the woods won't *distract him*. Come on, woman! Think! And . . . go!"

She pushed Rapunzel out into the path, careful not to touch her hair.

Rapunzel stood there and wondered what to say.

Hi?

Nice to meet you?

Excuse me?

But as it turned out none of this was necessary, because the path was twisty and Flynn Rider was focused on his running and breathing and generally living, not what might be on the trail ahead of him.

He appeared, Rapunzel opened her mouth, he slammed into her with the force of a man-sized embodiment of panic.

"Gah!" Rapunzel cried, hitting the ground hard.

"What the . . ." Flynn said, scissoring his arms and legs, trying to get off her. But he was tangled in her dress and hair.

"*NOT MY HAIR!*" Rapunzel shrieked, panicking and kicking out.

"I'm not—"

"*DON'T TOUCH MY HAIR!*" she screamed louder, flailing and trying to roll over.

Gina leapt out into the path behind them and stood at the ready with her small blade drawn. Those chasing Flynn had finally caught up: two large mean-looking men whose demeanors made the rest of the Snuggly Duckling characters look feeble by comparison. Their arms were as thick as Rapunzel's torso and their heavy jaws were set in repulsive sneers. One was missing an eye, and both of their noses were squashed flat from too many fights.

While Rapunzel knew little about real hand-to-hand matches, she was fairly certain that her new friend Gina, small and fast though she was, had no chance against them.

"Get off of me!" Rapunzel said desperately to Flynn, pushing at his chest.

"Oh, believe me, I'm *trying*," he snapped. "I would *really* like to get out of here."

"Oops, wait, I'm supposed to delay you," she suddenly remembered.

"*What?* You're with senior and junior ugly over there?" Rider asked in shock.

"Hold your ground," Gina told the Stabbington brothers in a clear, solid voice. "I need Flynn alive."

"No one needs Flynn alive," the one without an eye patch said. "*Mostly* everyone needs him dead. Mostly us."

"Back off, I warn you. I'm on a paid job to take him into possession," Gina said.

The two brothers looked at each other.

Then they began to bark out loud, harsh guffaws.

"Out of my way, wannabe," the one with the eye patch growled. He reached out a large paw-like hand and cuffed her, hard.

Gina didn't take the full force of the blow; she ducked at the last minute and spun on one heel. Then she dropped her arm and jammed the pommel of her weapon into the back of the large man's knee as hard as she could.

He groaned—more like an angry animal than a human in pain—and stumbled, landing hard on the other knee.

The one without the eye patch grunted and tried to grab Gina by her braid.

Rapunzel and Flynn had finally managed to disentangle

themselves. She rose upright uncertainly; he leapt onto his feet like cats were said to.

It was hard to believe that Flynn was the same species or gender as the Stabbingtons: he was smaller, lithe, muscled but slim. Few to no scars—or at least, only really fetching ones that accentuated his features. His face was built for all kinds of smiles; even cocky ones like the grin he sported right now.

His nose was *not at all* like in the posters.

Rapunzel felt a warmth wash over her and had to stop herself from staring.

Gina, still in the fight, kicked the other brother right in the . . . well, to be honest, Rapunzel didn't know the correct word for it. But it was apparently just as delicate—or maybe more so—than her own intimate parts, because the man fell over with no sound except for a sudden exhalation of all the breath in his body.

"Why you little," the first one (eye patch) said, getting up—but favoring his injured knee.

With one beautiful, flowing motion, Gina sprang away from him in a flip. As she righted herself she grabbed a stone from the path, windmilled her arm, and released it; the sharp-edged missile sailed through the air.

It smacked him just above his *good* eye.

"Run," Gina commanded.

"Will do," Rapunzel agreed.

"Oh no, I thought we'd hang around and see if these boys are okay," Flynn suggested fatuously.

The three took off, tearing down the path.

Rapunzel pumped her arms and forced her legs to move as fast as her brains could manage, but barely kept up with the other two.

"I don't know who you are," Flynn said, huffing, to Gina. "But I think I love you."

Rapunzel was surprised to feel herself miffed by this, despite the obvious casualness with which it was said. Wasn't *she* the pretty distraction in the road?

Gina said nothing, a grimace on her face that was maybe a smile.

All too soon came the unmistakable sounds of the large men getting up, running after them, and . . . roaring? Were they actually *roaring* in anger?

"I hope there's another part of your plan to rescue me," Flynn said. "Maybe one that involves horses? Or cannons? Or a small fortress?"

"It involves a lot of running, and hiding," Gina admitted.

"Same old same old," Flynn said disappointedly.

Rapunzel stumbled and pitched forward with a violence she didn't expect.

Without missing a beat Flynn turned and grabbed her, keeping her (mostly) upright.

Her first ever touch from a boy, and it burned, and was probably going to leave bruises on her wrist! Rapunzel felt cheated somehow.

"*Here,*" Gina suddenly commanded, diving off the path, deeper into the forest.

"Yeah, let's go someplace *less* populated so they can murder us in complete peace and quiet," Flynn muttered. But he followed her, and Rapunzel after him.

They were on what Rapunzel was pretty sure was a game trail, not a person or a horse or a cart trail. It was narrow and wobbled from side to side in shallow arcs, like the pace of something not used to going in perfectly straight lines—something small and not human.

"Tolson's Rock?" Flynn asked.

Gina shook her head. "Too obvious. Bear Knoll?"

"Too many bears."

"What about . . ."

"The Barrows!" they both cried at the same time.

Rapunzel felt a surge of confidence. Although things had gotten a little dangerous, she had obviously fallen in with the right company. They knew what they were doing and were familiar with the area.

(And *really* familiar with running away and hiding, it seemed.)

Now that they had a destination, Flynn ran up alongside Gina . . . and began to pass her.

Gina frowned and pushed her speed.

Rapunzel remained behind. She heaved and panted and her dress tore and she stumbled. She thought wryly about her initial enchantment with running on grass in the open; what it would be like to run forever. Seemed less charming now that she was actually doing it.

Her two new friends suddenly pitched to their left, narrowly avoiding the edge of a deep rocky gorge that had a thin trickle of water at its very bottom.

Rapunzel tried to stop herself, wavering at the top for a long moment—then started to tumble down into the ravine.

As her arms flew out, she thought quickly and grabbed her long "transport" braid, throwing it up and out into the branches of a tree. Gripping it tightly, she swung—*just* avoiding scraping her derriere on the pointy rocks below. As she began to pivot back up on her arcing path, she yanked; the braid came loose. She fell free . . . landing neatly on her toes.

Right in front of Gina and Flynn.

They were silent, literally speechless and gaping at what she had just done.

Without saying a word, Rapunzel methodically picked up her braid and wound it around her elbow and shoulder, firmly tucking it back into place.

"What . . ." Flynn began.

"How . . ." Gina continued.

Rapunzel shrugged. "So where are we going?" she asked innocently.

"The Barrows. You'll *love* it there. Lots of dark, damp hidey-holes, often inhabited by haunted corpses, but usually avoided by superstitious unsavory types," Flynn said.

"Except us," Gina said.

"We're not *unsavory*," Flynn objected. "We're *independent thinkers*."

They walked along a shallow green valley, which was cool and moist. Where the sides were too steep for grass, soft walls of moss grew. Rapunzel couldn't stop herself from continually pressing her hands into them.

Flynn gave Gina a look.

"Long story," Gina said. "I think."

"I'm so sorry, I don't believe we've been formally introduced. The name's Rider. *Flynn* Rider." He made a courtly little bow.

"We *have* been formally introduced. Several times," Gina said, glaring at him. "At the Snuggly Duckling. I'm Gina."

"And your lovely friend here?"

"I'm Rapunzel," she spoke up, not liking being discussed in the third person.

"Rapunzel, huh? Rapunzel of *what*? Of *whom*? What's your title, Silverlocks?" He indicated her dress, her hair, all of Rapunzel that was not at all like her companions. "Who are you, really?"

"I am . . . the one who hired Gina to find you," Rapunzel said primly, trying to sound adult. Or professional. Or something.

"Fair enough," Flynn said. "Secrets are trade in this line of work."

They came to the end of the gorge: a hollow so perfectly rounded on one side it had to have been man-made—or at least shaped with the help of man. Long ago all the sharp and rocky edges had been smoothed with dirt, leaves, time. Rapunzel tried to save the image in her head to paint later: a sweet but lonely scene, large trees sheltering it from above.

Dug into the sides of the hollow were regular holes that went blackly into the earth like cells in a wasp or beehive. Some had caved in or had their entrances filled by vines. Marking a sort of formal entrance were a pair of larger caves on either side of the bowl; gatehouses long missing their watchmen.

"We'll hang out here for a while," Gina said. But her eyes glanced quickly to Flynn, to see what the more experienced adventurer would do.

He shrugged "I don't have any pressing appointments anywhere. Though I *do* need to visit the local *branch* of my bank and make a quick withdrawal at some point."

Ha-ha, Rapunzel thought, unconsciously grasping her bag more tightly, feeling the edges of the crown. If he only knew!

". . . And maybe you can tell me what this is all about. Why you need me, what exactly is going on."

He sat down on a lichen-covered stone that tilted at an uneasy angle. Then he smiled and raised an eyebrow at Rapunzel . . . which made *her* feel uneasy.

His eyes were light, light brown like the dark honey that came at the end of the summer when the sumac and serious bushes bloomed. His eyebrows were heavy and expressive but didn't overwhelm his face. His mouth kept pulling to one side in that smile . . . there was something a little fake about it, but also something a little endearing. Like he was trying *very hard* to be suave and mysterious. And didn't realize how obvious it was.

"Hey," Gina said loudly, interrupting Rapunzel's train of not-really-thought. "Man wants a story."

"Right. So." Rapunzel cleared her head and took a deep

breath. "Once upon a time, in a lonely tower in the middle of the woods, a girl . . ."

"Who's this?" Flynn asked.

"Me," Rapunzel said, exasperated.

"Wait, you *lived* in that freakish plague tower?"

"Yes! Are you even listening? I and my mom lived there . . . well, she lived there more when I was younger. Now it's mostly me. Also, there was no plague," she added. "Those signs were put there to keep people away, I think."

"You lived by yourself in a tower your whole life?" It could have come out sounding sarcastic, or disbelieving . . . but there was a note of genuine horror in Flynn's tone. "Like a prisoner?"

She started to say no, but stopped: she had been literally sent to the tower for her crimes. "Kind of. This is the first time I've ever been down. I mean—outside."

"Whoa," Gina said.

Rapunzel didn't like the looks of pity on their faces. She had been happy there, mostly, and it was all for everyone's good. There was nothing to *pity* her for.

"Anyway, it was all pretty much the same, same things every day, same things out the window every season, except that every year around now, beautiful golden lights float up into the sky from somewhere northwest of here."

"You mean the lantern thing they do for the dead princess?" Gina and Flynn asked at the same time.

"Jinx!" they both immediately said.

"Buymeapint," they shouted at the same time, pointing at each other. Then they began laughing.

"Wait," Rapunzel said, completely mystified. She didn't *not* like the way her two new friends were becoming friends. But she didn't love it either. "Lanterns? That float?"

"Yeah, the little candles in the paper lantern make them rise up into the air," Flynn said with a shrug. "They do it every year to commemorate the death of the queen's only child."

"Oh. That's . . . sad."

All those years, all the things Rapunzel imagined the floating lights to be. She knew they weren't stars, because they didn't stay; she knew they weren't meteors or comets, because they went up, not down. Never did she guess it was a man-made phenomenon—well known, at that. And for such a sad reason! Not a very joyous marker of her birthday week after all.

"Well," she said aloud. "I want to see them. And I want *you* to guide me there," she added, to Flynn.

"I could totally take you to see the lanterns!" Gina protested. "You don't need this guy."

"Absolutely true," Flynn agreed. "You don't. This girl

can take you. Afraid I'm not on good terms with the kingdom at this moment."

"What'd you steal this time?" Gina asked interestedly.

"A crown. Nice one, too. Anyway, I'm not going anywhere near that place. And also, there's a lot of other things on my plate right now. The Stabbingtons are after me . . . I have to line up a buyer. . . . Really, it's not a good time."

"You haven't even asked what I'll pay you," Rapunzel said innocently.

"You don't have enough," Flynn promised. Then he turned to Gina and said in a theatrical whisper, "This is where she offers her necklace, or a bracelet, or some other rich girl trinket I couldn't pawn even if I wanted. . . ."

"How about a *crown*?" Rapunzel suggested.

Flynn grew very, very still.

"Uh-oh," Gina said with a wicked grin.

"What, um—what crown?" Flynn asked casually.

"The one that you stole. The one that the Stabbingtons want back. The one that you hid, rather obviously, in a tree hollow," Rapunzel said smugly, crossing her arms. "Diamonds, pearls, about my size . . . You know, *that* crown?"

"That's *my* crown! Give it back! I stole it fair and square!" Flynn cried, leaping up.

"You mean you stole it from the castle, or you stole it from the Stabbingtons?" Gina asked interestedly.

"Doesn't matter," Flynn said, crossing his arms and setting his jaw childishly. "It's mine now."

"Well, no, it's *mine*," Rapunzel said. "At least until you take me to see the lanterns, and home again. Then it's yours."

"You must have seen me hide it! In the tree!"

"Déduction très brillante," Rapunzel said archly.

"Really??" Gina asked, throwing her hands in the air—a lot like Mother Gothel when she was playacting exasperated anger. "You're paying him a whole crown to take you to see the stupid lights?"

"Well, you knew I didn't have anything to pay *you* with," Rapunzel protested.

"You have a crown," Gina shouted.

"But it's not yours," Rapunzel said.

"See?" Flynn nodded his head. "You *do* get it."

"I mean," Rapunzel added, "I figured this crown would be worth a lot more to the guy who originally stole it and is being chased, than, you know, just anyone."

Gina gave her a look.

"It's a *crown*," she pointed out. "Apparently one with diamonds and pearls. You could hire everyone at the Snuggly Duckling ten times over for that."

"But the wanted posters implied that *he's* dangerous, and a fugitive, and wily, and just the sort of antihero I need to protect people from my h—I mean, me." Rapunzel dug into her satchel—being *very* careful not to make any clinking noises around the crown—and pulled out the now very folded poster. "Sorry, Gina. I just didn't know about you."

"*No* one does," Gina mumbled, kicking a stone.

"No *way*," Flynn swore, tearing the poster from Rapunzel's hand. "They got my nose wrong *again*. This is like the fifth time. What do I have to do, pose for the royal guard?"

He held it up to his face and tried to copy the expression.

"Stop complaining," Gina snapped. "'Aw, I'm soooo famous that they print up soooo many different pictures of my face, getting them wrong.' Geez, tough life."

"All right, all right, I'll do it," Flynn said with a forced, world-weary sigh, ignoring Gina completely. "But only because my life is in danger and I really need that crown."

"And I get a share," Gina said.

"Why do you get anything?" Flynn demanded. "You're not taking the lady to see the lanterns."

"I led her to you. And I saved your life."

Gina and Flynn glared at each other.

Rapunzel now found herself wishing that her new friends were where they'd been five minutes ago, when they had been full of nothing but compliments and congratulations for each other.

"All right," Flynn said, rolling his eyes. "A share. I'm such a softie."

"Yes!" Gina whispered a little too loudly, pumping her fist in victory.

Rapunzel wanted to ask exactly what a share of a solid crown meant exactly (a single diamond? A broken-off flourish?) but decided that since the two were now working together to get her to where she wanted to go, she wasn't going to complicate things by bringing it up.

She was finally going to get to see the lanterns, and nothing could possibly go wrong.

Memorial Sloan Kettering

"They're all . . . together . . ." Daniella whispered, the slightest smile on her face. Her hand slipped from the covers she clutched to rest on the bed itself in a gesture that was far too reminiscent of death on a TV show. But her face was relaxed, and if not exactly healthy looking, then at least free of the pinched look she often got halfway through the chemo.

"Yeah," Brendan said quietly. "You can relax now. But trust me, there is trouble just around the corner for our heroes."

He pulled the blankets up around her neck. She would be freezing when she woke. He'd ask for another autoclaved blanket the next time a nurse came by.

He usually sketched or played on his phone while she slept, texting senseless half conversations with his friends that he could barely finish, randomly surfing on social media. None of it held his attention despite the utter absence of any real distractions in the tiny room—noises, movement, anything.

And despite the obvious similarity of his sister to the fairy-tale princesses who slept deeper and longer than they should have, Brendan immediately dismissed the comparison. Daniella wasn't a helpless princess any more than Rapunzel was. She was a tiny queen fighting for her kingdom—in this case, her body.

He found himself reaching for the book instead of his phone. Despite all the movie viewings and two book reads, he somehow still wasn't sure of some of the characters' names or physical details. Hook Hand was obvious, but what about Attila? And how *was* he going to work Maximus into the story?

He flipped through the book, taking notes, until his sister woke again.

Rapunzel

The next morning, after a surprisingly restful and unhaunted sleep in the Barrows, Rapunzel sorted her hair as best she could while Flynn and Gina vigorously discussed possible routes to where the lantern ceremony was held. The epicenter of which was, unfortunately, right in front of the castle on the island. Which was obviously bad for Flynn. But just as tricky was getting there; the Stabbingtons were now on the warpath for both him *and* Gina. Although the harbor could be easily reached in a day, the final itinerary they chose was circuitous, hidden, and would take at least two.

This worried Rapunzel a little; according to her calculations, they would be pushing it *very close* to arrive in time to see the lanterns.

She pulled out her journal. "The lights—I mean, lanterns—always appear a month and eight days before the summer solstice," she said, checking her figures and drawings for the thousandth time.

"May twelfth. Yeah," Flynn said.

"My ma took me once when I was younger," Gina said. "It was beautiful. Hundreds of the lanterns in the sky, all reflected in the water and everything. We actually had some coin, so my mom let me light one, but she was quiet the whole time. Sad. Almost as if she knew the baby princess."

"Your mother sounds wonderful," Rapunzel said.

"She's fine, I guess," Gina said with a shrug—but also a little smile, like she was secretly proud. "I mean, she's boring. It's all, *Gina, get your clothes off the floor, we don't live in a filthy hovel—just a hovel.* Or *Gina, I* really *need some skullcap—could you pick me some in the Western Fells?*"

"See, that's why I fled the orphanage. *Before* I was adopted," Flynn said with a sigh of contentment. "No one ever told me what to do. No *mom* doing all *mom* things like making me wash behind my ears or make a bed or whatever. Nope, I'm free as a bird."

"Wait, you're an orphan, too?" Gina asked in surprise. "What orphanage?"

"Mother Mary of the Blessed Little Children. You?"

"Same here!"

The two adventurers gawped at each other, and then began to laugh.

Rapunzel watched them with a mixture of amusement and envy. She was the one responsible for bringing these two together and discovering they had a shared past, true. But she wished that *she* had a past she could share with someone besides Gothel. *Hey, Pascal,* she could imagine herself saying. *Remember that time when it suddenly rained? And I forgot to close the shutters?*

And also . . . Flynn had escaped the orphanage as a *child*.

Rapunzel hadn't left the tower until her nineteenth birthday.

Had life been so pleasant that she had never even thought of escaping?

Of course there were hours of loneliness and sadness. Days, sometimes. Even the cheeriest person in the world would eventually be brought low by what was essentially solitary confinement.

But when she'd asked to leave the tower, she asked her mother to go with her. It wasn't really to *escape*. There hadn't been the thought that she wouldn't return to the tower afterward; return to endless hours by herself, painting, cleaning, playing, reading. Because . . .

Because . . . she was dangerous and needed—*deserved*—to stay there?

No, she realized. Nothing really so noble. It was simply because she didn't know anything else, or any other way to live. The tower was literally her entire world.

And here were these two strapping, energetic adventurers who had thought that orphanage was their tower, despite all the other people there, and just assumed that better things lay beyond it.

"Sorry," Gina said, seeing the faraway look on Rapunzel's face. "You had to be there. It was a *pit*."

"What do other children do, who don't, ah, escape the orphanage or get adopted?" Rapunzel asked quickly, wanting to think of something else.

Her two new friends shrugged.

"Get married, I guess?" Flynn said. "Become nuns? When you're fifteen you have to leave one way or the other. You're grown up. They started to make some changes before I left, I remember. The queen instituted some sort of improvement program. Better food, more classes, fewer lice—who cares. Glad I got out."

"I'm an orphan, too," Rapunzel said, trying not to sound desperate. "My parents . . . died when I was a baby. Mother Gothel adopted me."

"An orphan who was kept as a prisoner in a tower with plague signs to keep away?" Gina gently teased. "Seems like a lot of work. Nahh, I bet you're a princess of some sort."

Rapunzel stared at her. Then she began guffawing: big, hearty barks of laughter.

"She doesn't *sound* like one," Flynn observed.

"She wears a pretty dress like one," Gina pointed out.

"Your skin *is* creamy and perfect," Flynn said. "I mean, um, I guess."

"You have a crown," Gina said.

"It's not my crown," Rapunzel shouted, still laughing. "I grew up in two rooms . . . not a giant castle. I don't have any servants, or ladies-in-waiting . . ."

". . . or crowns you didn't steal," Flynn added.

". . . or a white horse, or velvet capes, or a scepter . . ."

"You *do* have that magnificent hair, though," Flynn pointed out. "I mean, just look at it. It *looks* fancy and expensive and royal. A normal person, even a lord or lady, couldn't manage locks half that long. Even if it ever came in silver, which seems reeealllly unlikely."

He leaned forward to get a better look, and at first Rapunzel did nothing, suddenly aware of his closeness. Whatever he said about *her* skin, Flynn's was also clear, healthy, and peachy. He had a little bit of hair on his chin (not a full beard like she had seen in pictures), a tiny feathery thing that she kind of wanted to touch. His eyes were bigger up close, which was silly, now that she thought about it, because of course they would be . . .

. . . and then she remembered she couldn't be normal.

"DON'T TOUCH MY HAIR!" she screamed, leaping backward and slapping at him crazily.

"Whoa, sorry, Your Highness!" Flynn said, stepping away. "I didn't realize milady's silvery tresses were so delicate."

"It's not that," Rapunzel said desperately. "Please, I'm sorry. It's just that . . ."

"Yeah, she's got a thing about touching her hair," Gina said. "Also about killing chickens, just FYI. She has some issues."

"All right, let's just keep going. Note to self: ix-nay on the air-hay."

Rapunzel wilted and padded along after them.

But Flynn didn't seem the type to hold a grudge or overthink things. Within a few minutes he was whistling, and humorously trying to trick Rapunzel into telling him where she had hidden the crown, and arguing with Gina about their journey.

And Rapunzel never stayed blue for long, either; soon enough she was almost skipping behind them, enjoying her adventure once again.

"The northern coast is so cold, hard, and, you know, salty," Flynn complained. "Let's just sneak through the royal gardens and come at the harbor from inside the island."

"I thought you said you were trying to avoid the city," Gina said.

"Yeah, but I like avoiding sea weather, too. Absolute nightmare on my skin."

"Wow. On that note, I need to find a private tree . . ."

"Why didn't you go *before* the adventure?" Flynn sighed, hands on hips. "You are such an amateur. I'll bet you didn't even pack a lunch."

"Go stuff yourself into a wasp nest," Gina told him amiably, and disappeared like a shadow into the woods. *"She has cheese,"* she shouted behind her.

"Cheese?" Flynn asked, raising an eyebrow at Rapunzel.

"Yes! I do!" Rapunzel replied eagerly. "And some roasted beans . . ."

"Hand 'em over. Let's just wander up this way . . . give your friend some privacy."

Rapunzel was suddenly aware that it was just the two of them. Mother had warned her about situations like this; it was one of the reasons she had to live in the tower. A boy would talk sweetly to her, lean in close, try to grab a kiss, and . . .

. . . be killed when Rapunzel panicked and fought back. And it would be all her fault.

Or was it he would he be killed if Rapunzel *didn't* fight back? If she just *kissed* him back? And somehow accidentally killed him anyway? It would be all her fault.

Or . . .

She couldn't remember which scenario her mother had particularly warned her about. Either way, it always ended with the boy's life taken and its being her fault. That was the point of the lectures.

And she was now in that very scenario. She was alone with a boy.

He caught her staring at him and gave her a sly look.

"Super impressed with being with a real live criminal, huh?" he asked, smiling with surprisingly nice white teeth.

"I'm super impressed with anyone who can fight and knows these woods and the world so well. I guess Gina does, too."

"Yes, Gina." He frowned. "She's kind of a weirdo. Nice weirdo, mind you. But very, very odd."

A flurry of thoughts winged their way through Rapunzel's head like a confused flock of birds on a late summer test flight. She couldn't separate the different feathered things out.

She was also puzzled by the look on Flynn's face: he raised his eyebrows and sort of gazed at her, turning his head so it was a little sideways. He smiled so that his lips stretched wide at the corners but remained partially closed over his teeth.

Obviously it was some sort of expression Gothel didn't make but that other people commonly used.

So she tried to copy him.

"What are you doing?" Flynn asked.

"I 'on't ow," Rapunzel responded, keeping her lips in the same half position. "'at ar*e oo* oing?"

"Okay, you're kind of a weirdo, too. No wonder you two get along so well," Flynn said, shaking his head and dropping the look. "Usually *the smolder* works on all the ladies."

"Oh, you were trying to . . ." Rapunzel began to giggle. Books #27 and #28 were tales of knights and damsels and adventures—with more than a touch of romance.

Flynn looked offended.

"No, please, try again!" Rapunzel begged.

"Oh, the mood's gone. Forget it," he said, rolling his eyes. But he smiled—a real smile this time, a natural one. "What did you do all day in the tower, anyway? I'm surprised you're not stark raving mad by now."

She sighed. "I have a *very* strict schedule. Six-thirty rise, chores until eight, first reading eight until eight-thirty. I mean, the first reading of the day, not of a book. I only have thirty-seven books. I've read them all hundreds of times. I keeping begging Mother for more . . . but she can only find one or two a year. Next is art. Then on Mondays and Fridays at ten is preparation for the night's astronomy. On Tuesdays and Thursdays it's writing and rehearsing puppet shows. On Wednesdays it's . . . Sorry, it's boring you, isn't it? I can tell."

"No . . . it's . . . I just . . . I don't know what to say," Flynn said softly. He *had* been staring at her—but it apparently wasn't with impatience; it was something else she couldn't name. "And believe you me, I *always* know what to say. Somehow you grew up, maintained a crazy amount of self-discipline . . . and managed to stay sane. I don't know how you're so constantly upbeat and cheery considering the hand life dealt you. You must be a truly amazing person."

Rapunzel blinked, unprepared for this response. But there was something so artlessly truthful about his remark that it must have bothered him as well, and he changed the subject before she had a chance to say anything.

"But then why do you want to see the lanterns so badly? I mean, of all the things you could do out in the wide world once you left . . . sail on a boat, date around, climb a mountain . . . why *that*?"

Rapunzel shrugged, and sort of danced with her feet as they continued down the path and she looked for the right words. "I don't know . . . It's the only thing I've ever really, really wanted. To see them up close. I thought if I could just do that . . . I could live happily ever after."

"Really? That's all you ever wanted out of life?"

"Really! But now . . ."

She looked around at the woods. The same woods she had seen from above, in her tower. It was different when you were down on the ground, and not just because of the way they looked. Everything was dirtier. Smellier, in a good way. *Realer*. Utterly different from what she'd thought, and all-consuming.

And there were Gina and Flynn. And the Snuggly Duckling. And kvass. And birds killed by someone else, roasted on a campfire.

Nothing she had ever imagined or wished for . . . but somehow the lanterns were fading a little in her mind, overshadowed by these other experiences. How strange!

"And now?" Flynn prodded.

"I don't know," Rapunzel said honestly. "I don't want *this* part to end. If I see the lanterns, then I will have seen the lanterns . . . and it will be over . . . and I'll go home. . . ."

"I really didn't think you were going to answer that," Flynn said, shaking his head. "You always seem to say exactly what's on your mind, or in your heart. It's new to me. As a daring criminal, lying is sort of par for the course."

"What do *you* want most of all? What dream have you had for your whole life?" Rapunzel asked curiously.

Flynn looked surprised—and then trapped, as if the question were a snare.

Finally he grinned, utterly erasing any previous emotion. He waved his hand nonchalantly in the air. "I mean, what does any thief wish for? To never have to thieve again! Piles and piles of money—"

But before he had a chance to finish, they rounded a corner and were faced by a trio of men waiting for them, weapons raised.

Rapunzel

"Hook Hand! Attila! Ulf!! What a *truly* pleasant surprise!"
Flynn exclaimed, hand going to his knife. "Don't you have
little girls to bully somewhere? A keg of ale that needs rescuing back at the Snuggly Duckling?"

"Hi again!" Rapunzel said with a grin and a little wave.
She pointed at Flynn. "I found him!"

Hook Hand's look, initially murderous, softened when
he saw her. All three of the pub thugs, including Attila (the
man in the full helm) and Ulf (silent and large) lowered their
weapons.

"You haven't heard, then," Hook Hand said slowly. "The
Snuggly Duckling was destroyed. It's all gone, burnt down."

"But we were just there . . ." Rapunzel murmured.

"You're kidding!" Flynn looked genuinely astonished. "*Nobody* would dare! Every villain in the kingdom would hunt down whoever did it. Who was it?"

"Countess Bathory and her manhunters—and her bloodhounds," Attila said from inside his helmet.

(Ulf mimed with his fingers a bunch of people breaking into a house and smashing it all to pieces.)

"Bathory?" Flynn's face went pale. "Why is she in this part of the country? What's going on?"

"Who's Countess Bathory?" Rapunzel added.

The thugs and Flynn didn't answer. Judging by the looks on their faces, it was less that they were ignoring her than that they really didn't *want* to answer.

"She's looking for a girl named Rapunzel," Hook Hand said softly.

Rapunzel swallowed. She had never introduced herself at the pub.

But if this man already knew who she was . . .

The only possible explanation was that her mother had discovered her absence and was having people look for her. But why not hire thugs who would take an easy job like that in a heartbeat—like these guys, from the Duckling? Why a *countess*? That was really strange. How did her mother know a countess? And how did she get in contact with her so quickly?

Young Rapunzel used to spend whole afternoons imagining what her mother did and saw when she left the tower, but after many years of questioning and only getting the same boring answers, she believed them: Gothel tended the home farm, gardened, and went to the market.

Did Gothel ever meet a countess at a farm stand? Haggling over turnips, maybe?

Poor Rapunzel had made a decision to change her life, to go outside . . . and not three days later, the inside was chasing *her*, wanting her back.

"I'm sorry, *who* is Countess Bathory?" she repeated.

All the men looked even more uncomfortable than before.

"She's a very bad lady," Flynn said carefully. He looked Hook Hand dead in the eye as he spoke, seemingly willing him to go along with whatever story he was about to tell. "She . . . likes to take girls . . . she kidnaps them. That's all."

"And dismembers them and bathes in their blood," Hook Hand said, also carefully—probably thinking he was saying it gently.

Flynn hit his forehead with the palm of his hand. Even Attila shook his metal-sheathed head sadly.

Rapunzel tried to process this terrible information.

She had never heard of, much less imagined in her worst stories, such a horrible thing.

Why would her mother send an evil creature like that after her?

"You must leave here at once," Attila said from inside his helm. "She has her bloodhounds out looking for you. They say one sniff of a person's shirt and they can track her across the country."

"Cool, cool, cool," Flynn said, nodding. "Yup, the worst stuff of my nightmares are all present and accounted for—including your own ugly mugs, of course. Speaking of, why exactly are you helping us?"

"We're not helping *you*," Hook Hand said with disgust. "We're helping the little lady here. No one deserves to be turned over to that monster . . . especially someone who came to the Snuggly Duckling just looking for help. I'm sorry for ignoring you," he added contritely.

"*And* Bathory destroyed the best pub in all the land," Attila growled. Ulf replayed his pantomime of the place being destroyed.

Just then Gina burst onto the little scene, her own knife out. "What's going on here?"

"Not what you think," Flynn said, putting his hands out to stop her. "Weirdly. We gotta go. These lovely refugees from social norms say that Bathory and her dogs are after our princess here—"

"Not a princess," Rapunzel interrupted.

"Bathory?" Gina asked, jaw dropping. "Her hounds? We gotta get to a river, confuse the scent trail. There's a small one east of us. . . ."

"Weasel Crick." Flynn nodded. "Let's go."

"Good luck," Hook Hand said.

"Thank you, kind sir!" Rapunzel stood on her toes and kissed him on the cheek before running off after her friends.

She couldn't, of course, *see* Hook Hand's face since they were running the opposite direction; but one could probably imagine the look of surprise and soft wonder that grew there, and the dawning of ideas and worlds that had never seemed possible before.

Weasel Crick had the honor of being the first body of water Rapunzel ever encountered. She was dazzled by the play of sunlight on the rocks and the water splashing and dividing over them: ripples and eddies and quick-lived bubbles in a thousand shades of white, silver, and black. Monochrome, and at the same time one of the most colorful things she had ever seen.

"Come on, into the current," Flynn said, already ankle deep in the middle of it. Gina rubbed her arms and boots with great handfuls she scooped up.

Rapunzel leapt in the stream eagerly and landed with a splash in between them. The water was *cold*. Some of the rocks were slippery. She wiggled her toes, wondering if her feet had ever felt this alive. She giggled as tiny fish swam in a flock over her feet, and shrieked happily when one tried to nibble her.

Gina and Flynn glared at her, dripping from where her water had hit them: face, nose, chin . . .

"This is *great!*" Rapunzel said, picking up her feet and putting them down again, letting her skin grow icy cold. "But why exactly are we doing this?"

"Throwing the bloodhounds off the scent," Gina explained. "The river doesn't carry smells, and will wash them off our feet."

"We'll go downstream through the water," Flynn added, "and exit it somewhere else. It will take them a while to go up and down the banks with the dogs and catch the trail again."

"Maybe *up*stream," Gina said thoughtfully. "They'll assume we'd go downstream 'cause that would be easier. But—um, whatever you think."

"Makes sense," Rapunzel said.

"And why should anything be easier?" Flynn said, sighing. "'Take me to the lanterns, that's all I want.'" He batted his eyes and imitated Rapunzel poorly. "And *boom*, suddenly the most bloodthirsty noble in all of Europe is after you. I feel like I should get a bonus for this. Hazard pay."

"Works for me," Gina said.

After a while, slogging through the cold stream wasn't *quite* as delightful as it had started out to be. Rapunzel's long skirts soaked up the water whenever she accidentally let them touch; soon heavy and wet fabric was slapping against her legs and chafing the skin of her inner thighs. But still. Pretty flowers grew on the banks in colors her books did not adequately re-create: pink, golden eggy yellow, bright white with the shadow of its own curled petal twinning next to it.

And funny little bugs that walked on the water where it slowed near the banks, delicately gliding across the surface like magic!

Pascal *might* have taken the opportunity to grab one as she leaned over to look more closely. She felt a little bad about that, but her friend had to eat.

When she stood up again Flynn was standing there, staring at her. Or rather, the lizard.

Oh, she had forgotten to introduce them!

"His name is Pascal," Rapunzel said, feeling strangely embarrassed. People had friends who were animals. *Pets.* Wasn't that a normal thing?

"Of course it is," Flynn said, and kept walking. "You know, if it turns out that he's your familiar and you're an ugly old witch in disguise—*who could have magically transported herself to the lanterns on her broom*—I'm going to be *very* disappointed in you."

"Hey, don't be mean," Gina said, hitting him on the shoulder. Rapunzel grinned smugly, defended by her other friend.

"Witches are *not* ugly and not always old. Be respectful," Gina continued.

Not what Rapunzel thought she was going to say.

"And how would you know? Actually, now it all makes sense," Flynn said thoughtfully, looking Gina over. "You escaped from a coven, yearning for an exciting life of banditry on the road. Sick of the same old newts' eyes for breakfast . . ."

There was no hesitation at all in Gina's decision to expertly hit him in the forehead with a ball of mud.

Eventually the two adventurers decided it was safe enough to leave Weasel Crick's cleansing waters. They wrung out their sopping garments in a sunny clearing where the trees were thin enough that they could see through the forest and over the fields, all the way to the sea.

"Well, there's our destination, Lady Silverlocks," Flynn said with a bow. Rapunzel pushed her way forward—and gasped.

There was the capital city.

She could see the wide stone bridge that connected the castle and its environs to the mainland, the sparkling ocean that lapped at its shores. Gleaming towers rose into the sky, topped with blue onion domes. Markets, keeps, pubs, and plazas cozied up to the palace like it was their mother. All the buildings had brightly tiled roofs, all the streets had prettily cobbled squares.

The ringing bell of a warning buoy just made itself heard over the distance, sounding more festive than forlorn.

Rapunzel was overcome with awe—and the sudden urge to hide. Cities! They were so big! And impressive!

"So, that's pretty great, right?" Flynn said, seeing the look on her face. "Bet we could see the lanterns *perfectly* from right here. People pay good money for seats like these, let me tell you. Above the crowds, away from the noise and garbage . . ."

Gina hit him.

"Do you see those guards down there?" he demanded. "Do you *see* them? They're probably looking for me right now!"

He wasn't wrong. A captain and two men, all mounted, were very obviously searching the open countryside that lay between the woods and the coast. As Rapunzel watched, they approached a pair of woodsmen coming back to town, stacks of small logs strapped to their backs. The captain spoke to one of the guards—sternly, it looked like—and he peeled off and began to trot back to the castle. The captain and the other one rode on, *toward the forest.*

"See?" Flynn demanded. "Are you seeing what I'm seeing?"

"Horses," Rapunzel breathed.

They were incredible—so much grander than the ones back at the Snuggly Duckling! Noble, huge, panting like gods. Shining white and rich, chestnut brown. All delicate legs but powerfully muscled, large eyes and manes and tails that *almost* put her own hair to shame.

"She sees horses," Flynn said, disbelieving.

"I see them, too," Gina said with a shrug. "Along with the guards. Raps? Thoughts? About our journey, I mean?"

"Um, yes," Rapunzel said, pulling herself together and facing Flynn. "The deal was you get your crown when I get to see the lanterns. *Up close.*"

"Do you really want to see *this face* behind bars?" Flynn asked, and gave her another smoldering smile, waggling his eyebrows.

"No, I want to see the lanterns. And no one can imprison you if *you don't have the crown.*" Rapunzel spun on her heel and began to walk jauntily down the path. "Well, you guys coming?"

"Gee, and I thought she was such a sweet and innocent thing," Flynn muttered.

"Shh!" Gina said.

"I don't care if she hears me! This is what the ruling classes always do! They *always* get their way, trampling us little folk. With their *fancy silver hair* and their *crowns* that I rightfully stole from them . . ."

"No, I mean it, *shhh!*" Gina said, holding her hand up.

Flynn cut his speech off immediately.

The clatter of men was coming toward them: boots on the path, swaggers made sound.

"Hide!" Flynn ordered Rapunzel. "We'll distract them."

It was so strange how he went from funny, chatting Flynn to serious and directed Flynn so quickly! Like there had been an actual thinking, planning person under all his faces and jokes all along. Intriguing . . .

Sadly, Rapunzel knew that if there was a fight, she would be useless. Her entangling with Flynn in front of the Stabbingtons was more than enough proof of that. And the fewer people who were anywhere near her hair the better. Despite her reluctance to abandon her new friends, Rapunzel ducked behind the thick trunk of an old tree (but poked her head out to watch).

Four armed men sauntered up the path to Flynn and Gina. They weren't more escapees from the Snuggly

Duckling, though. Nor did they look like the soldiers on horseback in their neat uniforms with shining buttons; they were like a cheaper, more evil version of them. Dirtier gear, caps rather than helms. The skull of a snarling boar decorated their jackets.

"Good afternoon, gentlemen. My, what a lovely day for a stroll, isn't it?" Flynn said with a winning smile.

"Is that the girl we're after?" the leader spat, not bothering to respond. He seemed particularly evil, with yellowed eyes and lank locks of hair hanging off his brow. "She doesn't look like the description we was told. Are you Rapunzel? *Did you cut off her hair?*"

"I'm not—" Gina began.

Flynn slapped a hand over her mouth.

"Why?" he asked. "Why do you want her? Is there a general call for ladies of unusual hair? For modeling, perhaps?"

The man ignored him and jerked his head. Two of the others quickly pushed behind Flynn and Gina, cutting off their escape. The friends reacted instantly, turning back-to-back, drawing their blades.

"This is hardly necessary. Any information you'd be willing to share might de-escalate this situation a bit," Flynn suggested. "Perhaps we can help each other out."

"All you need to know is that Baron Smeinhet wants

this 'Rapunzel' and is giving a nice reward to them what finds her."

"Fair enough. But why does Bathory want her, too? What's the deal? Can we get in on this?" Flynn sounded both suspicious and trustworthy: a villain another villain could trust. Rapunzel was deeply impressed.

But the man looked at him sharply. "*Bathory*? She know about you? Where you are? Grab her, boys! We got to get out of here before that wench and her dogs finds her."

"I'll gut the first one of you who puts a hand on me," Gina said calmly.

"You sure this is the right girl? She don't act like no princess," one of the men muttered.

Perhaps it was that word, more than anything else, that made Rapunzel stop watching and decide to do something.

He was right. She *wasn't* a princess.

(And neither was Gina.)

She looked around and saw a small, sharp-edged rock, like the one Gina had used against the Stabbingtons. She began to reach for it . . . then thought: *Nope, that's dumb.* There was no way she could take out even one of the four men with one rock, unless her aim was perfect. And that still left three.

She thought about jumping on the back of one of the

men, wrapping her arms around his neck, pulling him away. Like she used to do a long time ago to her mother, begging for piggyback rides.

. . . But if she flubbed it up, it was still four against two, and they would then have her, the real Rapunzel.

Also, if she panicked or the man hurt her, her hair would kill him. And anyone else it touched.

She looked around desperately for some answer to present itself from the scenery around her . . . and one did.

The horses!

Wait, no: the royal guard!

(*On* their horses.)

"HELP!" she yelled, running out from behind her tree and waving her arms at them. "Oh, help! Please! Help!"

She couldn't have asked for a more fairy-tale perfect response.

The captain, mounted on his beautiful horse, cocked his head, trying to pinpoint the location of the shouts. His man pointed to Rapunzel. The captain nodded and dug his heels into his horse's flanks, and together the two men galloped toward her.

Rapunzel was hypnotized for a moment, watching the grace and strength of the horses. Someday she would paint them. Someday she would capture the hooves, the bulging veins on the neck, the soft nostrils and eyelashes, the way no one ever had; the way horses were meant to be if frozen in paint.

When she pulled herself away she saw the situation with her friends had gotten worse: Flynn was on his knees, a sword at his neck. One of the men held Gina around her chest, her arms caught and immobile against her sides. She jumped and kicked and tried to get away but accomplished little, being not quite half his size.

Rapunzel ducked down behind her tree again, hoping they hadn't seen her.

"I was going to turn you over to the royal guards and get the reward," the greasy-haired man said, leering into Flynn's face. There was a bloody gash down the middle of his forehead. "Two birds with one stone. But it might be fun to try some butchery on you instead. I've a pig come Christmas and could use the practice."

"No fair!" one of the other soldiers complained. "We swore we'd split his reward four ways."

"*Who's leader here?*" The man whipped around with surprising speed for someone who seemed all laziness and low threats. His sword point was now at his comrade's neck.

"Who was that girl screaming?" another of them asked, pointing at the tree where Rapunzel (thought she) was hiding.

Before she could think of what to do, the cavalry

literally arrived. The two horses leapt into the middle of the clearing, snorting and rearing and having to be pulled back by their riders, so eager were they to plunge into battle. The captain sat high in his saddle—but honestly, he was a bit older than Rapunzel was expecting. His face was lined with years of leadership and worry, and it was hard to tell if his hair was pale with age or he was just a towhead.

(The man next to him was young and had nice hair, though, so that was something.)

"What the devil is going on?" he demanded, looking at the scene with more disgust than curiosity.

"Oh, hey there, Treggsy," Flynn called out. "Nice of you to drop in and save us. How's tricks at the castle?"

"Flynn Rider?" He looked, if it were possible, even more disgusted. "I heard a cry for help—but from someone a lot prettier than you. Thank you for apprehending this criminal, gentlemen. We will take him from here. But may I just ask what Lord Smeinhet's men are doing within the borders of our kingdom without a formal invitation?"

He spoke calmly despite the impatience of his horse, who turned left and right and stomped its feet, almost like it was sick of the talk and wanted enemies to crush.

"We was chasing a lost little girl what belongs to our lord," the leader of the men said, looking the captain defiantly in the face. "Our own private issues, Captain. Then we came upon this criminal here."

"Criminal*s*," Gina corrected.

"Your own private issues do not extend into these lands," Captain Tregsburg said crisply. "What you are doing here is a provocation, an act of war. Leave here at once, before you cause an international incident far above your pay grade."

The man's face went dark.

"You can't order us around! We report to Smeinhet. And with this girl here, he'll be the mightiest king in all the world, and you and your kingdom will be begging him for mercy."

"This girl?" the captain asked, confused. "This— common ruffian?"

Gina grinned, obviously proud to have been considered such.

"But wasn't there *another* girl? What is this all about, anyway?" Tregsburg demanded.

"Well, I can see you two have a *lot* to talk about," Flynn said, slowly getting up onto his feet. "I myself—and this common ruffian here—will simply be on our way, glad to have done our patriotic duty in letting you know about the incipient invasion of our beloved country. I assume all prices on my head have been made null and void in thanks for this. . . ."

"Stay where you are, Rider!" the captain bellowed, drawing his sword and pointing it at Flynn.

"Go on, take him," the leader of the Smeinhet men said with a shrug. "We'll take the girl and go back home."

"There are no negotiations here. Do not tell me what to do, and do not think you can abscond with a citizen of our kingdom, criminal though she may be. We will investigate this matter ourselves. Now start marching for the border—we'll see you out."

"Not unless we see you first!"

Suddenly—at no signal Rapunzel had seen—one of the Smeinhet men shot at the guards with a small crossbow affixed to his arm.

The missile hit the chestnut horse square in the shoulder. While it neither embedded itself nor even did much damage, it accomplished what it was supposed to: terrify and surprise the poor animal. It reared up and its rider scrambled to stay on.

The captain didn't bother looking around to see what had happened; he set his jaw and drove his own horse into the brigands, bringing his sword down on their leader.

The scene was chaos: the wounded horse screamed and lunged at anyone it could see. The guard on its back swung his sword while being nearly thrown left and right. The captain leveled a blow at one man and then another, wheeling his own horse around. One man still held Gina; the other two jumped to defend their leader.

No one even noticed Flynn slip through the fight and grab Rapunzel from her hiding place.

"Come *on!*" he cried.

"But Gina—" she said.

"She can take care of herself. *Run!*"

Rapunzel let herself be pulled along but looked behind them. Gina had indeed twirled out of her captor's grasp; she took one extra second to spit at him, then leapt nimbly through the panicking horses and fighting men, and fled into the trees.

Only the captain saw Rapunzel as she and Flynn escaped into the black forest. Their eyes met for a moment; his face fell in astonishment.

She would never be certain, but she could have sworn that his mouth made the words *It can't be.* . . .

And then she was plunging into the woods with her friends, away from the fight.

Rapunzel

They only stopped running when Rapunzel could literally not go any further, her legs spasming and seizing up.

Gina collapsed heavily on a boulder and pulled back her jerkin. The flesh underneath was ragged, ugly, torn, and bruised . . . Rapunzel suddenly realized that the strange, regular incisions were *bite marks*. From a horse. There were clear beads of sweat on her friend's pale face, but she just calmly and methodically pulled out her waterskin and washed the wounds, hissing when cold drops hit her flesh.

"You know, I was just saying to myself," Flynn said as soon as he caught his breath, "*Flynn*, you're getting a little saggy from lack of exercise and far too much foie gras. What you really need is a serious training program, where you're forced to run for your life *every second of the day*. I'd like to personally thank you, Princess, for making this man's six-pack ambitions come true."

"Not a princess," Rapunzel said weakly, still heaving and panting. There was a stitch in her side that was refusing to go away.

Her hair had come undone with all the running; some of her loops and whorls and braids now spread out around her like a silvery mass of fishing nets. She groaned thinking of the time it would take to redo it all.

"So, just for the record—and my own edification— where does 'getting hunted down by every hired heavy in the land' appear in the aforementioned contract of simply taking you to the lanterns and you giving me the crown?"

"*Us* the crown," Gina corrected, using the end of her shirt to dab at some drying blood.

"I didn't—" Rapunzel began.

"Out of the goodness of my heart, I decide to lend you my help . . . and then Bathory burns down the Snuggly Duckling. While hunting for *you*. And Smeinhet sends out what look like his ugliest evildoers after . . . *you*. 'You' being the common element here. What's actually going on? What aren't you telling us? I somehow feel it doesn't have anything to do with lanterns."

"Lady, it's time to fess up," Gina said, frankly but not meanly. She pointed at her wound.

Rapunzel put her head in her hands.

Her adventure had been going so well! It had been literally the best week of her life. She had made two entirely new friends who weren't puppets or paintings, she was finally on her way to see the floating lights . . . and now this.

She could have dealt with just Flynn yelling. He didn't seem to be *actually* angry at her, and most of what he said was just his usual drama, nothing serious. Plus she had a sneaking suspicion from the way he looked at her that if he was upset with her at all, he wouldn't stay that way for very long.

But Gina asking for the truth . . . and the way *she* looked at her . . .

Rapunzel sighed.

"I swear to you, all I wanted to do was see the lanterns. That's the *truth*. These men—they're all probably after me to protect the kingdom—the world, really. I was never supposed to leave my tower. All this beautiful hair? It's . . . murderhair."

The two stared at her. Flynn silently slid his feet back away from the hair where they had almost touched it.

Gina began to giggle. "Murderhair? Oh, come on . . ."

The story came out of Rapunzel with her breath, deflating her utterly.

"*That's* why I get upset when you try to touch my hair," she finished tiredly once she had told all there was to tell. "It's not vanity. If I lose my temper, or panic, or I—I don't know. I could kill you."

"Your own parents," Flynn murmured. "An orphan by your own hand. I can't imagine. . . ."

"Wait—is this part of why you're so freaky about killing birds somehow?" Gina asked. "It has something to do with your hair?"

Rapunzel nodded. She kind of wanted to cry. She focused on fixing her braids: the smooth, reassuring, and thick hanks that slid over each other seamlessly in a fisherman's plait.

(Flynn and Gina watched her put her hair away with newfound wonder—and maybe relief.)

When she felt together enough again, she spoke.

"Mother had me use my hair to kill them as a lesson about how dangerous I was to the world. How I needed to stay locked up in the tower and away from everyone forever."

"That seems excessive," Flynn said. "Like, 'maybe have someone else raise you' kind of excessive. I'm now having an even harder time understanding how you aren't completely nuts right now. To be locked up, punished, for something that you did as a baby? Your whole life?"

The man who had been swaggeringly trying to talk his way out of a situation with mercenaries and royal guards not that long ago now gazed at her with eyes that were bright and sad. Rapunzel couldn't look away.

"Why not—just cut off your hair?" he asked. "You could wear a wimple or wig or something. Not the most fashionable solution, but still. Problem solved!"

Rapunzel smiled wanly. "Sure, if that would work. But it's part of the magic. Cutting it would kill me."

"So they don't fear or hate you enough to kill you, but *just* enough to imprison you forever. *Nice,*" Flynn said, shaking his head.

"Wait, why lock you up at all?" Gina suddenly asked. "I mean, with your power, and stories about your power, you could rule the whole world. *The Queen with the Murderhair.* People would sing about you for centuries! Why wouldn't those who knew about your powers, those who imprisoned you, want that for themselves?"

Rapunzel was speechless. She had never even thought of that before.

Flynn nodded thoughtfully. "That's absolutely right. And I'll bet you're not the first one with that idea. Whatd'ya think is more likely: a bunch of warring, creepy lords and ladies running all over enemy territory to re-imprison a dangerous girl . . . or trying to *grab her for their own use?*"

Rapunzel shook her head. "The only person who knows about me and my powers is my mother, and she doesn't know any nobles."

"Are you sure? Maybe she has a big mouth. Also there's the people who saw what happened when you were a baby," Gina pointed out. "*And* those who made sure you wound up in a tower . . ."

"Yeah, something's fishy about all this. I'm sorry, Rapunzel," Flynn said. "I tend to see the devious and worst in most humans; hazard of the occupation. But all too often I'm right. You're being chased after like the Holy Grail. Like something out of an ancient saga. Not just being shot down as a potential danger to the public, like a dragon."

Gina nodded. "Yeah, people don't keep people in towers to keep the world safe. They *kill* people to keep the world safe."

All of them were quiet for a moment, letting this sink in.

"But no, I'm just . . ." Rapunzel trailed off. "I'm just . . . Rapunzel."

"Yes. You're also a weapon, or a bargaining chip, or a treasure. Someone they want alive in a tower, not at large or dead. Oh, what are we going to do with you?" Flynn sighed and slid down against a tree onto the ground—being careful to keep his feet away from Rapunzel's stray ends.

"I guess that means we're not going to get to see the floating lights," she said sadly.

But she also noticed that he said *what are* we *going to do with you.* He wasn't abandoning her. He was just trying to figure out what to do.

"Maybe I should just go back to my tower," she suggested, despite not liking that idea.

"No *way*," Gina said, angry. "You're *not* a doll with, um, murderhair, or a treasure, or a weapon—you're a person and you're not going to spend the next twenty years imprisoned. If it was punishment for a crime you committed, it's been enough anyway. The genie is out of the bottle and she's staying out."

Rapunzel smiled. She had never had someone so angry on her behalf before. It felt warm and sturdy, like a good chair you knew would hold you when you were down.

"We just need to take a moment to regroup—lay low while we figure all this out," Flynn said, tapping his chin.

Gina brightened. "We can go to my mom's! No one will find us there."

"I hardly think a smallholding is going to escape anyone's notice right now, no matter how small," Flynn objected. "Bathory's using bloodhounds. Folks seem to be literally combing the forest for Rapunzel here. Every and any house, hovel, and hut is going to be searched."

"Yeah, well, you don't know my mom," Gina said with a smile. "When she doesn't want to be found, she *really* doesn't want to be found. And besides, maybe she can help Rapunzel out with her hair."

"Why, is she a barber?" Flynn asked with a roll of his eyes.

"No," Gina answered with a grin. "She's a witch."

Memorial Sloan Kettering

"Wait, wait, wait, *wait*."

The chemo was over and they were just waiting for the nurse to unhook and release Daniella. She would pass out on the trip home, slackly asleep in the back seat like after a long day at the beach. Along the way she would throw up once or twice, and then not eat until the next morning.

"There are *no witches* in Rapunzel," she pointed out with the absolute authority of an expert. She crossed her arms to emphasize her expertness. "Except for *maybe* Mother Gothel. We don't really know the truth about her."

"Are you telling me that in a fairy-tale kingdom that has smart horses, *chameleons*, Sundrop Flowers, and an under-class of peasants perfectly happy to go out and perform menial labor for the royals and then dance ecstatically for them . . . there can't be *other* witches, too?" Brendan asked with a gentle smile.

"And speaking of Pascal and Maximus," Daniella said, ignoring him, "okay, there's horses now, but what's going on with Maximus? Why did you make him some dumb human? And why is Pascal just a normal, I dunno, European lizard who can't communicate or think or anything?"

"We're getting to that. Next time, I promise," her brother said. He reached forward to ruffle her hair like he normally would have . . . then paused because she didn't have any and it might be weird, the skin of his palm touching the skin of her head; that skin which on her should never touch *anything* besides hair. He continued with the gesture anyway because it would be weirder if he suddenly stopped. Her scalp was surprisingly cool, probably cooler than it should have been.

He began to pack away her books and things; their dad would be there soon to take him and the sick princess home. She was already falling asleep after her outburst. Brendan made himself continue thinking about that idea: the princess in the carriage after the ball, resting in the sleigh after the wild night out with the white wolves, on the back of a swan, nestled in warm white feathers after the tiring adventure was over.

All right, it was a Dodge Caravan, but still.

On the long, quiet ride home he could come up with ideas for the next session.

Rapunzel

Somehow the woods grew darker.

Rapunzel looked around in wonder and confusion. Pools of blackness gathered under trees and around bushes first, almost as if they were attracted to places where shadows would normally congregate in daylight.

Perhaps it was creepy or scary; certainly Flynn looked nonplussed by whatever silent thing was happening all around them. Moths, large and white and fluttering in a manner just a little too bat-like, came out of hiding to revel in this unexpected dismissal of day. So too did fireflies: Rapunzel squealed in delight when, like tiny candles, they twinkled in slow, unhurried loops around grass.

"Is this your mother's magic?" she shrieked, clawing at Gina's arm. *"ARE THOSE FAIRIES?"*

"No, those are lightning bugs, Princess," Flynn said with a sigh. "In-sects. Whose butts glow."

"Right. I'm an idiot," Rapunzel said, trying to get one to land on her. "Because in real life, fairies aren't real but witches are."

"Touché," he said good-naturedly, with a bow.

Rapunzel felt her chest flutter.

Yellow eyes peeked out of the darkness, from branches or unseen resting spots. An owl called. A spiderweb the size of a quilt, suggesting an owner the size of a dog, hung across a side path.

Gina ducked under it, brushing strands out of her hair.

"How do you know where we're going?" Flynn asked. "Actually, where *are* we going? None of this looks familiar to me."

"It's not so much where we're going, as *how* we're going," Gina admitted. "I don't get any of it myself. I never paid attention. It was all so boring. But like I told you, no one can find my mom if she doesn't want to be found."

She gestured smugly: the tiny, cobweb-covered trail broadened out and led to a green valley in the middle of which sat a perfect. Little. Cottage.

Rapunzel almost squealed again in delight.

The house was squashed like a mushroom by a thatched roof that hung far out over the walls. A pair of windows sparkled on either side of a rounded, heavy wooden door. There was nothing particularly creepy or witch-ish about it at all, except for maybe some leeks that grew on the roof around the higgledy-piggledy chimney (out of which wafted a lovely, homey-smelling smoke).

Next to the cottage was a small fenced-in kitchen garden, and even in the low light Rapunzel could see it wasn't given over just to herbs and vegetables. Tall rockets of flowers and pretty, feathery foliage shot colorfully out of the corners.

There was even a neat flagstone path that led up to the front door.

"Witch?" Flynn asked, skeptical. "Or, like . . . crunchy earth mother type who drinks herbal teas and pretends the goddess speaks to her?"

Gina hit him. As Flynn distractedly rubbed his arm, Rapunzel wondered: was this really a professional or personal rivalry? Or was it something else?

She felt a pout beginning to form on her lips, and marveled at this development. In the flattering orange light from the cottage, Flynn looked even more dashing than usual.

Then a hot, strange breath blew on her neck. She whirled around in surprise— and saw to her horror that the devil himself was facing her! Square pupils set the wrong way, a black widow's peak that arched menacingly, long, swirled, deadly horns . . .

Rapunzel opened her mouth to scream—

"Aw, didja miss me, boy?" Gina cooed, butting the creature's horns with the palms of her hands.

As they struggled in the pale glow of the cottage, the scene reset itself: Rapunzel saw her friend wrestling a large, warm animal who occasionally paused his playing to nose in her pockets, to see if she had anything good to eat there.

"That's normal," Flynn said. "A pet goat. Totally normal. Why have a dog? I mean, *that* would be weird. And a cat would just be jejune for a witch, am I right?"

Rapunzel inched around the animal, dying to hug it and stroke its long, silky hair that wasn't entirely unlike hers. But it was still large, and her fear hadn't entirely subsided despite its now harmless, slightly unfocused look and bucolic cud chewing.

"We have a whole herd of angoras," Gina said. "Dodger's just the friendliest. Now behave!" But whether she was talking to Dodger or Flynn was unclear. She threw open the front door of the cottage and shouted as if it were a giant house and her mother were in the upper reaches of the third floor somewhere. "Ma, I'm home! I brought some friends with me!"

"After you, milady," Flynn said, throwing his arm out chivalrously.

Rapunzel stepped into the witch's hut, sort of wishing she could hold his hand.

Inside was a wonder.

The ceiling was entirely obscured by bunches of herbs, flowers, and sweet rushes hanging to dry. Shelves lined every spare inch of wall, filled with bottles of potions, salves, and powders of all colors. A friendly fire blazed out of a flagstone hearth. Farthest away from this, in the back where it was cooler, was a dairy pantry filled with cheese, milk, and butter.

All goat, probably.

Growing through a window was a healthy spray of roses that looked like a neighbor poking her head in for news and a good gossip.

If this was a witch's hut, it was unlike any one Rapunzel had ever read about.

And the witch!

A tiny old lady sat in a comfortable chair next to the fire, her bare feet stretched out close to the flames, toes spread. Her dress was whitish, her apron whitish, the shawl around her shoulders whitish. Her hair was silver, which at first made Rapunzel start and gasp in hope, but as the little old lady turned to face them she saw it was markedly different from her own. It was coarser and frizzier, and while it was long and done up in coils around the witch's head, it wasn't a twentieth the length of Rapunzel's.

Her cheeks were plump and pink at the apples from the fire; her eyes were a startling blueberry color.

"Sorry for dropping in on you with guests like this, Ma," Gina said, going over and kissing her mother perfunctorily.

"It will be a sad day indeed when I am not prepared for the *gracious* return of my loving daughter, or the fact that she dragged along friends," the woman replied, a little dramatically.

Gina rolled her eyes and pointed at the tiny kitchen table. "She knew you were coming already."

Indeed, four places were already set at the table; four bowls, four mugs, and four spoons (oddly, three were wooden, one metal). Cloth-lined baskets contained cheese and bread, and there were small crocks of honey and butter. A dainty pot of pickled mushrooms and green onions served as condiments.

"Whoa," Flynn said, for once taken aback.

Rapunzel was confused, but not by the apparent predictive powers of the old lady.

She was more intrigued by how *this* mother and daughter were speaking: very casually, almost insultingly to each other. But it wasn't, really. Their exchanges felt both eternal and rehearsed, like something they acted out so often that it was almost a puppet show of reality. Underneath the surface there was a depth of familiarity full of warmth and love. Like the words themselves were unimportant; they were said only for the sake of anyone around who was listening, and didn't actually communicate the real and necessary things that lay underneath.

Rapunzel and Gothel never spoke to each other this way—

Well, Gothel was often a little insulting and disparaging, but that was different. And they were always telling each other how much they loved each other. She couldn't imagine these two saying *I love you more* and *I love you most*.

"I'm just glad you *have* friends. And decent ones it looks like, for a change. The—oh!" Suddenly the old woman saw Rapunzel clearly, as if she had moved a little into the firelight or a shadow had fallen from her face.

"Oh, dear girl, that's a fine head of hair you have there," she whispered.

Rapunzel felt herself blushing, as if she were naked, as if Gina's mother could see something inside her. The Goodwife rose from her chair with the help of a cane made from a gnarled root—but not with the difficulty Rapunzel imagined. She reached out a hand.

"No! *Don't touch it!*" Rapunzel hissed, stepping backward. "It could kill you!"

"Nonsense," the old woman said, and just like that, she grabbed a lock and pulled it through her fingers. Rapunzel tried to imagine calm things: the bluest sky with puffy clouds out her tower window, lazy afternoons when she dreamed and watched her mobiles spin, the morning after a night's snow when everything was silent and muffled.

Gina grinned. "Told you my ma could handle this."

"Oh, this is indeed a strange and powerful magic you have here, caught in your tresses." Unthinkingly the old woman combed her fingers through a tangled strand and adjusted a charm. "What sort of things do you do with it?"

She asked the question with calm curiosity and then patted the hair back in place as if it were nothing more than a farming tool.

"Do with it?" Rapunzel asked, a little darkly. "I try to bind it up out of the way so it doesn't kill anyone. That's all it does. It killed my parents, and . . . uh . . . various chickens."

"What silliness are you talking about? Wait—how old are you, girl?"

"Nineteen. This week."

Suddenly the woman looked tired, or old, or sad. Her face sort of crumpled up into itself and, once closed, her eyes became two lines in her face that rose up to almost meet above her nose.

"You were right to come here," she said after a moment,

opening her eyes again. "We have much to discuss. But first, let's fill your bellies and then sit by the fire so we can sort this mess out. Take your boots off!"

She suddenly whacked the side of Flynn's foot with her cane—not hard, just enough to make a point. But she grinned when she saw Rapunzel's bare feet.

"Ah, child! You're like me, you like to *feel* the world around you." She wiggled her toes.

Rapunzel found herself laughing, but couldn't tell if it was from the woman's simple delight or exhaustion bordering on hysteria.

The next few minutes were filled with as much commotion as could fill such a tiny space. Gina's mother ordered people around, shaking her cane for emphasis. Flynn and Rapunzel were told to wash their faces and hands at a silver basin filled with cool, clear water.

"Your *scrying* bowl, Ma?" Gina asked in surprise.

The old woman shrugged. "We have guests. Hospitality trumps magic."

Despite her excitement at the old woman's potential help with her hair, and the lateness of the hour, and exhaustion from constant running, Rapunzel found herself stuffing her face.

"The chèvre's real good this time, Ma. What's the herb?" Gina asked.

"Wild amaranth tips—seaseep. Your old friend Karl picked it for me from the Fenton."

Flynn grinned at Rapunzel over their meal. *Get a load of them,* he seemed to say, cocking his head at the two women.

Rapunzel smiled back, honey dripping out the side of her mouth.

He reached over without thinking and dabbed it off with his finger.

They both froze, looking at each other.

Then Flynn coughed and went back to eating.

As much as she wanted to hear what the old woman knew, perhaps the answers to all her questions and fears, Rapunzel wanted to bask in this moment just a little longer: the four of them eating and talking about nothing, like—

Like—

Well, Rapunzel had no idea what it was like. It was like nothing she had ever experienced. A warm home on the ground, friendly people around a table, talking . . . It was like her body instinctively longed for exactly this despite never having seen it.

Family?

Friends?

All too soon dinner was over, and Rapunzel—and Flynn, once she kicked him—helped wash up and put the crockery away.

"I know, I know, I'll make the tea," Gina said just as her mother opened her mouth. She turned to Rapunzel. "I'm not even going to bother telling you the choices. We have too many. I'll just brew up something that will hopefully ease your muscles a little and wake you up just long enough for a talk around the fire."

Flynn nudged Rapunzel. *"See? Earth goddess mother tea stuff."*

She giggled, unsure what that meant, but glad to be in on a joke.

The three young people sat on the floor, the old lady in her chair. The tea Gina made tasted very vaguely of mint and hope, and really did wake up Rapunzel a little. She wondered why her own mother, a witch powerful enough to protect herself from the murderhair, never displayed any of these other useful witchy skills: brewing magic tea, scrying the future, somehow getting roses to bloom indoors.

This time Rapunzel didn't make it even partway through her story; she had just described the tower when the old woman spat her tea out in surprise. "You lived as a prisoner for these past two decades? Alone, behind stone walls? For—*what*? What did they say you had done? *Killed your own parents?*

"But I wonder how much of this crime lies on my

shoulders," she added quietly, to herself. "Too slow, too lazy, unable to make decisions . . . well, the evil is spread around, and some of it may be mine, Princess."

"I. Am not. A *princess!*" Rapunzel tried to keep her voice under control in deference to the old lady. She ground her teeth to keep from screaming.

"But of course you are," the old lady said in mild surprise. "You are the Crown Princess Rapunzel, daughter of King Frederic and Queen Arianna, heir to the throne."

Rapunzel

Everyone sat silent, mouths agape at this.

Even Dodger, who had stuck his head through the window, stopped chewing his cud.

"HA! I knew it!" Flynn cried triumphantly. He pointed an accusing finger at Rapunzel. *"Princess!"*

"You serious, Ma?" Gina asked.

"And of course, not *any* princess," Flynn went on. "Oh, no. She's *the* princess. The *dead* princess. Wait—the dead princess. So the silver murderhair . . . she's a ghost?'"

"I'm not dead," Rapunzel said, not feeling as sure about this as she would have liked.

In stories (Book #17: *The Castle of Otranto and Other Diabolical Legends*) ghosts always looked markedly different from living people . . . with ghostly silver hair, maybe? And they haunted the same places, tied to a specific location and unable to leave—like the tower where she had lived for nineteen years? And few people could see them, but fewer still could converse with them, and only those with the Sight or whatever? *Like a powerful*—or maybe not-so-powerful—*witchy woman?* Mother Gothel?

Rapunzel felt a shiver go through her.

"She's obviously not dead, you young fool," the old woman said impatiently. "Of course, one wonders what that makes *you*, mooning over a ghost."

"I'm not . . ." Flynn said.

Rapunzel rubbed her temples wearily but made a note to think about the tone of Flynn's voice, later, and his less-than-enthusiastic denial.

"Let me tell you your own story, correctly this time," the old woman said, and proceeded to rock gently—which was startling, because Rapunzel could have sworn that a second earlier it had been just a normal chair, and not a rocker. "Once upon a time a king and queen wished for a baby and got one. When the queen fell sick near the baby's birth, she drank a magical infusion of the Sundrop Flower. Or so they thought. But I believe there was a mistake; I believe that it was the *Moon*drop Flower. Hence, the hair."

The old woman nodded sagely at them as if it was an obvious and foregone conclusion.

"*Hence, the hair,*" Flynn repeated heavily, for the three listeners. "What?"

"Well, if it was actually the Sundrop Flower, her hair would be golden, of course! Don't you people listen to stories anymore? Whenever there's a sun, moon, stars situation it's always gold, silver, and . . . I don't know. Opalescent or white or the like. Your mother drank the essence of the Moondrop Flower; it gave you silver hair and granted you unusual powers."

"*Murder*ous powers," Rapunzel said sadly.

"We'll get to that in a moment. The first and most important point is that you did *not* kill your parents—they are alive and well, thank you very much, good rulers and sad human beings. You did, however, kill a maid. They concocted a story at the castle that she died defending you from a poisonous adder, which killed you both. Or maybe it was a lizard, I really can't remember."

"There are no poisonous lizards in Europe, Mom," Gina pointed out.

(Rapunzel put a finger on Pascal's neck and stroked him: there were even lizards in this story!)

"Adder, then. It makes little difference because it was a lie. The baby was sent away until she learned to control her magic."

Then the old woman frowned.

"I may have made that last bit up. I don't really remember the details. I came in late with scanty information, and by then they had already found someone else. I was terribly disappointed, though—worked myself up to getting a wee babe and raising a daughter and apprentice.

"I wound up adopting this beautiful child instead. Best decision I've ever made. A lot of work, of course, but very blessed work."

She looked at Gina and smiled, patting her hair with her hand. Gina leaned into it and smiled sleepily.

"Wait—*you* would have adopted me?" Rapunzel asked, looking around the hut again in awe. "I could have grown up here?"

Her thoughts went crazy, like the starlings in early fall. Not a tower, a cottage. *Goats.* A woman who knew about the world and magic and was free in discussing all of it. Rapunzel loved Gothel, of course—their last conversation had been a little troubling, yes, but she was still her *mother*, after all. She had done so much for her. But . . . this was an alternate path. With grass, and a woman who knew magic.

"The past is over, child. Don't dwell overmuch on its echoes," the old woman said gently. "You will find no rest that way."

Rapunzel shook her head, trying to clear the birds out. "Yes, of course you're right. So . . . I really am a princess."

"Looks like I stole *your* crown," Flynn said, not really chagrined. "Sorry about that. It was smaller than the others and less carefully guarded. You should probably talk to your mom and dad about that sometime."

"Mom . . . and . . . dad . . ." Rapunzel said in wonder. Her eyes lit up. "*Mom and dad! Flynn! Gina! I have a mom and dad!*"

She leapt up excitedly.

Then she paused.

"I mean, Mother Gothel is my *real* mother. She raised me," she added, working out the complexities in her mind. "I mean, just like you're Gina's real mother."

"Doesn't really sound like Gothel was *anyone's* real mother," Flynn said. "Sounds like she was someone paid to take care of a tiny baby and locked her up instead. Also, not to belabor the point, but it also seems like Gothel was the one who made up that story about you killing your parents. And who kept telling it to you."

Rapunzel swallowed. True, she had not told Rapunzel any of the truth—or even a nicer version of the state-sponsored lie.

Why?

"Maybe she just did it to . . . make me understand how dangerous I was," Rapunzel said slowly, the only reason that made any sense to her at all. "A story that hid a deeper wisdom. Like a fairy tale."

The old woman huffed. "That's a load of goat dung, though you are sweet to forgive her so quick."

"Well, maybe she was *told* to say that?" Rapunzel protested weakly. "Isn't that likely? They wanted me to not have any hope of returning, so they royally ordered her to tell me all that."

"Then why give you anything with the *royal* sigil on it?" Flynn asked quietly. "If they didn't want you to know who you were? Like your pretty red bracelet there. Tirulian red coral, handwrought chain, pure gold clasp—yes, yes, I totally sized it up. *And the royal sun on the back.*"

Rapunzel looked at her bracelet in wonder. The little sun, constant companion of her childhood, in mobiles, embroidered on her clothing, on the little gifts Gothel sometimes gave her, *the crown* . . . That was the symbol of the royal house? Her whole life there had been hints of the truth, everywhere!

"The king and queen may not have known how you were 'taken care of,'" Flynn added gently, seeing the look on her face. "It sounds like Gothel was supposed to teach you, but kept you locked away, ignorant, instead. She lied to you, imprisoning you in a tower of your mind as well as the one of stone."

"I . . ." Rapunzel swallowed.

But Gothel loved her. She was her *mother*, for heaven's sake!

The cottage, cozy as it was, suddenly seemed smaller than the light-filled rooms in her tower. The ceiling hung much, much lower. There were many things in it that were breakable if she reacted, spun, or turned around too quickly; she was acutely aware that her hair could wreak massive damage of the decidedly non-magical kind. For just a moment, Rapunzel had a keen, nearly overwhelming desire to be back home, maybe slide down the railing of the gently curving stairs into the sunny, wide-open common room.

"I need to take a walk," she said shakily.

Gina leapt up. "Yeah, totally. It's a bit much in here. I can show you the goats and . . ."

The Goodwife gave Gina a look, kind but stern.

"I think maybe our guest needs to be *alone* for a bit," she said firmly. "It's been quite an evening of revelation. Rapunzel, you are perfectly safe as long as you stay in the vale. Just keep away from the forest and the paths, dear, and you'll be fine."

"Thank you," Rapunzel said, nodding, almost bowing her head—then wondered if that was a regal, royal gesture she somehow knew instinctively, or just something people did when exhausted and relieved that someone else was taking charge. As she padded to the door and went outside, she was also suddenly aware of her gait and bearing.

Did she walk like a royal princess?

She didn't know much about real princesses except for in fairy tales, and books like #27: *Legends from the Time of Knights*. Gawain and Roland and *his* tower and the like. Princesses were often the points on which plots turned, the fulcrum that sped the hero along on his journey of becoming legendary, dead, or both. Sometimes the princesses were good-hearted and the knights fought valiantly for their honor. Sometimes they were evil and used witchy machinations to control the people around them, lacking any real power over their own lives.

But honestly Rapunzel didn't remember a whole lot about either kind. They were boring. She loved the swordsmanship of the knights and did her best to reenact it with broom handles and frying pans, dancing back and forth on her feet to evade imaginary blows.

She stepped out into the night, head buzzing with these thoughts, and for a moment was confused; the doorway was small and the world so dark she imagined for half a moment that she was standing in her own window in the tower, poised over the empty ground far below her.

Then Pascal, not liking the draft of cold air he was suddenly exposed to, turned around and burrowed deeper into the hair on her neck. The feel of his delicate, tiny toes brought her to her senses. She reached around to stroke him and, thus fortified, kept walking.

The first thing she noticed was the cold, wet grass under her toes. It hadn't rained, and she wondered for a moment if this was more strange magic. But it was soft, and her feet were dirty from a long day of running and hiding, and she dragged her soles through it happily.

With a start she remembered something else about princesses: everybody wanted one.

Powerful men, lesser knights, random highway thieves. *Roaming bands of lords and their men.* That was where a lot of the "rescuing" plotlines came from.

And hadn't she been saved by her friends from a band of mercenaries?

"Gah," she said aloud, making a face. It was almost all too funny. She *was* a princess. The crown was hers, the attempts to snatch her real. Gina could very well be her noble knight, and Flynn . . .

Well, Flynn . . .

Rapunzel shook her head. She did not *want* to be a princess.

She also didn't like the idea of being given up, of

parents making the decision to abandon their child. But then again—oh, what noble rulers her parents must have been, worried about the fate of their people! Putting it above their own child!

And what of Gothel?

She hadn't merely lied to Rapunzel about her origins: she had repeated that lie almost daily, grinding it into her. *You are a powerful, horrible thing who killed your own parents.* Making her feel like she deserved to be trapped in a tower. Making her feel grateful to a woman who was "forced" to dedicate her life to serving the needs of her prisoner and child. Whom she was supposed to be teaching! So Rapunzel could return home someday, safe as houses!

"Pascal, I've lost my parents again today," she murmured. "I know, I know. It's like a fairy tale: I *found* my parents—they're right in that castle over there. But my real mother, the one who has been my mother my entire life . . . Pascal, I don't think she's . . . she's . . ."

But every time she tried to say it, to formulate the damning words even in her head, she couldn't. She would be interrupted by all sorts of memories presenting themselves in her mind: Gothel hugging her when she needed it. A surprise set of paints for no reason, in the middle of the year. Cookies that Gothel took the time to make at home and bring to the tower. Quiet, happy hours of the two of them reading or sewing together, no words, in the dusky light of the tower window.

"I love you."

"I love you more."

"I love you *most*."

The two versions of Gothel just couldn't exist together. Not in Rapunzel's head, anyway. The mean one who lied and kept her sad and scared—and okay, sometimes commented on her weight—and the one who brought so many good things into her life.

There was a rising of voices in the hut behind her as Gina and her mom fought about something loudly.

Rapunzel felt a strange surge of jealousy.

The little house looked so snug in the night, *on the ground*, with warm light pouring from its windows, the clink of things being moved around; even the domestic squabble had a strangely comforting ring to it.

Rapunzel looked up: the stars, her friends, surrounded her on all sides except below. She was closer to them when she was in her tower, but somehow now they seemed almost reachable.

Overcome with exhaustion—and unable to go back into that cozy little house—Rapunzel stretched out on the ground, and watched the heavens turn.

Captain Tregsburg

The usually unflappable, knife-keen mind of the captain of the guard was at this moment out in a field, racing with ponies.

All right, not ponies; *tolori*, the beautiful breed of horse that could be found only in this kingdom, descended from ancient Eastern lineages. They were a white so brilliant that they shone like angels in the sunlight. And while their legs weren't long and slender like those of Arabians or the racing breeds, they were incredibly muscular and powerful. They were meant for war, and long distances, and bearing stalwart riders along with their armor.

Of course there were no knights anymore, but the finest tolori became the steeds of the royal guard. Tregsburg's own was a lovely, huge mare without a spot of black on her except for her eyelashes (which were expressive and charcoal).

He wished he were riding her right then.

Pounding through the field of summer grass, pollen from the pines and fluffy seedpods flying up like snow behind them, leaping over sparkling streams filled with fish . . .

"Sir?"

The guard in front of him was not his right-hand man; that lieutenant was overseeing the change of watch this morning. With strange activity in the lands around the kingdom and the unsettling presence of foreign soldiers, Tregsburg had decided that the public would be reassured to see the capable, dashing young man organizing the maneuvers. But that lieutenant would have seen where the captain's eyes were just then and known immediately where his thoughts were as well.

And then waited before interrupting.

"Just trying to get this all straight in my mind," Tregsburg said, focusing again.

(This was his one weakness: horses. Even during training his eye always wandered to them. But there were worse things to be preoccupied with; he neither drank too much nor consorted with women, so horses were all right, he supposed.)

"I was just wondering, Captain. Do you think Smeinhet's men were lying? And do you think they are responsible for the destruction of the Snuggly Duckling?"

"Let us get one thing clear," Tregsburg said, grey eyes getting hard and cold. "I do not mind in the least that the Snuggly Duckling is gone. You will never find a more wretched hive of scum and villainy. A sweep of that place any day or night would have filled our jail cells to capacity with verifiable criminals. Good riddance, I say.

"*That being said*, it is extremely unusual that anything at all should have happened to the place. It is a favorite watering hole for malefactors of all kinds. No one would dare touch it—or the owner—for fear of retribution from the most violent and sadistic thugs in the realm. Why, old Rasko could walk through a graveyard at midnight wearing gold chains and no one would dare lay a hand on him."

"Old Rasko, sir?" the guard asked in surprise. "You mean you *know* the proprietor—"

"It was a long time ago! The point is, whoever did it doesn't worry about their personal health and safety. They feel untouchable. And that can only mean two things: arrogance bordering on psychosis, and power. Baron Smeinhet is a terrible person, but he knows just how weak he is militarily . . . one or two well-trained mercenaries could get to him quite easily.

"So while it's very suspicious that some men of Smeinhet just happen to be, let us not say *invading*, for that would indeed beget an international incident, but *crossing our borders* without permission, I do not believe that they had anything directly to do with the incident at the Duckling.

"Also, a witness mentioned *vérhounds*—which means Lady Bathory, who is both psychotic *and* powerful. She is undoubtedly the perpetrator. However, the fact is that multiple foreign nobles are seeking something in our fair country. Something strange is afoot."

"Perhaps they are chasing a terrible criminal from their own land. Or the Lady Bathory's," the young man suggested quite reasonably.

"Perhaps." Tregsburg nodded, but his mind drifted again. He didn't think they were all after a criminal. He suspected it was an innocent girl.

Well, a beautiful young woman, really; as comely as his niece Tasha, who was so clever with her loom and quick with her tongue. But this girl had extraordinary silver hair—a color so unusual the captain had seen it only once before in his long years in the guard.

On a royal princess, a tiny baby, dead to the world.

In fairy tales and myths, when children were given up because of a prophecy or because the family was starving, they *did* disappear into the world for a while—and then came back years later like a cicada, bringing the power of youth and the unavoidable anger of the gods with them.

Tregsburg nodded to himself slightly, liking the way this sounded. He had been raised on myths and stories of the great Romans. He even aspired to a military career just like an ancient centurion.

(Although it might be noticed that, lacking a formal education, he often mixed up ancient legend with real history.)

Yes, it made sense the girl was turning up now, from a mythic standpoint.

But from a real-world standpoint, there were a lot of actual facts that didn't make sense. And whatever the story with the princess was, people were running rampant across *his* country, attacking *his* criminals, wandering *his* roads. . . .

"I'll write up a full report of the incident myself. Dismissed."

The young guard saluted crisply, spun, and marched out of the room.

Tregsburg found himself looking out the window again.

Omitting potentially important details in a report was something he absolutely loathed. But far worse was the idea of telling the king and queen about their daughter's reappearance.

No doubt they would be upset, and overjoyed, and then probably go back on their vow to keep the kingdom safe from her—but maybe they wouldn't, and that would be hard, too. Tregsburg had seen the kingdom through rocky years as the stalwart but grieving and somehow diminished royal pair tried to govern normally. The kingdom shouldn't be put through that again.

He would wait to inform the king and queen until he had more information.

He wondered if he did this out of cold rationality—or weakness and fear.

The captain gazed out his window at the pasture set aside for the castle's retired horses. Even the oldest ones were whinnying for the sheer joy of life on this clear, dry summer day. The sun must have been warm on their achy backs, their short, greying coats.

Not a bad way to spend your declining years, he mused. In a meadow sweet with wildflowers and good companions by your side for company. Horses had it so much easier than captains of the royal guard. . . .

Rapunzel

She awoke a little after the sun rose. Someone had very thoughtfully put a blanket over her body and a soft bunch of hay under her head. That was three nights outside on the ground, now; up until leaving the tower she had slept only on a bed, with pillows.

"Like a princess," she said a little ruefully. She stuck her nose deeper into the hay and inhaled: it smelled amazing. Sometimes she caught that scent at the end of summer, when people she couldn't see slowly turned the faraway fields from blankets of gold into patches of tan and brown.

"Well, we *were* going to feed that to the goats . . . but maybe they won't want it now."

Rapunzel sat up. Flynn was leaning against the side of

the house, legs crossed, an ironic smile on his face. He must have been up for a while; he had obviously taken pains to wash his face and neck and arms (at least; that was just all Rapunzel could see) and straighten his hair so it was parted dashingly to one side. She wondered, for a moment, whose comb he had borrowed, or if he had his own stashed away somewhere like his knives.

He was stupidly, ridiculously handsome.

Even with the stupid, ridiculously fake smile on his face.

Not at all the worst thing to wake up to.

She suddenly felt her stomach clench: *princesses always married princes. Or kings.* If they did what they were told for the good of the family.

"I'll deal with that later," she told Pascal.

"What?" Flynn asked, leaning forward to hear better.

"Nothing," she called out, standing up. She grabbed the quilt as she did so and with a few well-practiced shakes and flourishes folded it in precise thirds, and thirds again, until she had a perfect little square to put away. "There, nice and neat!"

"I doubt many princesses could do *that*," Flynn drawled.

"Oh, please," she said, sweeping by him to the cottage. Nothing could take away from her good mood. Sleeping outside was intoxicating. The sky was that bright, clear shade of blue that spoke of a full day of good things and promise. She was hiding out at a *real white witch's* house with her two friends and Pascal, and was about to learn the secret of controlling her magical hair.

It appeared that everyone had been up hours before her: whatever they had slept on had all been straightened away now, perhaps the mats or mattresses rolled up and stored in a cupboard. Gina's mother stood as if waiting for her just inside the door, gnarled root cane in her hand.

"Ah, good morning, Sleeping Beauty! That Flynn fellow and my daughter have left to patrol the woods around us to make sure none of those bad men chasing you accidentally slip through my spells. Or are led through them by someone who knows the arts, I suppose—though that is highly unlikely."

That Flynn fellow did not seem to have made it far, Rapunzel noted. The thought pleased her immensely. She clasped her hands decorously behind her back and tried to sound as pleasant and polite as possible.

"So . . . After breakfast . . . I was wondering . . . If you have a moment . . . Can you counteract my magic somehow and stop my hair from murdering people?"

She wondered if that sounded too abrupt. Maybe she should have led in with something else, like *My, your goats seem healthy today! And speaking of goats . . .*

"Child, that is the wrong question," the old woman said

with a sigh. "We need to confirm my theory about the kind of magic you have so that you may learn how to *work* with it. Why would you ever want to get rid of your own powers?"

"So I stop *murdering people*," Rapunzel said wryly. "If I can control it, that would be great. But I don't want to kill anyone or anything again."

"Well, then, you might as well have cut it all off years ago and been done with it!" The Goodwife threw her hands in the air and waved her cane in exasperation.

"But cutting my hair will kill me!" Rapunzel shouted back, equally exasperated.

The other woman looked at Rapunzel with pity and sadness. "Poor child. How many lies did that . . . *not-witch* tell you? Of course cutting your hair won't kill you. It may reduce your powers until your hair grows back in fully from the root, but that is all. Whatever powers it may tap into, it is still just your *hair*, my dear. Not your heart or your soul."

"But . . ."

Why would Gothel lie about that, too? Rapunzel could have cut her hair off years ago; she would have shaved her head and worn a wimple if it meant she could go outside and be with other people.

The Goodwife stood back and looked at Rapunzel's hair with newfound seriousness. "The truth about you is all tangled, like your braids, Rapunzel. Bound up unnaturally.

It's time to let it all down, to let it out, to let it go. We must free you from the chains of your past—but first we need to free your beautiful hair. Let's go out and sit down over there. It looks like quite a job."

She took Rapunzel by the arm—firmly—and led her over to a gentle hummock beneath an ancient pear tree.

"Oh, I don't know if I can," Rapunzel said nervously, putting her hands to her longest braids. But whether she was protecting the old lady from them or them from the old lady she couldn't have said.

"Yes, you can. You *need* to." The old woman lowered herself down carefully onto the soft, moss-covered ground.

Biting her lip, Rapunzel reluctantly began to let down her hair.

Her fingers waved like grass back and forth, undoing her braids, taking down her buns, shaking out her tresses. Just like she did when she thoroughly brushed it out in the tower by herself, Rapunzel carefully laid out the pins, bands, ribbons, and charms in organized rows on the ground next to her.

The old woman watched interestedly, narrowing her eyes and squinting at the bits and bobs and pieces of jewelry.

"What is all this for?" she asked. "Oh my goodness—a hand of Hamsa. How lovely! But these aren't the sort of trinkets a young girl from around here usually sports."

"I read a lot about magic, I guess all of it wrong," Rapunzel said with a shrug. "I thought I could bind my hair, keep the magic in check."

"Aha! Clever! But these are not quite powerful enough."

Soon Rapunzel's hair spilled out around her like a silver pond sparkling in the sunlight, or a frozen one in the moonlight. When the breeze shifted the branches above, the sun hit her tresses and its light scattered everywhere. The whole area under the tree was illuminated with shifting, dappled scintillations.

Rapunzel wondered what it would look like from far away, from high above: would she look like a funny star? Were all the stars out there maidens with strange hair?

The old lady gasped in astonishment, sucking in her breath.

"Oh my, it's all so beautiful," she said, picking up a lock. "My hair started going silver—dull silver, not like yours—when I was sixteen. Had a streak of it right in front. Some said it aged me, but I always thought it was rather distinguished looking. Gave me gravitas at a time young women—and men—are usually sorely lacking in it."

Rapunzel brightened. "So our hair is silver because of magic? Both of ours?"

The old woman laughed. "No, mine went silver because my mother's family all goes grey before their time. In my case, it has nothing to do with magic. Tell me—when you, ah, killed the chickens for your mother, did you ever chant anything? Or sing? Or think of anything in particular?"

Rapunzel nodded, reluctant to say anything about it, afraid of summoning the deathly magic. She tried to pull her hair back.

The old lady lightly slapped her fingers.

Rapunzel whipped her hand away to her mouth, shocked and surprised. It didn't really hurt. But Gothel never hit her.

Maybe I really am a princess, Rapunzel thought with a mix of wonder and disappointment in herself. *Unaccustomed to hurt of any sort that I didn't cause myself.* Pillows, delicacy, owning a crown . . . the evidence was mounting up hard against her.

"Your magic cannot wound me, girl," the Goodwife chastised. "*Please.* And also, while we're on the subject of hurting people, it is not 'murderhair.' Now listen well, for here is your first, and perhaps most important, lesson in magic: *it is neither good nor evil.* It is a force of nature, a thing that just *is.* It is up to the person who wields it whether it's used for good or evil.

"Let us say your hair had the power to heal instead of kill—even that could be used for evil! What if it kept a tyrant alive forever, always in her prime, always in her youth, always in control? A lot of people would suffer for it."

Rapunzel thought about this. The Goodwife wasn't wrong, but she just couldn't see how the power to kill could ever be a positive thing. Even if you only used it for chickens you were going to eat.

"So please," the other woman said with a sigh, "keep that in mind when you get to the circle."

"Circle? What circle?"

"Oh, we hadn't gotten to that part yet. I forgot." The old lady chuckled to herself. "Your journey. To the ancient circle of stones that will hopefully shed some light on your situation, and confirm that you do bear the essence of the Moondrop Flower."

Rapunzel was torn between disappointment and excitement. On the one hand, she sort of knew deep down that answers wouldn't be as easy as just waving a magical spurtle over her hair or whatever. On the other hand: a *journey*! An adventure! The floating lanterns had been taken away—but replaced by this!

"Yes, we'll pack you up a lunch and set you off. The stones aren't too far from here, but you'll miss a meal or two. Follow an old cart track up into the Five-Claw Hills. Stay alert: the track dwindles to a walking path and then nothing more than a game trail, used by bears and those who keep to the old ways.

"Don't worry about the bears," she added quickly, seeing the look on Rapunzel's face. "You're not a child; the monstrous ones from any fairy stories you read have long ago disappeared, and their descendants fear grown men."

"Oh no, I was *hoping* to see a bear," Rapunzel explained. "I've always wanted to see one. Or a puppy."

The old woman narrowed her eyes but decided to ignore this.

"The circle sits on the top of the tallest hill like a crown, hard to miss unless your mind wanders far from your feet. The boulders may be covered with moss now—it's been a quite a few years since I last saw them. But it is there you may find your answers."

"Road to path to smaller path, hills, stones, got it," Rapunzel said, trying to etch the directions into her mind. It was hard because she had never needed directions before and rarely had to think in three dimensions.

The Goodwife slowly stood up and held her hand out—to help the younger girl up.

"Come, let's make a nice bag of snacks for you!"

Rapunzel padded after the old lady. For the first time ever, her hair flowed freely behind her. It didn't glow with magic; it merely shone with the reflected light of the sun.

She didn't even remember the protective charms and bands and ribbons she had left behind, under the tree.

Rapunzel

"On the road again! It's just you and me, Pascal," Rapunzel said brightly. He was perched on her shoulder, looking ahead down the path almost like he was enjoying the journey as well.

Sometimes she peeked behind her, hair trailing out like a long silver veil. Rarely did it snag on anything, which should have made Rapunzel stop and wonder. Nor did she consider how easily she skipped along the path despite the weight of all those locks behind her, how the ends danced and flowed over obstacles like they were weightless.

After a few hours the vegetation in the woods around her became worn down and tired; the air got muggy and close. Trees were now shorter and stuffed fuller of branches. Giant graceful leaves were replaced with tiny, drier, curling things that made the shapes of monsters when they fell in drifts. The grass was denser than before but somehow less lush.

(The heat, of course, made Pascal *more* alert. He trotted back and forth on her shoulder, sometimes coming down as far as her arm, and happily ate the gnats that also seemed to enjoy the warmth.)

Rapunzel noted the changes in the landscape with wonder. She closed one eye and held her thumb out, observing the differences in color and shadow.

"Pascal, do you know what all this means?" she whispered.

The lizard looked at her the same way he always did. Blankly.

"There is *so much more to learn!*" She picked him up in her hands and twirled around. "Like decades and decades! Shadow! Light! Angles! *Seasons!* Think of it! I'll have my hands full and so much painting for *years* . . . !"

She trailed off; the silence of the woods fell down on her again.

"If I were back in my tower again, I mean," she said, and her voice sounded funny all by itself, words and letters dwarfed by leaves.

"Which," she added nervously, "I . . . may not be?"

Pascal just looked at her.

"Right, nothing decided until I figure everything out," she agreed as if he had spoken. "My hair, all those random men after me . . ."

She adjusted her pack and continued down the path again.

"I mean, I guess I could go back to my tower if I had to, if I really turn out to be dangerous—or *in* danger," she continued conversationally. "But . . . maybe Flynn and Gina could drop by once in a while? Even if they stayed on the ground, outside. And oh! We could send things back and forth, on a rope. . . ."

Then she remembered what the Goodwife had said: *The circle sits on top of the tallest hill like a crown, hard to miss unless your mind wanders far from your feet.*

Her mind was definitely wandering. But it was a long-ingrained habit; her feet and body couldn't leave the tower, so for nineteen years her mind had wandered beyond its stony walls. What was it like to be a fish? Were there houses in the clouds? Why did Venus seem to have phases like the moon?

And that's how she nearly missed the bear.

Pascal had sensed it immediately and scurried up to her neck. Rapunzel didn't really notice, thoughtlessly putting her finger up to comfort him. It was only when she heard the low growl that she jumped.

Her initial fear was replaced by astonishment at how small the bear was, considering how large they seemed in fairy tales. Without the long fluffy tail, its body was really only the length of her arm. Its fur was astounding: a beautiful flame red with black ankles and (tiny!) paws, and lovely ruffs of white under its neck. Long whiskers framed its elegant face and narrow, aristocratic muzzle, and its eyes were a spectacular orange.

The poor bear was skinny and held its shoulders strangely, neither submissive nor brave. Threatening with a question mark. Ready to change its mind.

"Don't eat me," Rapunzel begged. "Please."

(Although she *did* wonder how something that size could eat a whole human anything—even a baby human being.)

The bear's orange eyes darted from side to side, either threatened by the tone of her voice or very, very confused by it.

It stepped to the side and back again and yipped. Slaver dripped from its mouth.

"Oh! You're drooling!" Rapunzel said with pity. "You *are* hungry! But I'm not good to eat at all. I've been cooped up in a tower all my life. No exercise at all; these muscles are all flabby and soft, and I've rarely seen the sun, so . . . actually, now that I think about, I do sound kind of tasty."

She put one hand to her hair. Even if she planned to do it, could she kill this bear? The way she did with the chickens? Would it be fast enough? She had no intention of harming such a magnificent tiny beast, but if it was a choice between her or it . . .

The bear barked once.

You were saying? maybe.

"But do you know what *is* tasty?" Rapunzel asked, suddenly inspired. "Goat cheese!"

She slowly reached into her bag, aware that any sudden movements could tip the situation. Which way she wasn't sure. She didn't want the bear to run away: scared, hungry, and hopeless. But she also didn't want it eating her. And she *definitely* didn't want it running a little bit away and then secretly following—only to pounce on her unexpectedly, later. At least if she was eaten now there wouldn't be the tension of waiting.

Her fingers found the cylinder of soft cheese wrapped in a large chestnut leaf, deep in the bag where it was cool. She started to break it in half—and then watched the bear lick its chops and let its tongue hang out. It whimpered slightly.

Rapunzel felt her heart break.

"You know, I don't think I've ever missed a single meal, even when Mother was punishing me. I may have been kept in a tower my whole life, but I've never known what it was like to be hungry." And with that she threw the entire cheese to it.

The bear caught it expertly in its narrow muzzle, then tossed it up into the air again to break the packet open. The cheese fell into a thousand tiny crumbles all over the ground and the bear fell to, devouring every morsel.

"Okay, then. I must be on my way now," Rapunzel said carefully—backing away, aware that the creature might have other plans. "Goodbye!"

The thing barely tipped one of its large ears toward her, too busy devouring the snack.

Rapunzel stopped dallying; the moment the path took the bear out of sight, she began to run. What had seemed like a grand adventure now took on more serious import; she had little food left and had finally realized that maybe not all meetings in the great world or wilderness necessarily ended happily.

(Pascal was relieved to be moving away from the fox as well; its kind ate lizards like candy. He *did* wonder vaguely, in his lizard brain, why the giant human didn't just kick the nasty thing.)

After trotting along for a while Rapunzel thought one of the hills up ahead looked a little diseased, as if rotten carbuncles were growing out of its skin. Soon it became clear that they were massive boulders that had been stood on their ends. A few were tipped over or leaning against each other.

The ancient circle of stones!

Someone else might have stopped here in wonder at the sight: monoliths unimaginably old loomed without meaning below an empty sky. The hilltop was lonely, devoid of birds and insects, and the wind whistled forlornly. Like the story of the swallow that wore away the mountainside one scratch at a time, this circle had been eroded by wind and rain and had already experienced the first second of eternity.

Perhaps Rapunzel felt a *little* of that; awe at something so large that had been built so long ago by people who worshipped strange gods. In the end she did pause, gawking a little.

But that moment quickly passed and she ran the rest of the way up the hill, eager to meet her destiny. Without another thought she ran right into the center of the ancient circle (which might have been a questionable decision in a world that contained witches and murderhair). She dropped her sack and opened her arms to embrace the day, the space, the grass, the answers, the joy of it all.

"I'm ready," Rapunzel said, closing her eyes.

But there was nothing.

After a moment of just standing, arms open, breathing the—admittedly sweet—air, she cautiously cracked one eye open again.

The round meadow she stood in, delineated by the stones, was disappointingly normal. There were pretty clumps of white star-shaped flowers—the kind she had seen around her tower. Their petals sparkled a little in the sunlight, but not unnaturally.

A dusty path circled around just inside the stones. Perhaps the dark spots on it were old scorch marks, remnants of respect, worship, or stains from grisly rites by people whose great-grandmothers barely remembered what they were for.

"All right," Rapunzel said brightly. "I'm here. Tell me about my hair!"

She waited expectantly.

"I mean, tell me about my powers," she added after a moment. "I wasn't looking for compliments or anything like that."

"Please?"

"Anyone?"

Did a breeze pick up? Did the little flowers bend their heads as if saying something? Was there a collective pause in the world, an even deeper silence from the stones?

Nope.

"Am I supposed to *do* something?" she asked the stones.

The stones said nothing.

She thought about the scorch marks, the dusty piles of nothing at the stones' bases.

"Do I need to offer something in return for an answer?"

She didn't know how she knew this; perhaps once again (like with the bear) she was drawing on some ancient instinct that lay deep in the bones of the human race. The gods gave nothing for nothing; people and things needed to be appeased.

She picked up her sack and rummaged through it. "I gave away my cheese. . . . Do you want water? Are you thirsty?"

Without a second thought she dumped her entire clay jar of water onto the closest stone.

The water very naturally dripped down the grey surface, sinking in where it was extra dry, but not in a startling way.

"No? All right. Let's see, I have . . . some dried apples, some nuts, some seeds, some . . . I don't know what this is; Gina's mom packed it. Oooh, is it some sort of sweet? Well, you can have it."

Each thing, once named, sailed over her shoulder to hit a stone, a different one each time, and fell down to its base.

Still nothing happened.

"Maybe you need something from *me*?" Rapunzel chewed her lip. "Maybe you want me to give something of myself? To learn something about me?"

"All right! Here is my knife and my travel paints . . . Oh, and a very tiny sketch on a wooden disk I made of what

I thought my father would look like. I gave him a moustache, which I tried to erase, so it kind of looks like a caterpillar is smudged on his upper lip? But I still like it and have had it for *years* . . ."

A little regretfully she placed that in the middle of the field, unwilling to throw it.

She waited.

Nothing.

The tiny sun moved across the sky; the moon rose into view: a bland white sickle easily missed in the pale blue sky.

Otherwise all was still.

An hour later Rapunzel was lying in the middle of the circle, head resting on her folded arms. The initially mysterious and imposing circle of stones was actually very disappointing. Whatever uses they originally had, whatever supernatural ends they were erected for, they had been forgotten, and perhaps they had wound up forgetting themselves.

So now they were just rocks. Not meriting any more or less respect than any other rock or feature of the landscape. Therefore . . .

Rapunzel leapt up and nimbly climbed a stone that had given in to time or weariness and leaned on its closest stony sister for support. The steepness of the incline was no match for her bare feet.

On top the view was lovely. A nearby hill had beautiful

white stones pushing up out of its grass. Their smooth surfaces shone like milk in the sunlight. The haze in the distance was mountains; their mist-cloaked tops were obscured, blending with the sky.

But there were no giant words etched in the ground, no cliffs with secret symbols carved into their faces. No ancient gods appeared. No—

"I wonder if I could run all the way around the ring without falling," Rapunzel said aloud.

At first frowning with concentration and then grinning in joy, teeth bare to the wind, she ran and leapt and ran and leapt. With only one terrifying stumble she made a complete circuit of the stones, silver hair flying out behind her.

"Wouldn't it be funny if *that* got their attention," she panted, still unsure who *they* were.

She lay down on her stomach on the top of the stone she had finished on, chin resting on her hands. Pascal, sensing a moment of calmness from his mistress—and the warmth radiating up from the rock in the sun—clambered off her neck and stood beside her, tail touching her arm as if for reassurance she wasn't going to leave. Rapunzel smiled and petted him absently and looked at the ground and the mess she had made throwing around the contents of her sack and all the pretty little clusters of white star-shaped flowers that bobbed gracefully in the slightest breeze.

"Look at that, Pascal," she said dreamily. "Those blossoms there, in a row? With the ones on either side and the one big one there? They almost look like a constellation of stars. Cygnus, actually. The swan. See—that big flower in its tail? It could be Deneb, one of the brightest stars in the sky."

What a funny thing, imagining the heavens *below* her instead of in the sky above.

"Let's see if we can complete the Summer Triangle," she said, craning her neck around to take in the whole meadow. "That's the three brightest stars in the sky in summer: Deneb, Altair, and Vega. Look: we can pretend that big one over there is Altair, and . . . yes! That one, next to where I threw my water jar, is Vega. Ha!"

"Actually, that's kind of funny. . . . They really *do* look like the constellations. Exactly. What an odd coincidence."

She frowned, narrowing her eyes in suspicion.

Rapunzel knew the stars like a lord knows the borders and details of his own land; her eyes traveled from one set of flowers to another like the meadow was a map.

"That looks an awful lot like Pegasus, those four stars there that make the big square. And look—that *W* is totally Cassiopeia!" She scooped up Pascal and leapt to the next stone, changing her perspective. "Is that *Hercules*? Over there? It absolutely is! And the Giant Fluffy Bunny!"

She imagined Pascal looking at her funny.

"Okay, that's not actually an ancient Greek constellation. That's one I made up," she admitted. "There are bunnies drawn in the margins of the *Farmer's Book of Days* (Book #34) and I just love their long tails.

"But seriously, what is going on? These flowers make a perfect map of the night sky as it appears *right now*, in this season. How is that possible? Did someone plant them that way? What if I came tomorrow, or in the winter? Would the constellations be correct? Would there be flowers at all in the snow? Would they be in the correct position to show Orion? Wait—is *this* magic?"

She bit her lip, puzzled.

"This isn't the way I imagined magic would work. I thought there would be sparkles or a fairy godmother or *something*. But perhaps they are still trying to show me something. . . ."

She carefully pushed her legs over the side of the monolith, dangling down the face of the stone until she felt she could let go. The distance between her feet and the ground was still surprisingly large, but Rapunzel only took a moment to recover from her painful landing before racing into the middle of the circle.

"Cygnus, Aquila, Hercules, Cassiopeia. Pegasus, Lyra, Draco . . ." She spun around as she named the constellations, pointing at each. "Okay, what now?

"WHAT?" she yelled in frustration, throwing her arms out and looking up the sky.

Now directly above her, transiting the meridian, was the new crescent moon. No longer a chalky white, it was as silver as a piece of polished jewelry, somehow shining and sparkling despite the fact that it should have been nearly invisible that close to the sun, traveling through his bright day.

"Oh, how pret—" Rapunzel started to say, but then she was distracted because her hair began to glow.

Just like when she killed the chickens—but *more.*

Brilliantly, with the white light of the diamonds of her (Flynn's) crown, with the whiteness she imagined the foam of a midnight sea would look like. She picked up a hank of hair and let it hang from her hands; it was like holding molten silver chains or all the distant rivers seen from her tower, gathered up together by some unimaginable fairy-tale giant.

"Pascal, do you *see* this?" she demanded, holding it out for him.

The lizard leaned forward, sniffing.

Rapunzel suddenly panicked and pulled it away. What if he *touched* it? What if it *killed* him?

And yet . . .

She couldn't put into words exactly what went through

her mind when she took the chickens' lives, but whatever it was, that wasn't happening now. She didn't feel a strange sinking feeling in the core of her being, the onset of death. She felt . . .

. . . bubbly? On the cusp of something? Like something deep within her was about to change, in a good way. Pushing out of her in all directions, trying to alter the shape of her soul.

Without knowing why, she brought her hair up to Pascal again. She *knew* he wouldn't be hurt. The little lizard was intrigued by whatever was going on; he nosed into her locks like a curious kitten.

Immediately the sparkles that pulsed through her hair danced around him, falling and flickering. Soon they completely covered the little lizard like snow. Rapunzel watched, enchanted.

Then he sneezed. Embers of magic flicked and faded as they fell to the earth.

Rapunzel gasped.

Pascal was perfectly fine.

He just wasn't—*Pascal*.

He was an entirely different lizard. A lizard Rapunzel had never seen before, in books or anywhere. His eyes were now two balls that perched on the sides of his head and looked around independently of each other. His back was a graceful arch. His feet had two pairs of strange toes that opened up in the middle like claws. And his tail! It curled around and around and clasped onto her arm—prehensile and grasping, not a limp thing that just hung there to help with balance (and to occasionally break off and confuse a predator).

And he was *looking* at himself! Holding his feet out one at a time and admiring them, thwacking the tip of his tail and snapping his mouth in satisfaction. Like a . . . person. He thoughtfully gazed back at his body, considering it.

His skin suddenly started to change color: a wave of brown, and then red, pulsed through him from nose to tail.

"Pascal!" Rapunzel cried. *"You're a dragon!"*

She only wished he had turned into a slightly larger dragon so she could ride and/or hug him.

Pascal experimentally licked an eyeball with his tongue. He didn't seem at all upset by this new shape or what appeared to be a distinct cognitive upgrade. He just slowly marched up her arm and planted himself on her shoulder, facing ahead like he had before, like he always did.

The pulsing silver of her hair slowed; she watched the last streak fade and die at the tips of her longest braid. Rapunzel looked up at the moon. Now it was silent and pale, a ghost no longer calling attention to itself. The nearly invisible crescent sailed innocently across the heavens on its westward path. If someone were just randomly looking up at the sky, her eyes would have been of course attracted to the sun and missed his twin entirely.

"It was the moon," Rapunzel said in wonder. "My hair has moon magic—just like Gina's mother said! From the Moondrop Flower!"

Pascal nodded.

Rapunzel's eyes widened at that; such a banal, human reaction from her pet.

"I have a *lot* of questions," she said slowly. "But I think . . . we're done here. This place somehow summoned my power—or the moon did, through this place. Or my hair summoned power from the moon? I don't know, and I don't think anyone is going to suddenly appear and explain it all . . . but maybe Gina's mom can. C'mon, Pascal! Let's try to make it home before it's too dark!"

She trotted off back toward the woods, so happy she could burst. Her hair didn't *just* kill. It didn't have to do that. It could change and make things.

"But why didn't Mother know?" she eventually asked.

Pascal gave her a look that she couldn't—or didn't want to—interpret.

They walked quietly; Rapunzel felt tired and thoughtful. Soon twilight descended. She held her hand out in front of her and saw its details clearly defined but in shades of grey. There was the tiny scar from one of her first attempts to bake a fruitcake; it wasn't a burn, but she had stupidly dragged the back of her hand against the sharp metal edge of the roasting rack. Someday there would be veins sticking out from the back of her hand like the Goodwife's. Someday there would be wrinkles around her knuckles. She thought about this with fascination, not fear or horror, and wondered how she would paint it.

"Isn't it funny, Pascal?" she said. "I'm a girl. Mother Gothel is—well, a mother. And the Goodwife is a crone. I mean, a *nice* crone. Old lady? Older lady of indeterminate years? Sorry, I don't know the right way of putting it. But we're like the three ancient goddesses, or the moon, or—life. I feel like that's not by accident."

When the night grew so dark that even the little white moths Pascal had been snacking on disappeared deeper into the woods, the little lizard nestled fearfully into her neck as he had before his change.

Rapunzel grinned. "Don't be scared, Pascal! I think I can do something about this."

She thought about the circle of stones and the feeling she had right before the sparkles, the presence of *change*. She imagined the moon—which maybe still hadn't set yet—as a delicate, gleaming silver boat. She tried to summon the feeling of *bubbling* inside her.

Something definitely began—but it didn't quite complete, like a stew that begins to simmer and then a wind comes and blows the fire out and the thick liquid slowly returns to its previous solid state, one or two final sticky bubbles popping at the surface.

Her hair glowed.

It shimmered and shone and pulsed, the full length of it flowing behind Rapunzel and lighting up the undersides of the trees and throwing soft illumination on all the paler leaves and mushrooms, gleaming for a moment where it hit a drop of dew or sap. The moths who had fled returned, like a fluttering train of silken flowers on a long, magical wedding veil, following the mesmerizing river of silver light.

Pascal's eyes couldn't widen, but both held stock-still for a moment, like he was taking in the beauty.

Rapunzel laughed and hurried home.

Rapunzel

Gina's house was all snug and glowing warmly, tucked inside the friendly night like an apple in a pocket. Rapunzel broke out into a grin when she saw it.

And then she heard the yelling.

Lots of yelling.

"How could you let her go on a trip like that by herself?"

"Ma, I know it's mostly safe, but she's an—I mean, she doesn't know anything about the world."

"Oh, you two! Young people think they know everything about the world and that no one else does!"

"I'm home!" Rapunzel called out gaily, throwing open the door.

"Of course you are," the Goodwife said, beaming.

"Thank the goddess," Gina muttered, shaking her head.

"Aha! I knew it!" Flynn cried, pointing an accusing finger at the mother and daughter. Then: "You're all right!" And he threw his arms around Rapunzel.

She enjoyed it immensely: he was much stronger than Mother Gothel—who didn't hug much anyway—and it was all-encompassing; she was so tiny compared to him.

After too short or too long, Flynn dropped his arms and clapped her on the back like a comrade.

"It's dark out there—don't you know what could have happened to you?" he demanded.

"No," Rapunzel admitted.

Flynn made a strangling noise in the back of his throat.

"Glad you're okay," Gina said, hugging her around the shoulders. This too was nice, but Rapunzel wished it were Flynn still embracing her.

"How did it go, dear?" the old lady asked.

"It was *amazing*!" Rapunzel said. "I didn't understand it at first . . . that the flowers were stars, all the constellations, aligned like they would be at night. Of course it was missing the moon because the waxing crescent moon rises *during the day*. And then I looked up—and there it was, exactly overhead! And it glittered, and then my hair glowed, and then Pascal became *this*!"

She plucked the lizard off her shoulder triumphantly and held him for all to see.

"A . . . chameleon?" the Goodwife asked in confusion. "They don't live anywhere near here. They're from the Sun Countries."

"Then he's a kind of dragon?" Rapunzel asked breathlessly.

"*Yes,*" Flynn answered before Gina or her mother could, giving them a look.

"Well, isn't he delightful?" the old woman said, putting her hand out. Pascal inched forward and gave her longest finger a tentative lick, then rubbed the spine of his skull against her like a cat. "You have transformed him. How amazing!

"And now we know for certain what I suspected. Those stones were placed there to chart the movements of the moon and harness her power. Your mother must have consumed the tea of the Moondrop and passed on its essence to you. Wonderful—if complicated.

"The power of the sun is simple: it heals, renews, refreshes, reinvigorates. Had you been imbued with it I could have taught you one simple incantation that would awaken its power and allow you to become the mightiest healer in the land—for good or for evil, as you would," she added with a wink. "The moon is not so simple . . . *varium et mutabile*, as an ancient, somewhat sexist phrase goes. Just as its phases wax and wane in the sky, so does all magic associated with it. When it is full, it comes closest to the power of the sun, glowing and round—but not quite. It heals, but not to the extent of the sun.

"And when it is new, and the sky is black for the lack of its light, its magic brings death."

Rapunzel frowned. "Wait . . . *just* during the new moon? A few days ago when I had to kill the poor chicken I think it was, so that's possible. . . . But when I was a baby it was because I lost my temper that I killed my p—I mean, my nurse. Who knows if it was the new moon at all?"

"You say you're an expert in the heavens," the old woman said, crossing her arms. "*You* work it out. Do the math."

Rapunzel frowned, thinking. Work it out? The moon was new a few days ago. This was her birthday week . . . did that have anything to do with it? Her birthday came at the same time every year on the solar calendar, every twelve months, of course, but the moon's months were shorter. The phase of the moon would have been different every year on her birthday, except . . . Then it came to her in a flash.

The moon repeated her phases on the exact same *solar* calendar day *once every nineteen years.*

And she had just turned nineteen! So nineteen years ago, at this time, the moon would have been new.

She would have been just born, and her magic would have been deadly. So that explained the nurse.

But the other times?

She couldn't remember. All she could clearly think of was that once when she was very, very upset about killing a game hen—more than usual—she had gone to weep and look out the window for hours. The sky was as black as her mind and spirit felt, and the usually comforting stars were pinprick harsh, untwinkling. Each was a stab into her heart. *There was no moon.*

"Maybe . . . ? I can't say for certain."

"Well, *I* can," the Goodwife said. "The moon has changed phases, and so has its power. Your familiar—"

"Friend," Rapunzel corrected, putting a hand on Pascal's head.

"—*changed*. He didn't die, and wasn't healed. That is another phase of lunar power. I don't know them all—you must start tracking your powers and how their effects work over the course of a lunar month."

Projects! Rapunzel's heart swelled. Imagine making magic *every night* and writing down how it worked, theorizing on it. Why, it would take up hours and hours of every day! She would need a whole new schedule!

Except she wasn't in the tower anymore.

Suddenly Rapunzel felt like she was in one of those funny, half-waking dreams. The ones in which you meet interesting characters or find a pretty cake or a treasure and are excited about showing or sharing them back home . . . in the real world . . . and then you wake up and realize the cake is a lie, the people aren't real, the treasure is a figment of your imagination; there is no meeting of the world of reality and dreaming, except for you, and you are a faulty medium, forgetting the other world as the day or night wears on.

The Goodwife didn't seem to notice that Rapunzel was lost in her thoughts.

"Also, we can now guess how your—most likely powerless, decidedly *un*witchy—mother dealt with you as an infant: she probably didn't. You may not be able to remember it, but I'll wager a bag of matsutake mushrooms that when you were a babe she either kept your hair swaddled or didn't touch you on those nights when the moon was new."

"You said you could have taught me an incantation to heal if I had the powers of the Sundrop Flower," Rapunzel said. "But I didn't need an incantation to kill anyone or anything. I sort of thought something and it happened. That's one of the reasons I thought I was so dangerous."

"Incantations are merely a way of reliably summoning the power out of something. As an infant you stumbled upon the right path, or way of thinking. It's true, if you were panicked now and it was the new moon, you might again accidentally call on those powers. But you are an adult now, so it is unlikely, and anyway—it's just once a month. The rest of the time your magic would do other things."

"*Like summon gold?*" Flynn whispered hopefully to Gina.

Rapunzel also wanted to press the Goodwife on that, but suddenly she noticed the food laid out on the tiny table: heels of bread, butter, the inevitable mushrooms . . .

"Sorry, I gabe all ma snax du circle," she said, reaching out and stuffing a bit of each into her mouth.

"You *gave* . . . You made an offering?" Gina's mother asked, blinking.

"'ooked 'ike other people did," she answered with a shrug.

The other woman laughed quietly. "An innocent of the world knows how to propitiate the old goddesses—you really are a natural, my dear. We must spend the next few days finding out as much as we can about your powers. While things are quiet, which I suspect they will not be for long. And I don't even need a scrying glass to predict that. If your path were different, I would beg you to stay here and study your powers, and learn about the universe with me."

"Sounds great," Flynn said approvingly. "We can hide out here for a nice long while, and live, if not happily ever after, then at least *live*. After a year I'll grow a beard and sneak off to Barcelona, where I'll become a highwayman and rob carts until I have enough money to buy a nice little place by the sea."

Rapunzel looked around at the pretty little hut. Everything was neat, in its place. The windows let in the smell of grass and summer flowers. The moon was almost out of view, a gleam at the edge of the pane obscured by rose branches; it could have been a bright star. Night was soft, dark. Somewhere close the goats bleated and muttered to themselves, not quite settled.

It was an ancient kind of heaven: peaceful. Full of life and good things.

If your path were different . . . stay here . . . .

"Can I ever come back here?" she asked, knowing in her heart that she would have to leave.

"A person cannot step into the same goat farm twice; for she is not the same woman, and it is not the same goat farm," the old woman quipped. "You are welcome at my house anytime, Rapunzel. The path will always be open to you. But you, and it, may not be the same."

And after a significant shake of her cane, the Goodwife went outside, to do who knew what in the moonless night.

"You've had a long day," Flynn said, unfolding himself from where he was leaning against the wall. "Maybe we should all call it a night."

Rapunzel warmed to this immediately; his concern for her was like a sun breaking through the clouds when he let it show.

But she shook her head.

"I'm too . . . I'm too excited. There's too many things to think about," she admitted. "I'll go to bed in a little while, but I want to think about and maybe write down what happened today, before I forget anything that might be important for the magic to work."

"Back to the hayloft with you," Gina said with a smirk, gently pushing Flynn out the door.

"All right, but the room service is *terrible* there. I want to lodge a complaint."

He let himself be steered, but turned back to look Rapunzel in the eye and say, "Good night, *Princess*."

She shook her head. "Good *night*, Flynn."

After they were gone she stood in the empty hut quietly for a moment, the only noise the crackling of the fire.

Then she got to work.

Thinking a bit of organization would help, Rapunzel took out the wanted poster of Flynn and made a chart on the back, dividing the rectangle into twenty-eight days. She wrote the moon phases neatly on each. On Day One, *New Moon*, she wrote *Murderhair*. Now it was Day Six; *Waxing Crescent*. Under this she wrote *Transformative—Lizard to*

Dragon. Day 8 would be *Waxing Half Moon*—that would be exciting, right? Maybe that would mean a really big change in her powers. For Day 15, *Full Moon*, she wrote *Healing?*

She looked at her neat little chart and felt very pleased with herself.

Projects.

They were the best.

Memorial Sloan Kettering

Daniella was almost impatient as they took her blood pressure and her temperature, put in the infusion lines, got her situated. She held out her arm and didn't flinch at the jabs.

"Want to get out of here quick today?" the nurse asked with a smile. This was Erik; he liked blackberry jelly doughnuts. His boyfriend was in finance. He had a pet clawed frog that ate fish, and he always brought *two* autoclaved blankets for Daniella.

(Her parents were quick to learn everything they could about those who were taking care of their baby—and they always brought the right doughnuts for everyone from Throop Patties and Pastries.)

"No, I want to hear more about Rapunzel," she answered with absolutely no embarrassment. "Brendan here is telling me his version of the story."

"Now *that's* a good brother," Erik said with a smile. "I'll leave you to it."

After he was gone—and the machines began pumping—Brendan pulled out his sketchbook.

It was a surprise he had been working on all week.

"Look, it's an illustrated story now!"

He held it out for her to see. Daniella leaned forward to study the pictures.

"Raps kind of looks like some sort of sixteenth-century French lady there, with her hair all up and all the little charms in it," she said thoughtfully.

"Eighteenth century, but I take your point."

"Whatever, history nerd. When she had her hair up, I sort of thought it would be more like . . . I don't know, like a skater girl, but crossed with a witch. You know? Kind of gutter punk? More of those braids, maybe ones that look like serpents. No, wait, a *fortune-teller*, but with Rapunzel's eyes and smile. Or an ancient priestess!"

"That sounds a little creepy," Brendan said, turning to the next picture.

"Nothing creepy about the goddess—which, by the way, I do appreciate you putting in. Oh! Pascal and Flynn!" she cried, seeing what he had drawn. "Pascal as he's supposed to be! Look at that face! That's *perfect*. Hello, Flynn, you're looking all right." She waggled her eyebrows.

"Um, all right, ew," Brendan said, quickly turning to the last one. It was Gina and her mother, and Captain Tregsburg.

"Where's Maximus?" Daniella demanded, chin out.

"Oh, come on. Just tell me—do they look like you imagined?"

"Yeah, exactly, no question," she said impatiently. "But *where is he*?"

"I have a plan," Brendan promised.

"You have a plan," Daniella humphed, crossing her arms (as best she could with the IVs). "You put in horses, and a guy who really likes horses, but no Maximus-the-horse. *Ridiculous*. Also—you didn't actually tell me the part where Gothel tells all the noble bad guys that Rapunzel has escaped, and sends them after her. In fact, where is she during all this? I'm missing some real bad guy action here."

"I thought it was pretty obvious what she had done. Didn't need to be shown *or* told," her brother protested. "You know, you're awfully eager to hear the next part of the story considering how you're constantly criticizing it. . . ."

"I constantly criticize your calc homework, and look

how much better you do. *Listen*. Learn from me," she suggested smugly.

"I cannot wait until you're better and I can give you a proper noogie," Brendan muttered, putting away his pictures and pulling out the book—more of a prop than a necessity, but at this point he still liked holding it.

"Me too," Daniella said wistfully.

Rapunzel

By the time Rapunzel woke the next morning the hearth was already swept and a fresh fire warmed an ancient fry pan filled with bubbly golden treats. The Goodwife was pouring a bowl of cream. Flynn was setting the table. Rapunzel sat herself down, guilty about having slept through it all. She had no idea what hour it was when she had finally collapsed, but made a mental promise to do *all* the cleanup.

Gina brought over the pancakes, plopping one expertly—if ungracefully—onto each plate.

"Funny, I didn't really see you as a master of the feminine arts," Flynn said.

The next pancake landed on top of his head.

He pretended not to care, ripping off pieces and eating

them as if it were the most normal thing in the world (but stopped short of putting butter on it, too).

"Say, Princess," he began casually. "When Gina and I were hunting yesterday we found this *super* pretty waterfall, perfect for a picnic—"

"Rapunzel here has a long day of study ahead of her, for which she needs total concentration," the Goodwife interrupted.

Rapunzel would have pouted, but she already had her own plans for the day. *And* plans for Flynn. Not all of her midnight thoughts were about magic. "I would love a picnic, but maybe tomorrow? Now that we're figuring out my hair, I think we also need to figure out what's going on with all of those people randomly looking for me. As you said, I can't stay here forever. So why don't you and Gina go find one of those men and bring him back here for questioning?"

"Listen—she's already sounding like a leader, a future queen," the old woman said happily, elbowing Gina in the side.

"It *isn't* 'randomly,'" Flynn pointed out. "*You* just left your tower for the first time in nineteen years. And now people are looking for you. Coincidence? I think not."

He smugly sipped his goat milk and tried not to make a face when the liquid hit his tongue.

"I'm in," Gina said with a shrug.

"This will take an extremely cunning plan," Flynn said thoughtfully, stroking his chin. "Wait, I know! We have Gina here dress up as Rapunzel. . . ."

"Never going to happen," Gina said immediately.

"Come on, it's just for a few hours. You'll be the bait."

"Nope. But *you* have a slender waist—maybe with the corset . . ."

"In your dreams."

"Oh, believe me, my dreams have nothing to do with you in a corset. My nightmares, on the other hand . . ."

"There's a reason I never wanted more than one kid," the Goodwife muttered.

Dodger let out an angry bleat from the window.

"*Human* kid," she added apologetically.

"Great! You guys finish, I'll clean up," Rapunzel said.

She began stacking the dirty dishes into piles and combining the remaining bowls of uneaten food. As she brought them over to the scrying bowl/washing basin, Flynn got up—with a quick look around to see if the mother and daughter noticed—and took her aside.

"Uh . . . hey . . . Rapunzel? These are for you."

She was more intrigued by the tone in his voice than what he held in his hand. The flirty, constantly joking Rider had a catch in his throat that was *almost* a stammer. What he held was nice, too, though; a bouquet of flowers. But not some quickly picked nosegay from a careless child; even Rapunzel with her limited experience could see that. They had been arranged with care and chosen for their colors, and the whole thing was tied up with plaited grass. When had he picked them?

(She did cringe a little at the giant pink mallow that was the centerpiece; it could only have come from the Goodwife's garden. And good though she might have been, so many fairy tales began poorly when someone plucked something illegally from a witch's garden. . . .)

"The lanterns would have been tonight," he said as she smelled and picked at the blossoms. "I'm really sorry. That was the only thing you wanted, for so many years—and we missed it."

Rapunzel was startled. She had actually forgotten about the floating lights since her adventure with the circle of stones and everything else.

And . . . it sounded like he actually cared. Not just about the crown. About her missing out.

Flynn opened his mouth as if he was going to say something else, his eyes caught in hers.

Then he grinned and tried to look charming.

"Not bad, right? I always thought if the whole adventurer thing didn't work out, I'd become a florist."

"But . . ."

Rapunzel wasn't sure what she wanted to say. Something like: *Bring back that Flynn from a moment ago! The nice, nervous one. The one who picked me flowers.*

"Don't you like them?" He waggled his eyebrows at her.

She would not be drawn into his dissembling. She would not let him off the hook. She stood on her tiptoes and kissed him on the cheek. "Thank you. That really means a lot to me."

When she turned away to do the dishes, she saw that his face was flushed.

"Your task is twofold," the Goodwife told her after the others had left. She had sat Rapunzel at her workbench, in a nook which hadn't seemed to be there before. "You must of course document your powers every day, see how they change throughout the lunar month. But more important, you must figure out how to bring them forth reliably. You will not always have the advantage of an ancient moon shrine, or the primal rage of a babe."

"It wasn't an *advantage*," Rapunzel said immediately. "It was murder."

"Nonsense!" The old woman's blueberry eyes blazed like a lightning storm in a lavender-grey sky. *"You were a baby.* It wasn't your fault. You could no more control yourself than you could control crying and breathing and wetting yourself. If you had been raised normally, you would have seen other babies in your life—oh, the tantrums that even the best of them throw! So angry they forget to breathe! Why, if any baby had powerful magic, even the sweetest-tempered child, everyone would be dead for a day's ride in any direction and all the world's seas turned into milk.

"Begin your nineteenth year by forgiving yourself, Rapunzel. That's a far better gift than floating lanterns."

Rapunzel was speechless.

As the old woman's words sank in, a sharp pain clove the front of her forehead. She felt everything at once: sadness for the dead nurse she didn't even know, despair for the parents she thought she killed, longing for the living parents she hadn't, regret for nineteen years of confinement for a crime that wasn't really her fault.

Anger. Because Gothel had never said anything like this.

You were a baby. It wasn't your fault.

It wasn't your fault.

The Goodwife reached out and squeezed Rapunzel's hand, seeing the pain on her face.

Rapunzel sucked in the tears she thought were going to start and gave a deep, shuddering sigh.

"Thank you," she murmured. "I . . . don't know if I can

forgive myself immediately, just like that, but just knowing that I can—that I *should*, that's a start."

"Well and honestly said. Now set it aside for later musing; you have work to do. Sit here and focus on the moon, anything that has to do with the moon. A poem, a song, something that *feels* right. You'll know."

Rapunzel tried. She really did.

It was bright morning out, and the moon was probably up. But even knowing that, she, like everyone else, still thought of the moon in association with the night. She couldn't fix it in her mind when it was so sunny.

She sang every moon song she could think of, every nursery rhyme. "Hey Diddle Diddle" and "The Man in the Moon came down too soon" and "Boys and girls come out to play / the moon doth shine as bright as day."

Nothing.

She could get the hair to glow—a little—by recapturing the feeling at the circle, sort of like she could fix death on the birds Gothel brought by refeeling what she had each time she performed that terrible rite. But she couldn't summon the fullness of power that had transformed Pascal.

The Goodwife came in to check on her once in a while, to bring her mugs of tea or broth—or little packets of dried herbs, crystals, stones, and even bones associated with the moon. She taught Rapunzel the few celestial incantations she knew, hoping one would work.

Nothing did.

Rapunzel decorated and redecorated her chart, filling in the margins with guesses: *Waxing Gibbous Moon—teleportation? 3rd Waning Crescent—making things smell different?*

At lunchtime Gina's mother, sensing Rapunzel's exhaustion and incipient despair, took her on a little tour of the goat farm and showed off her neatly laid-out patch of garden (which besides flowers and vegetables had several carefully placed rotting logs with mushrooms sprouting enthusiastically in suspiciously neat rows).

"I wish *Gina* had taken an interest in the magical arts the way you have," the old woman said with a sigh. "Goddess knows I tried. Potions that changed color, making small things explode, all the sorts of things that children love. Thought I would have a daughter *and* an apprentice. Ah well, that shows me, doesn't it? Imposing my will on another living being and making assumptions about how things worked. Just like a new parent. My Gina taught me some good lessons about life and expectations."

"But . . . so . . . was Gina always interested in becoming an . . . adventurer?"

In leaving the tower, seeing the world?

"Ever since she was little," the old woman said fondly.

"She was always taking my best knives and running outside to practice fighting. So physical! Climbing trees, slaying imaginary villains . . . and then as soon as she was old enough, rampaging through the woods looking for people to practice on, or join up with."

"And you didn't stop her?" Rapunzel asked as innocently as possible. It didn't come out that way at all.

The Goodwife laughed. "*Stop* Gina? Have you met my daughter? And besides, why would I want to? It's the only thing she has truly ever wanted to do or be. I'm her mother, not her guard dog. My work is to see that she is adequately prepared for whatever she wants to do in life—that she can feed herself, patch a tear in her clothes, find the right leaf for stomach cramps. And teach her that no matter what happens I will always love her. 'Go out for adventure, come home for love.' That's what I say."

They began to head back to the cottage. The old woman didn't have her cane but moved perfectly well on her own bare feet. Rapunzel followed thoughtfully. Princess, adventurer, enchantress . . . *mother*? She had never even thought about the word as it applied to herself, separate from Mother Gothel.

That was also a thing she could be. . . .

Back inside, the workbench mocked her with its witchy paraphernalia and magical bric-a-brac. Rapunzel gritted her teeth and refused to notice how the sunny day was passing and here she was yet again *inside*, doing strange little projects. Like back in her tower.

She tried to surprise her powers into working.

She even pretended to get up, to go do something else—then whipped back around and shouted, "Moon!"

Nothing.

She sighed and listlessly began to poke at the little things on the table, arranging and rearranging them into aesthetically pleasing combinations. Finally somewhat satisfied, she admired the shape she had made without really thinking: a crescent of crystals and moss.

I should paint that, she thought. *Make a nice little still life . . .*

Rapunzel blinked.

Of course!

She had been so oblivious!

She took out a charcoal stick and began to sketch—on the workbench itself. *Of course* the moon wouldn't come to her in songs or poems or crystals or whatever . . . she felt the most centered, the most tranquil, *when she was painting or drawing.* Lost in her own world or in new ones she imagined. She shouldn't have made a chart; she should have drawn a circle, with the moons going from waxing to waning all the way around . . .

She hummed to herself a little, the way she always did when she painted.

Her hair began to glow.

A little shading here, a few light strokes in the middle of the full moon for the face that Rapunzel saw there . . . Circles and shadows and crosshatching . . . She worked extra hard on the profile of the fatter waxing crescent, where the moon would be now. She *knew* what it looked like as she felt her hand shape it.

Her power surged; her hair began to sparkle.

She looked around frantically for something to release her magic on. The first thing she saw was her tea, so she grabbed the red clay cup and wrapped the end of a braid around it.

Just like with Pascal, sparks sprayed off her hair and over the object.

When they faded they revealed . . .

. . . a heavy, crude clay cup.

Rapunzel started to slump in disappointment—and then noticed something. Where the hair had touched the sides, the cup was now shiny black, like onyx or obsidian.

"Goodwife!" she cried excitedly. "*Gina's mom!* Come look!"

The old lady came pitter-pattering up as fast as she could.

"Oh, you did it!"

But rather than admiring the mug overmuch, she leaned over to peer at the illustrated moons now covering her workbench.

"A mandala!" she said. "*Very clever*, Rapunzel! I never would have thought of it myself. I know some folks who use them—not so much here, but in other lands. They are built and destroyed at each session. . . . Or is this a focus object for you? Something to gaze at, and strengthen your intentions?"

"I don't know," Rapunzel admitted. She looked at the black smudges on the cup. "But it looks like I'm only half-way there. I need something else. Something more . . ." As she pondered more *what,* she looked around the cottage, hoping for an answer. Her eyes lit up when she saw several crude wooden trays on which were piles of colored powders. "Hey! Can I use those?"

"Oh, my dyes, of course," the Goodwife said in surprise. "I hardly ever use them myself, except to remind myself of which potion is which, or sometimes for the goats' wool. Please, help yourself!"

Without wasting a second, Rapunzel did what she did best: she grabbed her supplies and began painting.

Gothel

In her mind, dominating all her thoughts, there was a map of the land such as a king or general going to war might have. Little toy men fanned out across the fields and hills, slowing down when they came to the woods, breaking up into smaller groups of twos and threes to search every path. Looking for Rapunzel.

The woods.

Gothel frowned.

These were not, of course, the great untamed and wild woods of centuries ago: there were paths through the deepest of them now and the largest boars and wolves were rare. Rarer still were sightings of fairies and goblins and ghosts and will-o'-the-wisps.

Or witches in huts made of candy.

Rapunzel had definitely been seen at the Snuggly Duckling—but before any details could be learned, Lady Bathory's men had burned it down in . . . anger? Retribution? Random act of violence? Who could say; she hired people like herself. Vicious, chaotic, and not that smart.

The countess did, however, have those fantastic *vérhounds*.

By good chance, one of Smeinhet's men, having escaped from a skirmish with the royal guard, claimed to have seen Rapunzel—with *Flynn Rider*, the reprobate from the wanted posters. Gothel had been right about the two of them conspiring together! What an idiot she was for bringing that poster back to her daughter as a birthday present. . . . No good deed ever went unpunished.

There was some confusion in the story, of course. Was Rapunzel "dressed up like a thug," in disguise—or *with* a girl dressed like a thug? It sounded like the latter, since this other girl didn't have silver hair. And of course all the lords and men then immediately dismissed this possible other girl—because how important could a girl be?

Gothel didn't dismiss her, however. The noble idiots didn't realize that any clue was a clue. A little snooping in the wrong places revealed that her name was Gina and her mother was a mysterious old goodwife who lived deep in the woods and occasionally healed—or yelled at—travelers in the forest.

A witch.

A *real* witch.

Someone who excelled at hiding from people. Someone whose daughter was now traveling with both a wanted felon and an escaped princess. Both of whom desperately needed to hide.

Not a single other person—not a single *man*—put those facts together.

Gothel might not have had any actual powers herself, but she knew some tricks. The right song to unlock the healing power of the Sundrop Flower. Silver for protection. Fresh running water from an ancient spring to dispel an evil enchantment.

A mixture of rabbit fat and usnea rubbed on the bottoms of your shoes to walk through glamours and illusions.

The question was . . . how best to make use of this new information?

And who would be the lucky noble to receive her help? She thought about the search parties of spies and soldiers, guards and mercenaries from all the rival houses on the hunt for Rapunzel. Kraske, Smeinhet, Thongel . . .

. . . Bathory . . .

Gothel really didn't like her. She had hoped the bidding would eliminate the countess naturally; there were certainly richer lords than she.

But that was a thought for later. There would be no auction if there was no prize.

It was time for Gothel to once again take an active part in securing her future.

And the first step was regaining her daughter's trust. . . .

Rapunzel

By the time the sun set and there was no good light left for working, Rapunzel was exhausted but pleased. She had painted a detailed mural of the phases of the moon on the workbench, colored in the soft pastels of the Goodwife's pigments mixed with a little water. Each of the moons had a different face and expression. There were also feathery flourishes and text labels in beautiful Gothic script (for Day 6 she wrote: *Change color?*).

She even put the royal sun in the middle to remind her who she was.

She managed to summon her powers twice more by gazing at her mandala, and was tickled with the results: she turned her bright red coral bracelet glittering black, and a dish of pale yellow dye a bluish black. Of course she had no idea if the color was set by the phase of the moon or if it was simply the way she thought about the moon, set in a blue-black sky. But imagine if she could summon any color! She would never have to worry about getting the right paints again. Mother Gothel wouldn't have to travel so far to that place to find the white pigment. . .

. . . and, of course, here it all fell apart again.

Rapunzel sighed and got up, going outside to clear her head. Also to wash in the stream; her arms and face—and even Pascal—were covered in soft smudges of color.

She knew a time of decision was coming up. She had an idea where her fate would lead her, and it probably wasn't back to her tower. Of course she wanted to *meet* her parents—but was she going to stay at their castle for the rest of her life? When there was so much else out in the world? Whatever a princess really did, Rapunzel was pretty sure she wouldn't have time for serious magical study.

(And she strongly doubted the Goodwife would come and live in the castle and tutor her.)

She strolled over to the goat pen, which was really more of a suggestion than something that would actually hold them in. One goat even balanced atop a post, looking down at Rapunzel and the world like it was her own kingdom. Amused, Rapunzel picked some flowers and began to braid a crown for her. Just the ability to pick as many flowers as she liked and not have to rely on her mother to bring them was a kind of freedom.

If . . . Gothel . . . really *was* a witch, despite the Goodwife's doubts, would she teach her daughter? If Rapunzel returned to the tower and her mother apologized for everything and admitted she was wrong, and they both cried . . . and then they lived on together as equals, and Flynn and Gina could visit, and maybe Flynn could stay, too . . .

Fantasies. Silliness.

Thoughts came and went and eventually settled. She finished the crown and set it on the goat's head.

"Now *you're* the royal princess," she said with a curtsy. "Good luck, Your Highness!"

The goat gave a bleat and promptly began to eat the crown, using her long tongue to pull it off her horns.

Rapunzel laughed. "Absolutely right!"

Then she sighed. It was time to go back in, with a quick stop to feed Dodger some more flowers she picked. He took them without expression or thanks, his agile lips ripping them from her grasp, chewing immediately. There was something to be learned from goats, Rapunzel decided. She made her way back to the house—and found a very strange scene inside.

"Can I have a drink now?"

In a space the cottage had conveniently opened up for him, there was a man tied to a chair, bruises on his cheeks and little intelligence in his eyes. He was dressed to fight or kill in thick boots, jacket, and gloves; the insignia on his jerkin was covered up by many, many layers of rope. Gina and Flynn stood on either side of him, looking dirty and tired but satisfied.

"You got one!" Rapunzel cried.

"Yup," Flynn said, crossing his arms—and for just a moment his eyes were angry, very, very angry. Frighteningly so. "And he was definitely looking for *you*."

"Hey! You're the girl with the silver hair," the man said excitedly. Then his face fell in disappointment. "The duke woulda given me a gold piece if I had gotten you."

"Shut it, cretin," Gina said, kicking the back of his stool.

"That would be Duke Kraske," Flynn said. "Known for small bouts of land-grabbing, the tightness of his purse strings, and, strangely enough, a thing for painting minia-tures. But his man here won't tell us or doesn't know *why* the duke wants you."

"You're very pretty," the man said helpfully. "He prob-ably wants to marry you."

"Nice try. The duke *has* a fiancée, a powerful one, the daughter of a Hugrian lord," Flynn pointed out, turning to Rapunzel. "He hasn't said anything about crown princesses or any magic, uh, H-A-I-R, and Witchy McTabitha over here won't help out with a little persuasive hocus-pocus."

"Magic should never be used for such evil purposes!" the Goodwife protested. "*I* suggested good old-fashioned torture. But it doesn't matter—he doesn't know anything. All he did was confirm what we thought: every lord in the land is looking for you, dear."

"*Witches!*" the captive began shrieking. "*I'm in a house of witches!*"

"Yeah, we told you that when we brought you here," Gina pointed out.

"Here, drink this," the Goodwife said impatiently. She took a ladle of water out of the bucket and discreetly crumbled some herbs in. When she held it out the man lapped at it like a dog, apparently having forgotten that just a moment ago he was screaming about being in a house full of witches. "Take him out to the shed. We'll deal with him later, when he wakes up. Let him go in the woods somewhere while he's still too sleepy to remember how he got there."

"What do you mean wake *uhh* . . ." the man started to demand, and then his eyes began to flutter.

"Quick, let's do this before he can't walk. I don't want to carry him," Flynn said.

"Agreed," Gina said. "But if he conks out, I get his head. You get his butt."

"Not likely, sister."

The two managed to get the man up, swaying and tipsy though he was, and out the door.

"It's almost like Yuletide around here," the Goodwife said a little wistfully when they were gone. "I mean with everyone around, in the house. Like when I was a girl. Before I left the world behind."

Before she left the world behind. . .

Rapunzel suddenly saw the peaceful vale in a new light: as a tower. A nicer one, but still hidden and lonely. Gina came and went like Gothel . . . the Goodwife *chose* to stay here. Why? Why would anyone turn away from a world full of so many magical things and people? Adventures, adventur*ers*, kvass, taverns, horses . . .

"Why did you leave the world behind? Is it dangerous for witches out there?"

"Certainly. But really I just didn't want anyone interrupting my studies, my meditations, my thoughts, my discoveries . . . I like peace and quiet."

"But if you learn something, how do you share it with the world?"

"Well, I don't usually, I suppose," the witch said with a

shrug. "I write it all down in my grimoires, and I have a few friends with whom I correspond occasionally, or see once in a blue moon. . . . It's really just my own curiosity I'm satisfying, you could say."

Rapunzel was silent. She wanted to love everything about the Goodwife. But this way of living seemed sort of . . . pointless. Imagine being a master of powerful, magical arts and just using them for your own personal studies and interest!

Rapunzel couldn't see herself doing that.

She poured herself a mug of tea and headed outside after the others (doorways to the outside were still enough of a novelty that she stepped back and forth through it several times, feeling and smelling the smoky little hut and then the flagstones outside that had their own mineral scent).

The evening was surprisingly warm; it was like a blanket of sweet, still air hung over the tiny valley, refusing to be moved by breeze or the icy airs of the heavens.

Her initial thought to watch Flynn and Gina and how they dealt with the prisoner was forgotten when she noticed something sparkling strangely under the pear tree. She went over to investigate. What at first she had thought were more fireflies or magic, she suddenly realized were her charms—all the pretty little silver things she had thought would protect the world from her hair. She sat down on the soft, mossy ground and dragged her fingers through them, felt their tiny weight, let them fall from her hand.

Eventually Flynn and Gina emerged from the black background of the valley, finished with whatever they had done with the passed-out mercenary. Rapunzel watched them say good night (she assumed) and wondered how things would have turned out if she had been a princess in a tower *over a city*. Or a small town. She would have been able to watch the comings and goings of people and animals all day, like ants, and keep notes on them, enjoy their little dramas playing out. That certainly would have alleviated the boredom and loneliness.

Flynn turned—he must have seen Rapunzel sitting there. When Gina went back inside, he continued up the path. He swung his arms and kept a cocky stride . . . but much more slowly than he usually did.

"Hey, Princess," he said as he drew near. "Mind if I sit down?"

"Only if you stop calling me that," she said, patting the ground beside her.

He gave a leering smile, but it faded quickly. There was, she saw, a rough stubble all over his face now, the shadow of what would be a full beard if he let it keep going. It made him look older, emphasized the hollows under his cheeks and around his eyes. He was exhausted from hunting, trapping, interrogating, and dealing with the only lead they had on her situation.

She kind of liked the look.

All his facial fakery, his posturing, had dropped away. It wasn't the weariness that was attractive; it was the fact that now there was nothing hiding the real Flynn, the right-before-he-fell-asleep or right-after-he-got-up-in-the-morning Flynn, the one who had seen things and done things and felt things and had no energy to lie.

"Well, *that* was a day ill spent," he said as he sat down next to her. "All we learned was that yes, everyone is after you. Still unclear why." He stretched; the shirt tightened around his torso, and he pulled up his sleeves, which were torn. A jagged, bloody cut ran down his entire left arm. He didn't notice her gasp; he was too busy closing his eyes and bending to the side, feeling around his stomach with his fist.

"If it's any consolation, I used my fantastic powers to turn things different colors today," she said with a smile. "Well, one color. Black."

"Very goth. And hey, more than I could do." He looked down at her trailing silver hair. "This is a *much* better look for you, by the way. Neoromantic. And . . . not actually deadly, I take it?"

"It's harmless," she said with a smile. "At least until the new moon. And even then, I have to be actually focusing and directing it to cause harm. I still have a lot to learn, but I feel . . . comfortable with it now. No more tying it up!"

Flynn smiled and for a moment looked like he was going to reach for her hair, now that it wasn't dangerous. His hand rose and floated in the air halfway between him and her . . . and then he quickly used it to slick his own hair back out of his face.

"Yeah. *My* hair can do things, too. But it's kind of dramatic and you have to ask nicely, sometimes with a little gel."

Rapunzel laughed. A chill breeze finally made its way from the forest to where they sat, ruffling the locks of willow branches and making its way under Rapunzel's skin. She shivered once, body already worn down from exhaustion. Without thinking she leaned up against Flynn. Without thinking he put his arm around her.

He was warm and smelled of . . . things she couldn't name precisely: work? Boy? Beard? It wasn't bad. It was just . . . Flynn.

They were quiet for a while. Rapunzel had her head back, watching the stars through the drifting willow leaves.

"This is all really strange," he said.

Rapunzel sat up. "Sorry! I'm sorry! Is this strange? I don't know. I always did this with my mother. . . ."

"No, no, the leaning? It's fine. Have at it!" Flynn said with a smile. "I mean . . . *all* of this is strange. A week ago my life was thieving, running from the law and *worse* thieves. Making a name for myself. Becoming a legend. Saving up for an early retirement. *Alone,* I might add.

"Now suddenly I'm surrounded by people and dealing with witches, international conspiracies, royal princesses, magic *hair*, goats . . ." He trailed off, looking around helplessly. "I don't know if I'm ever going to get back to my old life."

"Do you want to?" Rapunzel asked. "I've been asking myself the same thing."

"Well." He chuckled quietly. "*Your* life kind of stank, no offense. If you returned to your old life you'd be back by yourself in a tower. Me? If I had my old life, I'd have a crown, and maybe a girl, and a—"

"I'm a girl," Rapunzel pointed out.

"Yeah, but—" Flynn said.

"But what?"

Despite never having met a boy, much less dealt with one, Rapunzel knew he was going to kiss her. She could see it in the way he didn't blink, the way her own face was all that reflected in his eyes. His cheeks grew rosy and his lips parted a little.

And then the moment was over.

"You're a royal princess," he said, moving away from

her. He looked quickly here and there at other things as if to refresh his eyes. "That makes things . . . different."

Her disappointment existed for less than a moment before fury took over.

"Stop telling me who you think I am!" she shouted, slamming her fist on the ground. "Before I left the tower I was just Rapunzel! As soon as I met you, you were all like, *She looks like a princess.* You actually judged me because of the way I dressed. Despite my repeatedly telling you I had no servants, golden carriages, or even a single friend."

"But . . . you *are* a royal princess," Flynn said. "We know that now. And that really does change things."

"Maybe I was born a royal princess, but nothing at all has changed about *me*. I'm the same person I was yesterday. With a better grip on my powers and my hair. So why don't you call me *Witchy* instead? You could do your whole dumb 'Hey, look at me, the great Flynn Rider, I'm so funny with my nicknames and totally amazing stories and life, and aren't you jealous, Witchy?'"

"Hey now," Flynn said, sounding hurt. "I worked really hard to be who I am today. I came from *nothing*. I was an orphan, remember!? I had to claw my way up from being Eug—uh, a penniless nobody, to the great Flynn Rider!"

"I'm an orphan too, *remember?* And *I* don't even seem to have a choice in who I get to be!"

"Rapunzel, why are you upset?" Flynn asked, throwing his hands out in exasperation. "At the end of this little adventure you get to go off and be a royal princess. *With magic powers.* I get to either be executed for trying to kiss a royal princess, or be imprisoned, or . . . return to my usual life of thieving and adventure. Which is great, don't get me wrong, but it's not like being a royal prince.

"This . . . whatever this is, this moment between us, will just be an amusing memory for you years down the line when you're queen and looking back on your life. And I'm . . . nobody. Again."

"An amusing memory? You really think that's how I'll think of this? Your kindness, your risking your life for me, your . . . the flowers you picked? You think I'm that kind of person? That kind of princess?"

"Rapunzel, I . . ."

She began to dig through her bag.

"Here," she said, taking the crown out and thrusting it at him. "Here's your crown back. I'm sure you'll get extra bonus rewards for returning it along with the *princess.* And then this can all be just an amusing story for *you* to tell in a pub down the line when you're rich and retired and looking back at your life."

He blinked at the—slightly tarnished, dirty, sparkling, heavy—thing in his hands. . . .

And then said absolutely the wrong thing.

"You had this with you all along?"

Rapunzel's mouth hung open, as if breathing in such stupidity would allow her to understand it.

She stood up and looked at him just long enough to spit: "You're the *worst*, Flynn Rider!"

Then she stomped off.

Rapunzel

"You know, if you're going to keep doing this kind of thing, we're going to have to assign a watch goat to follow you around everywhere."

Rapunzel opened one eye to see Gina looking blandly down at her.

She was confused for a moment as to where she was lying, but the warm discomfort of being tucked in between a couple of goats made that evident immediately. So did the smell. What Rapunzel had at first thought was kind of unusual but somehow comforting now overpowered her to the point of nausea. She covered her nose with a lock of her hair—only to realize, with horror, that *it* smelled of goat, too.

"Yeah, uh, maybe you want to take a bath or

something . . . ?" Gina suggested. *She* looked fresh: for once out of her traveling and fighting clothes, dressed in a comfy-looking short green tunic and sandals, her braid slick and still wet, as if she had braided it up again immediately after washing it.

"Maybe," Rapunzel admitted, carefully extricating herself from between the goats, who seemed a little miffed she was going. Pascal waved goodbye to them, but it was unclear whether it was in triumph at leaving or sadness at going.

"There's a nice pool up the stream a bit," Gina suggested, handing her an old—but clean—rag and a small pot. While the semisolid oils or whatever inside had a very faint whiff of something animal (goat), it was overwhelmed by bright, clean herbs and dried flowers.

"I feel like you were planning this," Rapunzel said accusingly.

As they walked into the woods, Rapunzel's hair trailed out behind her; Gina kept on looking back at it as if it were a snake or something else unexpected and maybe just a little bit creepy. The sparkling pool of water they came to was absolutely beautiful—and *freezing*, as Rapunzel found when she dipped a toe in. She shivered and made a face.

"Sorry, Your Highness," Gina said. "It's all we got."

Rapunzel scooped up a handful of the water and pitched it at Gina.

"I'm so sick of the two of you calling me a princess! I don't even know what a real one looks or acts like!!"

"Okay," Gina said with a shrug as the water ran down her face. "If it bothers you that much I'll stop."

"Wait—really?"

"It's nothing serious, it's just a—game, I dunno. You've never had friends that you've goofed around with, I guess."

"No, I haven't." Rapunzel thought about this as she carefully set Pascal down in a puddle of sunlight on a warm rock. Then she undressed and forced herself to get into the water quickly, without any hesitation. She gritted her teeth and refused to shiver: whatever royal princesses were like, future queens had to be brave and stoic if they were going to get any respect from their people. Right?

Gina watched with fascination—and maybe a little bit of horror—as Rapunzel pulled all of her hair into the pool, armload after armload. "So . . . you and Flynn had a fight?"

"Did he tell you?" Rapunzel asked, unsure if she was curious angry or curious hopeful.

"Nahh, but it was pretty obvious after you went to sleep with the goats and he stomped around for a while outside."

"I gave him the crown back. Threw it at him, actually."

Gina's eyes popped open in shock.

Rapunzel suddenly realized what her thoughtless gesture meant to the other girl. "Ack—I promise, if and when I am ever, what's the word, *restored* to my kingdom, I'll make sure you get some other reward! Just as sparkly! Or I'll make him break it in half, or whatever."

"No, I, uh, I don't *need* half a crown," Gina said. Then she thought about this. "Well, actually, it would be kind of nice. I could get a horse. And a nicer cloak. Maybe if you get *another* crown, you could give it to me. Or a horse. I mean give *me* a horse, not give it to a horse."

"But about Flynn . . ."

"Oh, enough about him! He just wants to get this over with, grab his reward, and move on. I'm just . . . a side story in the epic of the great Flynn Rider he's made up about himself. The princess he rescued along the way to fame and fortune."

She angrily scrubbed herself and her hair in silence for a few minutes before getting out. Gina didn't say anything else.

The other girl had thoughtfully brought another tunic with her. It was undyed and off-white; Angora goat wool, of course. Not the linen and silk Rapunzel was used to. *"Princess!"* she hissed to herself ironically. It wasn't as scratchy as she feared, and soft with age.

"Sorry, one of Mom's," Gina said. "You and I are built, um, *differently*. Otherwise I'd loan you one of mine."

Rapunzel tried not to look at Gina's muscles and

curves, and then at her own, flatter chest. She wasn't embarrassed; merely curious.

She scooped up Pascal and they headed back out of the forest. Rapunzel felt like she had just engaged in some ancient rite, that she was some priestess who bathed in a sacred stream and then put on the vestments of ritual. Her silver hair solemnized the idea, trailing out behind her like elven robes.

"Maybe," Gina suddenly said out of nowhere—though it was obvious that the thought had been percolating slowly through her mind—"Maybe Flynn is saying all these things about getting his and getting out because he's afraid of being hurt. Maybe . . . he's *afraid* of having to leave, and losing you to your new life. Your new life as a princess, I mean. Maybe he can't say that, so he just says 'princess' a lot instead."

Rapunzel's eyes widened in surprise.

The thought had never even occurred to her.

Back at the cottage, her "new" plain wool dress offered a blank canvas and exciting opportunity to try her magic— and forget about Flynn for a while. On the chart it was Day 8; on her mural/mandala it was nearly a half moon. She stared at the image and retraced it with the plain end of her charcoal stick, *feeling* the shape of the moon.

Her hair began to glow.

"Stripes," she murmured. "I want stripes on my robe. Or—polka dots!"

She stood up and raised her arms, letting her hair fall all against the length of her dress, front and back, covering it entirely. There were sparkles everywhere, and then . . .

She felt something itchy and tickly on her arm.

Rapunzel shifted around in her, well, shift, and shrieked at what she saw: one end of a stray thread was waving slowly in the air, rising up from the garment and pulling away. It was a weft thread, one that weaves back and forth over the whole cloth and holds it all together . . . and it was unraveling. Rapidly.

When it was long enough to touch the ground it began to pool there, pulling faster and faster.

"Wait, no, stop, this isn't mine!" Rapunzel shouted. She grabbed at the yarn and tried to hold it still. It wriggled desperately out of her grasp—possibly like a worm—but it seemed that her command was enough. The sparkles dissipated and the unweaving stopped. Her hair ceased glowing; the dress was only partially undone at the top.

Feeling strangely exhausted, she fell back onto the stool and regarded the mess.

Why had it done that?

Did this moon phase mean *destruction*? *Unraveling*? The magic was still transformative, that much was clear; the dress had been acted on and changed. It hadn't disappeared or floated off or whatever else.

She sat quietly for a bit, drinking tea and resting and studying her mandala. Then she tried again, this time holding her black-smudged mug.

The change was too fast for her to stop: within moments the cup sort of thickened, then collapsed into a wet pile of clay.

"Pits," Rapunzel swore. She thought she would keep that mug as a memento of one of the first times she had performed magic correctly—without killing anything. Disheartened, she dolefully poked at the little glob of clay with one of her poky sticks. It seemed like the power of Day 8, the waxing half moon, was to "transform" an object into a pile of rubbish. Which kind of made sense; it was closer to a new moon, which was death, and nearly half a whole moon, which was healing. She shuddered to think what it would do to a chicken or Pascal.

Not feeling up to trying again immediately, she looked around for something else to do, magic related. On a scrap of bark she painted a full moon, on the other side of it a waxing crescent. A tiny token she could carry with her if she needed to use her magic and didn't have the mandala on the Goodwife's bench. Maybe someday she would have her own workshop (in her mind it looked a bit like the main room in her tower) with an entire wall that she painted with images of the moon . . . and maybe she would paint the floor, too.

Pleased with her work but done with it, she began to play with other things on the desk. A feather, a crystal, a pair of goat shears . . .

She picked this last thing up with interest.

Gothel had told her that cutting her hair would kill her. The Goodwife said that was nonsense; it would only affect her powers, if anything at all. And come to think of it, Rapunzel did lose the occasional hair when it caught on something, or when she was combing it out. The dead hairs turned a dull brown, and it used to panic her when she was little. Did it take a day off her life? A month? A year?

She thoughtfully wrapped a lock of hair around her fingers. Biting her lip, she brought the shears up. . . .

"Rapunzel? What are you doing? *No!*"

Flynn had quietly come in (and had paused at the door, preparing to say something theatrical) but immediately dropped all playing. He ran over and grabbed her hands, holding them away from her.

"What . . . oh," Rapunzel said, confused and taking a moment to figure out what he was doing. "You thought I was going to hurt myself. You didn't hear what the Goodwife said? Cutting my hair won't kill me."

"Oh. No, I did *not* hear that," Flynn said, collapsing

against the edge of the workbench. But he didn't let go of her right hand. "Maybe when the group learns something important like that, you could let me in on it? You know, keep me in the loop?"

"Sorry," she said, a little chagrined. "I guess this looked really bad, didn't it?"

"You have *no* idea. Rapunzel, I . . . I think I died a little when I saw that."

He opened his mouth, trying to say something else.

Was he going to go into full funny Flynn Rider mode? Or was he actually going to say something serious?

Rapunzel could hardly breathe, waiting to see.

And then he kissed her.

It wasn't like the night before, when there was a pause and a feeling of expectation. He took her face in his hands and pressed his lips to hers. With desperation, maybe as if she really had almost died.

Rapunzel shivered—and for the slightest moment panicked that it was her magic activating. But it wasn't. . . .

When he stopped, she reached up and touched his lips gently. She didn't want the moment to end.

"I don't want to lose you," he whispered. "But if I have to . . . I'd rather it be to your happy ending than to . . ."

"Brigands and mercenaries, or a hair-related death, I know. You *do* care, Flynn Rider!"

"It's a curse, really," he said with a dramatic sigh, backing away. Retreating into *full* Flynn Rider. "I'm too sensitive and caring. Ever since I was a boy."

That was funny, thinking of Flynn Rider as a boy, before he put on all these airs and . . .

Rapunzel's green eyes popped wide open.

A boy!

"They're not being *destroyed*," she cried, pushing him gently but firmly aside. "They're being . . . returned to earlier states!" She picked up the glob of clay and ran it through her fingers.

"Oh, yes, that was a *lovely* moment, Flynn; now can I get back to my witchy business?" he quipped.

Rapunzel ignored him.

"The power of the waxing half moon is to turn something younger, into a previous version of itself!" she explained triumphantly. "This was my mug—now it's back to being clay. And my dress also began to *unweave*! I'll bet if I hadn't stopped it would have gone back to being wool, or a whole fleece."

"Um—amazing? Yay, the goddess?"

"It *is* amazing," she said, beaming, and kissed him full on the lips again. "*Everything* is amazing."

"Look, I could stay and do this all day. I'm happy for you. But this also very, very strange, and kind of out of my

wheelhouse, so I'll leave you to it. We can pick this up later."
He turned to go, but stopped when he reached the door.
"Are you, are we . . ."

"I forgive you," Rapunzel said, reviewing her mandala,
pretending to be haughty.

"You forgive *me*? I'm pretty sure I wasn't the only par-
ticipant in our little tiff . . ."

"Begone! Before I turn you into a babe in arms—or a
toad!" She waved her arms menacingly above her head.

"Leaving!" He ducked his head and ran out. Rapunzel
collapsed into a fit of giggles, and tried to concentrate on
magic—and not what it was like kissing him.

It was hard.

A feather grew sleek and colorful and disappeared—back to
the bird it fell from? A bent nail became a lump of iron. A
rock stayed a rock, even when she sweated and concentrated
and almost passed out from using her magic. *Maybe* it got a
little bigger. It was sobering to think how many thousands of
years that rock had been almost exactly that size and shape.

An eggshell became a disgusting mess she resolved to
never think of again.

Exhausted and due for a break, Rapunzel decided to
go outside and get some fresh air. A goat followed her (she
kept feeding it handfuls of flowers), and the two wandered

together across the little vale to the far side, where her journey to the circle of stones had begun. There were some very tasty, as yet un-nibbled blossoms over there.

Suddenly the goat froze. One of its ears twitched. It turned its creepy eyes to look into the woods.

Rapunzel also stopped, unconsciously imitating the goat in the way it cocked its head. There *was* a distant sound, intermittent and garbled. Was it something crashing through the brush? Was it a deer making some sort of deer-y noise? The sounds of men shouting?

"Hello?" Rapunzel called out cautiously. There were woodsmen in the woods, of course, and hunters, and other people who occasionally stumbled onto the Goodwife's hidden valley. And now the forest was thick with Snuggly Duckling refugees.

And also men who were trying to capture her.

Was it better to hide, or run back to the cottage and warn everyone? Or should *she* confront the potential intruders? As future queen, and present sorceress?

The goat bleated once and began to awkwardly gallop away.

"Good choice," Rapunzel decided, following its lead. She put a hand onto Pascal to keep him steady and ran for the cottage. Flynn and Gina could fight anyone off, and the Goodwife would know what to do. She would either defend them with mighty powers or chide Rapunzel for fearing the locals.

As she passed under the pear tree, two men leapt from its branches and seized her.

One violently grabbed her arms, yanking hard; the other put a large gloved hand over her mouth so she couldn't scream or bite.

The noises in the woods were a ruse, she realized: a very clever and subtle one to distract her from the real danger.

She kicked and flailed. She tried to remember what Gina and Flynn had done when she had seen them fight.

And accomplished nothing. It was like attacking a wall.

With quick, efficient moves, the one who had put his hand on her face now forced a leather thong across her mouth and tied it around her head. The other held her down and tied her arms at her side. Finally they shoved her brutally down onto the ground and wound ropes around her ankles, pulling tight. That really hurt; the rough hemp chafed her bare skin.

Once she was bound up like a caterpillar, the first man— Rapunzel labeled him "Gagger"—grunted in approval. He then reached down and threw her over his shoulder as if she were no more than a doll.

Rapunzel twisted and struggled and tried to kick him

in the ribs with the points of her toes—but they did nothing against his leather jerkin. She lifted her head—just long enough to see the snug little cottage retreating into the distance—and let it fall back against his shoulder blade as hard as she could, but all it did was hurt her nose in a terrible *crunch*.

She tried to summon her magic—turning him into a boy wouldn't be deadly, and probably quite surprising—but she was exhausted. Nothing came, not a single sparkle.

She screamed incoherently, hoping they would think it was foul; nasty curses and swears.

(She didn't actually know any, but the intent was there.)

As soon as they had carried her far enough into the woods to be hidden from the house they stopped and threw her down to the ground.

"I'll go tell Kraske," Not-Gagger said. "You keep an eye on her."

She tried not to think about how *both* guards would have stayed to keep their eyes on Flynn or Gina.

When would anyone notice she was gone?

Would Flynn come to the cottage, looking for her?

She arched back and dug her heels into the ground, straining against her bonds. Her guard watched with bored amusement. His greasy jacket had a hound on it with some sort of tree in the upper right.

Pascal stuck a cautious nose through her hair, scenting the air to see if it was safe.

"Ascal," she whispered. "Oh et help. Ood-ife, Ynn, eena. Oh et help."

The previous version of Pascal could have skittered off, faster than sight, a liquid streak of color through the grass. But he would have understood nothing and returned after eating a fly or two.

This Pascal understood what she wanted perfectly and began, with obvious determination, to hurry back to the hut.

But dragons were apparently not made for walking on land. His strange toes were built for clasping onto branches and vines. Rapunzel watched in disappointment as he marched away: if she was lucky, he would make it to the cottage by dark.

Her captor, who had been paring his nails with a very sharp knife, began to spin the blade on his fingers thoughtfully. "Say, a lock of that hair of yours would make a nice trophy."

Even though she now knew that cutting it wouldn't do anything to her, the menace in his face and the glint of his blade was terrifying.

"Might make the whole thing worth it," he continued with a nasty grin. "Traipsing through these stinking, haunted woods. My cousin went missing, you know. Came back rambling on about witches and nonsense. Oh yes—this'll be my prize."

Rapunzel suddenly wasn't sure he was just going to take a lock of her hair. She began screaming again—

and the man's eyes popped wide and he fell forward.

She screeched and managed to roll out of the way just in time so his giant, partially armored body hit the ground next to her.

There, standing where he had been a moment ago, was Gothel—a heavy mallet in her hand.

"Uh-er," Rapunzel said in awe.

The dark-haired woman was extended to her full height on her tiptoes, arms raised, skinny neck straining with the effort of reaching the man's head for one perfect blow. She blinked slowly, as if shocked by her own boldness.

"Uh-er," Rapunzel said again.

"Rapunzel," Gothel said in a breath, putting a hand to her stomach. "I cannot *believe* I just did that. Can you?"

"Uh-er," Rapunzel said a third time, eyes filling with tears.

She wasn't sure why she was crying. Overcome with gratitude, certainly, but it was also seeing her mother, her *mother*, standing there, defeating the bad guys.

She had always said that Rapunzel needed her mother to protect her . . . and she was right.

"Here, let's get you out of this nasty mess and out of here," Gothel said, taking the knife from the unconscious man's hand with one efficient swoop. Rapunzel watched this with wonder—but she would think of it again, later. How easily and quickly her mother had grabbed a weapon out of a felled man's hand. It wasn't something a girl who spent her life in a tower would have necessarily thought of. She would have at least taken a moment to consider, look around, decide what her options were.

But that was later; right then, as her mother leaned over and began to methodically saw off the thongs and ropes, all Rapunzel could feel was relief and gratitude.

"Oh, my poor, poor dear," Gothel said, rubbing her daughter's arms to get the circulation back into them.

"*Mother!*" Rapunzel sobbed, and threw herself forward, hugging the other woman so tightly it was like she was trying to combine their bodies.

"Oh, all right now, all right," Gothel said, a little disturbed, as always, by her daughter's emotional response. It was like her hands, so nimble and efficient before, now didn't know what to do; they hung in the air uselessly, even the one with the knife in it.

"Everyone's after me, Mother," Rapunzel said, crying. "It's putting all my friends in danger, and there are mercenaries *everywhere*, and everything was just starting to be wonderful. . . ."

"There, there, all right, let's get you out of here before they come back and find us, and that fellow on the ground there." She stood and gave her daughter a hand up, then pinched one of her cheeks. "Enough with the tears. You know they age you prematurely. You can tell me *all* about it while we go home."

"Home?" Rapunzel repeated, a little thrown by this. She sniffed and wiped her nose.

(Pascal had paused in his hut-ward marathon to look back at this new development, and seemed to weigh the situation. He didn't immediately rush back to Rapunzel. It was almost as if he thought that it was still a good idea to go and inform the others what was happening.)

"Yes, home," Gothel said, straightening out the simple white shift that had gone askew on Rapunzel's shoulders. "What *is* this horrid thing? Are you playing a shepherd's wife in some sort of Christmas pageant? Ugh, look at the cut. We'll get you all cleaned up, and into one of your other dresses, and I'll make your favorite soup for you. . . ."

"But . . ." Rapunzel looked back over to where the hut was, where Pascal had decided to keep heading for reasons known only to himself. The shock and joy of having been rescued by her mother were now ebbing like morning mist from over the forest . . . and behind these initially good feelings was a mass of confusion: reasons, questions, issues, problems.

The simplest won out in its quest to get through her lips: "But I want to introduce you to my friends."

Gothel laughed, tinkling and long. "Oh I'm sure they don't want to meet little old me. No, it's best to get out while the getting's good, as they say. No time for long goodbyes. We want to avoid being caught again, don't we?"

"But—shouldn't we warn them, at least?' Rapunzel persisted. "They don't know what happened to me, or that there are dangerous men in the valley. They should be prepared for a—wait, how did *you* find me? This place? It's hidden magically somehow."

Gothel looked a little taken aback by this last question.

"Well, I have my own way with the arts, you know," her mother said. "I tracked you. . . ."

"If you have *your own way with the arts*, why didn't you know the truth about my hair?" Rapunzel demanded, pointing at the tresses that hung around her shoulders. "That it doesn't just kill. That it's harmless unless I purposefully summon the powers. That it can do other things—and that I won't die if it's cut?"

Gothel drew back, lips slightly parted, as if slowly inhaling the breath of the entire world.

Finally she spoke.

"I'm not perfect, dearest, I did my best. Imagine being given a child with powers that just killed her parents—"

"I didn't kill my parents," Rapunzel interrupted.

"Oh, so you know." Gothel bit her lip and looked sad. "The king and queen were only trying to do what was best for their country. Don't blame them."

"I wasn't," Rapunzel said in confusion. Her mother wasn't even trying to deny it?

"Look, we can sort this all out at home. We can maybe even arrange a meeting with your parents—would you like that? I think you're old enough to handle it. I'm new to this whole mothering business, Rapunzel. I've thought of you as *my* baby, my first and last, for too long. I didn't want to lose you, and that is selfish, I know." She sighed. "It was wrong of me. You should have known the truth years ago. Come now and I will fix everything. I promise. We'll get you cleaned up, get a good meal, have a good night's sleep, and then I'll see about the king and queen—*your parents*."

Rapunzel started to nod. It was all coming together; it was all so easy. After being violently seized and manhandled, the idea of being in her own bed, with her own things, and taking a nice long nap sounded heavenly. And her *parents*!

Maybe Gothel was changing? Maybe her mother just

needed a chance to see how serious Rapunzel was about wanting to leave and see the lanterns, the world. And now that she had, their relationship had shifted. She was seeing her daughter as an adult, ready to take on the truth about her background.

Only . . . she had accepted all the new things Rapunzel had said without contradicting anything or batting an eyelash. Wouldn't someone who genuinely believed for twenty years that her daughter's hair could kill maybe show some surprise at these revelations? Happiness at the way things actually were?

And . . . since Rapunzel was already out in the world, couldn't she maybe go see her parents? *Herself?* Now? Without going home first?

Gothel turned to leave—having put the knife in her belt, a little smugly—and was starting to walk away already.

"No . . ." Rapunzel said, quieter than she meant to, louder than she imagined.

The tip of Pascal's tail curled a little.

"*No,*" she repeated firmly.

Gothel stopped and turned—just a little, not all the way, as if it wasn't worth turning all the way around for, or maybe because turning all the way would mean a real line in the sand had been drawn. Admitting there was a challenge to her authority.

"No?" she asked neutrally.

"No, Mother—at least, not right away." Rapunzel wasn't sure if she should feel like a coward for saying that second bit. "I'm not abandoning my friends while there's dangerous men nearby, and I'm not leaving without saying goodbye. I'm not even sure I *am* leaving yet."

"But of course you are, dear," Gothel said with a bright smile that was maybe colder than she intended: the light of a failed wishing star rather than a warm fire. "Where else would you go? Mummy will take care of you, treat your wounds, feed you. . . ."

"No, I'm sorry, no," Rapunzel said, trying not to cross her arms. "Not yet. I have things to do."

"What *things*," Gothel asked, approaching her slowly and seeming to grow, looming over her daughter.

"Things." Rapunzel faltered a little, feeling stupid. "I want to study my hair, feed the goats, talk to Flynn. . . ."

"Listen to you! You're raving. *Feed the goats* indeed. You must have gotten a bad knock on the head, poor girl. Come with me before something worse happens." And with that Gothel took Rapunzel's hand and began to walk away again, forcibly pulling her behind.

"I said *no*," Rapunzel said, whipping her hand away. It stung with the friction. "Come with me if you want to meet the people who have helped me, or go home, by yourself—I am not going there with you now."

"*You will do as I say.* I am your *mother!*" Gothel hissed.

"I am nineteen," Rapunzel said calmly. "I'm an adult. Most girls are already married by this time."

At this Gothel unexpectedly began to laugh. It was ugly, and her eyes shone with evil irony.

"Oh, you have no idea," she whispered. "I was going to do this the easy way, I was going to make things straightforward and painless for you. But it seems like all you'll listen to is force."

"What are you talking about? Mother?" Rapunzel demanded, caught in the sharp, narrow place between anger and fear. "What are you saying?"

A voice rang out from somewhere in the forest: "*Rapunzel!*"

"Flynn?" Rapunzel spun, looking around for him.

"*Where are you?*" Gina cried, from someplace else nearby.

"I'm . . ." Rapunzel turned back, but her mother was *gone*. Faded into the shadows, away, no trace of her ever having been there at all but for the unconscious man on the ground and the knife missing from his belt.

"Here," she finished uneasily.

Rapunzel

The time it took for Gina and Flynn to find her was immeasurable: Rapunzel stared at the place her mother had last been and listened to the silence of the forest rush in her ears. Part of her hoped that it was all an hallucination, a summoned wish. She doubted that her mind could have come up with such specific details, however. Gothel's proficiency with the knife and the knocking out of the guard, for instance . . .

"Hey, you all right?" Gina got to her first, her own knife out. "Holy crow . . ." she added when she saw the unconscious man on the ground.

Flynn was close behind, his cheeks rosy with the effort of running and eyes wide with concern.

"My mother," Rapunzel said weakly.

"That guy is your mother?" Gina asked in confusion.

"No, she was here, she hit him on the head," Rapunzel said diffidently. Was she going to faint? She felt all empty inside. Not weak; more like hollowed out. Her skin was still strong and hard. It was her insides that were missing.

"Wait," Flynn said. "Your mother appeared in the middle of the woods, hit this guy on the head, and disappeared?"

Rapunzel nodded, unable to speak. *Stupid princess,* she told herself. *You're going to cry like a baby.* Flynn and Gina wouldn't be so weak. They'd grin and brag about the danger they were in.

She grinned.

"It was pretty scary there for a moment," she said brightly. "It was a trap. There were two men who grabbed me, and—"

"What's going on? Are you all right?" Flynn asked.

"What's wrong with your mouth?" Gina asked.

"How did your mother know where you were?" Flynn asked.

"How did your mother get here?" Gina asked. "Where is she now?"

"I think I need to sit down," Rapunzel admitted, putting a hand to her head.

"Home we go," Flynn said, taking her arm.

Rapunzel let herself be steered, thoughts pushing ahead to places she hadn't even considered yet like fingers of water on the floor from a dropped tankard, reaching to get under places that were hard to clean.

Her mother had found the Goodwife's secret valley and managed to enter it. Because, she said, she had a way with things.

But . . . the guards who had gotten into the valley before her. What about *them*? How had they gotten in? That was too much of a coincidence. Somehow Gothel must have wittingly or unwittingly brought them . . .

Or led them . . .

It was extremely, extremely convenient that she had shown up just in time to save the day. And she couldn't have arranged a better demonstration of how much safer Rapunzel was with her back in the tower. What had her mother said at the end there, threateningly? *I was going to do this the easy way. . . .*

Flynn spotted Pascal and scooped him up as they went without a thought, putting the creature he had initially called *vile* on his shoulder.

Rapunzel distractedly told herself to remember that. It was important.

The Goodwife was already standing at the cottage door, beckoning them to come in. New thorny brambles were growing around the edges of the house. They hadn't been there this morning. Big and black and fairy-tale-y, spikes as long as Rapunzel's fingers and thick as a knife. While one probably wouldn't *die* falling into them or impaling herself on one, it wouldn't be pleasant. Might even put an eye out.

"Quick," she said. "I have added some additional glamour to the hiding spell, but I don't know how long it will last. It's strongest around the house. Outsiders in my valley, can you believe it? Filthy vermin! *Bandits!*—Put her on the bed."

Rapunzel didn't remember seeing a bed in the hut before. Somehow she had missed the rustic lashed-together wood frame with an actual mattress.

"I'm all right," Rapunzel objected, sitting stiffly on it and refusing to be laid down. Queens, ancient queens of saga and myth, swords maidens and those who fought the Romans, bore everything with bravery.

(Princesses from fairy tales were so delicate they couldn't even sleep on a pile of mattresses if there was a pea hidden somewhere beneath.)

"Looks like you got into it," Gina's mother said with a low whistle, seeing the burns on Rapunzel's ankles where the ropes were tight.

"Things are a little out of hand," Rapunzel said softly. "I am so sorry about your valley. This is all my fault."

The old woman lashed out with her cane and rapped her smartly across the knuckles.

"Ow!" Rapunzel yelped.

"Ma!" Gina cried in horror.

"Oh, I'm sorry," the Goodwife said demurely, straightening out the wrinkles in her dress. "I was interrupting. You were just about to apologize for being tied up and nearly carried off by some hooligans? Pray continue."

"But they wouldn't be here if it wasn't for me," Rapunzel protested. "I've put you all in danger."

Flynn lunged forward and grabbed the cane before the Goodwife could use it again.

"Don't be daft, girl," she said, grumpy at being thwarted. "Would it have been nicer if violent men hadn't come into my peaceful valley? Absolutely. Is it *your* fault that someone ordered them to follow you and kidnap you? Unless you're not telling us something—like you drowned someone's favorite cat recently—I think we can put the blame squarely on the shoulders of whoever decided to kidnap you, and those who obeyed orders blindly."

Rapunzel took a deep breath. "Thank you. For pointing that out. And believing it."

"She said her mother was there—somehow rescued her from the baddies," Gina said.

The old lady frowned. "Where is she? And what did she say to you?"

"I have no idea, and—nothing that really means anything," Rapunzel said helplessly. "All she said is that she wanted me to come home. No, that she was going to *take* me home. She wouldn't take no for an answer. It was—scary. And . . . how did she get here? And the guards . . . She somehow knew to be right there. . . ."

"I'm not one to gossip maliciously about people I don't know, especially other people's mothers," the Goodwife said with a sniff, "but it all sounds very suspicious, I must say."

"All right. We can theorize about Moms and her motives later," Flynn said. "This safe house is officially no longer safe. We have to leave . . . but where do we go?"

The three began to argue, discuss different possibilities.

Rapunzel didn't really listen to them. How bright and unknown her future had looked just a few days ago! Terrifyingly blank but filled with possibilities, like a night sky covered in stars when it's so clear you can see forever, see all their shapes and the distances between them.

. . . And now it was narrowing back to one inevitable

line. The direction, Rapunzel suspected, it had pointed since her birth.

"There's only one place that makes sense," she said, interrupting her friends. "One place I'll be safe.

"The castle—back with my mother and father."

Everyone was silent, moodily thinking about this.

"Happily ever after, princess restored to the throne," Flynn finally said. "*Great*. A neat ending. I like it."

He didn't sound happy about it. And there was no patented Flynn Rider smile that went along with the words.

"I really don't *want* to go there yet," Rapunzel said with a sigh. "There are so many other things I want to see and do first—I don't even know what they are. I've lived so little outside my tower!"

"Just in case we're ever out in public anywhere or anything discussing this," Gina said, "try not to mention how upset you are about getting to be a princess—and then a queen—for the rest of your life? It might not go over well."

"What if your mother had stopped you from having adventures?" Rapunzel retorted. "What if she kept you at home, or something else did? And you knew there was a big wide world out there full of treasures to find? And you lived comfortably and got to eat sweets every night and had nice dresses, and a window from which you could watch the entire world go by, and you knew you would never be part of it?"

"Huh. It's strange when you put it that way," Gina said thoughtfully. "You can't really compare lack of . . . choice? To lack of clothes and food. But I guess I'd rather be hungry on the road than fat on a throne."

"Well said," Flynn said, putting a hand on Gina's shoulder. "I don't think either one of us would thrive in that world."

Rapunzel gave him a look.

"I mean, I *could*," he admitted. "Someday. I wouldn't say no to eventually having a nice estate somewhere warm with lots of servants and an *indoor* garderobe. That would be a nice thing in one's old age. Or your thirties . . ."

"All right," the Goodwife said, rolling her eyes at him. "How do you plan on *getting* our Rapunzel to this castle?"

"We'll stick to the original lantern plan." He grabbed the tiny dining table and rearranged the things on it, making a map of the kingdom and the lands around. "We'll head off the path and through the woods, bushwhacking. Come out by the northern coast, despite my sensitive skin, drop down—"

"But—" Gina said.

"I think the old king's road will be fine if we time it right and it's not high tide—"

"Wait," Gina tried again.

"*What,* Gina?"

"We don't need to hide the whole way this time, do we?"

"Oh no, I was thinking it would be fun to get beat up by *everyone* in the land: guards, thugs, nobles, mercenaries . . ." Flynn said with a wave of his hand. "Maybe we should hand out tickets?"

"No, I mean, yes, but . . . all we really need to do is avoid the rogues and men looking for Rapunzel."

"Yes, *that's all.* Do you hear yourself? Anyway, it should take us a day to get *here.* . . ."

Rapunzel cleared her throat. "*GINA,* do you have something to add?"

"It's just that . . ." She took a deep breath. "If our goal now is to get Rapunzel to safety, we don't need to avoid *everyone.* In fact, the sooner we run into Captain Tregsburg or one of his men, the better. Job done—they can take over, bring her to the castle."

Flynn looked at her for a long moment.

"Yeah, that could work, too," he decided, stroking his chin. "And no salty windburn from the sea!"

Gina gave Rapunzel a shy smile.

Rapunzel reached out and squeezed her hand. "Gina, you're a *great* adventurer. You don't need anyone else's permission to speak up, or approval. Just say what you think—and do it!"

"All right then, we'll just head on southwest to Harecross," Flynn said, pointing at a piece of the table near the salt. "It's the closest canton outside of the capital. Hopefully we can flag down a guard or join a merchant cart for safety from there to the castle."

"It's a plan," Gina said.

"You in on this, Prin—uh, Rapunzel?" Flynn asked.

She smiled. "With the two of you working together, I don't see how it could fail."

She allowed herself exactly one look back at the house in the valley. The thorns had grown higher while they packed up and prepared; vine-like canes reached over the windows, mostly covering them. The Goodwife waved from the doorway. She looked so much older, tinier, daintier; a teacup grandmother you could put in a corner and put a pretty crown of flowers on, maybe give some cake to. Not a mighty witch once again escaping from the world of troubles.

"What's going on in that head of yours?" Flynn asked curiously.

"You can't step into the same tower or goat farm twice," Rapunzel answered with a smile that was only slightly sad. "For it is not the same goat farm or tower, and you are not the same person."

"You know, you really are kind of weird," Flynn

said—but with admiration. "Weird and witchy. Yeah, that's definitely what I'm calling you from now on! Witchy!"

Rapunzel sighed and shook her head. "Do I need a nickname? Is there a problem with 'Rapunzel'?"

"Too long," Flynn said with a careless shrug. "Besides, if it's a choice between our hero being executed for kissing a princess or being turned into a frog for kissing a witch, well . . . I have no problem hanging out with ol' Pascal here and the other slimy amphibians."

He went to tap the lizard on his knuckles, but Pascal refused, pulling his feet in and turning his head away.

Flynn used the moment to kiss Rapunzel quickly, just below the ear—here and then gone, a moment of warmth that dissipated like magic sparkles. He gave her a mischievous grin.

"Lizards aren't amphibians, and aren't slimy," Gina said from behind them.

"Thanks, Professor," Flynn rejoined. "Can't you go find a lecture hall or someplace else to pontificate in?"

Rapunzel smiled to herself, and wished the three of them could have gone on that way forever.

Rapunzel

The canton of Harecross was, according to the two adventurers, "garbage." Larger than a smallholding, smaller than a village. It was still impressive to Rapunzel.

There were a dozen or so houses that were slightly larger than the Goodwife's (on the outside, at least). Small fields and grazing pastures surrounded them, but without the sort of neat rows of grain painted in Rapunzel's books; there were messy, squiggly plants and herbs, blobs of cabbage, rows of turnip or beet greens.

(Which excited Rapunzel very much. Once she had planted the top of a beet instead of throwing the leaves in a stew. The plant grew more leaves, but no more beet. Not living anywhere near the ground, she was fascinated by things that grew *under* it, and wondered if a royal princess might someday be allowed to pull out a beet, just to see it.)

There were sheep but no cows, a donkey but no horses. There were geese but no chickens. The road to the hamlet was little more than packed dirt.

But there were *people*.

Men and women in the fields with clunky-looking hoes and farming tools. Standing up in apple trees, doing who knew what. A woman trying to get a recalcitrant sheep to move, pulling it on a coarse rope lead. Sometimes the women had hats or wimple-like scarves wrapped around their heads, but mostly their faces were free, their hair bound up in intricate braids and whorls—none as complicated as Rapunzel's had been, of course, and all in shades of chestnut and wheat.

And *children*!

Rapunzel's heart almost stopped.

She immediately knew what they were—even without ever having seen a live child before except for the one in the mirror.

The game they played involved a stick that two girls held and that had to be either jumped over or hunched under, its height and the players' decisions based on some set of rules Rapunzel couldn't immediately discern. A line of seven children in varied but similar baggy clothing, regardless of gender, cheered on or jeered at each contestant.

Rapunzel rose up on her toes and danced on them in excitement. "Can we go closer?" she begged.

"To the . . . ankle biters? Sure, I guess," Flynn said with a shrug. "They're not wild animals, you know."

"Will I look strange to them? What should we do about my hair?"

"Something *really clever* we should have thought of an hour ago," Flynn suggested wryly. "If anyone asks, we'll say you're one of those mountain nuns, or some other religious thing—that'll shut them up and maybe keep you safe.

"And while you're, uh, child-watching, I think I'll find whoever's brewing the scrumpy," he decided. "A place like this doesn't have a tavern, so people just tend to hang out and gossip where they buy their cider. I want to hear if there's any news about you or all the international intrigue in the woods. Jeens, keep an eye on Witchy, would you?"

Gina nodded, set her eyes, and put her hands on her hips, obviously ready to fight anyone who came too close and very pleased to have been given the task. Rapunzel, already approaching the children, didn't notice.

"Hello!" she called cheerily, waving.

The children looked back at her with mixed expressions: apprehension, blankness, curiosity, delight. Some were only looking at her hair.

"Can I play?" Rapunzel asked hopefully.

A girl, holding one end of the stick and taller than most, looked skeptical. "*You* want to play high-low rod?"

"Growned-ups don't play," a little boy told her seriously. "Growned-ups work."

"Well, *I* play," Rapunzel said, hands on hips.

"Why is your hair so long?" the smallest girl who wasn't a toddler asked in carefully formed, polite words. "And the color of fishes?"

"It just grew that way!" Rapunzel answered with a smile. "So, how do you play?"

The other girl holding the stick shrugged. "You come at us shouting either *high rod* or *low rod*. If you shout *high* and you leap and make it, that's worth a golden frog. If you go under and it's above our waists, it's worth nothing. If we make it low anyway and you leap, that's also nothing. But if we make it low and you go under, that's a double golden frog. And if you shout *low*, it's all reversed. Got it?"

"Not a bit!" Rapunzel said happily. "But let's start, and I'll catch on."

Gina watched with an unreadable face as Rapunzel stood in line, bounced with excitement, clapped, and cried out as points were scored. She cheered the losers with equal enthusiasm. When it was finally her turn she leapt, ably and enthusiastically, with feet as bare as the rest of the children's. Her hair came after her in shining waves that brought a spontaneous explosion of shouts from everyone.

She never scored a single point—or *frog*—always shouting or doing the wrong thing at the wrong time, but doing it all energetically and pulling her hair in behind her with such force that it sometimes seemed like a pet. Then they played leapfrog and ring-around-the-rosy, the latter of which she liked best. She wasn't any taller than the tallest but still had to make her steps tiny so she didn't crash into the younger ones, or yank them out of line. When they spun around faster and faster her hair flew out like a ribband and encircled them in a silver crown . . . and then they all fell down, laughing and delighted.

"And you get to do this *every day*?" Rapunzel asked when she got her breath back. "All of you?"

"Most days," one of the boys said with a shrug. "Or we pretend we're knights and ladies."

"Or we climb the apple trees."

"Or in the winter, we go sledding."

"What's sledding?"

"You know, it's . . ." The oldest girl looked with exasperation to another child, possibly her brother. "You take a flat piece of wood, or something you've carved, or an old shield or something, and when the hills are covered in snow you go to the top and—well, it's better if you make a track, or someone else makes a track first—and you ride down it, on the snow."

"And snowball fights," the girl's brother added. "You make balls out of snow, with your hand, like this, and then you throw them at people."

Rapunzel strangely felt like crying. "This is one of the best days I've ever had," she said with a swallow. "But . . . I never had a brother, or a sister, or friends to play with. I feel like I missed out on *everything*."

"I'm sorry," the second-littlest girl said earnestly. "That sounds awful. But are you a princess?"

"Yes," Rapunzel said, wiping her nose on her sleeve.

"So don't you get feasts and dances and venison and carriages?" another little girl asked in awe.

"I don't know. I haven't been one for very long."

"But you *do* get at least two meals, every day?" a little boy asked. "Even at the end of winter?"

Rapunzel frowned and scooped the little boy closer to her (and was distracted by that for a moment—what a wonderful feeling! A tiny warm body that bent into her arm, *wanting* to be held and cuddled!). "I don't understand. What do you mean?"

He shrugged. "At the end of winter, you know. When all

the food your parents have saved is gone and there's nothing in the woods yet and the fat bunnies are asleep and if you have birds they aren't laying yet."

"And your parents and older siblings eat once a day, maybe—but they sneak you more, because you're little and it hurts more," another boy piped in eagerly.

"Once a day? There's no *food*?" Rapunzel asked, trying to understand. "But . . . but . . ."

She had too many questions, and the world flashed and changed behind her eyes. Where did Gothel always get their food? In the winter? Not having anything to eat had never been part of Rapunzel's world, except when she was being punished for bad behavior and not allowed a baked apple for dessert.

Rapunzel studied the children, who were not making fun of her or angry at her for not knowing the way of the world. Not *judging*. Maybe they were a little surprised, but that was all.

"No," she said, deciding to be as honest as they were. "I have never gone a day without food. I suppose that's one of the things that makes me a princess, even if I don't dance at balls and win the hearts of knights. I've never thought of that."

It was like Gina said: you couldn't really compare the two things. Rapunzel had been lonely her whole life but had more than enough food. Here were children who got to play with each other every day, had the infinite freedom of the woods and road—and went starving every year.

Why did it have to be a choice? Who got to choose?

"*I* think being a princess must be boring," the oldest girl said. "Having to dress in fancy clothes all the time and act all proper and learn Latin. *I* would rather climb trees and marry a highwayman."

"You don't *know* any highwaymen," another girl said, hitting her on the shoulder.

This was when Flynn returned from the cider maker's, brushing foam from his lip and handing Gina a tankard.

"Split it with Witchy here," Flynn said, nodding at Rapunzel. "And chug; I think we'd better get a hustle on."

The children made a collective, disappointed *awwwww*.

(Except for the girl who had said she would marry a highwayman; she nudged her friend, pointed at Flynn, and whispered, "Who's *he*?")

"Thank you for a lovely afternoon," Rapunzel said with a curtsy. "You have given me much to think about."

Gina offered the tankard for Rapunzel to drink first, and she gulped it thirstily. It was refreshing and dry and tasted like biting into a fresh autumn apple.

"Skoal," Gina said, taking it back and toasting.

"Well, there's definitely bad news on the horizon,"

Flynn said. "Too many sightings of mercenaries and armed men from outside the kingdom. People here are locking up their valuables and daughters, and sending complaints to the royal guards, but that's it. And there's no talk of royal princesses, evil witches, hidden towers, or magic hair."

"And what about missing crowns?" Gina asked innocently.

"There might be a little speculation on that," Flynn allowed. "We should probably head to the castle as soon as possible with the next group or merchant caravan we see."

"All right," Gina said, wiping her lips. "I'm going to return this mug—maybe get a refill. . . ."

Rapunzel and Flynn strolled through the village, looking at the little houses and watching the children re-form their playgroups, figuring out the rest of the afternoon that no longer had a princess in it. The fields had a haze hanging over them: pollen and dust and a thousand little spiders floating on whisper-silk parachutes, seeking out foreign ground to start their lives. Rarely did spiders ever make it as high as her tower, though it did happen. She caught one now and cupped it in her hands to peer at it. The tiny spider lifted up its front legs as if waving at her. She raised her arms high and let it go again, watching it spiral up into the winds with wonder and envy.

"Speaking of the crown, you'll probably be wanting

this back," Flynn said, producing it like a magic trick, balancing the rim on the tips of his fingers.

"I'm sorry I threw that at you," she said, not taking it.

"Please—I've had far worse thrown at me by women. If *only* more ladies would throw crowns at me. Instead of shoes, or goblets, or daggers . . ."

"How much of what you say is actually true?"

"Less than I'd like and more than a royal princess ever needs to hear," he said—and there was a trace of truth in his voice, something real.

"All right," she said, taking the crown and putting it back into her bag.

"What, you're not going to wear it?" he asked in mock shock. "It's still before the summer solstice: velvet dresses and crowns before five o'clock are totally acceptable."

She laughed and suddenly she realized that at some point, while she was playing with the children and he was supposedly getting news and cider, he had shaved. His cheeks were still a little raw from the blade, but their pinkness certainly didn't take away from his looks. And now his cheekbones were even more pronounced. And wait . . . had he combed his hair?

Was this all because he was saying goodbye?

Was this it?

By tonight she would be awkwardly meeting parents

she'd never known, living in a castle, and he would be gone—probably with a bag of gold for a reward, off to find even more somewhere, on some adventure. Maybe Gina with him. Free on the road.

She looked back to the forest, the road where they had come from.

"What if I just turned around?" she asked.

"Excuse me?"

"What if I just ran away with you and Gina?"

"Oh, I work strictly alone. No room for amateurs," he said, pointing a thumb back at Gina.

Rapunzel gave him a glowering look.

"All right, all right. I kid; she can hold her own. You, however, cannot. Unless your hair can also shoot Gina-style stone missiles . . ."

"Okay, and about that. Here I have this amazing magical head of hair," she said, tossing and swishing it for emphasis. "I don't fully understand its powers. Would it be so selfish to lock myself away as the Goodwife has, with her, to study and figure it all out? To truly become a sorcerer, a master of it? Even if it takes a hundred years?"

"I guess that all depends on what you want to do with your life," Flynn said, rubbing his chin with his hand. "My wants are pretty simple. What do you *want* to do?"

"You know, up until recently I had wondered that a lot.

Now I think it might be the wrong question. Maybe it's what *should* I do."

"Who cares what you *should* do? Life is short. People are cruel. Have fun while the sun shines and let everyone else sort themselves out."

"Oh, is that the great Flynn Rider dispensing advice?" Rapunzel asked, then immediately felt bad about it. "I'm sorry, that was uncalled for."

"No, you're spot on," he said a little sadly. "That *is* how Flynn Rider lives. But he also knows what he's talking about: the world doesn't appreciate *shoulds*. My parents should have lived, or should have kept me. The orphanage should have stopped the older kids beating me up. I should be able to earn a decent living doing something that was legal—if I wanted. Which I don't. But the point is, if you feel you *should* do something, then do it. But because you want to. Not because you have to."

"That's confusing," Rapunzel said with a smile. But what did she want to do?

Play with children. Every day.

Ride a horse.

Never, ever, live in a tower again.

Protect harmless old witches from cruelty.

Rebuild the Snuggly Duckling.

Stop people from starving in the winter.

Make a difference.

Not just float away into the distance like a glowing lantern. Above everyone, a spark quickly forgotten.

"I want to meet my parents," she said with more emotion than she had meant. "I can't choose anything until I see *all* my choices."

"But once you meet your parents, the royal couple, there's no turning back," Flynn warned her.

"I know."

They had somehow drawn closer together. She held her bag tightly in both hands, pressing it against her chest. There was the faintest scent of something foreign on his skin, sweet and deep—that didn't have even a trace of goat fat in it. A shaving oil, maybe . . .

Why am I thinking about shaving oils? she thought.

"So . . . what about you? You want to live happily ever after on a giant pile of money," she said softly. "And . . . nothing else?"

"It's pointless to waste time dreaming of things you can't have," he said, voice catching. "I *can* have lots of money."

"But *is* that all you want?" she pressed.

His eyes were wide and unblinking. And so soft and brown! She could fall into them, be dragged under . . .

"GUYS!"

Gina was shouting, running toward them at full tilt, pumping both her arms.

"Horsemen—a dozen of them," she huffed, out of breath. "Coming from the north. *Not* the royal guard, but I couldn't see their insignia."

"They couldn't know we're here," Flynn said, putting a hand on his blade.

Gina nodded. "I think they're just passing through—avoiding the city. But we should still get out of here."

Rapunzel frowned, looking. Raising up dust on a road that was mostly dust anyway was indeed a phalanx of horses, not quite trotting but not walking, either. There was something arrogant about their gait and the men who sat on them, stiff-backed and plumed. Rapunzel felt an ugly cramp in her stomach. The men who had grabbed her and tied her up were bad—but there was something even more ominous and immediately hateful about these fellows.

Maybe it was the grey whip-thin dogs that paced beside them, strangely pointed noses tasting the air like they were blind.

"The *vérhounds*—Bathory's dogs!" Flynn swore. "Run! Back to the forest!"

Suddenly one of the dogs began to howl: a high-pitched, ghostly keening that didn't sound at all like a dog.

The next thirty seconds were the worst Rapunzel ever experienced. Even including the days when she was young and alone and crying in the tower, when her mother didn't come.

They ran.

Gina and Flynn each took an arm to help her keep up. Rapunzel's body, already stretched from days of doing things she never had before, was once again put to the test. She forced her feet to move, her legs to open wider, dig the ground faster.

There was nothing but the pounding of their feet and ragged breaths. Everything else seemed strangely silent . . . until the hoofbeats began to clatter right behind them.

Gina stopped, let go of Rapunzel, and spun around, her sling out and aimed. Rapunzel stumbled. Confused, she tried to stay with her friend.

Flynn shoved Rapunzel forward. He *threw* her away from them, like an apple core, like a child. Then he too turned to face their pursuers.

Gina had already managed to knock one rider off with a missile and was winding up for another shot. Flynn ran forward, screaming and waving his hands and slashing his blade madly. These were battle horses, trained for chaos in the field, but one succumbed to his display. Its eyes rolled in panic and it veered away despite the terrible yanking its rider gave to the reins.

Heedless of the spiraling, dangerously sharp hooves, Gina dropped her sling and attacked the man closest to her.

She sank her dagger deep into the unprotected part of his leg, between boot and knee.

He screamed, the horses screamed . . .

Rapunzel knew she should keep running. But she also knew that she wouldn't be able to outrun anyone on horseback. And she couldn't look away; her fate depended on the next few moments, on the skill and strength of two people who just a few days ago didn't know her at all and were now risking their lives to save her. Despite there not *necessarily* being a reward.

Flynn managed to steal a sword from one of the men and wielded it adeptly, spinning and twirling—but he was surrounded.

What should she do? Should she—

She never got to figure it out, because then the dogs were on her.

They lunged and nosed and pawed and howled, knocking her backward. Teeth and claws and paws and sharp bony things were suffocating her, stepping on her, pecking, scratching . . .

But not biting.

They had found their quarry and were excited, alerting their masters to the fact. Beyond that they did nothing, trained to neither kill nor rend.

"Get *off*!" Rapunzel screeched, one hand protecting Pascal. She tried to roll onto her belly, instinct kicking in.

Suddenly she found herself lifted up and away from the dogs by rough hands under her armpits.

Spun in the air and held over someone's head she got a brief, terrifying view of the fight:

Gina was pulling a man off his horse, fingers dug deep in his side.

The last mounted mercenary hit at Flynn with the pommel of his sword, knocking him cleanly on the head.

Rapunzel screamed.

Flynn crumpled to the ground.

The man wheeled his horse around and changed his grasp on the sword, holding it more like a spear.

He hurled it down at Flynn.

Gina let go of the man she was fighting and threw herself at Flynn, grabbing him around the torso and pulling him out of the way. The sword still caught his arm—in what looked like the socket of his shoulder. Not entirely unconscious, Flynn screamed.

"NO!" Rapunzel shouted. "*NO!*"

And then she was being pulled through the woods, away from her friends, in the hands of the enemy.

Rapunzel

Now she was entirely alone.

Rapunzel had to rescue herself this time, and not rely on others—her mother, a random girl, a famous thief, a white witch—to save her.

She tried to focus on that while her hands were bound behind her and she was thrown across the back of a horse. Much more professionally than the previous time she had been tied up.

(Upon reflection, she realized that if she was becoming a connoisseur of how one is properly trussed up, there was something terribly wrong with either the entire world, or her own life.)

She tried to summon her powers. She couldn't quite

reach the moon charm she had made, but it didn't really matter. She was too exhausted to concentrate, and badly bruised with her head hitting the muscled, hard side of the horse with every hoofbeat. She couldn't even sleep for all the jostling and bouncing; she simply lay there in a dazed state, half upside down, watching the shadowy shapes of trees pass by.

At some point her weary and worn-out body must have finally given up. When she came to again they were still riding, but she was sat up this time, in front of—and leaning against—another rider, a giant man almost the size of the horse he rode.

Also, most of her hair had been bagged up—literally—and tied in a sack hanging off her head like a giant snood made out of burlap.

Pascal crept from his hiding place on her neck and put a delicate two-toed foot on her cheek.

"I'm okay," she whispered.

"What?" her guard demanded in a deep, guttural voice.

"What?" she asked back.

Confused and ultimately uninterested, the man lapsed into silence.

I think it's early morning—Day 9. Just past half moon— I wonder what my hair can do now. I wonder if I could . . . I wonder if I could do something to him.

A few tendrils of her hair had escaped the bag, delicately snaking down and touching the man's thigh.

But now that she could reach it—where *was* the little charm she had made, to help her focus? Rapunzel began to panic. She must have dropped it, or it had gotten lost somewhere since she had been kidnapped.

"Come on, moon; moon, do your thing," she murmured desperately, trying to visualize the moon as it would be now.

"Is it working?" she whispered, rolling her eyes to see if she could see the glow.

Pascal nodded quickly.

"Stop that," her captor hissed, whacking her on the back of the head.

It *hurt*. Rapunzel saw black and then stars for a moment.

"Save your tricks to impress the lady with."

Lady . . . ? Lady Bathory? The one whose name made Flynn and Gina shudder?

Rapunzel didn't try any incantations on her hair again. She would save that for *the lady*—as a last-ditch effort.

Soon they entered hilly scrublands. Fields larger than those of Harecross rolled up and down the landscape, devoted entirely to grain, but something about them seemed dry and barren. Lonely, run-down huts were few and far between, like islands in a fishless sea. The sun was hidden behind thin, soupy clouds and everything looked forlorn.

And then . . . of all the crazy things . . . a *carriage* rolled up to meet them.

A fancy, noble carriage, like out of a fairy tale.

It was coal black and drawn by four equally black horses. Painted on its side in blood red and corpse green was a slavering and ugly dragon, curled around what appeared to be the sharpened teeth of a monstrous ogre.

The driver was dressed in fine clothes and had a plume in his hat, and the footman dressed fancily as well. But neither was fair to look at, each as big as Rapunzel's captor, with muscles and scars to match. They looked like a pair of villains who had been forced into velvet and leggings to playact.

Not how she imagined the four-in-hand of Cinderella.

The footman leapt down—not lightly—and ran over to help ease her off the horse. She slid down ungracefully and pitched forward, almost hitting her head on the ground. Her fall was stopped just in time by the footman, who had, she noticed distractedly, nearly lashless grey eyes. That was all she could concentrate on as he led her, stumbling, over to the carriage.

"Apologies for my inappropriate handling of you," he said in a whisper that was lighter than she expected. "But

I fear you would fall and break your pretty neck if I let you go freely."

She wondered at the way he phrased that: almost as if she would do it on purpose.

She stepped up carefully into the carriage. Any further thought she had that this was a vehicle for a princess was immediately dashed. There were sturdy bars across the windows, a large dead bolt *on the outside* of the door. And personally, if she were designing a conveyance for comfortably traveling princesses, she would have covered the hard, plain bench with soft upholstery like velvet or chenille. Otherwise it was so shiny . . . easily wiped . . .

An order was cried, a whip applied to the horses' hind sides. The carriage began to roll.

What would Flynn Rider do?

He would somehow pick the lock of the door, even with his hands tied.

She had no chance of that; she had no idea *how.* So she turned her attentions to the outside, to try to figure out where she was going—in case she managed to escape, and needed to find her way home.

They passed through a very dismal-looking town, seemingly empty. Only hints of its inhabitants appeared in its cracks and alleys: shadows of bodies slipping away into doorways, the sounds of running. The few old people who remained on the streets turned from the carriage, spitting or making signs of the cross.

It was like Rapunzel had wandered into one of the scarier parables about what happens to little girls who don't behave.

After the terrible village, the road climbed steeply into a range of sharp stony peaks. Grey escarpments rose like thick pages in a book, layers and slices falling away into gorges, crumbling into dust. What little greenery there was in these desolate highlands clung to the sides of the road and the series of alpine meadows it connected.

Suddenly the carriage was on a straightaway, a high bridge across a deep gorge. Rapunzel pressed her face against the window as hard as she could to get a look at her destination.

It was a castle.

A small one, far smaller than the palace on the island. Honestly, it wasn't more than a few Rapunzel-towers thrown together behind a wall, with some interconnected build-ings. These towers were pointed, polygonal, angry-looking. This was a keep at the end of the world—garrisoned against any and all intruders.

If Rapunzel was still hoping for a rescue, the sight of the bleak, dull fortress before her utterly dashed that.

The horses shuffled to a stop; men in black-and-red

outfits ran out and began to tend to them. The footman put out a set of steps for Rapunzel to descend, unlocked the door, and gave her his—kid-gloved—hand for balance.

Really, he circled her wrist with his thumb and finger; a slight squeeze let her knew immediately what would happen if she tried to run. He would break her arm in two.

Inside, the castle seemed even colder than the chill mountain air despite the preponderance of tapestries, rugs, mirrors, candles, and even flowering branches and bowls of blossoms that crowded the space. All the furniture was ebony; all the decorations were in shades of black, red, and the green of the heraldic dragon. The suits of armor standing forever at attention in the halls were smeary with tarnish, some of their banners falling apart with mold.

The mixture of feminine touches and brutal reminders of the past was terribly confusing to Rapunzel's already-rattled mind.

"Here, My Lady," the footman said, shoving her into a small room. He took out a sharp black knife and sliced through the bonds around her wrists. "You can take your hair down now, if you like. But if a single strand gets anywhere near the countess I'll stab you in the heart myself. Now wash yourself from the trip—you will sup with Bathory tonight. She likes her girls clean."

He didn't leer, and he didn't stick around, either,

slamming—and locking—the door behind him. Rapunzel shook the handle, but it was solidly bolted. She examined the tiny room in despair: there was a basin of water, a linen washrag, and even a bowl of scented oil and a brush for her nails.

"Not doing it," Rapunzel decided.

She *did* look in the mirror (there were a lot of mirrors in the castle; the extravagance was unthinkable). Her cheeks were a little streaked with dust, and there were dry tracks where there had been tears. Did her face seem a little different? Changed in the quick week, the strange week, the most adventurous week she'd ever had? Pascal nuzzled her sadly.

"I think we're in trouble," she murmured.

And then she sat down, knees drawn up, to wait.

Memorial Sloan Kettering

"Whoa, that got real dark real quick," Daniella whispered.

"Told you Bathory was coming back," Brendan said with a grin.

His sister moved her legs a little uncomfortably under the blankets.

"This isn't going to get, like—you have a plan to get Rapunzel out, right?"

"Afraid of a little blood?"

"You *know* I love horror movies. But this is—like, Rapunzel! *And also.* What happened to Flynn and Gina? How badly hurt is Flynn? And what did Gothel do, just fly away and disappear after her and Raps's fight?"

"Ohhhh no." Brendan shook his head. "Gothel isn't done yet. She's way too clever and greedy for that. In fact, she's coming up real soon. . . ."

Rapunzel

No one came to get her for a long time—the candle in the washroom had burned down to nearly half. It was as if they had forgotten her. Every time she started to fall asleep she splashed a little of the water on her face (but not enough to wash it).

When the door finally opened it was by a new person: a thin, hollow-eyed girl who made even the neat black-and-scarlet servant's dress she wore look drab and unappealing.

"The countess awaits you for dinner," she whispered.

When Rapunzel pushed through the door, she saw that her old friend the footman was *also* there, obviously to prevent her escaping.

She began to have serious doubts that he was really a footman at all.

This was, despite all appearances, Rapunzel's first noble-to-noble meeting and meal; she decided to act like it was voluntary. No—that it was her *pleasure.* She held herself tall and followed the girl at a decorous distance, though she desperately wanted to get close and whisper a thousand questions. The footman said nothing. He followed them both like this was the most normal thing in the world.

They came to a long and narrow feasting hall with a positively enormous fireplace—in which there burned a tiny, smoky fire in the middle of its mostly empty stones. The table was set for only two, with dishes and bowls decorated with sparkling jet and goblets of red crystal. There were no knives, only spoons, and their handles were bone.

Everything was horrible and ridiculous, tasteless and terrifying at the same time. *A cup of goat milk poured into one of the glasses would look like creamy blood,* Rapunzel realized. *Disgusting.*

The footman pulled out a chair and she sat, adjusting her simple woolen dress as if it were fancy robes and skirts. She was too busy looking at the things on the table and trying not to be nervous to notice her hostess actually arrive.

"Well, well. We finally meet."

The countess—for it must have been she—lurked at the other end of the room, a decidedly fake smile set around her mouth and her hands clasped tightly like she was trying to keep something from escaping them. She was small but voluptuous and had a neck like a swan. Her skin, where it was exposed on her face and hands, was white as a cloud and flawless. She wore a white silk dress with gold at the cuffs, a bodice and overskirt of scarlet. Her snood was thickly netted gold wire set with pearls; more of a crown, really.

She would have been an absolute vision of loveliness if not for the malicious insanity in her eyes. It was so obvious, so decidedly *there* that it was shocking; Rapunzel looked at the servant and the footman to see if they noticed, but both had their faces turned down to the ground.

The corners of the woman's perfect mouth twitched constantly.

"Countess Bathory, I presume," Rapunzel said, not getting up—as Flynn would have reminded her, she was a royal princess and far outranked the villain in the corner. Until she could summon her powers (and somehow touch the other woman with her hair), she might as well play the one card she had.

The woman's mouth twitched even more.

"Of course. And you are Princess Rapunzel, which fact is entirely irrelevant from here on out."

The woman sat down. As if that was the signal, a servant came in with a plate of sliced meat, cheese, bread, grapes, and hard sausages. All easily eaten without a knife. At the countess's seat was placed what looked like a piece of venison, barely roasted, pink to the bone. Two large knives were set next to it. One was a normal carving knife, the other a glittering thing that was more suited to violence than viands.

The countess immediately picked up the sinuous, evil-looking knife and began to saw through her meat with gusto and relish.

Rapunzel kept her hands at her sides.

"Well, go on," the countess said, with a casual gesture of the knife. "It's not poisoned. I could have you killed a thousand times already without lifting a finger. I wouldn't need to poison you."

Reluctantly, Rapunzel picked up a tiny piece of cheese and began to nibble on it.

"Why have you brought me here?" she asked as calmly as she could.

"Are you daft?" the countess asked, looking up, genuinely surprised. "Your *hair*. Your beautiful, magical hair that can kill. I'm going to rule all of Europe."

And with that, the countess went back to attacking her meat and shoving it into her mouth.

Rapunzel blinked.

Flynn's words came back to her: *Whatd'ya think is more likely: a bunch of warring, creepy lords and ladies running all over enemy territory to re-imprison a dangerous girl . . . or trying to grab her for their own use?*

He and Gina had been right. Rapunzel wasn't a prisoner because she was dangerous; she was a treasure kept safe because of her power. They all wanted her for her hair—somehow they all knew what it could do. But . . .

"It doesn't work like that," Rapunzel said despite herself.

"It had better," the countess said with a shrug. "Otherwise you're dead."

Rapunzel tried not to panic at the casual, matter-of-fact way the woman had spoken.

"It's been a while since I've had one of my baths," the countess went on, suddenly admiring her right hand, turning it this way and that. The knife it held glinted. "Do you know what I discovered, when I was young?"

Rapunzel shook her head. She kept forcing herself to eat bits of cheese through her terror. Flynn—and Gina—would tell her not to show fear. To pretend she had the upper hand, was unconcerned.

It was hard.

"A clumsy servant cut herself with a fruit knife once, and where the blood landed on me, like magic, my skin was remade. Youthful, soft, moist, supple. It was a revelation—no, an inflection point, you might say." She held her gaze on her hand for another moment, then shrugged and went back to eating.

"So I had her killed for her clumsiness and washed my entire body in her blood. And kept it up, with others. Works best with maidens, of course, but they are getting harder and harder to come by. I've used up almost all of them in Čachtice and have had to seek them further afield.

"So here is how it stands.

"You use your powers to help me defeat my enemies and conquer the land, or I cut you and bathe in your blood. And, probably, take your beautiful hair and have something woven out of it. A tapestry or a counterpane or something. Waste not, want not!"

Rapunzel swallowed, but suddenly the back of her throat was very dry.

This was the world outside her tower? This was a real thing that happened in it?

"Whoever told you about my hair didn't understand its magic fully," Rapunzel said slowly, forcing herself to pick up a piece of—dark red—sausage and eat it. Obviously and slowly, as if she were enjoying it.

"Well," the countess said, thinking. "I would *like* to rule all of the land. If that doesn't pan out, perhaps you will still be useful. I have been running out of ways to . . . subdue and drain my girls. It's grown very boring. Perhaps you might make it interesting again!"

Rapunzel tried not to shudder, tried not to imagine her hair around the servant girl's neck, being told to kill her like a bird.

"How, ah, how *did* you come to know about the secret of my hair?" she asked casually, using a spoon to pick up a grape. "I've been hidden from the world for nearly twenty years."

"The information was imparted to a select few. You were put up for auction after we received trustworthy proof of your powers. The highest bidder would win your hand in marriage. Or, in my case, just your hand."

Rapunzel nearly choked on her grape. Being sold into marriage wasn't that surprising; it was a common occurrence in all the fairy tales and knights' quests she had read. Princesses were always being handed off to the best fighter, or the foreign king with the most land, or whoever defeated the ogre, or whatnot.

It was more the idea that this group of people, these nameless nobles, had known *all about* her and her hair, and had been watching her—even if not directly—for years. Rapunzel had thought she was all alone in the tower. This was far worse: she *wasn't* entirely alone. She imagined faceless heads surrounding her bedroom, looking in. . . .

"So, ah, you won the auction," Rapunzel stammered, trying to stay focused.

"No, it wasn't even half over yet. We were in the middle of the second round of bidding. You *fled*." She said this accusingly, levelling a knife at Rapunzel. "You escaped. A less trusting person might wonder if the disappearance was all contrived, to drive up the price or whatnot. *I* believe in the inherent goodness of people, however."

Rapunzel couldn't hide the expression on her face and was glad the countess was too busy picking a piece of gristle out of her meat to notice.

"We all set off like idiots through the countryside to find you—like that was our *job*. Like I don't have better things to do. This was supposed to be neat and easy. Clean. But there it is. I happen to have a little more skill than my fellow lords and ladies at hunting down and rounding up wanted girls. My beloved *vérhounds*! So I found you first.

"And now that I've found you, I think I'll keep you. To hell with the auction! If they don't like it, well . . . good luck storming my castle, especially with my new weapon of mass destruction."

The countess smiled (with dimples!), very pleased with herself.

After a moment, perhaps disappointed with Rapunzel's lack of response, she added: "That's you, you know."

"I know," Rapunzel said, trying not to sound exasperated. Couldn't the countess be one thing—sadistic, disgusting, or evil? Not *also* boring and needy?

And there was one piece of the puzzle missing. *Who* arranged the auction? Who knew all about her powers, and all the other nobles? Who was it who managed this while keeping her locked up in secret for twenty years?

There was only one answer, of course, obvious and crushingly disappointing.

The king and queen—her parents.

Gothel

Gothel raged for hours after she fled the hidden vale. That girl just didn't understand how much she owed her mother! *Nearly two decades of her life* had been wasted on a child who wasn't really hers.

Of course in the end Gothel was more practical than emotional; once she calmed down she immediately began plotting her next move. There was no sense returning home yet; all the pieces were still in play, and, ironically, *because* of the stupid "real" witch, Rapunzel had so far avoided winding up in the hands of any one noble.

(Gothel was under no illusion that anyone would nicely hand her over and continue the auction. No, there would be bloodshed before this was over.)

And then she heard a chilling bit of news: the wretched girl had gone and let herself be caught by Countess Bathory! Was there any limit to that child's incompetence?

Disgraceful.

Even worse, Gothel hadn't seen a single cent of the dowry—er, auction money—that was so rightfully hers.

Bathory was irrational and violent, her fortress difficult to breach. There was no way to prize Rapunzel out of the situation. It would take an army.

Luckily, *that* was something Gothel could arrange. Tempers were high; unemployed armed men were all over the place. Armies were easily assembled in such situations. And she knew just where to start.

Despite the endless petty wars and border squabbles across the land, wherever there was a large enough campfire and skin of wine, men forgot their loyalties and sang songs and told stories instead. Sometimes even the lords and counts joined in.

Especially if that campfire was the Snuggly Duckling Pop-Up, a little bit of the old tavern returned to life.

Gothel entered the cheery circle of revelers from the shadows like a rat, the absolutely enormous bonfire reflected large in her eyes. A thrown-together bar stood in one corner of the clearing, barrels of ale holding up a halved log for a tabletop. All the old serving wenches were there, and they tried to keep the spirit of the original place, flirting with customers and handing out flagons with threats.

"Excuse me, m'lady," a tiny old man said, suddenly appearing before—and blocking—Gothel. It was the thug known as Shorty, often underestimated by the authorities (but always a little into his cups). "For enjoyment of the fire and access to the quality refreshment you were accustomed to at the original Snuggly Duckling, we are asking for a *pittance* of a donation, all of which will be put toward a brave new Snuggly Duckling establishment."

"You must be joking," Gothel said with a sneer, trying to look over his shoulder.

When Shorty continued to bounce up and around to block her view she finally gave in, throwing a copper piece at him with disgust.

"Most appreciated, beautiful lady," Shorty continued with great dignity. "Tonight the entertainment will be from Henry John Deutschendorf Jr., son of the Baron Deutschendorf and durn handy with a banjo and lute, if I do say so myself. Also, we're having a Tuesday Takeover of the grub: Ikram and Ayanna from the Sun Countries are preparing a magnificent—and vegetarian—stew for your enjoyment."

Gothel growled and pushed the little man out of her way.

Someone else might have thoroughly enjoyed the night;

it was almost like old times at the Duckling (albeit with more forced hilarity and a few extra knife fights). The old regulars were in the back, keeping to themselves.

The unusual presence of *multiple* lords there with their men meant the silver flowed freer—and so, therefore, did the ale (and vegetarian stew). They loudly toasted Gothel when she made herself known . . . but also roundly cursed the straits they were now in.

"All of this running around chasing the girl, and what have we to show for it?" Duke Kraske complained. "No girl, no hair, no marriage, no magical powers . . . Can't you keep control of your own daughter?"

Viscount Thongel raised his tankard in salute of these words. "You mean Frederic and Arianna's daughter. And *my* future queen."

"But haven't you heard?" Gothel asked innocently. "I was overwhelmed. Flynn Rider and his evil compatriots *stole* her . . . and delivered her to *Countess Bathory*! Who plans to keep her . . . and avoid the auction entirely."

Duke Kraske made a grunt of anger and disgust in the back of his throat. He slugged down the rest of his drink and wiped his red, fleshy lips with the back of his hand.

"I hate that woman," Baron Smeinhet growled. "There's something unnatural about her."

"She's started prowling *our* lands for victims," Thongel

added reluctantly. "Apparently she used up all the young women in her own country."

"I'll never say anything against an independent woman or a nobleman's . . . *hobbies*," Gothel drawled. "But the fact is that *she has Rapunzel*. Without paying a cent. You have all been cheated out of your chance . . . and by such a villain! Why, Lord Kraske, didn't you say your cousin's daughter was kidnapped by her?"

"From her boarding school, aye, that's what he claims," Kraske said. "She disappeared one night, no trace—but Bathory's carriage was supposedly seen near the place earlier."

"Well, if she's moved on to our noble girls, it's long past time we stopped her," Smeinhet said, slamming his fist down. "Rapunzel is as good an excuse as any. And a better prize than most. Down with Bathory!"

Men cheered, raising their tankards in the air.

Serving wenches looked at each other and shook their heads: how long had girls like *them* been disappearing and no one cared?

Gothel let a small, demure smile cross her lips. Let them have Rapunzel, Bathory, whatever. Let them raise their swords and kill each other for glory or gold.

This was what she craved: to make men and women do her will . . . without coin, a throne, threats, or magic.

This was power.

Rapunzel

Her parents had sold her.

The very people she was running to. The only people who *could* legally auction her off under the laws of the land. The folks who had probably wanted a son instead, to inherit the kingdom and rule at their death. The king and queen who had immediately sent her away once it became clear what a dangerous baby she was, and hidden her in a tower until she was old enough to marry.

"When was . . . all this arranged? When I was baby?" Rapunzel asked, trying to sound casual.

"I am not precisely sure when, exactly. I suppose word got out at some point—it became a *thing*, as they say, among us chosen few, around the time you were a child. Before or around your first blood. When your powers really began to grow. Those of us who might be interested in such a thing were contacted and told you would be available in a few years."

Rapunzel's head spun. This didn't make any sense. Her powers hadn't changed that much over the years; up until recently she had only and always killed chickens. Nothing more or less, ever since she was little.

But also, were the king and queen somehow actively spying on her? Did they get weekly reports from Gothel?

"Pray forgive my confusion," Rapunzel said, trying to sound as formal as a person in one of her knight stories. "I'm curious how my parents kept such close eyes on the situation, hidden away as I was."

"Your parents? You mean the king and queen? What are you talking about?" the countess asked in surprise. "I don't think they know anything about this. I believe the plan is to just sort of present it as a fait accompli: here is your daughter, married to some stupid lord, good luck with the idiot son she'll produce that will give her husband control over all of the kingdom legally. Luckily for you, you're in *my* hands. At least you'll be spared that nasty son business."

"Wait—I mean, *hold*," Rapunzel said, forgetting her put-on manners in her confusion. "If it wasn't my parents who did this, who was it?"

"Are you daft, girl? Your marriage, the auction, was all arranged by the witch who kept you captive—Mother Gothel."

The secret part of Rapunzel that seemed to know things before she actively did accepted this information immediately; almost expected it. This answer connected all the dots far more neatly than any other possible explanation: all the lies about her parenthood and hair and danger, why she was kept a prisoner, Gothel showing up out of nowhere to "take her home" . . . All the little bits and pieces that didn't add up quite right but certainly didn't point to a normal, good-hearted mother.

Despite this, despite fully understanding all of this, to the girl still partially trapped in the tower it was the final pain in a long-coming heartbreak.

"All right, I think that's enough questions," the countess declared. "It's been quite a day and I'm tired. Magda here will show you to your room."

Bathory gestured at the serving girl with her knife.

But not at the footman! Rapunzel felt a surge of hope. She would think like Flynn and find a way to get out!

Bathory had started using her meat knife—yuck—on an

apple, and was very quickly peeling it, flaying the shiny red skin off in perfect spirals.

"If you try to escape, I will of course punish you—you don't need your hands to work magic with your hair, I am told. But first we will punish *Magda*. And it will be slow, I promise. . . ."

Rapunzel's stomach turned. Magda didn't even pale. Resigned, with an exhaustion that could have come only from being terrified every moment she was alive, the maid motioned weakly for Rapunzel to follow her out of the room.

"Do not forget, Magda: she is a royal prin*cess*," Bathory said with a nasty smile. "You will curtsy to her and show her all appropriate forms of respect."

Rapunzel couldn't even tell if the woman was being ironic—or simply stating matters as she saw them.

In the end, she supposed, it didn't really matter.

Rapunzel's room was at the top of the tallest turret in the castle, up a seemingly endless and dizzying spiral flight of stairs. Despite the placement, it was a fairly large room and had its own garderobe. There were furs of all kind of animals hung on the walls for insulation; mismatched, random, some with holes. No artistry or respect for the animal. Like everything in Lady Bathory's castle, nauseating.

Hysterical laughter almost overwhelmed Rapunzel

when she looked out of the high, narrow windows in her room.

"I'm in a tower again," she explained to Magda.

The girl nodded uncertainly, bowed—then corrected herself, curtsying.

"All this stuff about the blood and the girls—it's true?" Rapunzel pressed.

Magda's hazel eyes looked like distant moons, bleak and alien, that rolled tiredly over an infertile land.

"There are almost no women left in my village because of her—habits," she answered tonelessly. "I suppose I'm next. I will bring you another meal later," she added with almost no pause between her thoughts. She took out a large black key (with a skull on its end, of course) and left to go on with her other tasks.

The moment she was gone Rapunzel fell on her bed in despair, overwhelmed by the idea of a person who had so completely given up: there was no fight, no desire, no *anything* left in Magda.

If Rapunzel could escape—*would* she? Knowing Magda would die? Knowing she might lose her own hands?

(Although she suspected that Gothel actually knew so little about her powers, and told her bidders so little, and Bathory seemed so easily impressed and confused by magic, that she could easily convince the countess that hands were indeed necessary. Then again, the hideous woman might choose to cut off her nose or something else instead.)

Pascal crawled out of her hair and took a few tentative steps down her arm toward the end of the bed, toward the fireplace, and then stopped when he seemed to realize it was unlit. And likely to stay unlit. He looked back at her, an unreadable expression on his saurian face.

Rapunzel raised her arm so he was in the air, looking down at her. He licked his left eye, tasted the currents with his long sticky tongue, and patted her with one of his front feet.

"Hey, can you see or smell things I can't?" Rapunzel asked. "Can you help me find a way out of here?"

Pascal looked at the very solid, locked, banded-with-iron oaken door. He looked around the rest of the room, thinking. Then he gestured to the window—too narrow for even a small girl like Rapunzel—and she placed him carefully on the sill. He easily slipped through to the outside. A moment later he was back: he shrugged. Perhaps he could make his way down—eventually—and then what? How long would it take for him to find help? What form would that help take? It would take an army to storm the castle, or the most elite sneak thief ever (Rider), provided he survived his wound.

And even then Magda's life hung in the balance.

"She's dead already," Rapunzel said aloud, thinking about the girl's eyes. It was the darkest thing she had ever thought.

Another thing to thank Mother Gothel for.

"Mother," Rapunzel muttered.

She had lied for *nineteen years* about Rapunzel's real parentage, and what had happened to them—and then quickly "apologized" when she was found out and said it was for her own good. Rapunzel could almost swallow that in her desperation for someone to love her, the only person she had a connection to her entire life. A *mother,* even a bad one.

But this . . . mother . . . had told a bunch of rich strangers about her murderhair. Had promised her daughter's hand to the one who paid the most.

In fairy tales things happened like this. So often, in fact, that a reader might even say that the princesses always *knew* it was their fates to be used as pawns. That's why they ran away when they could, or relaxed when the beast they had been promised to turned out to be actually nice after all despite his tusks.

But in none of the stories did a mother and daughter say:

"I love you."

"I love you more."

"I love you *most.*"

Was that just pure deception on Gothel's part? Were all her professions of love—even to infant, toddler Rapunzel—a lie?

Bathory was a straight-up monster who was honest about her desires and motivation. She wanted to rule the world. She believed killing young women would allow her to stay young forever.

Was that worse than a woman who sold a person she called daughter?

"Don't be so dramatic, Raps," she said aloud, stroking Pascal. "Girls . . . lots of girls . . . have *lost their lives* to that beast downstairs. You're upset now because you've met Magda, and now you know her story. But you haven't *been* Magda.

"You've been lied to and made to feel loved and then realized you weren't. Which is sad but not deadly. You can't compare the two at all.

"Right, Pascal?"

She turned over, facedown into the pillow, and wept.

Gina and Flynn

"Stay *still!*"

Flynn groaned but kept trying to sit up. Gina put a hand on his chest and pushed him back down.

He groaned louder.

"Daughter, remind me not to come to you with a migraine," the Goodwife muttered.

After the men had fled with Rapunzel, Gina had managed to grab the reins of one of the horses. She had hoisted Flynn up in front of her as quickly and carefully as she could and taken off into the forest. As soon as they were deep enough, she had called out: "*Mother!* Someone tell Mother I need help—one of us is hurt."

Whether birds, trees, or the invisible fungal threads that

connected all things under the forest floor wound up being the vector for communicating this request, Gina didn't know. But she was unsurprised when the shadows suddenly grew long and shapes became indistinct and the Goodwife stepped out of the bushes as if she had been merely behind the tree the whole time, waiting for them.

All the usual greetings, ironic exchanges, and conversational sparring between mother and daughter were silenced: the Goodwife took one look at the wounds on Flynn's head and her face grew grim.

"Follow me" was all she said, and Gina complied without a peep.

Now the three were in a tiny magical clearing in the forest: lime-green moss and tiny, sweet-scented flowers not seen elsewhere in the dark woods grew in profusion. In the middle of it a crystal-clear spring burbled whose waters were supposed to have healing properties. No one said it aloud, but it was very clear this was exactly the sort of place the king—or queen—of the forest would live: a golden-antlered stag, a snow-white hart, or . . .

Flynn was laid down on the thickest tuffets of moss, his head cradled in the Goodwife's shawl. She bathed his head and hair in water from the stream and laid whole, unblemished leaves of strange herbs on his eyes and forehead, and in his shoulder wound. When he finally began to breathe regularly, she tipped a tiny clay pot of a highly aromatic extract onto his tongue.

"Boneset for the skull," she muttered. "Gentian for the eyes. Mud from a cemetery stream to keep necrosis out. *Samui, tarseia, feun eys moida* . . . Where's Rapunzel?"

"They stole her," Gina answered, used to her mother's multitasking and sudden conversation switches.

"Bathory's men . . ." Flynn whispered. "Green dragon . . . teeth . . ."

The Goodwife looked grim. "You need to go after her."

"Flynn's okay with you?" Gina asked, getting up and putting her cloak on.

"No!" Flynn pushed himself up on his elbows, ripping open the wound in his head that had just begun to (magically) knit itself together. Scarlet blood trickled down his face again. "I'll go. . . ."

"You gotta be kidding me," Gina said. "*Look* at you."

"'m okay. . . ." He rolled over onto his side, trying to push himself up.

"You don't think I can rescue her by myself?" Gina demanded. "You *still* think I can't do anything?"

"Oh, do calm down, Gina," her mother said in irritation. "Not everything is about you and what you can and can't do. He's not even thinking about that. He loves Rapunzel. He just wants to help."

Gina's eyes widened in genuine surprise. "Really?" she asked, leaning over him. "You love her? Like, *love*?"

"Nnf . . . I dunno . . . why are we talking . . . should be riding . . ." Flynn forced his eyes open, tried to look like he was together. He did a remarkably good job, giving an old Flynn Rider style smile: all teeth, eyebrows raised suggestively, mouth pulled to the side in a way he obviously thought was devilishly handsome. He winked at the two ladies, but they were distracted by how that only spattered more blood on his cheek.

"If you get on a horse now, none of my fixes will stay," the Goodwife warned him.

It was like she had skipped over the part where they argued, and gone straight to the end where they had all given up and agreed he was going—despite the fact that he was so weak that with one bony old hand she could have kept him down on the ground. "Your head wounds are serious, Rider. With serious consequences. You get up now, I can't promise you'll stay alive."

"Or that you won't turn into even *more* of a drooling idiot," Gina added.

"Chance I'll have to take." He put a hand—somewhat unsteadily—on Gina's shoulder and looked into her eyes. "I *know* you'll do everything you can to rescue her. There's a castle and a bloodthirsty psycho, and the odds are totally stacked against you. But if there's anyone I believe could do it, it would be you, Gina. You're amazing. It's crazy the rest of the world hasn't realized that yet.

"But if I don't go and help . . . I'll never forgive myself."

"Aw," Gina said, trying not to smile. "You're so dumb. But right, this one time."

"All right, boy," the Goodwife said with a sigh. "Give me ten more minutes and two more cantrips. I can at least stabilize you—or, I could stabilize a goat. It's been a while since I've done this with a person. I'm sure it will be fine. And I'll pack up a little kit of draughts and poultices so you can keep going . . . for a bit. Gina, come watch how to apply them."

For Flynn the ten minutes might as well have been forever. The world around him faded out in different shades of dark; he watched them and debated whether or not to stay conscious.

And then he was waking up.

"Whoa," he said, blinking. "I feel . . . not bad."

Gina helped him sit up fully. They had washed his face and neck; he felt new and clean and ready to go.

And then a bolt of pain hit him in the forehead, worse than the worst morning after, like he had been punched through the skull with a mallet made of tacks.

"I wasn't kidding when I said it was a serious head

wound, Rider," the Goodwife said softly. "I have no magic that will really *fix* it all immediately—I don't know if anyone does, besides Rapunzel when the moon is full. You will be kept alive, and mostly functioning. But it isn't perfect."

"It's all good." Flynn put a hand to his head, gritted his teeth, *willed* himself to get up despite the pain.

Gina kept a hand on his arm and helped him when he seemed to need it, but otherwise stood there patiently as an object for him to lean on.

"You're going to need to ride seated *behind* Gina," the Goodwife insisted, hands on hips. "Keeping your neck straight. And sleep as much as you can."

"Oh, you don't need to worry about any male pride issues here," he assured them. "If you told me Gina had to carry me piggyback, I'd be all right with that, too."

Gina took the little packets and skins from her mother and tucked them away in the horse's panniers, tightened the saddle strap, and straightened the blanket. Then she helped Flynn get up, lacing her fingers for him to step in like a child so he wouldn't have to twist into the stirrup. Finally she swung herself up, as gracefully as anyone who had been riding her entire life. She grinned, obviously loving the feeling.

Then Flynn flopped against her back.

"Your braid's a little scratchy . . . can you maybe make it into a soft, pillow-like bun?" he murmured.

"Good luck," the Goodwife said, meaning it. "I'm relocating our home. I may not be easy to find when you get back, but we'll see each other again. Home will always be home."

"Bye, Ma," Gina said—no jokes, no digs.

She wheeled the horse around and they galloped into the darkness.

What seemed like scant seconds later Flynn was jolted painfully awake by the horse rearing up and screaming.

Three soldiers blocked their way—*led by Captain Tregsburg.* Their weapons were drawn and they were cool as ice: a well-trained group, not the chaotic mercenaries of the other nobles. Gina and Flynn knew they didn't have a chance.

"No, Treggsy, please," Flynn said, trying to sit up, putting a hand out. "Not now. . . ."

"Flynn Rider," the captain drawled. His horse, as if it could sense its human friend's extreme pleasure in this, casually kicked its front hooves. "You are under arrest for . . . so many different things I can't even be bothered to list them all here. Dismount quickly to turn yourself in and we will go lightly on your accomplice."

"Because I'm a *girl?*" Gina demanded angrily.

"No, because we have no idea who you are and there are no warrants for your arrest."

"Please, Captain, *sir*," Flynn said, summoning all his strength. The soldiers drew their swords. One false move and Flynn would be hacked apart, thrown from the horse, beaten, or trod upon—it didn't matter. It wouldn't be good. "*Please listen.* We're on our way to save Rapunzel. . . ."

The captain's eyes widened.

"Rapunzel," Gina repeated. "The crown princess."

"There *is* no crown princess here," one of the other soldiers spat. It wasn't a pretty look for his otherwise Roman-perfect bearing and shiny armored bits. "The girl died as an infant."

The captain held up his hand to quiet him.

"What do you know of this?" he demanded.

Flynn took a deep breath.

"The king and queen had a daughter who killed her nurse in a fit of, uh, baby magic probably from the Moon-drop Flower the queen ate when she was ill. To keep anyone else from being hurt, the royal couple had Rapunzel sent away and raised by a witch who could handle the baby's magic. This was nineteen years ago."

The soldiers all looked to their captain in disbelief.

"He isn't wrong," Tregsburg said, adjusting his grip on

his horse's reins. His men's eyes widened in shock, but they remained silent. "I was there. Continue, Rider. Though I fail to see what this has to do with saving your sorry hide."

"Long story short, she escaped the tower where the witch basically had her imprisoned. We, we . . . um . . . were introduced, and were all set to take her to see the floating lanterns, which is all she wanted . . ."

"You're leaving out the bit about the crown," Gina pointed out.

"Shut *up*, Gina; no one cares about the crown. Okay, there might have been a crown involved. Anyway, we were attacked by several different groups of men from different noble houses—it seems like a surprising number of people *also* had maybe known about the princess and her powers and wanted a piece of that now that she was out of the tower. We were actually on our way to return her to the castle . . . *No*, really," he added, seeing the look on the captain's face.

"It's true," Gina added. "It seemed like the safest option for her."

"We stopped in Harecross to scout out the terrain. Our plan was to join the next merchant caravan or any guards we saw and make sure she got safely into the capital. You can ask at the village—everyone saw us there."

Tregsburg narrowed his eyes, a strange combination of suspicious and thoughtful. Like he didn't *want* to believe what Flynn was saying but that unfortunately it had the tang of truth about it.

"And everyone saw what happened there," Flynn went on desperately. "Bathory's men came with her *vérhounds* and found Rapunzel, and grabbed her. The two of us tried to fight them off, but it wasn't enough . . . they escaped with her, and gave me this. . . ."

He lifted up the edge of his poultice. One of the guards sucked in his breath; another went pale. The captain said nothing. He had obviously seen wounds like that and worse in his times; he neither acknowledged nor dismissed its severity.

"Look," Flynn said, after a deep, ragged breath. "*Rapunzel* has the crown. I gave it back to her. You can lock me up when this is all over. I promise. But please, I am actually *begging* you, let us go rescue her. Help us, even! Rapunzel is at the mercy of Countess Bathory. I don't need to tell you what that means."

As if sensing its rider's discomfort and indecision, the captain's horse took steps to the left and right, impatient and antsy.

"We have no proof this is in fact the crown princess," Tregsburg said aloud.

"Yeah, and God forbid the kingdom's finest go rescue a citizen of the realm who's *not* a princess," Flynn growled, suddenly feeling exhausted. It wasn't fair. The world was a random, unkind place; he had always known that. Or at least he had believed that until he had spent time with Rapunzel and Gina and her mother. It was just too much that the world asked of Flynn Rider, forgotten orphan turned adventurer: to fight brigands, witches, sadistic murderesses, and now *bureaucracy* to save an entirely innocent girl.

The captain was silent a moment, thinking.

"Sternwalt," he finally said, turning to one of his men. "Go to Harecross immediately and ask around—verify if what he says is true. When you are done, return to the castle and report to the lieutenant."

"Yes, sir!"

"Verris, you return to the castle and tell the lieutenant everything that occurred here. Tell him that by my order he is to get the cavalry ready for a potential assault on Castle Bathory. None of the large siege weapons—the smaller trebuchet and ram will do."

The soldier smiled a hard smile. "I have family in Čachtice—they will be more than pleased by the destruction of that monster. Absolutely, sir!"

The two men turned their horses and took off. Flynn regarded the one remaining and the captain with weariness, and a *tiny* bit of hope. His head was throbbing and he would pass out soon without another poultice or draught.

"We'll go to Bathory together," Tregsburg said. "To investigate if you're telling the truth. If you are, Konrad here will get a message to the castle, to send the troops. Am I clear?"

"As goat's cheese," Flynn said, saluting sloppily—and then flopping forward onto Gina.

He missed the one—fleeting—human look the old guard gave Gina: actual worry, and a questioning raise of his eyebrows. Nor did he see or hear how Gina responded.

"Forward, then," the captain said aloud.

"I'm not obeying orders," Gina muttered.

Flynn *did* hear this, and smiled a little, right before he passed out.

Rapunzel

When she woke up it was daylight. There was still no fire in the fireplace, and a bowl of soup—which had been placed terrifyingly silently on a table near the door—was also cold. Her bare feet were *freezing*. She was loath to touch any of the furs scattered around or on the wall. With barely any amusement, she wrapped her hair around her shoulders and chest like a shawl.

Never in her life had she felt so empty. A completely negative, blank version of Rapunzel rattled inside her skin.

If she were plopped back into her old tower again, knowing what she knew now about the world and her friends (and magic), she would just escape it again. Here she couldn't escape—either the tower itself, or the one thought that raced around and around the stony tower inside her mind: her "mother" only kept her around to sell her when she was old enough.

"If Gothel had been unfriendly and cruel, would it have been better?" she wondered, stroking Pascal (who stayed hidden deep behind her neck, trying to stay awake in the lizard-killing chill). "I would have been miserable growing up, but I wouldn't have been surprised or hurt by any of this *now*.

"Was it possible she loved me at all? In her own strange way? Can someone be so complicated? Can you love a person and also treat her as a disposable object?

"Or . . . could she have actually loved me when I was little, and . . . stopped when I grew old enough to argue, to disagree? Do mothers do that?"

She pulled Pascal off her neck so she could see his response. He crossed his arms and frowned.

"Yes, bad mothers do, I guess. I guess 'mother' is a complicated word. There's a difference between taking care of a thing and loving a person. 'Go out for adventure, come home for love.' The Goodwife was right—she's exactly the sort of mother I'd want to be, if I were a mother someday.

"But . . . not the kind of *sorceress* I'd want to be. I've already spent nineteen years alone in a tower studying things. Once I figured out my powers, I'd want to use them. Spectacularly."

Rapunzel frowned in thought.

"It's funny; Gothel only pretended she had powers. And yet she still managed to get all these lords—and lady—in the palm of her hand. By acting all spooky and promising to sell them her spooky daughter. I suppose that's a kind of power.

"Bathory was *born* with land, money, and power; she has everything anyone could want—and yet all she does is slake her thirst for gore and violence with innocent people.

"Three powerful women—and all of their powers used for ill, or nothing at all. But how do you *get* power in the world, if you're not born a princess or a witch?"

Pascal was giving her a look.

"What?" she asked.

He pointed out the window, the direction of the castle where her parents ruled.

"Oh, I know," she said with smile. "*I* was born a crown princess. *And* a witch. In some ways, the most powerful woman of all. I should be able to do the most good: help the hungry villagers, save Magda, destroy Bathory . . . I know the only answer is to go home, whatever it winds up being."

The lizard nodded.

"Unfortunately, I'm trapped—really trapped, this time, unless I can get my magic to work usefully. There's no way out of this room, and I can't leave Magda. Once again I'm all alone in a tower with no help at all."

And that's when a small rock flew into her room, sailed past Pascal, and rolled into a corner.

Rapunzel looked out the window but saw nothing: not a bird, a strange storm, or anything. And the rock wasn't burning the way a fallen star would.

Curious, she picked it up.

Scratched on its surface in soot were the unmistakable initials F & G.

Flynn and Gina

Gina's horse kept trying to speed up as they climbed into the highlands, excited to be returning home. Gina kept trying to get her to slow down, whispering and pulling on the reins.

"Here, sit back, like this," Captain Tregsburg suggested at one point, gruffly. "If you act tense, the horse will be tense, too. She thinks you're *also* eager to go."

"We are," Flynn murmured.

When they stopped for a rest the captain looked over the horse, checked her teeth, and ran his hand along her flanks.

"Could be fed more oats," he muttered. "Other than that, Bathory seems to at least treat her horses all right."

"You really like them, huh," Gina said, chewing on a piece of pemmican her mother had slipped in with the medicines. She offered him a stick and he didn't refuse, ripping off the end with his giant square teeth like it was nothing.

"They are often better than people. Loyal, honest, brave, courteous . . ."

"Courteous . . . ?" Flynn asked from where he lay on the ground.

"Hey, you're awake! The cap'n here says the castle is just past the village," Gina said. "I think it's time we really hit you with all of Mom's healing stuff."

"Agreed," Flynn said through teeth gritted in pain.

Swiftly, efficiently, but not half as gently as her mother, Gina replaced the poultice on his head with a fresh one dripping with the extracts her mother had made. She held the tiny bottle of elixir while he gulped. It burned and he coughed, but he pressed his lips together to hold it all down.

By the time they saddled up again Flynn was clear-eyed and alert. He was able to hold himself perfectly upright and not have to lean against Gina. He even smiled at the people they passed in the village. None smiled back. Not even the one or two ladies they saw.

"This place is foul," Tregsburg muttered. "Preyed upon by their own lady like sheep kept for a vampire."

And for the first time ever, perhaps, Flynn was silent, in complete agreement with him.

They dismounted and led their horses off the road as they approached the castle, entering the feeble woods so they wouldn't be spotted easily.

"So if we're sticking to the storyline here," Flynn said as they drew close and surveilled the fort, "I'd bet that Rapunzel is stuck in that high tower there."

"If she is here at all and is being treated *differently* than Bathory's other prisoners," the captain pointed out. "If not, then she will be in the dungeons."

"Why don't you and your man here ride up there and ask them?" Flynn suggested. "They'd have to listen to buttoned-up, official types."

Tregsburg gave him a withering look. "I am not here under the aegis of my liege—she would immediately be suspicious."

"Okay, then how *do* we figure out where she is?" Gina asked. "That'll determine what to do next."

"We start by can eliminating the options," Flynn said, staring thoughtfully at the tower windows. "Gina, now's your chance. Prove to me you're a legendary adventurer type. You think you can get a stone missile through those tiny windows with your sling?"

Gina grinned.

Rapunzel

"Pascal! Pascal! It's from my friends!" Rapunzel started to shout—and then lowered her voice immediately.

"Pascal, I have *friends*. And they came to rescue me!"

She grinned in shock, this information so new and spectacular. Flynn and Gina weren't just a moment in time, a hobby, a passing phase, something that happened and then was over. She was *real* to them. She had left an impression. They had survived the fight for her life and weren't giving up on her.

She leapt into the air with a (quiet) yelp of joy, then ran to the window and looked out. They were really too far up to see anything clearly, and for the rock to have gone cleanly through the window it must have come from somewhere outside the castle grounds, in the trees. She waved desperately, putting her hand out the window, but wasn't sure anyone would be able to see it.

"What can I do? What can I do to show them that I'm here, I'm alive, it's me?" she wailed.

Pascal just looked at her.

"Oh, right," she said. "Not thinking at all. Thanks, buddy."

She gathered up as much of her hair as she could and flung it through the window. Hard.

Like a thousand baby spiders parachuting into the sky, it glittered and sparkled—completely unmagically, just because of the sunlight—before falling down to hang along the wall of the tower, rippling in the wind.

Flynn and Gina

"That's her! It's Rapunzel!" Flynn cried, throwing his arms around Gina.

She smiled a small Gina smile.

"That hair . . ." Captain Tregsburg said in awe. "The baby princess . . . Silver hair, like the moon . . ." He recovered himself quickly. "Well, I don't know what the full ramifications of all this are, but certainly something strange is afoot and you were, against all odds, telling the truth.

"Konrad, ride straight back to the castle as fast as you can and update the lieutenant on everything. But also, and this is very important: *the king and queen must know.*" He took out a tiny dagger, more of a decorated fruit knife than a serious weapon, and handed it to his man. "This was their gift to me after the Battle of Gronden. They will know you speak for me and that this is serious."

"At once, sir," the guard said, saluting. He leapt on his horse and galloped off.

"Now what?" Gina asked. "We wait until your army comes and we storm the castle?"

"Nothing doing," Flynn said, stretching. "I'm going in."

The captain looked at him hard, obviously trying to figure out something.

"You're serious . . . ?" he finally said.

"Yup."

"You know if they catch you—which they will—the countess will torture you until you *wish* that you had died under the headsman's ax back home."

"Yes, Treggsy, thank you. I am aware of that."

"This is an entirely new side of Flynn Rider we haven't seen before," the older man said thoughtfully.

"Good luck," Gina said. "There's more of a chance of us getting caught if we both go. I'll stay back and rescue you *and* Rapunzel if it comes to that."

"Couldn't have said it better myself," Flynn said. "Except for that part about me needing rescue. That was garbage."

Konrad rode back to the castle with the dagger and the message, and Flynn Rider marched toward Castle Bathory to sneak in and save the princess.

Flynn

. . . And was caught, only ten minutes after he slipped inside.

"I smell blood," the countess said, suddenly looking up from her papers. "*Fresh* blood. And not of my doing."

Her pale nose twitched and she called for the guards.

Of course Flynn couldn't help that his wounds were weeping a bit around the edges.

(While he was squeezing himself through a window, whatever healing magic had begun to knit his flesh popped.)

Or that the villain was nearly supernatural in her disquieting olfactive abilities . . .

Gina

Gina watched the tower and fretted. It had been several hours and there was no sign of Flynn or Rapunzel.

"I should go in after them," she decided.

"And be killed just as certainly as Flynn?" the captain demanded. "Think strategically, girl: even when my men come, we will be attacking *Bathory*; the castle as a whole. Our aim will be to rescue the girl who may or may not be the royal princess, and probably to take out the countess once and for all. Saving Flynn Rider will be at the bottom of our priority list. That's where you come in."

Gina narrowed her eyes at the captain. "You sound like you actually care about him."

"Don't try to deconstruct my reasons!" Tregsburg

snapped. "It has nothing to do with the fact that Rider seems to have turned his life around and I never had a son of my own!"

"Uh, I wasn't—"

"I'm just thinking logically, since no one else here seems to be doing it. You want to save your friend Flynn, you wait until the cavalry comes. Literally."

"Okay," Gina said, grinning. The captain suddenly found something to adjust on his greaves, and his greying eyebrows scrunched up in concentration.

But all desire to tease the serious military man disappeared when she heard the sounds of hoofbeats. "Wait, what's that? That can't be your men already, can it?"

In the distance, clouds of dust began to rise above the road. A motley assortment of men on horse and on foot soon came into view. But not as one army: there were clearly distinct little groups marching together under individual banners. At least three of the riders looked like lords, with expensive trappings and bells.

"What the—that's Lords Kraske and Thongel," Tregsburg declared. "What in blazes is going on here?"

Bathory castle guards saw the threat immediately: they ran to the gates and hastily began to pull the giant wooden doors closed.

"It's not our men, but it *is* some kind of coordinated

siege," the captain said in wonder. There was almost a note of delight in his voice.

One of the mounted riders from the strange company saw the gates closing and immediately urged his horse into a gallop. Just before they slammed shut, he threw something in between them; a spear or end of a lance or something; Gina couldn't tell. There was a giant *crack* and the gates shuddered and bounced back open. The attackers cheered.

Someone blew a horn, one of the lords shouted:

"*Bathory!* Release the girl immediately! Or we will besiege your castle and take you—and her—by force!"

"*NOT BLOODY LIKELY!*"

This was shouted from the top of the wall: the countess stood there, hands on hips, laughing hysterically at her own joke. "This castle has stood for a thousand years. I'm going to fetch my secret weapon now. And when I command her, Rapunzel will release a rain of death upon you all!"

The captain's eyes widened and he turned to Gina. "Can she do that?" he asked.

Gina shook her head and shrugged. "She turned a lizard into a—um—different lizard. And changes things different colors. That's all I saw her do. Also she told me she used to kill chickens occasionally."

"It hasn't stood for a thousand years," one of the lords

in the army scoffed. "Her husband built it for her as a present for her disgusting hobbies! It's garbage!"

"This," Captain Tregsburg said, "is going to be *very* interesting."

Rapunzel

She paced back and forth round her room, fretting over what to do.

"My friends are coming," she murmured. "But I mustn't entirely rely on them. I must be ready—I must try to rescue myself, or meet them at least halfway. First, soup!"

Rapunzel made herself drink the gelid, nasty mass that sorely needed salt. But she would have to keep her strength up, especially if there was running involved.

"Now, let's see if I can help myself, a little!" She pushed up her half-raveled sleeves and plunked a lock of hair into the now-empty bowl. "All right . . . this is Day 10 since the new moon, I think? I've lost track! Still half-moon-ish? Or closer to healing? More transformations, maybe?"

Her fingers twitched where she had once held her charcoal pencil, wishing they cupped the little moon charm she had made. She had nothing to focus on. She didn't even know exactly what the moon looked like right then.

She tried to visualize the mandala she had painted, tried to remember how calm and centered she was in the cottage. Peace and magic and moons . . .

But the feeling kept slipping away. A cold breeze snaked through the tower windows and thoughts of Bathory snaked through her subconscious. She closed her eyes and tried harder: moon MOON *moon* moon. . . .

Her hair began to sparkle. It was working!

She opened her eyes before the embers faded, picked up the bowl even as it changed—to a much smaller bowl.

"Huh," she said, turning the doll-sized thing over in her hands. "Interesting. Ooh! Maybe I could shrink the door, and get out!"

She went over to investigate how best to drape her hair along the length of it, when suddenly there was a knock, heavy and ominous, like the hand was gloved in mail.

Rapunzel's heart nearly stopped in fright.

"Princessssss, you have a vissssssitor." The countess's voice, unsuited to sweet platitudes, grated terribly. Pascal shook his head, trying to get it out of his ears.

Rapunzel jumped back. The (skull) key was put in the

lock; the door creaked open. Bathory was grinning like a gargoyle, wearing a reverse of the outfit she had upon Rapunzel's arrival: a blood-red underdress with a cream-colored overskirt and bodice. She strode into the room, flanked by two giant men whose faces were hidden behind spiked metal helms. Behind them were two more men, and between them they carried . . .

"Flynn!" Rapunzel cried.

He was bound rather overmuch to a chair: ankles, legs, torso, arms behind his back, iron chains and shackles running back and forth as if he were a dangerous, rabid beast rather than a slender thief. He grinned up at her, a little woozily. His hair was matted with blood and there was a bandage coming off the top of his head.

"Heya, Witchy," he said. "Sorry about the rescue attempt."

Rapunzel flung herself at him. She was torn between the urge to embrace him, to treat him gently, to look at his wounds, to question his presence, and maybe even to kiss him—all at once.

"Quite the brave lover boy," the countess observed. "And he did put up quite a fight until he fainted."

""Snothing, just dizzy from the wound before," he said, rolling his eyes and blowing a puff of hair off his forehead.

"You can't kill him," Rapunzel said, standing up, fury in her eyes. "I won't let you."

"Honestly, I'd be relieved and impressed to actually see those tresses of yours working," the countess said, eying her (slightly soupy) silver hair. "But don't worry, darling, he is absolutely safe with me—as long as you do exactly as I say.

"Give me proof of your hair's power before the sun goes down or both he and Magda will be drained of their blood. Not for my bath, of course—he's a boy and a filthy one at that. . . ."

Flynn gave her a devilish grin.

"Disgusting," she muttered, and turned to go.

Two of the guards followed. Two stayed—one on either side of Flynn.

"You're leaving him here?" Rapunzel asked in surprise.

"Why not? How does it hurt to let you spend time with him?" the countess asked curiously, as if she really didn't understand the question. "Spending time together will only bring you closer. Which means you'll be even less likely to want him to die. I suggest you talk quickly."

The door slammed shut. The room grew quiet.

The two guards remained motionless, undistinguished and ghoulish behind their helms.

Flynn let his head sink out of exhaustion, unable to keep it upright any longer.

"I really blew it, huh?" he muttered.

"Oh, don't be ridiculous," Rapunzel said. "There's still"—she just barely stopped herself from saying *Gina* aloud—"hope," she finished instead, a little awkwardly.

The guards didn't appear to notice her near slipup.

She took some of the pillows off her bed and tried to prop them behind Flynn's neck. The guards didn't even move: she wasn't worth worrying about. As she adjusted the lumps and fluffy bits, she got a better look at the top of Flynn's head. She tried not to gasp. Despite her lack of experience with any kind of serious wound, it really, *really* didn't look good.

Not knowing what else to do, she held his hand and squeezed it.

He smiled. "See, that made it all worth it."

"I can't believe you came here. I can't believe you followed me, and found me! You know, when I first saw you from up in my tower—wow, like ages ago—and then the pictures of you on the posters . . . I had ideas of what I *wanted* you to be. And you wound up being almost exactly that!"

"Rapunzel, I'm not anything heroic or wonderful or whatever you thought," he said sadly. "I'm a sneak thief mostly out for my own good. The rest of it's a lie. My name isn't even Flynn Rider."

"Um, what?"

Of all the many things she thought he might say, this was not one of them.

"My real name is Eugene Fitzherbert. At least, that was what was on record at the orphanage."

There *might* have been a glint from inside a guard's helmet at that, as if he couldn't help sniggering a little.

Rapunzel's jaw actually fell open.

"Eugene?" she asked.

"Yes."

"And doesn't Fitz mean—"

"Yes, it does," he interrupted in annoyance. "But who knows if that's really my family name, or a real name, or whatever. I think of myself as Flynn Rider. Daring hero, escape artist, adventurer extraordinaire . . . Eugene is some one who wastes away in an orphanage, who nobody wants. *Eugene* eats porridge once or twice a day, maybe, and wears the old clothes that bigger kids grew out of a generation ago."

"I like Eugene," Rapunzel protested, patting his hand. "I like it better than Flynn. It sounds more . . . real. Like who you really are."

"Thanks," he muttered.

"No, really! *Eugene* doesn't abandon his friends. *Eugene* makes snarky remarks . . . and then hangs around witchy goat farms to see how he can help. *Eugene* pauses his wild, adventurous life to make sure the people around him get their happy endings. Eugene gives crowns back to their rightful owners."

"*Eugene* winds up drained of his blood in a castle ruled by a demonic she-beast," Flynn said, looking up to gauge his captors' possibly violent response. They didn't move. "Flynn Rider is somewhere off riding into the sunset—"

"*Without* his princess," Rapunzel interrupted, hands on hips.

Flynn smiled sadly at her.

She tried to frown and continue looking stern . . . but instead wound up leaning closer. Very deliberately, she pushed her lips into his.

Flynn leaned forward as far as his ropes allowed. His nose pressed into hers; she tilted her head.

A moment later Flynn looked up to see if the captors, again, were doing anything.

Nope.

Rapunzel broke off the kiss, laughing.

"My second kiss," she sighed. "What a disaster."

"*My* first kiss under lock and key," Flynn said. Then he thought about it. "Okay, second. Mayyyybe third."

"We have to get out of here," Rapunzel said, shaking her head.

"I gotta tell you, I don't have high hopes for the situation resolving itself happily. But whatever happens, Rapunzel, I am *not* sorry you saw me hide the crown in the tree and came after me. Even if it winds up, ah, shortening my life unexpectedly, it's the best ending someone like me could have hoped for."

"But what about your piles of money?" she asked, only half teasing.

He shrugged—which was difficult given all of the chains and ropes. "Money is a . . . it's like a place saver for happiness. You know? I grew up poor, so I figured having food, and a comfortable place to live, and servants, and a really nice couch would make me happy."

"A really nice couch . . . ?"

"Look, shush, it's just part of the whole thing. The point is, I didn't really know what happiness was until the last few days. I didn't think a *person* could make me happy. It was a weird and wonderful discovery. And if I was a jerk earlier, I'm sorry—all I saw was that happiness being taken away from me again."

Rapunzel kissed him on the cheek, overwhelmed. "I'm sorry we fought. I'm a big, spoiled princess who doesn't understand the real world."

"*You* are a wonderful human being who has been locked up for her entire life," Flynn said, appalled. "I don't think 'spoiled' is the word for it."

"Thank you," Rapunzel murmured.

She couldn't help wondering if she would ever know what being a regular person was like. It crossed her mind that maybe, in some ways, her quest for the lanterns was a fill-in for that, like Flynn's piles of money: she wasn't chasing distant lights; she was pursuing an unrealized dream of normalcy.

If it turned out her entire life was a dream, and she woke up to find out she was just a common village girl with chores like taking care of the goats, and she had Eugene for a sweetheart and Gina for a friend . . . for a sister . . . would she be happy?

Or would some part of her look around at the world, and feel something was wrong with it? What if she lived in Čachtice? What if her little cousins were starving?

Or would peasant-Rapunzel still try to change the world, regardless of her station in it, or of the witchy powers she didn't have?

"Gold piece for your thoughts," Flynn said.

Rapunzel put her arms around his neck. "Oh, just thinking of other lives, other times." She went to kiss him on the neck, below his ear.

"What's Gina's plan?" she whispered.

"Get Tregsburg's army," he whispered back.

Her heart leapt at this strange news. But how . . . ?

Suddenly there were the sounds of shouting from outside. Even the guards shifted and looked at each other. Rapunzel ran to the window. "That was fast," she said, impressed.

"What's going on?" Flynn asked, as antsy as any child denied knowledge of something *at that minute.*

"It . . . looks like an army is attacking the castle. Sort of."

In books she had read, the armies that besieged castles were large and stayed in orderly rows; they wore shining armor and rode brilliant chestnut horses, carried banners and horns and lances and pushed along machines for destroying walls and catapults.

Below her was a strangely mismatched crowd of people sporting heraldic imagery from a half dozen different houses. None of it was shiny or new. No group was doing the same thing as any other; there was no coordinated attack. They looked more like a large version of the loosely organized groups of brigands who had been trying to grab Rapunzel for the past week. Horses and men like ants were pacing around the main gates almost aimlessly.

"Say, out of curiosity, what would Tregsburg's army look like?" she asked casually.

"Oh, you know, all spit-polished buttons and boots, marching lockstep, shiny horses, helmets with those funny brushy things on top . . ."

"So this is probably not them," Rapunzel decided.

The door unlocked and creaked open; Magda came padding in. "I've brought some ale. . . ."

"We're a little busy," Flynn said fatuously.

"Oh, yes, the attack," Magda said listlessly. She put down the jug and mugs she was carrying and joined Rapunzel at the window. Looking down at the chaos below, her eyes, for just a moment, showed a hint of life. "It's like out of a fairy story," she said softly. "All the princes of the kingdom come to rescue the princess."

"They aren't princes—they are barons and lesser nobility," Rapunzel said. "For starters. And for second, they do not want me because they are all madly in love with me; they want me because of my magic hair. I am a weapon or a treasure or an oddity, not an object of affection. And thirdly—most importantly—I am *not* an *object* to be fought over, whether it's as a wife or a weapon. I am a person."

Magda regarded her with blank, lizard-like eyes. "No one came to rescue *me*, for any reason."

Rapunzel wilted like she had been punched in the gut, feeling stupid and undone once again.

"You're . . . right," she finally said. "I have this magical hair because my mother was a queen and managed to get an entire kingdom to look for a magical flower to save her and her baby. It was all privilege."

"For which you were hidden away in a tower for twenty years!" Flynn shouted.

One of the guards kicked his chair.

"Also true. Life is complicated. Like mothers and power. There are two things I know for certain, however. One is that I *don't need someone telling my story for me,*" she said pointedly to Flynn. Then she took the other girl's hands in her own. "And two. Magda, if I get out of here, *you* get out of here. I promise."

Magda blinked slowly, looking at her hands, and then at Rapunzel's face. The ghost of a smile played about her lips.

"All right," she said, which was strange.

Rapunzel was beginning to realize that not everyone reacted to imprisonment with the same resilience she had.

"So . . . *can* you do something with your hair?" the other girl asked.

The Battle for Castle Bathory

The mishmash army charged forward and attacked.

Some were organized enough to make a concerted effort to push on the gates. Mostly, however, it was individual men attacking individual guards.

With a strange look on his face, Captain Tregsburg got back on his horse.

"What are you doing?" Gina hissed.

"The enemy of my enemy is my friend . . . for a while," he answered, adjusting his reins and stirrups, straightening up in the saddle. "I can help them until my own men come."

"*Now* who's not thinking logically?" Gina demanded. "What will your men do when they arrive? Won't they need a leader?"

"They'll see me," he said distractedly—and rode into the fray, a steely grin on his face.

"He's gone berserker," Gina murmured.

She didn't know anything about formal military battles. She didn't even have access to the sorts of books Rapunzel grew up with. To her it all looked like chaos. Horses were screaming. The constant clang of swords was neither merry nor legendary; it was muted and frenetic. Men grunted and hissed like animals. Lords called orders to men, but their words got lost in the scramble. Swords rose and fell methodically, hacking and slashing, creating ugly results. Two men were scuffling like crabs in the dirt, trying to throttle each other but impeded by helms, armor, boots, jackets. . . .

More than anything else, it all seemed like a children's scrum with real weapons and animals instead of sticks. Angry, violent, and with no real direction.

. . . on the "good guys" team, that is. The bad guys were much more together.

When the large gates were finally forced open, the ragtag army of lords cheered . . . only to break off when they realized the truth of the situation. Bathory had all the resources of a castle, all the men and supplies of a small town. A dozen soldiers, armored and heavily armed, marched out from the bailey as one. There was a deadly pause, and then the two sides clashed.

Even with the addition of Tregsburg, it didn't look good. Whether the castle had stood for twenty years or a thousand made no difference; in the end it was still a stone castle full of trained and weaponed men.

Gina considered her "orders," such as they were: to wait until the royal army arrived, then slip in during the chaos and rescue Flynn. Did this unexpected battle change things? There was indeed chaos, but it hadn't made it all the way into the castle yet. Could she slip in anyway?

Rapunzel would be rescued by her kingdom's soldiers . . . if and when they came. How long would that be?

If those fighting now were the villains who were all after her, and they got to her first . . .

"Hey! You!"

Gina spun around. One of the "good guys" had seen her. Who knew what he thought? Maybe he assumed she was part of Bathory's force, sneaking around the back to attack from behind. Maybe he thought she was a messenger from the castle trying to send for help. Maybe he was too caught up in bloodlust to care anymore. Whatever else, she presented an obviously less difficult target than Bathory's armored men. He raised his sword and ran at her. . . .

What could she possibly do to help anything right now? Or anyone? Rapunzel, Flynn, Tregsburg—even herself?

Gina, you're a great *adventurer. You don't need anyone else's permission to speak up, or approval. Just say what you think—and do it!* The words came echoing back to her.

So she grabbed her horse, leapt on, and galloped away from the battle and castle as fast as she could.

Rapunzel

"You're supposed to be this terrible witch—*do* something with your silver hair," Magda said impatiently. "Save us!"

"I can't see the moon," Rapunzel said. "I'm having a hard time focusing. And all the moon can do now is make things smaller."

"What?" the other girl asked, looking at Flynn for an explanation of what obviously sounded like crazy talk.

"I have literally no idea," Flynn admitted.

A key turned in the lock, and the door creaked open. One of Flynn's guards drew his giant sword, ready to lop the head off any potential rescue.

But it was Bathory.

"Here's your last chance, *Princess Rapunzel*," Bathory

said. "My apologies at not being able to wait until sundown. One does as needs must. Should the besiegers make any headway, you will unleash the full power of your hair . . . or be thrown onto our enemies below. Along with your lover."

"But it doesn't look like it's going so badly for you," Rapunzel observed, looking out the window.

"A demonstration of your power would end things quickly," Countess Bathory said crisply. "And if you do not have the power, then . . . your body will *still* set things to rest quickly. So I suggest you begin whatever magical preparations or incantations you require immediately."

"Absolutely," Rapunzel agreed.

"Uh-oh," Flynn said.

"Moon, oh moon, please," she chanted or begged, closing her eyes and wrapping her arms around her hair.

"Come on, come on; we haven't got all day," Bathory growled.

"I'm working on it!" Rapunzel snapped. She felt the *pre-magic* building and ebbing, but every time she was interrupted—or panicked—it faded away.

"*Focus,*" she muttered to herself. She tried to remember images of the moon, but couldn't pick just one; multiple versions in all its different phases slipped quickly through her mind.

"All right, him first," Bathory said to the guards, pointing to Flynn.

They nodded. One took out a knife and cut the straps holding him to the chair, pulled the chains from his legs. The other lifted him up easily with one hand and tried to stand him up like a puppet. Flynn swayed and had trouble staying on his feet.

"*NO!*" Rapunzel wailed. "Moon moon moon-MOONmoon!"

Maybe the countess would be happy with *some* display—any display of power. If she could just get her hair to glow . . .

"Boys and girls come out to play?" Magda suggested timidly.

"*What?*" Rapunzel demanded distractedly.

"The children's rhyme?" The poor maid obviously had no idea what was going on beyond Rapunzel seeming to need something about the moon. " 'Boys and girls come out to play . . .' "

"*The moon doth shine as bright as day!*" Rapunzel finished.

She thought of the bright, cold winter full moon that cast a light so strong that windows in her tower lit up like magic, and instead of sunbeams, blue moonbeams traced the floor. She would run to the tower window. . . .

Leave your supper and leave your sleep . . .

. . . and the whole world would be white and blue, as bright as daytime, but with a glowing, magical scrim. Rapunzel had felt like she could dive into it, fly over the whole world in its strange state.

And join your playfellows in the street.

Her hair began to glow.

Bathory's eyes widened—less with pleasure and more with surprise. It was almost like she had never really thought that the magic was real, that it had all been a trick.

But a nasty, smug look grew on her face regardless.

The guards were outright stunned.

"What the—" the one on the right said.

"Witch!" the other cried.

And then Flynn, who had looked like he was on the point of passing out, suddenly spun and drove his fist straight into the man's groin.

The injured guard didn't fall over, but he did kind of collapse into himself, clutching and groaning.

Pausing only a moment to put a hand to his bandage, Flynn ducked under the blow from the second guard. He dropped to the ground and rolled hard into his opponent's knees.

The guard fell heavily—into Bathory, knocking her over.

The countess screamed hysterically, flailing her arms and trying to get out from under the heavy man who now dragged her to the floor with him.

"Any time now, Rapunzel," Flynn said, panting heavily.

"Trying!" Rapunzel said. *What should she shrink?* What *could* she shrink?

And suddenly she *saw* it.

Saw the castle as the moon might, saw the world from above and the fight below and the stupid, stupid tower where fate had ironically conspired to lock her up again. Hateful tower—as small as a doll's tower, really, when seen from the height of the moon. Insignificant. *Nothing.*

Strange things began to happen.

The light in the room changed as if shadow and illumination were switched.

Flynn cried out—the wall he had been leaning heavily against suddenly *wasn't* . . . It melted away and then reappeared under his hand, which he hastily yanked back.

The whole structure of the tower seemed to be there and not, like in a dream when you realize something shouldn't be, and so it suddenly isn't.

"Is this it?" Bathory demanded, finally managing to stand up. No one was listening.

The first guard apparently didn't notice what was going

on around him, too filled with personal fury. He ran at Flynn, helmeted head down for ramming.

Flynn managed to spin mostly out of his way. The spiked helmet smashed into the bony part of his hip—the best of all possible alternatives, but still not great.

Rider cried out from the pain as his neck snapped back, jarring his already injured head.

"Come *on*," Rapunzel cried, stepping over and around the guards, grabbing Flynn's arm.

"*. . . where . . . ?*" he gasped. It was a fair question: the second guard and Bathory had sorted themselves out and blocked the only exit from the room. The windows were still too narrow to get through, and the walls still weren't making any sense. Everything was covered in sparkles. Rapunzel could feel what the magic wanted to do. And if she was in the wrong place at the wrong time, it wouldn't matter who had summoned the magic: her ending would be short and stony.

"Not here," she answered, grabbing Magda with her other hand. Pascal wrapped his tail around her neck tightly.

The world swayed and warbled and transformed. The wall with the door disappeared entirely.

Rapunzel yanked her friends through, ducking around the countess and her guard.

Just as they made it over, the world shifted; Rapunzel could see straight down to the ground, a thousand feet below.

Magda finally screamed.

The three companions started down precarious stony steps that spiraled around the outside of a now much, much smaller tower. It had shut up inside itself somehow; the outer wall on their right was now an inner wall. On their left was . . . *nothing.* Empty space all the way to the cold, hard ground.

"Keep moving," Rapunzel urged Magda when she froze (which was often).

The princess had, of course, no vertigo or fear of heights. Flynn looked uneasy—and dizzy besides—but worked his way methodically down, clinging to the wall like he was trying to hug it.

Rapunzel made the mistake of looking back and saw that Bathory and at least one of the guards had regained their bearings and were coming down after them. She tightened her grip on Magda's hand and counted the stairs as they went.

Below, the fighting had paused. Whereas Rapunzel's magic made no sound in itself, one couldn't just magically change and displace carefully lodged stones without some repercussions in the physical world. The resulting shifting—and occasional collapse—of structures resulted in lithic screams, like an entire mountain was twisting, like a mining disaster, like a landslide, like nothing any of the men gleefully shedding blood had heard before.

"What the blazes," someone said.

"An earthquake," Tregsburg said, taking the moment to pant and straighten his grip on his sword. He wasn't as young as many of the soldiers by half. Skill and experience only made up for so much.

"Witchcraft!" a Bathory soldier shouted in dismay at the changed castle.

"You would know about witches," the captain of the guard snorted, and struck him a fatal blow to the neck.

And so it went: those who recovered first from shock at the strange sight immediately returned to their bloody work and got some extra licks in; those who were stupefied either came around quickly or lost their lives.

It was into this newly chaotic, violent scene that Rapunzel, Flynn, and Magda finally descended (Magda was still crying). Despite Flynn's apparent return to vigor, he collapsed when they hit the bottom step; evidently all his willpower was used up now that they were safe on the ground. Rapunzel grabbed him and wrapped her hair around his shoulders to help steady him.

It was impossible at first to get her bearings; the world itself seemed to have turned upside down. Her magic had not bothered to neatly deal with how the tower in its shrunken state would remain connected to the rest of the castle. Random walls, steps to nowhere, rooms without ceilings, and scattered plinths now made an obscene obstacle course, a dollhouse from a fever dream.

Servants and other inhabitants of the castle were pouring out from everywhere, screaming and running away from the unnatural disaster. Rapunzel made a note that when this was all over they should check for any remaining prisoners or people trapped in the rubble.

But for now her responsibility was to get her little group to safety.

She focused on just placing one foot in front of the other—while trying to balance the swaying Flynn, and forcing Magda to keep up.

"Can I have a little help here?" she finally demanded of the other girl when Flynn listed heavily to the side.

Getting a direct order seemed to clear Magda's head; she took his other arm and slung it around her neck.

Now they were confronted with the fighting that they had heard from above, but at eye level. Poor Rapunzel had never seen that many people in one spot before, the battle was even louder and more confusing to her long-isolated ears and eyes.

"But we've made it," she told herself. And because she had done some changing over the course of her adventures, *but hadn't finished yet*, she assumed this was the end. Everyone would drop their weapons when they saw that the prisoners were free, that *she* was free, and things would work out. If nothing else, she could rely on the fact that she was a royal princess to impart some authority to the mess.

And indeed the soldiers did notice her, after minute.

"It's Rapunzel!" someone yelled, pointing at her hair.

"GRAB HER!"

Instead of complying with his demand, a soldier of Bathory's used that opportunity to stab the man who shouted.

"Gina. Get Gina. Or Tregsburg," Flynn wheezed. "Big towheaded guy. Flashy sun on his armor. He'll help you get out of here."

Rapunzel ignored the "help *you*" and looked around desperately for the man Flynn described. She had seen him before, she remembered, but only at a distance. Was that him, fighting from the ground, grimacing and trying to stand? Or . . .

By then the countess had also managed to get down to the bottom of the tower, her two guards behind her.

"Get the girl and return to me!" she ordered, her voice ringing across the battlements.

Rapunzel wished she had that command, that powerful a voice. Did one have to be a sadistic murderer to get it?

She looked around desperately: there was no way to get to the captain, no path that wasn't blocked by fighting. It was only a matter of time before someone else spotted her.

"Rapunzel, to me!"

Like a dream, suddenly her mother was before her.

Again.

She wore a tightly wrapped cloak and a hood to hide her face. Her hand was out, reaching, imploring.

"Let's get you out of here," she said.

Rapunzel's body moved forward out of instinct, responding to a voice and body she had known her entire life. *Help* and *comfort* and *warmth.*

Her mind froze her feet.

She stared at this woman, out of place in the battlefield, neither fighting nor scared. Not even nervous.

"Rapunzel," Gothel repeated. "Now! Before they see you!"

"They?" Rapunzel demanded. She felt anger boiling up

from her stomach, bile and venom. "Which *they*, Mother? The ones who were *bidding for my hand in marriage*—or just the ones in the employ of a sadistic monster?"

Gothel's face twitched between impatience and irritation.

"Rapunzel, I never meant for you to wind up with Bathory. She's a terrible woman. I was coming to save you from her!"

"Who *did* you mean for me to *wind up with*, then? The one who gave you the most money?"

"Oh, hey, Moms." Flynn waved weakly. "Good to finally meet you."

"My child, this world is dangerous and full of woe," Gothel said, ignoring him. "I was only trying to secure a safe and prosperous future for you. You may not agree with my methods, but when you're older you'll see a mother has to make choices to protect and provide for her children—"

"Oh, *stop it!*" Rapunzel snapped. Part of her *still* wanted to believe the comforting lies. Part of her still wanted things to go back to the way they were—a very, very tiny part of her that now needed to be managed, moved out of the way, and made to shut up. "You're a liar, and worse— you broke my heart. You're not a mother. *You're a villain.*"

Gothel's eyes went wide. Her mouth opened and hung

there as though even she was a little curious as to what she would say, what words would come and bring the situation back under her control.

"I would rather take my chances with an honest villain like Bathory!" Rapunzel hissed. "Get out of my sight and never let me see you again!"

"Or *what*?" Gothel asked, a knowing, nasty tone in her voice: her real voice. "What could *you* do to *me*, Rapunzel? I am your mother, and besides that I control all of these sword-playing idiots."

"Did you forget that I'm a crown princess? *And* a powerful witch who can control her hair now. Or did you think the castle just fell on its own today?

"Either way, your time with me is over, if you know what is good for you."

The two women glared at each other.

And after a moment, Rapunzel realized that's what they were: two *women*. Despite being younger and shorter than Gothel, she wasn't a girl anymore. She had power and will and a stubborn disposition.

"Go. *Now*," she ordered. "Never approach me again."

Her mother started to growl something—

"What's that? I can't hear you. All that mumbling," Rapunzel said airily, and walked away, turning her back on the woman forever.

Just a few Rapunzel-lengths away, however, she allowed herself exactly one sob of relief and loss. She knew she might someday change her mind; the heart was a fickle beast. But for now she truly didn't ever want to see her mother again. And that was a terrible, terrible thing to admit, as justified as it was.

Flynn squeezed Rapunzel's shoulder in comfort—when she was suddenly pulled away.

"Got you!"

A dangerous, dagger-wielding man with blood on his face and torn insignia on his chest nearly broke her wrist grabbing her to him. The smell of sweat and blood on him was overpowering.

"Hands off her, you—" Flynn began before falling to the ground in a faint.

"I am a *crown princess*," Rapunzel shouted as haughtily as she could. "You will remove your foul hands from me at once!"

"I've got her!" the man yelled, shaking her to be quiet as though she were a child or cat he hated.

"Get *off* her!" Magda shouted, pounding her fists on his back.

"Shut up, you," the man said, shaking the maid off like a gnat. "Wait . . . what's that noise? More magic? Is the whole castle falling?"

There *was* a low rumble, and a strange noise with it; a barely audible whistle that rose to a constant, unceasing shriek.

Had she done that? Rapunzel wondered in a daze.

But no . . .

It was Gina!

Mounted on the horse she had commandeered, leading a band of the ugliest, most muscled and *dangerous*-looking men the world had ever seen. They were running like berserkers, screaming like madmen, waving their weapons and angry as hell.

The Snuggly Duckling thugs.

The big guy with the nose, the large one with what looked like ghostly white paint on his face, the helmeted man with the arm painting of the cupcakes . . . And Hook Hand, screaming loudest of all, a look of senseless rapture on his face. His eyes were not even focusing properly. He ran into the battle swinging his ax, not caring whom he hit, but mostly trying to aim for the real bad guys.

Bathory's men were used to the terrible and vicious habits of their mistress, and the other soldiers were certainly no strangers to violence and war. But when they saw the approaching horde, even the bravest of them trembled. These were the thugs who terrified lesser villains; these were the Stabbingtons times ten; these were men who had no other recourse in life but to pursue the most shadowy and deadly of careers.

Several lords chose that moment to simply leave, not knowing where the fight was going but simply having had enough of it, and of bloody countesses, and of supposedly magical princesses with silver hair.

Gina quickly spotted Rapunzel and Flynn and waved. Then, in one incredibly graceful movement, she slid down off her horse and into the fray—*while* the horse was still galloping. She let out a terrifying war cry and joined the fight, spinning, bobbing, and parrying with her long, slim knife.

"I don't really understand what's happening," Rapunzel said. "But I think I love Gina."

Flynn worked up enough energy to pout and hit her wearily in the leg before passing out again.

Rapunzel

From there on out the battle was short—but extremely intense. Once Bathory was defeated the friends' main task was to prevent the Snuggly Ducklings from turning on everyone else—it was hard to get them to calm down once they began fighting. On the bright side, however, no one had any issue when they ran through the castle afterward, looting and pillaging more than they had ever dreamed.

(The quiet one with the white face paint made the mistake of entering Bathory's private workshop. . . . He emerged looking even paler than before.)

Rapunzel made her way through the slowly recovering battlefield, feeling for the first time in days like she could take a breath and not be in danger. Gina was tending to Flynn with the medicines from her saddlebags. Magda was standing quietly by, smiling a little to herself as if she was in a dream and couldn't quite believe it was all real. Some of the not-the-worst lords and men were going methodically through the castle releasing all the prisoners and liberating the servants.

(The footman's body was discovered with a paring knife stuck in his back.)

Countess Bathory was quickly captured and held at unflinching sword point. Still sneering.

Gothel was nowhere to be found.

Hook Hand wandered through the mess, enjoying clubbing the occasional Bathory soldier who made the poor decision to try to rise from the ground. He did the same thing to the soldiers who, at their lords' request, had tried to grab Rapunzel.

"Cease that at once, scoundrel," the Baron of Smeinhet said. "Your help in defeating that vile woman will be rewarded adequately. But now the auction can proceed as planned."

"Anyone wants that girl can come through me first," Hook Hand said. Big Nose came and stood behind him, one hand on his sword (the other hand on a sack of jewelry he had found).

"Not that I don't appreciate this," Rapunzel said, "but *why* are you helping me?"

Hook Hand looked a little hurt.

"Like I said, you was just an innocent girl trying to get our help back at the Duckling—if we'da actually helped, none of this would have happened. Holding up a carriage and stealing jewels ain't the same thing as buying and selling a person like a *thing*, or a girl into a marriage she don't want."

"Plus ransom's got *rules*," another pub thug said thoughtfully.

"*And* Bathory destroyed the Snuggly Duckling," the man with the large horns said. "No one touches the Snuggly Duckling. No one."

"No one ever will again, that's for sure," Hook Hand said, running his fingers along the side of his sword.

"Yeah, and I'm sure sucking up to a future queen probably doesn't hurt, either," Flynn muttered from where he lay. "Speaking of, you ever find your dashing captain? The only reason we got here at all is because he let me go. . . ."

"Old Tregsburg's over there, dyin'," Big Nose said, pointing. "Can't say I feel strongly about it, but he was a man of integrity, for all that'll get you."

Rapunzel ran over to the large man, lying untended among the dead. He was as pale as if he had already gone.

"Captain? Sir?" she pleaded, kneeling down beside him.

"My Lady," he said, eyes fluttering open. "I'm . . . so . . . sorry . . . for everything. . . ."

"Shh, come on." Rapunzel looked around desperately. Gina stood there with the poultices and serums but shook her head sadly, pointing. No medicine in the world would heal the giant wound in his side, cut so deep they could see organs pulsing within. He lay in a dark pool of his own blood.

"Can't you magic him, or something?" Gina asked.

Rapunzel shook her head. "I can't heal until the full moon—it's all weird change-y magic right now."

"Okay, can't you change him, then? Into something— *not* dying?"

"I can't! I don't know what to do—I can't really control it! Right now it just wants to change the size of things. . . ."

Tregsburg let out the faintest whisper of a groan; his body seemed to relax and stiffen at the same time.

Despite her unfamiliarity with death, Rapunzel knew she was out of time.

She gritted her teeth and chanted.

"Boys and girls come out to play, the moon doth shine as bright as day. . . ."

She wrapped her hair around the captain as best she could. She closed her eyes and felt for the magic.

There was little to draw on; whatever had happened

with the tower had exhausted her, or the magic, or *something*. It took all of Rapunzel's willpower just to stay focused, much less bend the magic into doing something useful. Like not just making the man *smaller*, as with the bowl and the tower—or larger, which she felt was also a possibility.

Think of Pascal! Think of his change! It wasn't so long ago . . . Mold the form and flesh. . . . The moon's phase wasn't *that* different now, really, was it . . . ?

Had Pascal wanted to transform? Did his own wishes somehow inform the magic? What would Tregsburg want?

She tried. She really tried.

Finally she slumped, unable to do any more.

"Wondrous . . ." was the last thing Captain Tregsburg ever said.

When Rapunzel wearily opened her eyes, there was a magnificent white horse where the captain had been.

There was dried blood on its pure white flanks, what looked like an old, healed wound on its belly—and an ecstatic look in its eye.

It rose onto its feet, trumpeting out a whinny of triumph, kicking its front legs and tossing its mane back and forth.

"Oh," Rapunzel said, dismayed. "I didn't—I'm sorry—"

But Justin "Maximus" Tregsburg, captain of the royal guard and now shining white stallion, gently nuzzled her cheek. He was . . . happy.

"I'm glad you're all right," Rapunzel said, hugging him. "I'm sorry we never got to talk."

The stallion rolled his eyes and tossed his head: What's the use of *talk*, he seemed to say. Then he lowered himself on his front legs and encouraged her to get on.

Feeling strange, Rapunzel marveled at how easily she waved to everyone from horseback and spoke with them: the villains and thugs who freed her, the servants and prisoners who were also freed, the lords and their men who reluctantly gave up trying to own the girl whose magic they finally saw in action. She was cold but polite to these, and made a mental note of their names for future diplomacy.

She led a slow and triumphant parade of everyone back to the kingdom on her magical white horse, accompanied by cheers, singing, and general merriment.

Flynn had to ride behind Gina again; apparently Maximus's softening of heart didn't go far enough to let the thief ride on his back.

Memorial Sloan Kettering

Daniella chuckled.

"That was clever, I'll give you that," she murmured, eyes closed. "I thought you totally forgot about Maximus. But you had a plan."

"Like I did for Pascal. And no Stormtroopers or robots or anything," Brendan said, snapping the book shut. "So. Happily ever after and all; Raps and Flynn get married, Gothel gets hers, and Rapunzel becomes the best queen the kingdom ever had. The end."

"*What?*" His sister's eyes shot open. "No, you can't do that. That's not how it ends."

"But they did everything. They *won*," he protested.

"No, you gotta drag that stuff out," she growled. "Like,

that's the reward. Her meeting her mom and dad, the final really good kiss, you know?"

"Ugh—another kiss? C'mon. . . ."

"BRENDAN!"

Rapunzel

By the time they made it to the castle, the crowd of people marching home had whittled down to just Rapunzel (on Maximus, with Pascal) and Flynn and Gina (on her horse). Some lords and their mercenaries stayed behind at Castle Bathory to take the countess to trial; some went back to their own lands. Bathory's prisoners and servants joyfully returned to their families. The Snuggly Duckling thugs went to the pop-up in the woods, where they would present Rasko with more than enough gold to rebuild his tavern.

As the three (six) friends tiredly approached the small, painted gates, so different from Bathory's, Rapunzel found her heart beating wildly. Despite calm reassurances to herself that she belonged there; that she was the fairy-tale crown princess coming home.

Because she *didn't* belong there. Not really. She had never seen this castle up close, at least not since she was a baby.

And she had outgrown her tower.

The forest and the Goodwife's valley called to her; the idea of sleeping behind stone walls again filled her with dread. Who were these people she was finally meeting? What if they turned out to be more Bathory than King David? What if, having given her away nineteen years ago, they wanted nothing to do with her now?

"Hey, uh." Gina pulled her horse to a halt at the foot of the bridge. "I think this is all you from here on out."

"Yeah," Flynn said with a weak smile. "Gina and I . . . don't really belong here. Officially."

"You will do no such thing," Rapunzel said in a commanding tone, only realizing halfway through that what she said didn't make a whole lot of sense. "I'm only here *because* of the two of you. If they accept me, they accept all of us. If they reject me, I'm going to burden you until you figure out what to do with me."

"I would give all the stolen crowns in the world for you to burden me," Flynn said—giving his old, devilish smile at the end.

And so they rode over the bridge together.

The guards immediately saw that something unusual was up: Rapunzel, still in her white goats'-wool tunic, sitting straight upon a magnificent shining tolori horse, her silver hair around her like Lady Godiva's. By the time the three (six) friends crossed the bridge, more guards had emerged from the castle, flanking either side of the doors.

This was both a relief and a surprise to Rapunzel, who had literally no idea what to say when she got up close.

Hello, I'm Rapunzel, the very much not dead daughter of your king and queen.

Well met. This is your captain Maximus I'm riding here, and . . .

Hey, so I know Flynn Rider behind me is a wanted criminal, but he's also in dire need of a doctor. You see, he helped rescue your crown princess and . . .

A dozen or so Rapunzel-lengths away from the gate she slipped down from her horse—who stood very straight and unhorselike at attention in front of his men. While she kept waiting for the right words to come, the guards looked at her curiously and also waited for something.

All at once a middle-aged woman pushed her way through the men, her silver-streaked hair and expensive dress flapping somehow both crazily and elegantly around her. Despite her naked face and lack of crown, Rapunzel recognized her at once: *the queen*.

And a moment later recognized her again, in the shape of her eyes and brow, the hang of her surprised, open mouth: *Mother*.

"Rapunzel," the woman whispered, stopping for a moment to stare.

Then she ran forward again and enveloped Rapunzel in her arms, weeping and pressing her face against her daughter's chest.

Rapunzel was overwhelmed; her first urge was to hug back, something she always wanted to do but Gothel never reciprocated. Any idea of a *speech* or the *questions* flew away forever as this woman received and accepted Rapunzel and sobbed all at once.

And held a lock of her hair tightly in a fist, wrapping it around her knuckles as if she meant to keep Rapunzel from fleeing.

"Mother . . . ?" Rapunzel finally said, trying it out.

"I'm sorry I'm sorry I'm sorry I'm sorry," came the response, whispered and choked.

The woman was terrified. She was expecting rebuke and hatred. Maybe even welcoming it.

"Mother," Rapunzel said with a smile, putting her arms

around her as she might a goat or a little girl. "Aren't you afraid of my hair?"

"No," the queen said emphatically. "If I died now, I would be happy. All I ever wanted to do was hold you again."

And then Rapunzel felt her face screw up all ugly and she began to sob; loud, horrible, unprincessly noises that gulped at the air like she had been suffocating her whole life. There were no remaining doubts that this was her *real mother*: a woman who hugged, cried, loved, and wasn't afraid.

A silent man stood behind them, face crossed with far too many lines for his age, a simple crown upon his head.

"Dad?" Rapunzel asked. *Father* sounded too . . .

He came forward hesitantly, tears streaking down those hollow cheeks, and he wrapped his giant arms around both of the women.

Rapunzel had no idea how long they stayed that way, or—having grown up in a tower—how unusual it was for a king and queen to kneel, weeping, on the cobblestones in front of a castle, engaged in a very private family moment.

The accidental clop of a horse, interpreting the nervousness of her rider, woke Rapunzel up from the softest, best moment she'd ever had.

"Mom, Dad," she said, wiping her face. "This is . . .

Eugene and Gina. They saved me and rescued me and brought me here. Not quite in that order."

The king raised an eyebrow at Flynn, who saluted him as best he could.

"Isn't that Flynn Rider, the *very* wanted thief?" he demanded in a rich, rolling voice. "The one who stole the goblet? And the *crown*?"

"No, dear," the queen said, wiping her eyes. "Our daughter just told you: that's *Eugene*. Who saved her. No relation at all to that other man."

She gave Flynn a sharp look and the corner of her lips twitched into a hastily smothered smile.

Flynn blinked in surprise.

"And I have the crown back, anyway," Rapunzel said quickly. She would have to ask about the goblet later. "And this . . . is Captain Tregsburg, who also helped rescue me . . . and whose life I sort of saved by turning him into a horse."

Rapunzel would not forget the look on the king's and queen's faces for the rest of her life.

Maximus bowed, one front leg curled under and the other splayed out, his neck extended gracefully.

"I thought I recognized him," one of the guards whispered to another in wonder.

Despite the insistent tapping on her neck, Rapunzel decided to wait on introducing Pascal. Things had already gotten a little out of hand. There would be time for every-thing later.

Later took a little while to sort out.

Gina was given a generous reward in gold coin, along with new clothes and boots and a decorated set of tack and equipment for her horse—and was also invited to stay in the castle for as long as she wanted. After she bathed and put on the new clothes and outfitted her horse, she proceeded to wander around the castle a little nervously, obviously wanting to be somewhere else but not wanting to appear ungrateful.

Maximus was put through some fairly comedic paces because, as was human nature, few people immediately believed who he was. Once his identity was determined without a doubt (many whinnies and hoof-taps later), it then had to be determined whether he still wanted a role in the castle guard or whether he would prefer to literally be put out to pasture. In the end it was decided that for now he would oversee the transition of leadership to his lieutenant . . . while enjoying the kingdom's finest apples served to him on a silver platter.

Flynn was immediately put in the care of Signore Dottore Alzi, who was concerned—resigned, really—about his head wound. Rapunzel wasn't worried; the full moon was in a few nights, and according to Gina's mother that meant her powers would be the most sunlike, and therefore healing.

The king and queen watched as their daughter sat by him and laughed softly and brought him food and drink.

"So, ah, this Eugene," the king said, clearing his throat. "Who exactly is he?"

Rapunzel tried not to giggle, watching the king of a country take faltering steps in a new role: that of *father*. She might have been raised in a tower, but she had spent the last couple of weeks running, adventuring, meeting witches and human demons, seeing violence firsthand, and learning about life. She would do her best to be daughtered, but she wasn't a little girl.

"He's my—" She couldn't think of a word. *Hero* was closest but, for obvious reasons, straight out. Rescuer? Friend? *Sweetheart* sounded stupid. ". . . ine," she finished.

"He's mine," she repeated simply.

"Is this true?" the queen asked Flynn archly.

"Yes, ma'am, uh—Your Majesty," he said. With his cheeks properly shaved and washed and his hair combed back, despite his bandage, Flynn fairly glowed against the white pillow. Rapunzel could have kissed him then and there. "I am entirely at your daughter's command. One

WHAT ONCE WAS MINE

hundred percent. Devoted and unflagging and whatever she says I am."

"Oh, because"—the queen and king exchanged looks—"you were riding with Gina, and . . ."

Gina looked up with big, terrified eyes.

"Max wouldn't let him ride," Rapunzel began to explain. "I think he still holds Eugene's . . . uh . . . background against him. And . . ."

"*BLECH,*" Gina spat out before she could stop herself.

"*Her?* No way. No offense," Flynn said.

"None taken. I mean, are you kidding?"

"She's *kind of* a handful."

"He's *definitely* an idiot."

"Totally not my type."

"Yeah, and my type is 'human.'"

The queen laughed. "You're better than court jesters. Rapunzel said you were both orphans. Is that true?"

"Yup! From Mother Mary of the Blessed Little Children," Flynn said, almost proudly.

"Oh, that place." The king's eyes went dark. "You must have been there before the queen became involved. It was terrible. She poured all her sorrow and guilt from giving up Rapunzel into improving the orphanage, and the lives of children all over the kingdom. It's much nicer now."

Rapunzel was glad to hear that. She had . . . ideas for the

country. Ones she wanted to start putting into place *before* she became queen. It was good that there was precedent.

"But look at the two of you," the queen pressed. "And Eu-*gene* and *Gina*! Didn't you ever think about that?"

Flynn and Gina looked at each other, confused. With, now that Rapunzel thought about, strangely similar faces.

"I wonder if there's any way to prove it," Flynn said in wonder.

"OH MY GOD!" Rapunzel shrieked, unable to help herself. She bounced. "*I have a sister! A real sister!*"

She threw her arms around Gina and squeezed her tight. The other girl looked a little uncomfortable, but also a little happy.

"This is the happily ever afterest ever," she added when she calmed down, leaning over and kissing Flynn so familiarly on the lips that her overjoyed and mostly accepting parents still squeezed each other's hands nervously.

"I wish we could have begun it nineteen years ago," the queen said softly.

Eventually, of course, came the fairy-tale royal wedding—modified a bit; Flynn was not royalty. He was named "royal consort," which sent Gina into a fit of giggles whenever his title was announced (Flynn always unroyally tried to whack her). Everyone was there, even Gina's mother, who had made the big trip from the forest and wore a crown of flowering brambles for the occasion.

Rapunzel had no problem fitting into castle life. In fact, her parents seemed almost fragile with her around, undone by a mistake nearly twenty years ago that they would never forgive themselves for.

But the girl who had spent so long in a tower didn't have a habit of looking backward. Who knew if she would be where she was today, with *whom* she was, if things had worked out differently?

It was a lesson she made sure all the children of the kingdom learned in the schools she set up. She also built an extension to the orphanage with an apprenticeship program for boys and girls who were too old to be adopted but too young or unwilling to marry. No one was ever "adopted" into servitude again. They would learn to be smithies or healers, scholars or weavers—whatever they wanted.

The crowning touch of this plan was that . . .

"Gina will be directing the school!" Rapunzel announced proudly.

"No thank you," Gina said almost immediately.

"Uh, what?"

As the happily ever after had unrolled, nothing at all had interrupted the princess's wishes and desires. So this was a bit of a surprise.

"I . . . want to have more adventures," Gina said with a shrug. Her braid was now tied off with a silver clasp, but she still stood and spoke like her old self: with few words, and lots of shyness. "I said all I wanted was a horse of my own and the chance to make a name for myself. I can do that now. I'll miss you and Flynn. I'll come back. But I have legends of my own I want to make."

"Oh, pits," Rapunzel said. "I understand. I just thought we'd all live together like a family."

"I'll be here for Christmas," Gina promised.

They hugged and Rapunzel cried a little, and laughed.

After Gina left, the princess walked the rose garden by herself, feeling melancholy and moody. She wondered about the ends of things, and if happily ever afters ever lasted.

That's how Flynn found her. Sensing her mood, he took her by the hand and pulled her over to the little bench by the apple trees.

"What are we doing?" Rapunzel asked curiously.

"I think you need a break from princessing," Flynn said. "Besides, it's after eight. *Wayyyyy* past time for reading."

He held up a book whose cover he had replaced with one he made; it said *Book #38.*

Rapunzel, overwhelmed by how much he understood and loved her, reached up and kissed him fully on the lips.

Reading would have to wait until later.

Epilogue

And what happened to Crespin the spy, who played such a small but vital role at the beginning of all these events? Little is known, unfortunately; he disappeared after collecting his gold. It is said he pursued his own interests from there on out, finally eschewing all pretense of loyalty to anything or anyone—including gold. Perhaps he took off to some foreign land; perhaps he even escaped to the New World.

Or perhaps he spent his time satisfying his curiosity about a certain witch who kept her pretty daughter in a tower until she was old enough to sell.

For it certainly looked like *his* hand that ripped the Sundrop Flower from its roots—

And it was definitely Gothel's screams that tore through the land, dying suddenly at the end—

Memorial Sloan Kettering

"You just had to go dark again, didn't you?" Daniella asked with a grin.

"Oh, come on. You *love* Gothel actively getting her just deserts."

"Didn't say I didn't." She yawned and stretched, forgetting that her arm was still tethered by tubes. She looked at them with resigned acceptance. "Maybe when this is all over we could go to the Cloisters sometime. That's like a castle. I wanna see the tapestries . . . and the armor. . . ."

"Okay, but this Rapunzel was supposed to take place at the beginning of the Renaissance, not—"

"Shut up, Brendan," she said with a smile, snuggling down into her pillow.

"*Thank you,*" she added, and it was so real, and so quiet, he almost didn't believe she said anything at all.

He flipped through his sketchbook, a little sad now that it was all over. He wanted to spend more time with his friends back in the magical kingdom. After all his complaining, it wasn't much, really, making up a story for his sister.

He liked to think Flynn would have done the same.

Author's Note

My baby sister had cancer.

Okay, she was in her thirties, but she's nine years younger than me and will *always* be my baby sister.

We look a lot alike; our mother calls us "twins born a decade apart." We're both tall (she's taller); we both have big feet (mine are bigger) and very pale skin (she tans, I burst into flame).

We have weirdly different hair; it's all dark brown, but mine is fine and mostly straight, and hers is thick with waves and curls that get out of hand without constant maintenance or keeping short.

Even as our lives and locations have drifted apart, we remain close, though not in a greeting-card, *sisterhood* sort of way: we text gross jokes, watch the latest horror movies together, and weather the news and family dynamics with rolled eyes and inappropriate comments like both of us are still thirteen years old.

I sat with her through many of her chemo sessions. I watched her get sick from the chemicals and the radiation that would ultimately cure her. I watched her lose her hair in patches until she shaved her head.

There are three important facts you need to know for the rest of this story.

One: the Silver Star diner on Second and Sixty-Fifth makes damn good egg creams.

(All right, that is not *strictly* necessary to know for the rest of the story, but my sister and I consumed many dozens of chocolate egg creams before and around her doctor appointments. Their turkey clubs ain't so bad, either.)

Two: New York City has some of the most amazing wig shops in the world. This is thanks to the presence of great theater, a glorious spectrum of gender nonconformity, and a melting pot of cultures that highly value wigs—from the Caribbean to Crown Heights.

Three: at the time of my sister's cancer there was a very popular adult fantasy series on HBO that everybody was addicted to (including us).

So when my sister went to choose a wig, she did not

pick a short brown style, which is what she had before she got sick.

She chose a *fabulous*, long, platinum-blond train of hair that pretty much exactly matched the queen (um, Khaleesi) in the aforementioned HBO fantasy series. A lovely friend of hers, a professional stylist, trimmed it and shaped it to her face.

When my sister walked outside wearing it—with a bit of makeup for her missing brows and pale cheeks—she strutted. No, for real: she walked and behaved like the queen she felt like in the wig.

Up until that moment, I had never fully understood the allure of wearing Rapunzel's golden hair, especially if it wasn't at all like your real hair (my own hair is still natural brown, with natural streaks of silver in it now). For many Halloweens after *Tangled* came out, I watched girls—including my own daughter—with hair of all colors and textures trick-or-treat with yards and yards of long golden braids piled on their heads in a crown or trailing down their backs.

When I saw my sister's eyes light up as she looked in the mirror wearing the wig, I finally got it.

(And kinda wanted to try it on myself.)

I could go on and on here about the significance of hair in mythology, race, and history, but that's not really the point of this story. This story is about the importance of hair to one person only, one of my favorite people in the world.

My sister's hair grew back in and is once again the short brown it used to be. She is perfectly healthy except for something of a chocolate egg cream addiction.

She has a baby girl, and everyone is living happily ever after.